Praise for

ANNETTE VALLON

"Tipton's marvelous novel proves French women through history . . . delectably soignée and self-confident, even facing the blood-soaked terror of the Revolution. . . . Annette is both an authentic free spirit and believably eighteenth century. You understand why Wordsworth was mad for her."

—*USA Today*

"James Tipton has taken a little-known story about a famous English poet in his formative years, and has created a fine novel which is a pleasure to read. This is a book which will be enjoyed on many levels—as a romance, as a well-researched historical novel, and not least as an exciting adventure story."

—Janet Aylmer, author of *Darcy's Story*

"James Tipton has woven a complex and engrossing historical tapestry, centered on the radiant, rebellious figure of William Wordsworth's first great love, the mother of his 'illegitimate' French daughter Caroline. Dashing and desirous, Tipton's Annette is more than worthy of a Romantic poet's devotion, while their romance, set against the turmoil of the French Revolution, will fascinate contemporary readers."

—Sandra Gilbert, coauthor of *Madwoman in the Attic*

"The romance of the novel is secondary to Tipton's portrait of Annette as a spirited heroine in a time of desperation and danger. . . . Tipton is able to balance the action with the history. A pleasing literary fancy set against the terrors of the French Revolution."

—*Kirkus Reviews*

"Annette—and those who help her along the way—are believable in their struggles through the best and the worst of times."

—*Publishers Weekly*

© Devin Merner

About the Author

JAMES TIPTON holds a Ph.D. in English literature
and teaches in the San Francisco Bay Area, where he
lives with his family.

Annette Vallon

ANNETTE VALLON

A NOVEL

of the

FRENCH
REVOLUTION

JAMES TIPTON

HARPER

NEW YORK · LONDON · TORONTO · SYDNEY

HARPER

A hardcover edition of this book was published in 2007 by HarperCollins Publishers.

HarperCollins books may be purchased for educational, business, or sales promotional use. For information please write: Special Markets Department, HarperCollins Publishers, 10 East 53rd Street, New York, NY 10022.

FIRST HARPER PAPERBACK PUBLISHED 2008.

Designed by Leah Carlson-Stanisic

Library of Congress Cataloging-in-Publication Data is available upon request.

ISBN 978-0-06-082222-4 (pbk.)

08 09 10 11 12   OV/RRD   10 9 8 7 6 5 4 3 2 1

For Lorraine

Bliss was it in that dawn to be alive.
But to be young was very heaven.

WILLIAM WORDSWORTH, *The Prelude*, BOOK X

Adieu, mon ami. . . . Aime toujours ta petite fille et
ton Annette qui t'embrasse mil fois sur la bouche,
sur les yeux. . . . Adieu, je t'aime pour la vie.

ANNETTE VALLON, FROM A LETTER TO WILLIAM WORDSWORTH

ANNETTE VALLON

PREFACE

January 4, 1821, Paris

It's raining. Through the veiled January day I can still see the river, as if unmoving, in the distance. But it is moving. My God, we saw the world change. I want to get it down before I am old. The window, slightly ajar, brings in the rain-fresh air that mixes with the smell of aged leather on the three diaries in front of me. But it is not all in the diaries, and I had to stop writing them, for fear they would fall into the wrong hands. My memories remain fresh and cool. I remember the feel of a silk sleeve on my skin, the lightness of taffeta when I danced, and the big riding cloak when I could feel the reassuring weight of a pistol in each pocket. I remember the river flowing through it all, glazed with sunsets or cracking with ice. We were all young then. So many minds thought France was bringing about a new world of freedom and equality and brotherhood. I loved a young poet, who had come from England full of those thoughts and of a love of words with which to build his own vision. Some tried to change the world. I just tried to live in it, which became increasingly difficult.

I loved a young poet then.

BOOK I

The Loire Valley, France,

1785–1791

"ut may you never have a revolution in *this* country," the tall American said.

We were dining at the grand house of my older sister and her husband. The American gentleman had come down from Paris in a golden carriage on some business regarding my brother-in-law's vineyard. I had not paid attention to what it was: I was only sixteen and fresh out of convent school.

"In France you enjoy the most graceful lifestyle in the world," he continued. "You value philosophy, literature, art, music, all the sciences, more than any culture I know, including my own," and he laughed. "But your people do not have any representation in the government. To that end, I hope they may be educated, but gradually— for if they were thrust headlong into a freedom which they have never known, it would be chaos. A revolution here would not be as it was in my country, against a foreign power; a revolution here would be . . . a disaster. But forgive me for presuming to speak on a subject of which you know far more than I. What do *you* think, Mademoiselle?" And his blue eyes suddenly looked directly at me.

I frantically tried to think of something, one line from Rousseau that I had talked about with the girls because I had applied it to the despotic Sister Angèle.

"I think that since Might cannot produce Right, the only legitimate authority in human societies is *agreement*."

The American laughed. "That must be an enlightened convent school your parents sent you to," he said.

"I'm afraid, Monsieur, that some of us read Rousseau in secret."

"Well, for now," he said, "Rousseau may be best kept behind closed doors in France and pondered upon by fine young minds." And he turned to the men.

We were on to the duck with orange now. Our guest took a bite of the meat but held back on the sauce. I was impatient for the steaming sauceboat, placed in front of him, with its mélange of caramelized sugar, lemon and orange juices, white wine, and red currant jelly.

A servant poured a ruby wine into the one glass I was allowed at dinner. I was sure it was my brother-in-law's vintage, which he said smelled of green peppers and pea pods. He was championing a red wine in the land of famous whites. I reached for my glass, then caught Papa's eye and became aware of a curious tension at the table. Our guest, my father had told me, was the finest wine connoisseur in the New World and had a peculiarity about trying new wines. He thought they were only truly appreciated in the context of food, so he waited until dinner to make his final decisions. He had come all the way from Paris now for this moment. All his pleasant and insightful conversation, all of my sister's dinner plans and Cook's lengthy preparations, were leading to this.

The American drank some water, raised his wineglass, inspected the color within—I noticed a flame from the hearth reflected, shimmering, in the burgundy depths—swirled it gently, tipped, sniffed it—would he smell peppers and pea pods? He closed his eyes, sipped, held, and almost chewed the wine. He seemed oblivious to us, in a world of pure concentration.

I could smell the sauce, see its curling steam, and very much wanted him to pass it to me. But there was no rushing the moment. A smile gradually spread across his handsome face. He opened his blue eyes. "Monsieur Vincent," he said, "it exceeds all expectations. It must be those cool limestone caves you keep it in."

The table relaxed. Maybe he would now pour the sauce. But he held the eye of my brother-in-law. This was a moment of business transacted between gentlemen, at a table laden with duck and wine. "I will take ten cases and, with your permission, the soil samples I collected today back to Paris," the foreigner said.

I liked his hair. My father and brother-in-law had powdered wigs, and here was this bright red hair that seemed to shine in the candle-light.

Our guest lifted the porcelain boat and discreetly lavished his duck with the sauce that was now coming my way. He paused a moment and took in the fragrance. Then he returned to business. "And I will accept your offer to ship some vines to Virginia."

"I would be honored," my brother-in-law said.

"I will call it," said the American, "the Shenandoah grape."

I liked the name. "Pardon, Monsieur?"

"Yes, Mademoiselle?"

"Could you please say that name again?"

"Shenandoah," he said. "It is the river that runs near my home. Like your great river here. It is very beautiful, and I miss it. When I think of America, I do not think of the vast Atlantic seaboard and of our victory against the British Empire; I think of one small patch of rocky land on top of a cliff overlooking the river. So you remember that, Mademoiselle," and he looked at me again, his eyes twinkling.

"Remember what, Monsieur?"

"To thine own land be true," and he smiled, and my brother-in-law asked him to sample another wine, and their conversation went on, but it isn't part of my story.

NYMPHS AND SATYRS

I liked watching the slanting evening light that gleamed on the wild strawberries in the woods on either side of the road.

We had endured a long carriage ride, and it felt good now to be walking toward the château de Chenonceaux, its iron gates and front arches and tower just visible at the end of a long aisle of plane trees. I liked this château. As a girl one summer we had stayed here a week, and my older sister, Marguerite, and I once ran through the long hall that crosses the river, our steps echoing on the black-and-white-checkered floor, river light catching in the panes of the dormer windows, its shadows dancing over the walls, and I stopped and leaned out an open window over the dazzling water and felt that I was not in a stone château at all, but in a *gabare*, a large vessel on the Loire, its sails full. I also got delightfully lost in the maze one evening. As I turned the corners between the hedges, it was like going from one green glade into another. Marguerite finally had to come and fetch me.

Now I was going to my first end-of-the-season fête at this grand château. Maman had pointed out what a privilege it was for a girl just out of convent school, and Marguerite, who wasn't coming this year, said you never knew *what* to expect at the last fête. Papa, who had work to do in town, said these fêtes were silly things and it would be far more enlightening for me to become more familiar with his library at home.

But I couldn't pass up this opportunity. This was life, coming to greet me. And like Julie in my favorite novel, I would open my arms to it. The day had started simply, with finding the right satin ribbon that matched the decoration in my wide-brimmed hat. Then we had the long journey, following the river west. And tonight I would observe the elegant dancers, the folded fans swaying from the ladies' wrists as they took the hand of the gentlemen who bowed, and they both moved in unison to a music of mathematical precision. The heavenly spheres themselves, hanging in space, were governed by the same harmony that regulated the dancers, I believed. I myself hoped to learn all the intricate steps this summer. Now it was enough just to watch.

Maman held the arm of our old family friend, Count Thibaut of the château de Beauregard.

"Come now, ladies, we're late," he said.

"Why wouldn't dear Madame Dupin allow us this year to drive our carriages to the door? This is not in good taste or style," Maman said.

I was teetering on my heels, trying not to look gauche.

"Man was born to suffer," the count said.

"Oh, you can say that," said Maman, "with your buckled shoes and walking cane. I think it's most inconsiderate of Madame. As if we're peasants. Who's ever heard of *walking* to a ball?"

"It *is* just the entryway, my dear. We will all deserve our refreshments. And you know what an old eccentric Madame Dupin is."

Just then I thought I saw something coming toward us in the woods to my right. I looked on the other side of the drive and saw it there too: a flicker of a shape, darting swiftly between the trees, then hiding behind them. We were almost to the entrance of the château.

In a sudden flurry of movement, figures leaped from behind the trees and surrounded us. The light was dim now, and I could only make out that they didn't look quite human. They had horns on their heads, were bare-chested, and, as they pranced around us, appeared to have hooves. The count drew his sword. The creatures were wailing in a demented way and leering at us, especially at me. One tugged at the long sash on my dress. I slapped its hairy hand. Another leaped by and wisped his fingers through my hair.

"Get away. Get away," Maman cried, waving the back of her hand at them. The count set himself in the *en garde* position, his cane balanced in one hand and the sword in the other, ready to lunge against the beasts from another world. Then he laughed and sheathed his sword. "They're in costume! The fools we are. This is Madame Dupin's way to usher us to the party."

As if in assent, one of the satyrlike creatures motioned us to follow him toward the château. Maman and the count started, and I held back. "Annette, don't be afraid," Maman said. "These are *Madame Dupin*'s satyrs; they won't hurt you."

Then one pranced by my side, nodded his head, bent down, and lifted my silk dress and underskirts well above my knees, and ran off. But Maman had turned her back and didn't notice.

"She always does something strange for the last fête," she said to the count.

The satyrs leaped ahead of us now in the dusk. At the moat they melted into a crowd of waiting guests, bobbing among them, pinching and dancing. Torches hung in sconces set in the château wall. Everyone was staring down into the moat. I heard lovely pastoral music. I am small and couldn't see over women's ostrich plumes, palmlike feathers, or hats with lace brims.

Not walking on my feet but balancing on the heels, I must have said "Pardon me" a hundred times, weaving my way through a sea of satin-covered hip pads or long trains falling on the ground.

Then I saw it too: a small barge with an orchestra on it, coming gently toward us on the current of the river Cher, diverted here into the moat. Silver candlesticks sat on veneer wood tables beside the musicians. As if we were one person, the crowd sighed in appreciation. A gentleman shouted, "Bravo!" and we all applauded. Then we gasped. From a door in the wall just above the level of the moat, six young women dove, one after another, into the water and swam around the raft. Their gossamer-thin muslin gowns, once wet, made them appear naked. Their slender arms, dipping in and out of the water, shone in the torchlight; then they floated directly below us, their faces upturned, and every one of them was beautiful.

They began to sing—something I vaguely recognized from an opera Papa had taken me to long ago—

The denizens of our sacred groves
Have prepared for you a glorious festival!
And already their sweet pipes
Announce the happy moment
When you shall reign over them.

At the end of the last phrase, six satyrs jumped into the water and proceeded to caress or kiss the lovely maidens. "The nymphs and the satyrs!" a gentleman cried. "Bravo, Madame Dupin. You have out-done yourself."

We all applauded again, and the crowd swept across the draw-bridge to the terrace as the barge and the nymphs floated around the bend in the moat. I was glad for the swimmers that it was such a warm night.

And four years later, when the Revolution began, I was often glad that, because the villagers loved old Madame Dupin, the château de Chenonceaux was not sacked or burned.

NOVELS

*B*e careful, reader: my troubles started because I read novels. Rousseau was my favorite author—not necessarily *The Social Contract*, but his fiction, especially the one about Julie and her true love. So that was my problem.

Novels had ruined me by the age of sixteen, when Maman invited me into her salon and told me in a hushed and solemn manner, as if she were imparting to me my catechism, that she was arranging for me a *mariage de raison* with a wealthy sugar merchant from Tours. Instead of thanking her and being blushingly excited, as was proper, I merely said that I was honored by her consideration, but I would wait. I was waiting for true love, you see, for my novels had told me that it existed, somewhere. They had also given me a suspicion that maman's *arrangement* had more to do with money and position and less to do with love—in fact, she hadn't even used that word when she outlined for me my future happiness. My novels had also told me that true love rarely had an auspicious ending, but that seemed of little importance to me at the time.

So my wise mother said, "Very well, then, I will prepare you for society, to meet your perfect mate." I thanked her profusely. I knew I was a gauche girl, so I welcomed this opportunity, especially when she told me the next day that she had hired me a tutor. Now tutors figured prominently in two of the novels I had read. It seems gauche girls couldn't refuse them, and well-intentioned mothers kept hiring them. I half hoped mine would turn out to be an old music master, whose hands trembled when he turned the pages of the music, whose voice was dry and crackly when he sang. Yet I also knew my teacher would be nothing of the sort and that, as in my favorite novels, my destiny was laid out before me.

My tutor was an accomplished music and dance master from Orléans, who, Maman pointed out, only came to the finest houses. His name was Raoul Leforges, and when I met him he was dressed fashionably in black silk, from the ribbon on the queue of his powdered wig to his high-collared coat to his knee breeches and black-and-white-striped stockings. He held a black beaver-skin hat in his left hand and bowed graciously to me. No one had ever bowed to me before, and I thought I had never seen a more handsome or a more striking man.

Rousseau's *La Nouvelle Héloïse* had prepared me for such a thing, and so had other novels that we circulated in secret at the convent school, especially the one reserved only for girls in their last year: Laclos's *Les Liaisons dangereuses*. Even then, to read it you had to be *approved* by a committee of head girls and swear oaths that could send you straight to hell, and you could only have the book for twenty-four hours at a time.

The first lesson started with Monsieur Leforges presenting his hand, without saying a word. He nodded, and I stepped back, thinking we were going to dance, and stopped.

"No, no," he said, "look at your feet."

I did, and was embarrassed for them.

Monsieur Leforges had Maman's permission to break the gaucherie out of me all summer, and he did it through chastisement, rigorous hours, and occasional encouragement. More than once, as I performed a particularly shameful step, he tapped me firmly on the behind with his bamboo cane, and I glowed beneath and above my muslin.

He was preparing me for my first ball, which would be at the château de Beauregard, the home of the count. As well as my entrance into society, it was the first fête of the new season, and the count wanted to make sure no one wanted for anything and that his fête would set the standard for all the rest to come. That warm September night, as the orchestra played some gentle Lully and before I had to hasten up the marble stairs so I could descend them in slow, graceful steps, I lingered by the refreshment tables. I was too nervous to sample anything, but I swore to myself I would have my fill after I danced my first dance, which I was sure would be in a kind of daze. Then I would retire here for most of the night.

On a table that stretched the length of the room lay rows of *corniottes*, little three-cornered hats made out of cheese pastries; *religieuses*, also known as nun cakes; almond pastries in the shape of yellow, green, and red fish; puff pastry with almond filling (which I loved when I escaped from convent school and sat in a *pâtisserie* in Orléans last winter); plum, lemon, and strawberry tarts; pear cake with red currant jelly; and pears cooked in wine, lemon, and sugar. I leaned over the bowls to breathe in the fragrant syrup. And then, in a hundred glasses set in bright silver cups, gleamed strawberry ices. At the end rose a pyramid of candies: dark chocolate, sweet lemon, almond macaroon. And at every pillar, under every arch, stood a sober servant holding a silver tray of tall glasses of sparkling white wine.

I had worked harder than I ever had in my life all that summer to become a lady; to play piano passably; to know how to curtsy with subtle nuances of difference to a marquis, to a count, to a father; to talk to servants in a firm yet gentle tone; to walk with grace and dignity; to converse by asking questions and by making witty interjections; to sing somewhat respectable duets; and especially, to master the art of the dance. And Monsieur Leforges, the nonpareil of style and taste, had been my taskmaster in all of these. I deserved all the rewards I could reap now of pastries, tarts, ices, and wine. But I had grown to worship my stern and handsome tutor, who said I dare not lose my concentration through even one taste or sip until I had proven myself on the ballroom floor—and through those curtsies that I would bestow on the crowd first, which we had worked on all of a particularly sultry August afternoon. He said he deserved his reward too, although I was sure Maman was paying him well.

Then before I knew it the count had me by the arm, had guided me past the perfumed pear bowls and to the top of the stairs. I was afraid for a moment and thought I might dash into the corridor behind me, which led, in flickering light, to a long hall where loomed tiles of marching musketeers and portraits of every king of France and his queen up to Louis XIII. It wasn't an attractive thought to run in the half-dark in that direction, and the count still held my arm, as if he intuited my fear.

The music stopped. The count whispered, "May the Virgin be with you," though I never thought of him as a devout man, and we began the slow descent, then paused halfway, so everyone could regard me. Now it was disconcerting and wonderful at once, hovering as if in midair in a gauze gown and white taffeta skirt with tiny red roses. All the silk-clad crowd looked up at me, a hundred candles lighting their faces, powdered wigs, and coiffured hair, their smiling, expectant faces, the proud faces of my parents. Everyone I loved was there, with a soft glow over them all.

My nervousness melted, and I felt ready to enter their world, to be one of those who moved with grace and dignity and beauty under crystal chandeliers and marble stairways. The gauche girl had suddenly dropped away, and now I, too, would lightly touch gloved hand to gloved hand, a fan dangling from my own wrist, my satin-slippered feet gliding over the bright floor to the beauty and order of Rameau's music, which dictated the orderly and beautiful movements of the dance. The music started again, and I descended.

It's a marvelous thing to be young and at the radiant center of one's world. The problem, of course, is that so often that radiance is purely of one's own imagination, and its light of such short duration.

One thinks differently when one is young, if one thinks at all. It seemed to me that Monsieur Leforges was the world of charm and grace. I gave my heart to that world. My tutor religiously followed Rameau's *Art of the Dance*, and I religiously followed him in everything, and by the end of that evening I had followed him too far.

I never made it to the tables waiting for me with their sweet rewards. After I had been the center of all the world and had danced with ease in a circle of taffeta and perfumed lace cuffs, Monsieur Leforges claimed his own reward. The night of my triumph I was vanquished by my tutor in the small room built for a secretary of state in the Renaissance, at the end of the portrait gallery of kings and musketeers. The tiny red roses on my taffeta skirt were crushed. I stared at the gold bells in the coat of arms of the lords of Beauregard that hung from the gilt ceiling. Monsieur Leforges abruptly got up, saying he had to return to the ballroom. He had to dance late into the night, he said, with the guests. As a professional dancer, that was his *duty*. He did not ask me to go. I didn't know whether to follow him or wait for him to ask me, and all of a sudden I was alone. At first it seemed intolerable, and I couldn't move from my position on the Turkish carpet. Then it seemed a relief to be alone in the dim room, with the glow of one wall sconce reaching up to the Beauregard coat of arms. I stayed a long time with the golden bells. They seemed, in the sagacity of their silence, their ancient age, and their loftiness in the shadows, mildly comforting.

A fortnight later I made my way down the steep streets and the old stone stairways in the falling dusk. I pulled my collar high and my broad hat down as the first, fine September rain made slick the cobble-stones and softened the dusty streets. Maman had put a date to my marriage now with the sugar merchant, and I would lay the matter before Raoul.

He always had an answer.

I had left my chaperone, the stern Agnès, at the market and went early for a lesson at my tutor's. Feeling the urgency of the situation, I walked past his protesting valet, opened the tall doors of the salon, and saw my dance master on the settee on the far side of the piano, engaged with a wealthy widow of the town. Yards of velvet skirt lay crumpled about her hips, revealing fine legs (far longer than mine). A few days earlier I had been so naïve as to believe that settee was reserved solely for me.

"Oh, it's your little convent-school girl, Raoul," the widow said languidly, not shifting her position. "*She* must have been quite a chal-lenge."

Monsieur Leforges's game with me was up, and he ended it with a cold panache all his own. "Madame Lambert," my tutor said evenly, not taking his arms from around her, "is having her lesson. You may return at your proper time."

I will never forget how then, without lifting her head from a silk pillow, Madame Lambert let loose a lazy peal of humiliating, vulgar laughter.

Monsieur Leforges chuckled too.

*M*y father taught me to ride to the hunt that autumn.

He had found out about my liaison with the dance tutor through a letter I had lost at the count's château. The count had informed him. I never knew what Papa went through then, but the count's discretion and Papa's forgiveness kept a foolish girl from social disgrace. My father didn't let Maman know, but made her abandon her plans for the *mariage de raison* with the sugar merchant. He told her I wasn't *ready*, and Maman declared to me that because I wanted to choose my own husband like a butcher or a baker's daughter, I was decidedly *common*. She had reserved for me her worst insult, and the matter was closed. She had made a success with her first daughter's marriage and had one more daughter besides me with which she could make another success. Maman had washed her hands of me, and she handed me over to my father. He told her he was going to drive the silliness out of me by teaching me to hunt. That was fine with me. I had had enough of dancing instruction.

The hounds were kept in a kennel at the side of the hunting lodge and fed a huge slab of very red deer carcass every evening at five o'clock. The count's young groom, Benoît, stood between the meat and the lean, even emaciated hounds and kept them at bay with a whip. He finally let them at the meat, and they tore at it and fought and jumped on each other to get at it. It was not a big enough piece of meat for all the hounds. I always felt sorry for the ones that could not make it in for their dinner.

That autumn the Revolution was still years away. The gold leaves fell from the chestnut trees, and my father taught me to shoot. In the morning we gathered outside the count's hunting lodge. It was well off the main road, buried in the woods on the grounds of his château. You could smell the forest of pines and chestnuts as soon as you walked out the door.

The hounds, tails wagging, barking in anticipation, milled about the legs of the horses. We sat on horseback in a circle now, an odd assortment: my father, tall and gaunt in an old cloak; the count, of perfect physique with gold braid on his coat; the baron de Tardiff, short, portly, and dark; my brother-in-law, Paul, tall, slender, and fair; Philippe, the count's son, a year younger than I, skinny, swimming in his coat; and I in my riding cloak, three-cornered hat, and jockey boots, all in the English style, as my maidservant, the wise Claudette, prescribed.

I was on the horse that my father had given me, a three-year-old sorrel mare I named La Belle Rouge, shortened to La Rouge, after my father's stallion, Le Bleu. (He wasn't really blue but a dappled gray.) The men's grooms sat on horseback just behind them, each with a pistol and a musket just in case one had a problem with a wounded stag or wild boar or a horse with a broken leg.

The count's horse took the lead down the narrow track to the meadow, our customary starting point. The horses grew more excited as we approached it, La Rouge's ears forward and Le Bleu, in front of me, wanting to break out, stepping to the side of the path. Then we heard the hounds.

When they reached the meadow, the men let the horses have their head. From the cold shadow of the forest I saw the count's stallion streak out in the early sunlight, followed quickly by the others, their servants bouncing faithfully behind them. Now, my father and I together at the dividing line between shade and light, we let Le Bleu and La Rouge go. I had raced my mare against stallions along roads that summer and had felt her speed, but she was young and uncertain and followed Papa's lead. Yet she was running flat out now, and my boot heels skimmed the meadow, and I could smell the grass, fresh with the morning, as we flew through it. It was as smooth as walking, twirling my bonnet in my hand, but a thousand times more exhilarating.

The leaders were nearly across the meadow when a stag bounded out of the grass in front of them; it hung in the air for an instant and disappeared into the thicket on the other side of the meadow. They took off after it. Papa and Jean, his groom, plunged into the thicket after the others, and La Rouge continued her pace, unslackened, so I pulled hard at her reins to turn her left, to slow her down just at the thicket's edge. I was still not far behind Papa when I heard him curse as a low branch swiped his cheek. But following Papa's groan was another squealing sound in the brush.

The commotion of the hounds and horses had flushed a boar, who now charged through the thicket with Papa after him. La Rouge heard the sound too, and its shifting unfamiliarity, as if the brush itself were squealing, frightened her. She bolted back toward the meadow, and I reined her in there and had just calmed her down when I heard a shot from the direction in which Papa and Jean had gone. La Rouge whinnied but got no response from the other horses. We rushed through the thicket in their wake; both Rouge and I could sense where the others were. She dashed headlong down a gulley; I was obliged to stand upright in the stirrup, her rump above me, it was so steep. Ahead of us lay a dry streambed, strewn with leaves under a sheer rock face. Le Bleu, riderless, stood under the lee of the rock.

On the ground, amid copper leaves and stones, lay Papa. Le Bleu must have bolted and thrown his master when the boar, cornered in a rocky gulley, turned on its pursuers. Jean had shot his musket, wounding the boar and increasing its desperation, and was now reloading. The hounds leaped and barked at the boar; it grunted, lunged at them, hating them, its tusks thrusting in the air and the hounds leaping back. Then the boar went after the source of what had caused him pain and, before Jean could fire again, charged through the dogs and gored him in the ankle. Jean dropped the musket on the rocks.

Jean's scream, the boar's fierce grunts, the hound's howling, and the horse's whinnies filled the gulley; then the boar paused, the dogs keeping back, and it turned toward my father, a welcome quarry down on its level among the stones. In the seconds that the boar paused to consider its second prey, I pulled as hard as I could at Rouge's bit, and we reached the bottom of the gorge. As the boar charged my father, I jumped down from my saddle, snatched up the musket, and shot into the nape of its tough neck. The boar lay still among the leaf-littered stones, a few inches from my father's chest. The hounds were on it in an instant.

That night at the count's table we enjoyed boar's head along with haunch of venison in chestnuts, though I myself did not partake of the boar. Above us hung a tapestry of the hunt: a man in a red-and-blue cloak on a white steed leaping over a log, in the grasses a white hart not far before him, about to disappear into a forest of a hundred shades of green. I always preferred to think he got away, across the meadow strewn with the *mille-fleurs*, the thousand flowers, into the woods out of which rabbits peek: the hunter still has his crossbow slung across his back. The joy is obviously in the chase. The enormous hearth flames licked massive logs; light and shadows flickered across the oak paneling.

My father had attended Jean's wound and said Jean might always walk with a slight limp. Papa himself had a twisted ankle from his fall, and he had his foot up on an embroidered cushion and was in jovial spirits.

He insisted that I sit at table with the men. The count's son had retired early; Paul had gone home to spend the evening with my older sister Marguerite and their little daughter, Marie, and the men of the château de Beauregard were toasting me now.

"To Annette, a huntress the likes of whom haven't been seen since the days of Diane de Poitiers," the baron said, which made Papa beam. Diane was his heroine from the days when the kings and queens hunted through these forests.

"To the huntress!" they cried.

Everyone laughed and drained their glasses, and with my father glancing proudly over at me, I felt I belonged just as much here, with the huge fireplace and the wine and laughter, as in the ballroom under a thousand tapers of shining chandeliers and the carefully timed movements of hand and leg and foot, the fan swinging or lifted for coy messages.

What else might I do now? I was glad now Raoul Leforges had his rich widow and dozens of other naïve or not-so-naïve girls, and that I was free. What a purgatory to live only through another—him or a sugar merchant in Tours. How odd life was, with its twists and turns.

I was not sure it was proper in a woman to do, but I raised my glass, and in a voice that sounded strangely high, I proposed a toast of my own.

"To my father," I said, "who taught me to ride, to hunt, and who would have stared that old boar down if I had not made that unnecessary shot."

"To Jean-Paul Vallon!" they sang out, and the firelight flickered on the hunter's white stallion and on the oak beams high above.

That was the autumn of my sixteenth year, when there was nothing more frightening than difficult dance steps, untrue lovers, ambitious mothers, and wounded wild boars.

CHAMPAGNE AND OMELETTES

Other nations can live on rice or pasta or potatoes. The French need their bread. For two seasons the harvests had been bitter failures, and in the summer shortage the grain prices rose so no ordinary citizen could afford to pay them. You can read what you like about the political and social causes for what happened that July of 1789, and those books will all be right, in their way. But the Revolution started over bread.

We had heard that a city magistrate in Orléans, who himself had no children, remarked that if all the little girls died, there would be plenty of bread. This comment especially disturbed my younger sister, Angelique, who at fifteen wondered if she still fell into the category of *little girl*. (I, at twenty, felt exempt.) That complacency only lasted a night, though. The next day the rumor was corrected: the magistrate had actually said, "*All* children should be thrown into the river because bread is too expensive."

Throughout that summer the grand châteaux of the Loire were looted and burned. The grandest château, Chambord, with four hundred chimneys and a double spiral staircase on which I had once played hide-and-seek, was one of the first to go. Every velvet armchair and rich tapestry was dragged down that staircase and piled below it and set alight. The fire spread rapidly, and soon even the coffered ceiling and the sun rays painted on the shutters of the room where the Sun King himself had stayed were scorched beyond recognition. Such was the fate of all the châteaux where kings had stayed. And the Loire Valley had been the playground of the kings.

We lived in the town of Blois, just north and west from Chambord, along the river Loire. There were riots in town whenever a grain barge arrived at the quai, and by the end of the summer the château de Blois, too, had been sacked. No one went out at night. No one knew how it had got out of hand so quickly, nor when it would ever end.

But I had never seen any of the effects of the Revolution myself. I had only heard about them. The Revolution as conversation topic was considered impolite, so we never talked about our fears and lived almost happily in this way through that summer.

My father, a respected doctor in town, still visited patients, riots or no. His friend the count also remained unfazed that the world we had always known was changing before our eyes. The count himself had inherited the château de Beauregard, but since it was one of the lesser châteaux of the Loire and since he always provided his peasants and tenants with bread, he was not worried. My own parents thought it actually safer to be out of the town, and my younger brother Etienne and I were staying now, at the end of the summer, with the count.

I had known him as a type of uncle most of my life. When my father taught me to ride to the hunt, the count was there. When I had the liaison with the dance tutor, it was the count who kept my father from challenging the musical Casanova to a duel, who used his influence so that the tutor's reputation was ruined and not my own, and made him quietly and permanently leave town. It was at the count's château that the finest dinners and dances had always been held. So when the streets in town weren't safe, and beautiful châteaux went up in flames, I was happy to visit the count.

In the fall Etienne was to start at the university in Paris, at the Sorbonne. Revolution or no, it was continuing; in its many centuries it had known worse than the fall of the Bastille. So my brother and I had this time together. He was a good friend to me, and I did not look forward to him going away. That September he and I rode through the count's fields and woods and raced through the meadow where the hunts had always started. The count was not continuing them this year. There was never a year in anyone's memory that the château de Beauregard did not hold its autumn hunt and ball. But the extent to which the Revolution had turned the world upside down was not fully made clear to me until one day when Etienne and I were returning from a ride in the meadow. Those days we always went armed.

We saw peasants walking on the road toward the château as if they were going to a fair. A young man had a drum; many carried rakes or scythes like muskets on their shoulders. Young women picked poppies and put them in their straw hats. They all seemed happy and as if on holiday, and indeed, they were not harvesting the count's fields that day. "We're going for dinner at the château," they shouted to us. "The count is waiting." But we had heard of no general invitation for dinner to all peasants on his lands.

As we crossed the narrow stone bridge over the Beuvron River, they surrounded our horses and held on to their reins as we walked. A women caressed my riding skirt and undid its lower buttons up to the saddle (I already had the bottom two undone, myself, for freedom when I rode) and fingered my petticoats and tore lace fragments off.

Our strange procession wound its way up the long tree-lined entryway to the château, a road most of them had probably never been on. "Long live the Third Estate," they began chanting. Now the Third Estate literally meant all Frenchmen except the clergy and the nobles (the First and Second Estates), and this, of course, included Etienne and me, though the peasants seemed surprised when we shrugged and joined in the chanting. "I'll always say *long life* to myself," Etienne said to me.

My escort now grabbed the bridle tight as La Rouge snorted at another woman who tore off a large handful of petticoat, exposing part of my left leg, and I dared not lower my crop at them, for they surrounded us so our horses could hardly move, and although they all seemed jolly, and some now, tired of the chant, started singing, it was prudent, I thought, especially in these days, not to aggravate a crowd.

We stopped by the ruins of the chapel in front of the château. The count had told me this chapel was three hundred years older than the original château: matins were sung here long before our dances graced his gilded ballroom. Today a few peasants, warm from the walk, lounged in the shade of the chancel and leaned against the toppled stones that would have once vaulted over their heads. Now the green woods beckoned through the fallen ceiling.

Most of the peasants stood, still chanting or singing their own songs. They stared at the impassive face of the château. Suddenly the count emerged from his broad doors and stood in front of them, his arms crossed, surveying the crowd. The chanting and singing ceased abruptly. The count wore his velvet dressing gown and soft indoor shoes, and his eyes fell on Etienne and me, on our horses toward the back, the bridles of both of our frightened horses held by more than one pair of hands. Then he smiled and spread his arms wide, "Welcome, citizens," he cried out, and they all cheered, and he himself pulled the ancient iron knocker and opened the doors of the château de Beauregard to people I'm sure he had never dreamed would enter it. "Leave your tools in the courtyard, please," he said.

Etienne and I rode to the stables and quickly unsaddled and brushed our horses. We wanted to see how the count was faring with the crowd, and I took the big iron lock from behind the stable door and closed and locked the doors. If I so much as saw anyone approaching where La Rouge was kept, I'd be there with my pistol.

We hastened to the château and found the count as if leading the crowd on a tour of his home. "This," he said, "is our kitchen." It was, in fact, almost as big as the chapel; it certainly held within it a religion, I think, which the count practiced more regularly. "Observe," he said, "how we can have two capons or haunch of venison turning at once in two different fireplaces."

I'm not sure if at first he thought they just wanted to look at the château, or if he thought that if he could charm them, then they would leave, but they seemed still in awe of the château, or of him. "You see there, bread freshly baked for supper—have your fill; I wish we had more." And in a second two loaves were grabbed, then fought over and torn for general consumption. The count saw men heading down some stairs. Etienne and I looked at each other. The count pushed his way to the front of the crowd and held up his hand. "My special gift, for this day in which we honor the Third Estate" (he must have heard the chant coming up his drive), "is that those of you who are old enough—not you, *ma petite*," he said to a girl my sister Angelique's age, scampering past him, "are welcome to sample my superb cellar, with the best of wines from throughout the Loire Valley—" No one but Etienne and I heard the last words, as men rushed by us over the flagstone floor. But others, mainly women, now ran in a predatory frenzy into the other rooms as well. His stand before the cellar door had been the count's last semblance of authority over the crowd, his act of giving to them so they would not be stealing from him.

Etienne and I blanched as we saw men emerge from the cellar with bottles in their hands, breaking their tops off before us in the kitchen and grabbing crystal glasses, in their hurry breaking others, or, in a fit of bravado, a man drinking gingerly from the jagged top of a broken bottle, then giving it, as a challenge, to his neighbor. "You should go," Etienne said to me. "I'll stay here and see that the count's all right."

"Then I'll stay too," I said, and we went into the front salon and saw a man drinking straight from a bottle of Chinon red with his feet up on one of the new embroidered chairs. But most of the count's guests seemed in a hurry to grab something before someone else did—porcelain teacups disappearing into giant apron pockets; on top of the lace tablecloth of the dining room table, women in dirty bare feet reaching up to pull candles out of the chandelier; other women ripping large sections off the tablecloth or jerking at the velvet draperies, pulling them down, and one taking a knife from her pocket to cut sizable portions to carry home.

I saw the count calmly talking to an outraged Edouard—the only time I ever saw the count's valet other than imperturbable—and patting Edouard on the back and sending him out of the house. Now Etienne and I sat on stools by one of the fireplaces in the kitchen. I had hardly ever been in the kitchen before, and I noticed writing inside the chimney, on the stones above the spit that turned the game. I got up, peered into the sooty emptiness, and read: *Those who keep their promises have no enemies.*

The count had opened one of his own bottles of champagne and was coming toward us with three glasses. But he never reached us, for one of his guests grabbed the bottle, another the glasses, and a third one, a big man, swaying back and forth, stopped him. "O great Count," he said in a voice that carried throughout the kitchen. "I would like . . . an omelette!"

"Why not?" the count said. His cook and all his servants had left when they saw the mob coming, so he looked over at my brother and me. "Now it's your turn to help the Third Estate," he shouted to us.

"Fetch eggs and cheese and butter from the pantry before they're all gone, please." He reached up to a tall shelf and threw us two baskets each. The pantry had not been ravaged yet—grabbing *things* seemed more important first—and we returned with perhaps more than the count wanted, but we stood beside him, and Etienne stoked the fire and I mixed the ingredients and the count prepared omelette after omelette. Some took it in their hands, others pulled porcelain plates off shelves. "The Vallons always come through in a pinch. Didn't know you knew how to mix so well, Annette."

"Didn't know you could cook so well. Count," I said, "what promises have you broken? I'm referring to—" I motioned with my head towards where I had been sitting.

"The old fireplace motto! That's been here at least two hundred years. As a child I'd visit Cook and she showed me that once and made me promise I wouldn't break promises. But all these people—" he waved a hand and held a pan with the other. "They are not my enemies. If they were, they would have left my body pierced with a pitchfork before my own door—and believe me, that has happened to others of late—no, they are just a bit *on fire* with the opportunity, suddenly available this summer, to get something more for themselves or for their families. If any promises have been broken, I'm afraid they are right about the Third Estate—it's been by those in love with power in the First and Second Estates. No, they may ransack my château, but they are not my enemies, and I am not theirs. Still, I must make precautions."

He told Etienne to take what was left of the finest champagne and hide it in the garden and bring us a few bottles in here. Etienne returned sometime later with three bottles and put them before us. "I've heard of people in châteaux burying jewels and silver in the garden, but only you, Count, would think of burying champagne."

"Jewelry and silver don't taste the same as a Vouvray *pétillant*," said the count, "nor do they soothe the soul," and he took three glasses miraculously from his coat pockets and filled them. "To the Third Estate," he said, and we drank as he continued to cook and hand out omelettes. When we had used all the ingredients, he said, "I am going to sit down awhile and finish this bottle. Perhaps it would be prudent if you two retired to what is left of your rooms and rested until the tide recedes. It may be beginning to ebb. Even looting gets to be a bore, you know. It's the new *ennui* of the Revolution," and he lifted his glass to us. "Meet me for supper," he said, and made his way over to the stool I had sat on. He looked very tired, and perhaps, even for the first time, old.

A stench of unwashed bodies suffocated me now in the warm afternoon, and I opened the French doors to the inner courtyard and stepped out and looked in the direction of the stables, but saw no one. They were too occupied with the glories of the house. I turned and saw a woman standing on a velvet chair and tearing down the hunting tapestry from the wall in the dining room. She got down from the chair and pulled out her knife. "No, no," the count came running in from the kitchen, glass in hand. Then he stopped himself. He bent to put his glass on a table, noticed the table wasn't there, and put his glass on the wine-stained parquet floor. "One must roll it up, like this—if you put it on a wall, it will keep the cold down. If you cut it in small portions, it can't keep your home warm. Keep it like this, it will serve you well, Citizeness." And he finished rolling it up, ripped a tassel from a drapery piece on the floor, and tied up the tapestry. He put it in the arms of the woman. "This is for you," he said, "from the château de Beauregard. Keep it well."

I went up the long marble staircase, partway down the corridor, and knocked on Etienne's door. A looter carrying an armchair calmly walked by me. No one seemed interested in the paintings of kings.

"Who is it?" my brother asked.

"I just wanted to see that you were safe," I said through the door. "How are you?"

"I should have taken one of the bottles of champagne with me. All my things are gone except for what I have on me. I'll see you when the mob goes, Annette. You lock your door, now."

It was horrible not being able to help my brother. And, at seventeen, I think it was harder for him when everything he knew was falling apart. I had already felt something like that, once. I didn't really care if my things were gone—all except one: my diary, which had in it my writings since my sixteenth birthday. And it was where I had always kept it since convent school.

I entered my room, locked the door, and opened the heavy oak wardrobe: in the back of the shelf at the top I saw the hatbox. I grabbed a footstool—the chair had been taken—and stood on my tiptoes and pulled the box down. Either no one had looked inside or they didn't care for my plumed hat; underneath it rested my diary. Habits developed in convent school still held me in good stead. I shoved the box back up and lay on my carved beechwood bed, far too heavy to move. All my draperies, bed curtains, sheets, and blankets were gone, as was the writing desk, the bedside table and the small mahogany commode, and my silk and muslin dresses and velvet redingote that had hung in the wardrobe. Even the châteaux' old bronze chamberpot with, for some unknown reason, the likeness of the American Benjamin Franklin engraved on its bowl was gone from under the bed. My copies of medieval epics, though, *Eric and Enide* and *The Romance of the Rose*, lay unharmed on the floor where the bedside table had been. Those had marginalia in them from when I was sixteen and seventeen, and would have been harder to replace than any fine muslin gown. My pistol was still in the pocket of my riding skirt.

Our world was turning on its head, and the count, through his clever solicitousness, was keeping us all safe. Most of the noise and activity came from below, where the wine still flowed: drunken, raised male voices. Perhaps the count had a strategy in opening his cellar first: many would get so drunk they would be no good at more extensive looting.

Still aware, though, of the possibilities of a drunken mob, I kept my hand in the pocket of my skirt that held my pistol. I heard male voices outside my door and someone trying to turn the doorknob, then kicking the door, lunging his shoulder against it. Then he was criticized by his friend, who himself now tried the door, with more force. My finger lay quietly on the trigger and my thumb uncocked the pistol, but I kept it in my pocket. I didn't want the men to see me pointing it at them if they entered the room, and have an excuse for violence. The doors of the château de Beauregard were made strong, and the looters must have grown tired of trying it, or their shoulders hurt, and I gratefully heard their steps retreat down the hall, then others passing by but not stopping, then silence, and the noise slowly subsiding below.

It seemed that they had all had enough. I cautiously walked downstairs and saw the count's ravaged salons and the last of the rioters leaving, their arms full of live chickens, bottles, copper pots and pans, kitchen knives, silver utensils, long strips of velvet drapery, porcelain plates and cups and teapots, even the pair of wolves from the mantel in the library. With no women living in the house, there seemed to be no jewelry available, but the count's guests made up for it in furniture: pairs of men carrying out the Turkish couch, a woven silk one embroidered with figures of peacocks, the Moroccan leather one with a brass boar's head (I didn't mind seeing that go), an ottoman, a mahogany writing table mounted in bronze, a veneered tea table, a silver candelabrum, a carved oak armoire that four men tried to take down the stairs, then dropped it halfway and left it there, a clock in gilded bronze, and so many carved and gilt wood chairs I couldn't tell you.

The count stood in the vestibule and watched the furnishings of his house, some of which I am sure had been there for decades or even for over a century, leave and wished all his departing guests good day, as if, after dancing dozens of quadrilles, they were about to have their footmen help them into waiting carriages. As one grizzled old man, smiling and carrying one of the embroidered armchairs, passed him, the count clapped him on the back and said, "Rest well in that now, Father." The count only left the vestibule, ostensibly to get himself another glass of the champagne Etienne had brought, when he saw the hunting tapestry being carried out.

My brother now sat by me on the marble stairs, beside the fallen oak armoire. It was also our childhood being carried out: the chairs and couches we remembered ourselves or others we knew using, or the tables we had rested our refreshments on, or the clock we had heard chime. The count finally closed the great doors. He waved his arms—"*Things*," he said, "all *things*. They mean nothing in themselves—except the tapestry, except the tapestry, but even that—we're safe, aren't we? No one harmed; a peaceful, happy crowd. It could be so much worse. And the finest pieces, of course, like the dining table, my bureau upstairs, our beds—too heavy to carry. The Beauregard coat of arms is pinioned too high for any to reach. Etienne—where's that champagne hidden in the garden? I stuck some cheese up on a high shelf in the kitchen. Annette, see if there's any eggs left in the nests in the barn—I doubt that any hens are left—what's the matter with you two?" He opened his arms wide, as when he had welcomed the peasants. "It is our distinct privilege to dine tonight on omelette and champagne." Etienne went to fetch the hidden bottles. The count's arms were still spread wide, as if he were welcoming something that hadn't arrived. I embraced him, and his big arms went around me. I felt his body shake and heard a sob that he caught in his throat. "This is my home," he said. "This is my home."

tienne and I left the château de Beauregard the day after the looting; the countryside was quiet, and some of the peasants were even back working in the count's fields. It had been quite a holiday for them.

In spite of the turmoils of the summer, in the back of my mind I always knew Etienne would be leaving to start his medical studies, as my father had at his age. We had to act in our everyday life as if the world had not changed. I had partly hoped, though, that the Revolution would keep the Sorbonne from starting, but suddenly the day was here, looming like the old stone church before us, immovable, blocking out the light. Jean, Papa's groom, had driven us down to Louis XII Square for Etienne to get the *diligence* that would take him east, through Chartres, to Paris, the violent heart of the Revolution.

He had said good-bye to Maman and the others the night before. Paul and Marguerite had come to dinner. We had said the sacking of the château de Beauregard was just some peasants wanting gifts and to see the irony of the most powerful man in the region making them omelettes. It was really quite amusing, we said. Papa and Paul knew better, and we talked to them after dinner.

Now it was a chilly autumn dawn. The square was deserted. The ornate Louis XII fountain lapped by us in the quiet morning.

"Be careful," I said. "Don't trust new friends. They may not be your friends nowadays."

My bold brother had turned eighteen at the end of August. No older sister was going to give him advice. He wore his invincibility like a cloak. I had felt like that once, when I was sixteen. Monsieur Leforges's dancing instructions had taken that away.

Etienne thanked me and looked over my shoulder for the *diligence* coming into the square. We could hear it lumbering through the slowly awakening streets. I touched his arm. "I have something for you," I said.

The coach was entering the square. It stopped by the fountain. I pressed into Etienne's hand a watch that I had bought for him, on a silver chain with a miniature attached to it. He opened the miniature, saw the likeness of me, and quickly shut it again. I kissed him, and he stepped into the *diligence*. He waved from the window and I waved back; then I watched his carriage roll noisily out of the square, and the only sound again was that of the ancient fountain.

Etienne had been my best friend for these past several years. Marguerite was my confidante in many things, but she had her family. Etienne was my companion. I wrapped my shawl tighter around me. The cathedral was still in shadow. The cobbles were wet with dew. I had never been here at this hour, and I didn't know how cold and dark Louis XII Square was at dawn.

Now I would move to chez Vincent, the house of Marguerite's family on top of the steep hill across the river in Vienne. Maman had already resumed her old theme of marriage. It was tiresome for me; I still had no taste for it, and now with Etienne gone I would be more vulnerable.

Papa was at the hospital all the time or attending patients. Besides, I had a job to do at chez Vincent. Marguerite's attention was taken up with her two-year-old son, Gérard, and I was to entertain and tutor her eight-year-old daughter, Marie.

She and I read together, practiced piano, and drew pictures of the vine rows that stretched down the steep hill of her father's property toward the river, or of the small fountain in the courtyard in the sunlight. She took her drawings seriously, and they frequently had much more style and precision than mine. I also taught her dance steps that we practiced together, as at a ball, songs by Lully, and some simple things about writing one's thoughts down and making observations.

Today was a gray day over the river, with an early autumn crispness that made me think of the beginning of the hunting season, of the contentment that shone on Papa's face as if the world held no greater joy than this moment in the early morning: with the smoke of the breath of horses and of men on the air; with his daughter mounted beside him; with the hounds barking about the heels of the horses; just before we dashed through the waist-high grass in the meadow and pursued whatever adventure the day had in store. I decided my next job would be to teach Marie to ride.

This morning I started the lesson with a passage for Marie to read from Rousseau's *Emile*: "The only moral lesson which is suited for a child—the most important lesson for every time of life—is this: 'Never hurt anybody.'" I had her memorize those three words and who said them. "Imagine," I said, "what the world would be like if everyone tried to follow Rousseau's *most important lesson?*"

Marie said it would be a very nice world.

She also liked word games, and in the late morning we were looking out the dormer windows at a funnel of fog creeping up the river.

"I have a riddle for you, Marie."

"What is it?"

"Why is the fog like a magician?"

She thought awhile. "Because they both make things disappear," she said and smiled.

"You're right." The riddle was too elementary for her, but it was all I could think up, and I wanted it to lead me to another lesson. "For instance, can you see the river?"

"No."

"It has disappeared, but that doesn't mean it's not there. Is knowledge through the senses the only knowledge we go by? In this case, which is true: the senses that tell you the river isn't there, or your intellect that remembers that it is?"

"The intellect."

"According to what I see, the sun travels in his golden chariot across the sky every day. Is that true?"

"No, the sun never moves."

"Precisely. So sometimes if we go only by what the senses perceive, we can be misled. We hold by what the intellect knows to be true. You'll find that in the quotidian, the world of the senses, especially in these days, people will make up excuses and justifications for hurting someone, but Rousseau said his lesson was *for every time of life,* so the intellect holds on to that truth."

"I will test the senses now," she said. "Maybe I can see the river from the terrace."

I followed her out. We were both hatless and without our shawls, and I could feel the cold fog piercing my linen dress. I could see it swirling in front of the chestnut tree, veiling half of its limbs.

"What is that?"

Marie pointed to a dead bird amid yellow leaves beneath the tree. I could not tell whether the bird had died of cold or from the attentions of one of Marguerite's cats or both. "It's a dead bird."

Marie walked slowly up to it and looked at it closely.

"Let's go back in the house."

"It's beautiful," she said, and lingered, then followed me. Then she went back to the bird, and I followed her. You could see the spine of each blue-black feather, and the short ribs that arched off to either side, whitish against the dark feathers. You could look at all the things you could not see when it was moving so fast in the sky or skittishly in the branches. The little body in the middle was lost in the wide fan of dark feathers, and Marie was squatting by it.

"May I bring the bird inside?"

"Just remember how it looks, and we'll draw a picture of it, as if it's still flying in the sky."

We sat near the fire and held our palms out to it until they were as hot as we could stand it, then Marie spread her paper out on the floor, where she liked to lie on her stomach on the Savonnerie rug by the fire and draw. Once when my parents visited, my mother took this opportunity to explain to little Marie that this was not a very ladylike position, to which my father immediately replied, "Look at her fine drawing. This is the position in which inspiration strikes her. I would not sacrifice art for vanity." Marie kept working on the floor by the fire, and it became her regular place.

At the noon meal the chestnut tree outside the windows had now completely disappeared in the fog. "Why is the fog like a magician?" Marie asked her mother. She never received an answer because Françoise, Marguerite's maidservant, announced that someone was at the front door. Marguerite got up to answer the call: muffled voices, then her piercing scream. I told Marie to stay at the table and ran to my sister.

"Papa," she sobbed. "Papa's been killed. A riot, a grain riot, on the embankment," she got out. I looked at the boy from the *préfecture*, as if Marguerite had got it wrong. I didn't break down at the time, like my sister, because I didn't believe the messenger. Papa could handle himself. He had gone through riots before this summer. He just stayed calm when everyone else was insane. He had even administered to fallen rioters. He was known in the town. There was some mistake.

"There is some mistake," I said to the boy, uncomfortable in the doorway with all the crying.

"A mob was looting a grain barge, Mademoiselle," he said to me. When I didn't answer, he added pleadingly, as if it would help me believe him, "You know what the bread prices have been, Mademoiselle. People were hurt. Some had been beaten by the bargemen. Your father was on his way to attend to a patient . . . "

He trailed off, and it seemed silent for a long time.

When I was younger, I had accompanied Papa on some of his rounds, and he had sent a note yesterday to chez Vincent, asking me to join him this morning. I had not seen him for a month, since Etienne left for Paris. "Papa asked me if I wanted to come today," I said to my sister, "and I said I was busy tutoring Marie—Marguerite, perhaps I could have—"

"Annette, you just would have been harmed too—"

The messenger stood there watching us.

"I'm sorry," I said to him. "Please go on."

Marguerite sank now to a carved settee in the vestibule. It took all my effort to stand there and listen to the boy tell me something that I could not, in reality, acknowledge.

"Monsieur Vallon had stopped to attend to their wounds—"

"Whose wounds?" I said.

"The rioters hurt by the bargemen. Those bargemen are big. It's just that there were so many of the rioters. Monsieur Vallon was kneeling by one of them when the mob rushed again on the barge. It is thought that because of his dress he was taken for an aristocrat."

"How was he—"

"Monsieur Vallon was struck on the head, and the crowd—"

"How do you know this?"

"A bargeman, Mademoiselle, escaped."

"Where is . . . Papa?"

"At the Bishop's Palace—pardon me, it's the Town Hall now. They burned the barge; the captain might survive."

"My mother?"

"She has already been notified, as has Monsieur Vincent."

"Then you are free to go. Here, for your pains." I rummaged in the purse in the pocket of my skirt. "This can't have been pleasant news for you to relate, either."

"Thank you, Mademoiselle."

I shut the door and turned to my sister. She looked strange, crumpled on the bench where people sat in their finery, waiting for a footman to bring around a carriage. Marie was now by her side. "What's wrong, Maman? What's wrong, Maman?" she said, her voice rising as she repeated it, but Marguerite could not answer the child.

I sat now with my arms around her on the couch. She could not lift hers. I felt the sobs rack her body now, and I also saw Marie, distressed, beside me. I would hold my tears until I was alone.

"Come to the fire, *ma pauvre*. Grandpère's been hurt," I said to Marie. "Please help me get your mother to the drawing room. She can rest better there."

"Come, Maman, come and rest," Marie said, and lifted her mother's arm.

At the touch of her child, Marguerite seemed to become suddenly conscious of us around her, and said, "I'm sorry," and we led her into the room with Marie's drawing material still on the floor by the fire, with the bird's wings spread out against a blue sky, and I lay my sister down on a chaise longue there and took Marie back into the dining room. I hoped Marguerite's scream had not waked Gérard from his nap.

We sat silently, not touching the plum tart that still sat before us. The fog had cleared now, and an autumn wind ripped more leaves from the chestnut tree. You could hear the wind in the eaves of the house, like a low moan. The room was cold.

"Would you like some water?" I said to Marie. She nodded.

Every one of my movements, even the slightest, now required a great effort. I wanted to curl into a ball in my bed for months, for years. Someone though, for now, needed to sit with Marie. I could hibernate later.

I poured Marie, then myself, some water from the porcelain jug. I stared at the Chinese-style drawing of plum blossoms, poised forever against a blue sky on the jug, as I lifted it. I felt the coolness of the water through the fine porcelain of the handle, the sound, as of snow-melt racing down a hill, filling first Marie's glass, then my own.

"You could continue your drawing," I said, my voice sounding strange. "It's a good drawing."

"You think so? I could do another one."

"What of?"

"I could draw the bird as we saw it, by the yellow leaves. Will Grandpère die, Aunt Annette?"

"He is already gone." It was not easy to say it. I really did not believe it.

"I knew it." She paused, and we sipped our cool water. "Aunt Annette, is death when you can't see the person anymore?"

I nodded.

"Then it's like the fog covering the river."

I nodded again.

My own words coming back to me shocked me. Her interpretation of my simple lesson about the senses was so much more clear and to the point than any theological dogma I could use to comfort her or myself. It comprised all the loss and all the certainty of a life continuing completely out of our realm.

"Thank you," I said. "You are very wise. Now you must comfort your mother, just as she has comforted you many times."

Marie nodded.

"And now I need to rest, myself," I said.

I held her hand and went back to the drawing room. Marguerite held her arms out to her daughter, who let go of my hand and ran to her mother. I brought a cushioned chair over for Marie to sit on, beside the chaise longue. Françoise, keeping an eye on her mistress, was knitting by the fire and didn't look up, as if it were rude to intrude.

I handed my sister a glass of the cool water. "Thank you," she said. "You take care of both of us. How are you?"

"Marie took care of me. You have a wise daughter." Of my own feelings, I didn't care to speak. The only one who understood me had crossed the river that morning in the fog. I will go to the old Bishop's Palace later today, I thought, and wash his wounds.

I pressed my sister's hand and left mother and daughter and slowly climbed the curving staircase to my room. It seemed to take a long time to reach the top, and I had to stop more than once and hold on to the walnut banister. I forced myself to take one step after the other up the steep stairs and then down the long hall to my room and flung myself on the bed and wept. I could hold myself together in front of Marguerite and Marie, but now the loss flooded in.

The room around me seemed to have such a passing existence as to be entirely illusory. I clutched the bed curtains to feel that they were real. What was the purpose of anything? I thought. Papa's death had revealed how thin the fabric of life is. Everything seemed trivial and absurd. Why teach a child dance steps, or even logic or art? And for me, the foundation of my world, the source of understanding and love, had just been reft from me like a cold wind whipping through fog, and I was left alone in an emptiness that knew no end. That wind was blowing everywhere through the universe, revealing our shadow world for what it was: the field of death. I should have been there to help him, I thought. Then the vanity of my thoughts seemed as absurd and trivial as everything else.

Suddenly I saw my father on the morning of a hunt, alive and loving life; defending Marie's decision to draw on the floor by the fire because that inspired her; smiling at me the night I had shot the boar. And that day in front of the stable when he had given me La Rouge, when he never said a thing about my disgrace with Monsieur Leforges, and I knew he had forgiven me.

I wiped away my tears and put on my riding habit and boots, and without seeing anyone walked down to the stables, saddled La Rouge, and was soon riding in the mist on the chalk cliffs above the river, feeling the cold wind snatch away my tears, the thundering life smoothly moving below me, and the gray river glinting through spaces in the fog.

Etienne returned for the mass said for Papa at Saint-Louis Cathedral. He was strange and full of his new burdens of head of the household. At the mass he took our younger sister Angelique's arm; Marguerite was on Paul's, and my mother leaned on the arm of the count. She was stoic, but we embraced. I noticed the count's eyes bright with unshed tears. I had no one to take my arm, so Marie and I stood and knelt and prayed together. It felt good to hear her soft child's voice next to me and feel her small arm, firmly locked in mine. She is the one who enlightened me, I thought, that the finality of death is only for the living.

Papa in his goodness had provided for the living—he had left substantial gifts for each child, not to be confused with inheritance, complicated as that was by issues of gender and by the fact that my mother was still alive. These were gifts to be used when needed, and, twenty and unmarried, I appreciated the security that such a gift might offer me one day.

I repeated softly

Ave, verum corpus, natum de Maria virgine

and looked up at the vast arches of the cathedral. How can they make a ceiling of stone so that it doesn't fall down, as if it's floating far above us? There were so many things I didn't understand.

I felt Marie's small hand in mine, and the touch of that hand kept me linked to the mortal world. Otherwise, I thought, I wish I could just pass right up along those arches where the incense curls and disappears, where a single, thin sun shaft comes down.

A SAFE PLACE

*M*y nephew, Gérard Vincent, learned to speak as the disturbed air of the Revolution moved about him. Sometime after his fourth birthday in 1791, he began referring regularly to demons, and I was never quite sure how much of this was his own active child's imagination and how much was influenced by those conversations that children overhear and of which they understand not the meaning but the feeling. He had his own ways of dealing with these demons, before whom his parents were powerless. Marguerite and Paul, though, did their best to keep Gérard and his sister in their own happy world.

I had returned to live with my mother and Angelique, but Maman's criticisms of my riding and her insistence that I follow her advice on suitors agitated me. Less than a year after Papa's death, perhaps out of her need for stability in the changing times, she married an ambitious lawyer in town, who came to live at chez Vallon, now chez Vergez, which was his name. It wasn't my home anymore, and I returned to chez Vincent, grateful to be part of a family, but apart from it as well. I tutored and played with little Gérard as well as Marie. He was a talkative four-year-old, and we spent so much time together, he was rapidly becoming my very good friend.

On a sunny October afternoon we made up spontaneous songs about things we saw from Marguerite's terrace. Gérard sang first about how the sun was bright on the water and how the river looked small because it was far away, then he sang about how it would be winter soon because the grapes had all been picked. I had been teaching him about seasons. Then it was my turn, and I made up a verse about how the red roses no longer flared at the end of the vine rows, and that was how you knew the harvest was over and winter was coming.

Gérard was telling me how his hoop, which he could not roll well yet with his stick, was actually a circle to catch demons in. I told him demons were only in the imagination and to use his imagination for good things, and he said he had two imaginations, one good and one bad, and when the bad one came it took over his whole body; that is why he needed the hoop.

How much did he know, in his fine world of song and play, of the way the world he was growing into was falling down outside the walls of his father's beautiful house? I was afraid that his haven would suddenly collapse in upon itself. I gave him a little hug and kissed his cheek, and he went right on singing his song about the demons.

Marguerite joined us at the table by the small fountain, and we poured iced water into our glasses of juice squeezed from lemons, then, with gleaming silver pincers, dropped in two or three cubes of sugar. I made a third, very sweet *citron pressé* for Gérard, who was playing under the table and surfaced for a sip from his wooden cup, hummed delightedly at the sweet, cold taste, then disappeared again.

But before he ducked under the table, he told us we were in a carriage. "It is going to Paris, very fast," he said.

"I don't want to go to Paris," I said.

"Yes, you do. We're going to see a riot."

"Gérard, that is enough," said his mother, who, even in the world of make-believe wanted to keep her son from danger. Paul made a point of reading the papers and keeping himself informed. Marguerite did not want to hear much of the news from Paris. But she knew it was there. "If you want to go to Paris, we will see the opera," she said.

"We are there, now. Everybody out of the carriage. Look at those people throwing that man off the tower!"

"Gérard, go back under the table," said Marguerite. "Take us somewhere else."

"Yes, take us to the seaside, Gérard. I want to see the ocean. You can build in the sand," I said. Gérard disappeared under the table, and I could hear the clip-clopping of the horses' hooves as he clicked his tongue.

"I would love to go to Paris again," said Marguerite. "I would like to give my children the same exposure to society that I received."

"There is plenty of society here."

"I think I was born in the wrong time. I would have loved to have been one of the ladies at the court of the Cavalier King."

"It would be stifling always to be expected to dress so perfectly. I prefer my muslin tea dress to that heavy velvet."

"Or perhaps I could be one of those girls in silk who flirted and listened at court and informed the queen of any intrigues. Do you know the National Assembly has closed the silk factories in Tours? Said they were decadent."

"We have plenty of silks."

"We are at the seaside, now," announced Gérard.

"I will stay here and watch you, for I hate getting sandy."

"Come, Marguerite, the breezes are fine," I said. "You can even see the cliffs of England."

"The season is approaching, Annette. Will anyone be accompanying you to the fêtes in Orléans?"

No one was accompanying me, and I preferred to stay at the beach.

"Please don't start on Maman's favorite subject, Marguerite. Now what if you could be Marguerite d'Angoulême, one of the great ancient queens of the Loire?"

"Well, I wouldn't want to be a queen nowadays. Marie-Antoinette is not one of the more beloved creatures in France. And I would not want Gérard to be a prince and be taken, at the point of a pike, from his château." She clasped her hand over her mouth. "Was I talking too loud?"

Gérard ran to the shade of the enormous horse chestnut tree that overhung the terrace and then disappeared. I had almost forgotten that he was under the table. I thought he was playing hide-and-seek, so I looked behind the tree and along the side of the terrace and couldn't find him. Then Marguerite looked in the same places, and the littlest Vincent was nowhere. She called for him; then we both called his name.

Finally, we heard his own impatient piping: "Find me." We followed the voice and found him, over the short wall that surrounded the terrace. He was perched on a steep ledge with a sheer drop just below him. Marguerite screamed, and Gérard froze and started crying. I leaned way over, had my sister hold my waist, and extended my arm down to him. My back ached, and my arm felt like lead as his entire weight swung from it; my fingers, suddenly sweaty and slippery, grasped his small hand.

"You're almost there," I said to him, and his little boots scraped the cliffs. I didn't know how he had scrambled down there.

When he was back up on the terrace, I made out, amid his sniffles, "I am a good climber. When the demons come, I know a good place to hide."

It was worth having a safe place. Maman's was with a lawyer who was able to play both sides. And Gérard, alone among us at chez Vincent, had realized the need for one of his own.

I was rereading Rousseau's *Héloïse* in the window seat with the coldness and the growing dark outside, while Marie drew stretched out in front of the fire and Marguerite worked on her needlepoint. Gérard played a game with a tiny carved figure of a mounted knight, prancing upon an embroidered chair. I was filled with love for this small, quiet world, with the snapping fire the only conversation. I thought that I didn't need anybody or anything else. I just wanted it to stay like this, always. Why couldn't it, if the Revolution settled down with the new constitution, as Paul predicted, and if I could stay away from Maman's insistence that I marry? I was content with being an old maid at twenty-two.

But *Héloïse* reminded me of the dances we would soon be a part of in the Christmas season at Orléans:

> *In the evening, the whole house assembled to dance. Claire seemed to be adorned by the hand of the graces; she had never been so brilliant as she was that day. She danced, she chatted, she laughed, she gave orders, she was equal to everything.*

Now snow sifted steadily down as I watched the half-dark of the day slip into the deeper dark of the night. The servants silently lighted fifty candles. I saw the moon rise full over the bare horse-chestnut tree; its shadows twisted and curved over the untouched snow that glimmered a little in the moonlight.

"I want you to help me make a carriage. That's what I want you to do," said a voice at my elbow. Gérard beckoned me to follow him, and I knew what this meant—moving some chairs together and sitting on them, facing each other, as if we were in a carriage. But I didn't want to leave my window seat. "Come, come," he said, and I let him draw me to the great fireplace, where he had herded Marguerite, Marie, and

Nurse. I sat by my sister in the carriage and listened to Gérard jabber to himself: "Now we are going to England," he said. I didn't even know he knew there was such a country. I was sure he didn't know you had to cross the Channel to get there.

"Monsieur and Madame Varache have left France," my sister said to me, from her seat in the carriage. "I didn't think they'd actually do it. They're going to England." I stood up to walk to the fire.

"You're standing in the water! Get out of the water!" Gérard shouted. I sat back down. I guess he did know about the Channel. It must be a magical carriage.

"You still hear of all sorts of people emigrating," Marguerite said.

"I don't want to go to England," Marie said.

"Nobody's going anywhere," I said. "Except Gérard."

"Aunt Annette and I are planning what we are going to wear to the first fête of the Christmas season in Orléans," Marguerite said to her daughter. "It will be nice to stay with the Dubourgs again."

Nurse ushered the children away for supper and bed, and my sister continued working on an embroidery pattern, green on white, of a tree with flowering branches, and I wrote in a little book.

"What do you write in that thing?" asked Marguerite. "You're jotting in it every evening."

"I like to keep track of my thoughts."

"Do you ever," she said, and looked down at her flowering tree, "write about love?"

"You know I tried that when I was a girl. It turned out to be rather deceptive."

"Well, that was one rotten man." She paused again. "Do you ever think Maman is right, and perhaps you ought to think about it again? I know you're different and always have been different—riding and hunting, and having dozens of suitors who never get anything more than a consent to dance with you. We love having you here, but it is selfish of me to rely on you to take care of Gérard. You should have a life of your own. You do know one *can* be happily married. Look at Paul and me."

"How many men are like Paul? Intelligent, honorable, kind? Your luck is rare. His sort's not what I see, in my many conversations with clever or not-so-clever young men. No, thank you, if I may continue to take advantage of your hospitality, I'm very happy here with you and your family, and with riding La Rouge by the river. And with dancing with gentlemen without being overmastered by some sudden and uncontrollable emotion—except that excited by the music."

"Annette, I like you to stay here simply because I find your conversation amusing. No one I know talks like you."

"When I was a girl, I was a fool," I said. "And now I prefer to watch the snow."

It swirled in the pale evening on the terrace and looked as if it blew in every direction at once. I wanted to ride out in it and stop in the woods along the river and watch the world transformed before me. Everything that was ordinary gained some new grace: the weight of hours of snow balanced on one twig, on the old shovel, leaning against the terrace wall.

"Well, I hope this snow stops soon or we'll never get to Orléans," said Marguerite. "And there, you see, I have forgotten all about England and Monsieur and Madame Varache," she added.

"I wonder if they're happy?"

I looked over my shoulder, and the snow had indeed stopped. The fire was a good sight and warm on my legs, but I thought this was the time.

"I'm going out," I said.

"It's the blue hour, almost dark."

"La Rouge needs her exercise. It will be pretty; you want to come?"

"Ask me in the spring."

I put on my long English riding cloak with a high collar that was the style of a few years ago, and the rabbit fur gloves and the hat, in which Marguerite said I looked like a Cossack.

I opened the wide old stable doors and walked into the familiar smell of hay and alfalfa, of manure, and the earthy smell of the horses themselves: the realm that stayed the same no matter what went on outside those stable doors. La Rouge nickered at my approach. I talked softly while I saddled her, and we rode out onto the fresh snow. We walked down the steep, narrow street, cantered the quai on which lumbered only one late cart, laden with wood, and I let her out farther down the left bank. I rode and rode, until the heavy cares of past, present, and future had dropped off far behind.

I sat still and allowed La Rouge to paw through the snow for a mouthful of grass, and as dark descended and hardly a breeze whispered and a new set of flakes fell, I felt a peace that rose up out of the winter earth and enveloped me. I felt a presence of something vast and intimate, of which I was a small yet conscious part. I had felt it before, when I paused by the river or at the edge of the woods. I called it the presence of the Virgin, for I was taught to give it that name, but one could, I suppose, just as easily give it the pagan name of some spirit of the water or the trees.

I thought, then, that I could only feel this presence by myself. If anyone else were here, I would be thinking about that person and would miss it all.

And yet I wanted to share, deeply. I yearned for a day, far in the future of a peaceful France, when I'd ride here with a man who himself knew the vast and intimate presence suddenly felt in solitude by a rushing river. I dreamed that we'd talk and ride and not have to talk at all. I shook my head. I cherished my contentment by the fire with my niece and nephew and book.

I thought, therefore, of my dream of writing. I'd fill my journals with thoughts and descriptions, and one day, perhaps as an old woman, I'd publish them under the name of a man.

I watched the moonlight on snow and water. I knew of few things as beautiful. The earth became a map of light and dark. Orion and Canus Major glittered in clear coldness. Above and below stretched a shining world. I dreamed, too, that the peace that dwelt here, just beyond my fingertips, I could know and carry with me as I carried my own limbs, and pass it on. What else was life for?

I was getting cold, standing still with my thoughts. I mounted La Rouge and rode swiftly, the snow and moonlight-bright sparks shed from her hooves.

LUXURY

*I*t was the third Christmas without Papa, and each one passing did not make it easier. Part of me did not want to make the traditional journey to the Dubourgs in Orléans, where we always had fine parties and dances. Part of me didn't even care that Etienne would be there; that Angelique was already there, and the family would be together again. Part of me just wanted to stay with my two quiet friends: La Rouge and the river.

It was still considered bad manners to talk about the Revolution in social gatherings where one was supposed to be happy, and many of my parents' friends kept up the pretense that the Revolution had never happened.

The first Christmas after Papa was killed and the Revolution began, no one discussed how, in October of that year, the royal family had been rousted at pike's point from their palace in Versailles by a mob led by market women who had walked all the way from Paris. Marie-Antoinette only missed being hacked to pieces in her bedchamber by escaping through a secret passageway designed for the King's assignations with her when they were trying to produce an heir. Now, in the storming of the palace she ran to meet the King and her two children, huddling with their nurse in his chamber. Once they had arrived, the mob shunted them into a carriage, and they left their home and began a long, slow, ignominious ride to Paris. The crowd marched on all sides of the carriage, shouted insults to the King and Queen, and proudly carried, bobbing on pikes that they regularly dipped beside the windows, the bloody heads of the royal family's personal Swiss Guards. The family was then immured in the Tuileries, an unused, rat-infested palace along the Seine, where the people of Paris and the new National Assembly could keep a close watch on them. That seemed worth discussing, but no one mentioned it that year at chez Dubourg. No one could do anything about it anyway.

This present Christmas saw the royal family truly *imprisoned* in the Tuileries. They had tried to escape in June, but had bungled it and were caught close to the border near a town called Varennes. The National Guard escorted them back to Paris in shame, disgrace, and utter mistrust. If the King had any credibility left, it was gone after the flight to Varennes. It would be improper to discuss this final blow to the sham authority of the King, though, among the people in silks and velvets at chez Dubourg. Nevertheless, my family, in private, had gone over the what-ifs of the aborted escape many times.

Paul held out hope that things could settle down now. He thought we could have a constitutional monarchy, like Great Britain with their king and parliament. He said *that* would be the most stable government, for struggles were already rife within the National Assembly that ruled France, power shifting almost monthly between different men, like a ball they kicked to or stole from each other.

Anyone who still believed in having a king of any sort was called a royalist. But there were different types of royalists: those like Paul, who wanted a peaceful transformation; those, like the Varaches, who, threatened by the instability, simply emigrated; and those who secretly accepted no change and quietly waited for the King's restoration to power, to be brought about by his brothers and their émigré armies forming abroad. Chez Dubourg was a royalist household, perhaps of the third category.

The greatest change for me, though, on our way to Orléans, was that Monsieur Vergez, a poor substitute, was sitting in Papa's place in the old family carriage in which Vergez had installed new velveteen curtains. He said he wanted to keep out the glares of the commoners. As a lawyer, though, he supported all the new laws that supported them.

Vergez became garrulous about business matters regarding Grégoire, the new constitutional bishop of Blois. Grégoire had secured his title by taking an oath that his first priority of allegiance was to the republican constitution and not to his religion, an oath any self-respecting priest would not take and which would, in the near future, cause much strife throughout France. Vergez said he planned to please Grégoire in a case involving a priest who would not take the new oath, though Vergez loathed Grégoire for being a revolutionary.

My stepfather was also planning to ask the bishop to recommend him, Vergez, to a seat on the new trade tribunal. My mother seemed untroubled by this hypocrisy.

I opened the *Romance of the Rose*:

> *I bathed my face in clear water,*
> *The bottom paved with shining stones*

and Maman took that moment to enumerate to me the young men I'd meet in the coming season in Orléans. I reflected, not for the first or last time, that when you are reading, others think they can disturb you because you are not *doing* anything.

So I asked, in my own non sequitur, had she noticed that we were traveling the same route, north along the river, that Joan of Arc's troops had taken in 1429 to end the siege of Orléans? She didn't seem interested in my historical allusion. His own speech finished, Vergez was asleep, his head against the velvet.

I peeked out the heavy curtains at the endless brown and white, stubbly wintry fields and bare poplars that marched up long narrow roads to isolated farms and searched out the two towers of Sainte-Croix Cathedral that would signal that we were approaching Orléans.

Finally we arrived, driving down the rue Royale. After the long hours of empty road the street was suddenly crowded with carts and carriages, its shops lit in the wintry dusk, and men and women hurrying home in their long coats with high collars or in billowing capes. I was impatient to get out of the carriage.

Slowed at times to a standstill by the traffic, we finally turned left on the rue de Bourgogne, which led to the old *porte* through which Joan had entered to the cheers of the people. We stopped in front of a large stone house with two lanterns lit outside, and the Dubourgs' footman rushed out to greet us. Soon we were in the lit vestibule, enfolded by the embraces of the Dubourgs and of the Vincents, who had journeyed in their own carriage.

Monsieur Dubourg, small and portly, with a powdered and curled wig, bent over my hand and smiled with real affection. His tall, thin wife, with a heaped-up coiffure that made her still taller, loomed above him and lowered herself, giraffelike, to bestow on me two kisses and a lavender scent, and the words that I still looked as young and pretty as ever. Twenty-two and unmarried, I wasn't sure if this was a compliment. She was my mother's best friend, and they disappeared into the front salon, already lost in low and urgent gossip.

Monsieur Dubourg took my arm and led me into another room, firelit, with a couch embroidered with Chinese-style boughs. I took my perch on a branch with Marie and Gérard on either side, and Monsieur Dubourg offered me a glass of eau-de-vie. Angelique had arrived at chez Dubourg to start the round of fêtes a week early, and now she and Etienne entered together with delight at our reunion. The Christmas season had arrived, and the first dance would be here, tomorrow night, in chez Dubourg's small but elegant ballroom, walls festooned with ribbons and gilded flowers, as real as if they were alive.

Etienne pulled a small box, tied in saffron silk ribbon, from his pocket and insisted that I open it straightaway. It was a watch on a gold chain, and inside it I beheld a painted miniature of a sorrel horse— the likeness of La Rouge. My brother laughed. "I thought you would rather look at a portrait of your horse than of me," he said.

"La Rouge does have smaller ears."

"So you like my longer hair," he said, and I stood up and kissed him on both cheeks. It was good, after all, to be together again. One could almost imagine Papa, shedding his cloak in the vestibule, hastening to join us. I could hear his deep voice as he entered the room. I could see us all rushing up to him.

I sat there on an oriental bough, with a golden bird behind me, and allowed myself the luxury of imagining, for a moment, that our world had not changed, not changed at all.

BOOK II

1791–1792

THE FOREIGNER

The harpsichord music chimed pleasantly through the drone of voices. I sat sipping Monsieur Dubourg's felicitous Poire William and enjoying its warmth when I accidentally caught the eye of a young man in dark green silk stockings. He asked if he could sit down, and I was angry that now I would not be alone with the music and the taste of the wine. A servant came by. "What are you drinking?" asked green stockings.

"Eau-de-vie."

"You're too young to drink that by yourself." He requested one. "Enjoying the fête?"

"Very much so."

"It's good to see so many elegantly dressed ladies in these republican times. What are you called?"

"Mademoiselle Annette Vallon."

"I am Monsieur Letour of Bordeaux. My father owns a grand vineyard in the Médoc, and I'm the personal guest of the vicomte and vicomtesse de Fresne d'Aguesseau. Perhaps you've heard of them?"

I nodded. The vicomtesse had snubbed my mother once because, though my father's family was old and respected in the Loire region, it had no title. Then, as if to make up for a rudeness that, after all, wasn't intentional but just a reflex of her class, the vicomtesse said to Maman, "What a lovely coiffure," and to me, "What nice amber ringlets."

"Are you from Orléans?" Monsieur Letour asked.

"From Blois."

"I visited the grand château there on my tour. It is an amazing montage, this wing of one century, that wing two centuries before, old Catherine de Medici's room with secret panels hiding shelves where she kept poisons."

"I never really liked her."

"But she was better than her son Henri III."

I could hear the oboes stepping lightly over the buzz of voices. It had been months since I had talked at a fête to a strange and eager young man. It can be very tedious. Monsieur Letour from Bordeaux continued to tell me about the history of my city. "I was in the actual room on the second floor where Henri III murdered the duc de Guise, who ruled Paris. Do you believe in phantoms?"

"It depends."

"I think I heard the ghost of Henri telling his mother, 'I alone rule France! The King of Paris is dead!' Do you know what I heard her phantom answer?"

I remembered the line that every schoolchild in Blois knows. "I forget," I said.

"She said, 'I hope that you have not now become the King of Nothing!' Isn't that clever? 'The King of Nothing'!"

"Perhaps that could be said about our present king, shut away, as he is, in the Tuileries."

I had willfully committed an indiscretion, and Monsieur Letour regarded me as if trying to assess if I were a revolutionary in a blue satin gown with a lawn kerchief and sleeve ruffles. I was bored with acting as if nothing had changed, as if the King were still hunting happily on the vast grounds of Versailles. Monsieur Letour finally decided to overlook my bad manners. I was just a woman, after all.

"The King of Nothing," he went on, "then killed the duke's brother, just to make sure, I guess, then burned both bodies and let the Loire take the ashes. He thought of everything."

"I like that the windows aren't symmetrical," I said.

"What windows?" asked my guest.

"Of the château."

"Oh, they are horrible."

"They were made to harmonize with what was inside. No one cared about symmetry," I said.

"That wouldn't happen now," said the man from Bordeaux, "though the vicomte and vicomtessee both say contemporary architecture—"

Then from the door I heard a familiar voice calling, "Annette! Annette!"

"Pardon me. It's my sister." I went to greet Marguerite and Paul, handsome in his gray velvet coat but looking a little tired, and my younger sister, Angelique.

"The dancing is going to start," said Marguerite. "I know how you hate to miss the first one."

"You will join us, won't you?" Paul asked.

"And bring your new friend," whispered Angelique. "He's already missing you."

I could feel his eyes on me and wanted to slip with my sisters into the ballroom. Instead, remembering my manners, I returned to the table. "Who are your sister's friends?" my guest asked.

"Her husband and my other sister."

"You have a good-looking family."

"Thank you. They say the dancing is beginning."

"Shall we go?" We left our glasses on the table. My heart lifted at the sight of dancers forming into circles in the little jewel of a ballroom. Angelique raised the tip of her fan, and we joined them.

"Who is your friend?" she whispered to me. I had forgotten his name. I only remembered whom he wanted me to associate him with, the vicomte and vicomtesse. He stood beside me, conspicuous in his nonidentity, and I looked helplessly at Angelique.

"May I present myself. I am Monsieur Letour of Bordeaux and guest of the vicomte and vicomtesse de Fresne d'Aguesseau." I noticed Angelique raise her eyebrows. I presented my family, and he had just time to kiss Angelique's hand before the music started.

I love dancing. I do not care who my partner is. When I move to music, nothing else exists for that time. My partners sometimes think the enchantment is of their making. I let them think that, as long as it does not interfere with my transport. This was a lovely minuet, and I recognized in it the lightness of the young Austrian composer who had recently died. His music belongs to the old world of refined movements, of lace and silk rustling, of courtesy and charm (though Papa had seen him play in Paris once, and it seems from what he said, Herr Mozart would be now what is called a citizen, not a subject, and would not have cared for ceremony, though his music soars in an ordered universe of grace).

I could see the gloved hand of Monsieur Letour being extended toward me. I smiled and whisked forward and back. Gloves are convenient things. His powdered face smiled back, and the lace at his wrist brushed the folded fan dangling at mine. Under the chandelier of a hundred wax tapers his powdered wig gleamed white, and the music picked up my feet. They knew the right steps, and I had no thought of them. Over the green silk collar of Monsieur Letour I saw a wigless, fair-haired stranger standing by himself at the door. His hair was wet from the rain and hung loosely to his shoulders. He looked like a citizen. His face was suntanned and without powder. He stood there unsmiling and seemed nervous, as if he would at any minute bolt back out into the winter night.

When the minuet was over, Marguerite brushed by me, waving her fan, and smiled. It was cold outside, but the fire in the hearth and the warmth of the dancers in their velvets and silks were making pearls of perspiration under the ringlets on the back of my neck. I excused myself and walked toward the door and felt the cool air from the hall on my bare shoulders and throat. The strange fair-haired man stood at the edge of the hall and the ballroom, as if he were about to enter either one, but having no immediate purpose, hovered there, glancing at the thronging people and fingering one of the buttons on his plain brown frock coat. For a moment I was in the path of his glance. He stared at me, then purposefully looked at the orchestra, as if he were inspecting to see if the candles were properly fixed on the music stands.

The cooler air in the hall felt good, and the music started again, sounding beautiful without anyone to interrupt it.

"Mademoiselle Vallon." Madame Dubourg was dressed for a grand occasion in a *robe à la turque*, an embroidered red satin robe, over a skirt of Chinese silk with stripes that looked faintly like bamboo. "Are you enjoying yourself?"

"Yes, thank you. A fine chamber orchestra."

"I forgot that you know so much about music. You studied singing and dancing some years ago with that handsome teacher, did you not? I saw you dance with him at the château de Beauregard. Both so charming and accomplished."

"Thank you."

"Annette, I want you to do me a favor. Will you talk for a moment with an Englishman from Cambridge University? He was invited here tonight by his landlord on the rue Royale, Monsieur du Vivier, who is a friend of my husband. Monsieur du Vivier made the mistake of promising the Englishman he would introduce him to Orléans society. So now he is here, and I don't know what to do with him. He doesn't know anyone; his French is poor, and his clothes are worse. But I hear he is an educated gentleman. I will introduce you."

She ushered me over to the damp-headed stranger, and when she presented me to him, his eyes regarded me sharply. Madame Dubourg mumbled an awful foreign surname. As she left us she said in my ear, "Get him to practice his French. If he is going to come to our fêtes, it is embarrassing to have him looming around in silence." Then he and I were standing alone together at the entrance of the ballroom.

"How long have you been in France?" I asked.

"About a month."

"How do you like it?"

"I like it very well." His French was not as bad as Madame Dubourg had said. It was just slow.

"Lovely music, isn't it?"

"It's very pretty." Then he ventured on a longer sentence. "I like watching the people dance. Do you like to dance?"

"Yes, very much." In the long pause I thought he was going to ask me to accompany him to the floor.

"I am afraid I do not dance very well," he said. I could see him translating and conjugating verbs in his head. His eyes would wander to the ceiling as he spoke. When they returned to me, they were the opposite of his speech. They looked on after his sentence had ended, as if they were speaking after his words had stopped. They certainly made more interesting conversation. What were we going to do if he could not dance?

"Shall we sit over there?" I asked. We sat down on a small settee in the music room, but the harpsichordist had gone to have his brief supper. Only two or three people were left in the room. I saw the unfinished liqueur glasses still sitting on the table. On the wallpaper next to us a bird, its tiny mouth open, sang surrounded by a forest of blossoms. As soon as the foreigner sat down, he looked at me again with his eyes that seemed not embarrassed to stare, and now it was I who looked away.

He started on his own: "This is a very grand house. I have seen something very interesting here." He was out of his depth. He could not tell me what was so interesting. "On the . . . walls there are . . . " He flapped his arms, as if he were about to take off from the settee. I almost laughed and stopped myself. I didn't want to embarrass him. He was wonderfully different.

"Birds," I said.

"Birds, of course," he said. "I know that word. How stupid of me. Isn't that amusing that *bête*, 'stupid,' is the same word in French as *beasts*. I don't think that beasts are necessarily stupid. I know many humans who are more stupid than some horses I've known."

Now I did laugh, not at him, but at his delightful insight.

"What did you say you were called?"

"William Wordsworth."

"You have an unpronounceable name."

"Try it." He had a gently mischievous smile.

I could not get my tongue and lips around his foreign name, and mangled it.

"Close," he said. "William, with an *L* as in 'Loire.' Then Words-worth."

"Willam."

"Very good."

Then I mangled his surname again. It came out something like "Woodswoods," and he laughed and said he preferred it.

"I am supposed to be helping *you* with French."

"Who says?"

"Madame Dubourg."

"Ah, that's why you are talking to me."

"Why do the English have such difficult names, when so many of their names are French?"

"From William the Conqueror."

"William," I repeated.

"Yes, that's right."

"I will call you Monsieur William and never try your horrible surname again."

"Monsieur *Williams* would be better."

"Why?"

"Because it is an actual name."

"What does that matter? I am making up your name."

"What is yours again?"

"You have forgotten? It's easy to remember."

"Tell it to me."

"Annette Vallon."

"Annette Vallon." He said it to himself, softly. "I have not talked to many people since . . . I have been in France."

I smiled at his effort and his success. "People need to have more patience," I said.

"I want to engage a tutor, but it's expensive."

He stared at me with his glowing blue eyes. His hands were straight out in front of him and folded on the table. They were near mine. "Will you teach me French?"

He was so sincere and intense, he made me laugh again. "I will be your tutor for a night." He looked at me and smiled, waiting. "Have you seen Paris, Monsieur *William*?" I pronounced his name with difficulty, and he nodded.

Now he had to perform. He looked at the ceiling, then started enthusiastically: "I visited the Champ de Mars . . . where in July, the National Guard shot innocent people . . . who were demanding the abdication of a worthless king—"

There was no one else in the room, but it was still a royalist house, and I didn't want the Dubourgs or their servants to hear their foreign guest abuse the King. "Did you see any of the historic sights?"

"I loved the Pantheon. I took my shoes off so I . . . could feel the same cool marble on my feet as the ancient Romans. I loved their worship of . . . forces, intelligences in nature, all complementing each other."

The Dubourgs, devout Catholics, would also find this disagreeable, but I liked it. At least he was practicing his French. A servant entered and was clearing away the liqueur glasses and sweeping crumbs from another table. "Monsieur William, as a foreigner, what was the most interesting thing you saw?"

He didn't pause at all. "Without question, it was the Legislative Assembly. I had a letter of introduction from an English lady, a fine poet named Charlotte Smith, which allowed me to listen to a debate in the assembly on . . . a revolt of the negroes in Saint-Domingue. They spoke too fast for me, and everyone was agitated. I'm afraid I didn't follow it well. . . . But I thought it was noble that they even debated these people's fate. In England the negroes aren't even . . . considered people. The Revolution has brought such new thinking."

"Did you see anything else?" I thought he might mention something to do with the arts.

"Charlotte Smith's letter also . . . admitted me to the Jacobin Club. I met a fascinating man there, who dined with me, for he spoke English, having traveled in England and America. His father was a caterer, and now this man is one of the most eloquent and altruistic voices of the new France. He founded the newspaper *La Patriote Française.* Perhaps you've heard of him, Jacques-Pierre Brissot."

I had heard of him, informed of political events through Paul. Brissot had recently proposed a decree by which property of families such as the Varaches, who had emigrated, was to be confiscated. Why had Monsieur William gone to the Jacobin Club, that revolutionary hotbed? I wondered. These are not sights for the casual tourist. Nor were these the times. "What made you want to travel to France?" I said out loud.

"I want to learn your language better and become a tour guide for gentlemen. I liked France when I was here before." Some of the candles had guttered and gone out, and Monsieur William's face was partly in shadow. It made his eyes stand out. They held me.

"When was that?"

"I arrived at Calais on the night of July 13, 1790, the eve of the first anniversary of the Revolution."

His long, fair, reddish brown hair caught the light from candles still lit on the table behind him. I could hear the music calling from the ballroom.

"Everyone was dancing. When my friend and I walked south, through the villages, people danced in the streets at night. The celebrations went on for a week. At one town they invited us for dinner, and toasted us, as free Englishmen, and we toasted them as *citizens*. Then they took our hands and led us, dancing, back out into the street."

Didn't his landlord tell him he is not supposed to talk of such things here? "How far south did you go?" I asked.

"Save for a few boat rides, we walked all the way from London to Lake Como and back. About thirty miles a day."

I had never been farther than Nantes or, once, Paris.

"We . . . had to be back in time for university. My family did not want me to go on that trip because they wanted me to study for exams. My friends did not want me to go because they thought France was dangerous."

"Was it?"

"Only the Italian mosquitoes." He stretched his arm to its full length and with his finger mimicked a mosquito coming at him. He made a high-pitched whine, hit his face several times quickly from different directions, and laughed. It was a good hearty laugh and made me laugh too.

"What did your family think of you going to France this time?"

"My parents are dead. I refer to my uncles. They did not want me to go. They wanted me to find a job. So I am looking." He laughed again.

"Tell me about London."

"More people than Paris. I can pass the whole day just looking at all the people. But two things I do not like. The many people who come for executions, as if it's entertainment, and the many . . . women of the streets. They seemed more sad than those types of women in Paris."

"How do you know?" I was shocked, though, that the foreigner had talked in polite society of women of the streets.

"How long do you intend to stay in France?"

He smiled. "Is this how you teach me French? Ask me questions?"

"Who else here would listen to you talk so slowly?"

"I will stay here until I have learned more French, until I have no more money, until I have seen what I have come to see." I had never seen eyes like his in an adult. They were so excited and so innocent.

Their frankness could disarm anyone, I thought. He pulled something from his pocket and put it on the empty table. In the dim light I could not see it clearly, but it looked like a rock. He rolled it in his hands and threw it up in the air a little and caught it and put it back down on the table. "Do you know what this is?" he asked.

"It looks like a rock."

"Here, touch it." It felt like a rock.

"Is it from your homeland?"

"It's from your homeland. It's from the rubble of the Bastille. It's a symbol of great change."

"It's a rough and ugly rock. There are more beautiful ones along the banks of the Loire." Someone stood in shadow at the doorway in front of the light from the hall.

"There you are, Annette. We have been looking for you." Paul looked inquiringly at Monsieur William.

"Madame Dubourg instructed me to help her foreign guest practice his French. May I present Monsieur William."

He stood and, picking up the rock, put it back in his pocket.

"Monsieur William, Monsieur Paul Vincent, the husband of my sister."

"Annette, they are going to start the last dance. Would you like to come? And you, Monsieur."

"I prefer to watch. Thank you for the lesson, Mademoiselle Vallon."

"It was nothing."

My brother-in-law took my arm, and we walked into the ballroom for the last dance. It seemed very bright and loud. I noticed that outside the glass doors it was beginning to snow. "You have been gone a long time," he said to me with a teasing smile. Over his shoulder of mouse-colored velvet I saw Monsieur William leaning against the wall at the entrance of the ballroom and regarding me with those sharp and innocent eyes.

CUT-HEAD JOURDAN

*L*ate that night, after all the guests had left chez Dubourg, Paul accompanied me to my room. The upstairs hall was deserted, and we walked past the children's rooms and stopped outside my door at the end of the corridor. Paul almost spoke and stopped himself. His eyes seemed tight and tired. I waited.

"We are all pretending," he said.

"Pretending what?"

"Things have changed, Annette. Cultivate a friendship with the Englishman. We all may follow Monsieur and Madame Varache."

"What more has happened?"

"Just the tenor of the times. Things seem set against us. After the royal family's flight in the summer, a more severe reaction has set in against them, and against anyone who sympathizes with them. If you are for the King, you are for the Austrian Empire, since the Queen is Austrian. Now the emperors of Austria and Prussia have threatened armed intervention in France if there's any further outrage to Louis and his family. That is just what the extreme revolutionists want— an excuse to accuse us all of being in league with the enemies of France. That includes the priests: any who do not take the new oath of allegiance to the constitution are declared in conspiracy against the nation. I do not want to tell Marguerite any of this. She worries so about the children. I know she doesn't want to leave Blois. When I do talk about it, she points out correctly that we ourselves are not threatened in any way. But I can only think it will get worse."

Paul took off his powdered wig and leaned against the wall. He ran his fingers through his cropped blond hair. He must have been pretending all night.

"I'm sorry," he said. "I shouldn't burden you with this."

"Do. I know Marguerite cannot bear to talk about it. I thought you said things would settle down with the new constitution."

"Yes, but there are those now who want more. They want first to strip the King of his last vestiges of power, then—they want to kill him. I know they do. I misjudged the hatred, Annette. Anyone who is considered a royalist can be called a conspirator against France. And one can do anything to conspirators. I misjudged the violence this whole thing has unleashed. I don't know what kind of world we're in. In September, in Provence, *moderate* aristocrats *and their families* were murdered in prisons by a band whose leader they call 'Cut-Head Jourdan.' That's the name they give to their local hero. If in Avignon, why not in Orléans, even in Blois?"

He saw my face. "They were probably just fanatics in the south in hot September. The Loire Valley is different. It was a wonderful party tonight. Angelique had more than one dance with your Monsieur Letour."

"Now you're pretending again. And I never cared for green silk stockings."

"Thank you for letting me unburden to you, Annette. You are a good friend, and a good aunt to Marie and Gérard."

"They are so charming I don't have to try."

"Good night."

"Good night." I watched him walk away down the hall and pause slightly before he opened the door into the room where my sister lay, probably already asleep.

Our personal servants had stayed behind in Blois, for the Dubourgs supplied us with all our needs, including servants to look after us. But I did not ask for one for my room. I missed my maidservant, Claudette. She would have had something funny to say about Monsieur Letour, something insightful to say about Monsieur William, to take my mind off Paul's news. The fire in my room was low, and as I undressed I looked out the window at the new snow on the roofs of the old half-timbered houses of Orléans. I suddenly wanted to be in my hometown. I always liked Orléans and our stay here, but now everything felt unfamiliar and cold. I shoveled hot coals into the bed-warmer and thrust it deep under the covers, then jumped in after it and reached my bare feet down until the soles were almost touching it and were as hot as I could stand. The rest of me was still chilled.

I was tired. My eyes and feet ached. I looked forward to sleep and closed my eyes and involuntarily pictured families helpless in prison in Avignon, and the faces of those who murdered them, led by a man they called Cut-Head Jourdan. I heard their cries and tried to think of ways I could help them escape.

Then I thought of Monsieur William and the rock. I wasn't against all the rock symbolized as much as I was against the violent emotions it let loose, of which Monsieur William, as a foreigner, seemed blatantly unaware. He had visited the Jacobin Club, that seat of revolutionary fervor, but I thought of him, and the tightness in my body that went with the other thoughts relaxed and I heard his voice, speaking slowly and deliberately, saw his eyes looking at me in the half-dark room, and I fell asleep.

Every year, for a little present for Madame Dubourg, Marguerite brought a few pots of jam made from the apricot trees that lined the warm brick wall at the back of the garden at chez Vincent. At breakfast, I sipped the hot coffee from the West Indies, where Monsieur Dubourg's company did a brisk business in the sugar trade: from Martinique and Guadeloupe to Nantes, upriver to Orléans, and from there to Paris.

I spread last summer's jam on my roll; little Gérard and I had picked many of these apricots. It had taken all afternoon, and I had held Gérard up so he could pull some off the branches above his head. The apricots were beautiful: softly furred, orange, and round in the thick green leaves with specks of blue sky showing through. It had been hard hot work, and we were proud of the basketfuls we had brought back to the kitchen. I was making a good citizeness. I helped Cook make the apricots into the jam the next day and sat Gérard up on the counter to watch. I held the boiling wax too close to the curtains by the window, and the curtains caught fire and Cook and I threw bowls of water at them and hit them with towels, laughing as hard as we could. Gérard did not know whether it was scary or funny, and neither did his mother, when she walked in. She always thought of me, fondly, as a bit of a fool.

Now I scooped the golden jam out of the pot and smoothed it over my just-warm roll and tasted the sweetness of summer, and looked out the window at the new snow below, lining the busy rue de Bourgogne, carts and wagons rattling along already, east-west, as they had done on this road since before the Romans came and will do long after us. What was one more summer or winter to the ancient road? What was a revolution; what were kings?

And I thought now of a young Englishman walking the roads

across France. "Marguerite, do you think men are mostly liars when it comes to their physical feats and adventures?"

"You always say things out of nowhere."

"This is not out of nowhere. It's very logical. I am referring to a conversation I had last night."

"With Monsieur Letour?"

"Why would I remember anything that bore said to me? Marguerite, would you believe it if a man told you he had virtually walked all the way from London to the other side of the Alps and back?"

"Oh, the Englishman. All men are hiding something."

"What would Monsieur William hide?"

"Why is he here?"

"You're not answering my question."

"I would believe that he was trying to impress you. Whether it's true or not isn't important."

"He probably walked here from Paris."

"And walked from London across the Channel."

I got up from the table. "I am going on a walk this morning."

"In this weather, and by yourself? Don't be foolish."

"The sun's coming out. And I haven't visited the quai du Châtelet in a year. I'll be back at noon."

After breakfast, I put on my fur-lined cloak and, my hands lost in a large muff, joined the current of pedestrians going west on the rue de Bourgogne; then I turned south along a narrow alley lined with half-timbered houses almost leaning over me. I passed Saint-Pierre-le-Puellier, the dark little church built six hundred years ago, when they didn't know how to make grand cathedrals yet. I liked to go there for Christmas mass rather than to the colossal Cathedral of the Holy Cross that they were still rebuilding, where one was dwarfed by the statues of the four apostles as soon as one reached the door. Soon I was out of the narrow alleys, the river gleaming suddenly before me in the winter sun.

Gabares, with their huge sails, and their smaller, attendant vessels, each pulling a yet smaller one upriver, lined the quais. They had just made the long trip—over a fortnight—up from Nantes, even in December frost. Men without gloves unloaded wood and coal from a barge. Others herded livestock and carried hay onto a barge without rigging, headed downstream, perhaps just to Blois or Tours. Behind the busy ships lay the Bridge Royal, on the spot where Joan of Arc's troops had charged across the broken arches of a bridge, the spring water swirling beneath them, to drive the English out of the boulevard des Tourelles just across the river. There, leaning against a post of the bridge and writing in a small book, seemingly oblivious to bargemen shouting at each other nearby, was the tall Englishman I had met the night before.

Affected gentlemen never used to *wear* hats, but only hold them under their arms so as not to disturb their powdered wigs. Yet this Englishman had his hat under his arm, but no wig to put in disarray. His long fair hair blew in the crisp breeze, and he brushed it out of his eyes as if without noticing it had got in his way, as he didn't notice me when I walked past, staring at the strange, unmoving figure with the tide of the world moving around him and the river, brightly, before him. I walked on.

When I was past the bridge I heard, "Mademoiselle Vallon! Annette Vallon!" I turned and saw Monsieur William, running through a passel of bargemen, each twice as wide as he. He stopped beside me, slightly out of breath. "It's a beautiful morning," he got out.

"I wonder you notice it, Monsieur William; you seemed to give it little account."

"Ah, I was writing."

"What do you write?"

"I scribble poems. It is what I do."

"A scribbler? I was reading the scribbling of Jean de Meung's *Romance of the Rose* on my way to Orléans."

"I know that poem, in its translation by our poet Chaucer, of course."

"You should read it in French sometime, Monsieur. What were you scribbling about, may I ask?"

"I'm trying to . . . capture my sensations when I saw the Alps, on the journey I told you about last night. I walked by the river to help me remember the torrent at Chamouny."

"You weren't walking."

"May I join you now?"

I nodded and he took the river side as we headed west with the current. We were silent, and I began to wonder if this was a good idea, to promenade with an odd foreigner along the quai. Would a friend of my mother's see us and remark to her that I, who refused to see young men of good families outside of a ballroom or a musical soirée, had been seen strolling unchaperoned by the river? But those proprieties had relaxed somewhat with the Revolution, even among conservative families. It was no longer strange to see a young woman walk by herself, or talk with a gentleman without her mother or an older lady nearby. But I also wondered if it would be comfortable for me to converse more with this poet who had found the Legislative Assembly, the Jacobin Club, and the ruins of the Bastille such fascinating sights. He was looking away from me, down at the banks of the river.

"I am looking," he said, "for those beautiful stones you said were along the Loire."

"I think you will have a hard time this time of year," I said.

"Why do you say they are more beautiful?"

"They are round and smooth and do not have the rough edges of the rock you showed me last night."

We were near stairs on the quai Cypierre, and Monsieur William ran ahead down the stone steps and strolled slowly along the banks, eyeing the shallows. I thought, what do I have better to do than to play this game with the odd Englishman? And I followed him along the banks of the Loire. There were still barges here, but not the fleet of *gabares*. Monsieur William suddenly clapped his tricorne hat on his head and stuck his bare hand into the icy water.

"How's this one?" He held a small, smooth stone up to me.

"Like that, but more round." I stepped in my high boots to the edge of the bank. Under my long cloak my skirts trailed in the slush of mud and snow, then in the water, as I knelt by the bank and heard the thin ice under my boots crackle. I looked down into the cold water and took my glove off, stuck it in my teeth, and thrust my hand into the glassy river. My hand ached instantly, and I ran my fingers over the different textures of the stones, and finally pulled one out. It was cold and dripping in my hand as I took it up to Monsieur William and placed it into his hand. "It's smoother and larger and has beautiful specks in it."

"But you've had more practice." He threw his stone far out into the current.

"You'll have to do that with your one from the Bastille now, too."

"It's my souvenir for my friends in England."

"You can find better souvenirs."

"I shall keep this one," and he tossed it up and down. We walked back to the stairs. "You're the first French lady I've really talked to. Are they all so . . . " I looked over at him in his pause, wondering what he was trying to say about me, "knowledgeable about the geology of their region?"

I laughed. In our short acquaintance, this was not the first time that his freshness and ingenuousness had made me laugh. "Monsieur William, I'm sure, if I were visiting England, that English ladies could tell me just as much about rocks and rivers from their region."

"I think it is a unique ability," he said, forming his phrases with deliberation, "to look closely at objects, to really see them." We were on the quai again now, going back in the direction from which we had come. Two carts, one laden high with wood, the other with coal, creaked and lumbered past us from the quai du Châtelet. "That is one of the . . . distinctions a poet must make, between merely *looking* and truly *seeing*. Did I get my verbs right?"

"I believe so. I am not a poet, though, Monsieur William."

"Ah, but you are," he said. His words seemed to come more quickly when he talked about poetry. "The first task is to develop the ability to perceive, to *see*, and you, Mademoiselle, have that."

"You can tell all that from how I talked about rocks?"

He made a peculiarly Gallic shrug and said, "But of course."

"What is the second task, Monsieur Poet?"

"The second is . . . look across the river, and tell me what you see."

"I see the aspens shimmering on the quai des Tourelles, where Joan of Arc, after being wounded with an arrow that went through her shoulder and out the back of her neck, pulled it out herself; after the saints appeared before her and calmed her pain, she again attacked the hated English, who, convinced now that she had supernatural aid, surrendered on the spot."

Now it was Monsieur William's turn to laugh. "You've proved my point. You are a poet. The second task is the use of the *imagination* . . . blended with perception. You have two eyes that both must be used to an extent one rarely uses them: the naked eye, and what Plato calls 'the eye of the mind.' "

"What about the heart?"

"You're ahead of me. The third task is, the poet must teach. He is either a teacher, or nothing. And to teach anything worthwhile, one must know the language of the heart."

"I thought only children and lovers knew that."

"The poet is a child, or sees with the child's eyes, and he is always in love."

"With what, Monsieur? For surely you don't mean that the poet is a libertine."

"With his life, with rivers, with woods, with mountains."

"What about people—does he love them?"

"He sees the ones whom others don't see, the beggar under the bridge, the orphan in the doorway, the widow by the window."

"Monsieur William, you are doing well with your French."

"I just need to practice it more. With someone who will listen. Others with whom I tried to converse don't have the patience. Then you also ask the right questions."

He had been looking out over the river or at the ground as he was talking, concentrating on his words; now he looked directly at me, and his bright blue eyes stunned me again. I could hardly tell whether the rest of his face was attractive or plain. His eyes looked at me, and that was all. "I find you are agreeable to listen to. Few men converse with such passion, especially in a language that is not their own." We had just walked past the narrow street I was to turn into. "We may speak just a little more before I must return to chez Dubourg. Tell me about where you are from."

"From the north of England. I am always in love with our mountains, and when I am away from them, I want to return to them—except when I was in Switzerland last year. Other young men, fresh from universities, make the tour of Europe to see the great capital cities. I wanted to see the Alps. I also love rivers. I was born with a river running behind my house."

"So was I—well, almost—I could see it from my window. Pardon me, continue." His reddish brown hair looked very fair in the winter sun. He had an aquiline nose, what is called a nose of strong character.

"Tell me more about the house," I said.

"I liked the library. I opened the window, even in the rain, so I . . . could hear the river while I read." He stopped and smiled. I felt honored for some reason, that he was sharing that with me. "We lost the house when my parents died—first my mother, then a few years later, my father," William said.

It was less noisy along this part of the quai, and the river made no sound against the ice at its banks. I didn't say anything.

"When my parents died, I was sent to live with my grandparents. My grandfather was very strict, and I was . . . punished often."

"Why?"

"One time I destroyed a family portrait with a riding whip. I was very proud of being punished." He paused again, and a horseman suddenly rode past, splashing mud on us. Monsieur William didn't seem to notice. "I remembered the house in which I was a child, Mademoiselle, in that house where I . . . could always hear the river, and the river was very blue from the small stones of its bed." Then his tone shifted: "I was wrong—I've just remembered the third task of the poet, or you've made me remember it, and it is not teaching, as I said; I apologize; it precedes that, for it is part of the art of composition: the task of *memory*, of course."

He stopped. He had so much to say and had to say it so slowly.

"I'm listening," I said. "Take as long as you like. Take all the time in the world. Most men talk quickly and say nothing. It's far preferable that you speak slowly and say everything—at least about poetry. You're already far more eloquent than when I met you." He glanced keenly at me, perhaps to make sure that I was not being ironic, and, with his eyes on his feet or the river, and pausing after every phrase, he continued.

"You know the muses themselves are the daughters of Memory, in Greek mythology."

I didn't know that.

"Think what that must mean, according to the ancient Greeks,

regarding the relationship of memory to inspiration, of how important it is. Let me illustrate with you as an example. First you do not
merely look, but *see* the quai des Tourelles, across the river, secondly,
you reshape it through your *imagination*, perhaps touched by compassion; lastly, if you write about it, you will conjure your perception
of the quai up again out of *memory*, which shall add to it the power of
calm reflection and the greater value that only time can bestow upon
it. Then all those together may *teach* the reader something, if you are
lucky."

"Monsieur William, you ought to be a professor."

"I—excuse me; I am slow with the conditional tense—"

I waited and smiled. His phrases were worth waiting for.

"I *would not have* the patience to mark exams," he said, and
laughed. "Especially ones from a student such as I was. When everyone else was studying hard, I was reading Richardson's *Clarissa*. I
knew enough to pass. An exam, unlike a poem, does not have to be
perfect."

"Monsieur William," I said, "since you have enlightened me so
much regarding poetry today, I have a thought of my own about
writing. It's a secret, though."

"I like secrets."

"I like to write too."

He laughed again.

"I said that you were a poet."

"Oh, I aspire not to write poetry, Monsieur. That is beyond me. I
remain in the earthly sphere."

"What is your subject?"

"I observe. I listen."

"That you do. I wish you well, Mademoiselle, in your literary
endeavors." He made a slight bow.

"And you too, Monsieur."

He stopped walking. He put his hat on, then took it off again.

"Mademoiselle, *would* you . . . "

"Yes?"

" . . . care to be my French professor again, if I . . . *were*—I hate
the subjunctive—to bring to you a translation at chez Dubourg,

perhaps at a future fête to which Monsieur du Vivier, my landlord . . . *might* invite me? All of that was hard to say."

"That would be very kind of you to work on a poem on my behalf. And it will be highly edifying. Now, if you please, I must be returning to chez Dubourg. I am a guest there, you know. I am really from Blois."

"Then we are both foreigners," he said. "Joan of Arc was blessed by the archbishop in Blois; that's all I know about the town, I'm afraid. Until the next fête, Mademoiselle. It has been a great pleasure."

"Until, then, Monsieur." And, "Yes, it has," I added softly to myself, as I turned. Then I looked back at Monsieur William, already distant on the quai. He must have really walked all the way from London to Lake Como and back, I thought. *Some* men do not lie.

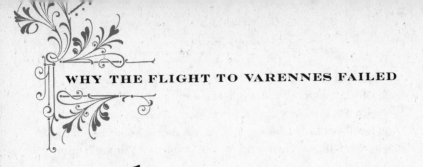

I glanced at Gérard's intense face as he molded shapes out of dough. I was keeping the children occupied on Christmas afternoon while Maman and Marguerite rested, and we were sitting at the zinc-covered servant's dining table in the kitchen. Marie and I were creating horses out of dough, but hers were much better than mine. She already had four good ones beside her. I had one that resembled an amphibious dog and was well into my second, which I was really trying to make look more like a horse.

"Gérard, what are you making now?" I asked. He had one rabbit beside him. It was all ears.

"I don't know," he said.

"Have you seen your papa and Etienne?" I asked Marie.

"Talking in the library," said Marie, without raising her eyes from the curve of the horse's tail. "They're always talking in the library about politics." She had recently turned ten and had begun to be aware of the volatile nature of the world around her. The Varaches' daughter, Louise, had been Marie's friend. I don't know what she had told Marie of the reasons her family was emigrating, but I do know Marie missed her, and now, confronted with a life without her best friend, found herself helping me more in tutoring her younger brother and engaging him in some of her own old childhood pastimes. Perhaps she was too old to make shapes out of dough, but this was a cherished tradition, which she had done every year since before Gérard was born. They baked their animal shapes that then became Christmas cookies.

"You would think that they would get tired of talking about politics, especially on Christmas," Marie said.

"It is a mouse. There are his ears. There are his eyes," Gérard said.

"It is just the head of the mouse," I said.

"The mouse is eating potatoes. These are the potatoes," Gérard said.

"He is getting bigger as he eats," I said.

"Louise said we'll all have to go to England sooner or later," said Marie. "It's not far away."

I had nothing to say to that, so I said, "Your horse looks as if it's galloping across a meadow."

"But its mane would be flowing in the wind, wouldn't it?" I had taught her to ride last summer, and she already wanted a horse for her next birthday. She looked over at my figure of dough. She laughed. "Aunt Annette, I'm afraid yours looks a bit like a cow."

"Cows can gallop fast," I said. "Shall my cow and your horse have a race?"

"Now it is a man hopping on his bottom," Gérard said.

"Where are his legs?" I asked.

"He doesn't need them. He is hopping," Gérard said.

"Do they still celebrate Christmas in England?" asked Marie, "even if they are Protestant?"

"I believe so," I said. "They just have different songs."

"Let's sing," Marie said.

And we sang "*Il est né le divin enfant*," and I took the alto harmony.

Now Gérard was pounding the dough on a mat with a small mallet used for beating cutlets flat.

"This next one is a horse, but it is not real good," he said.

"I see its tail. It's running fast," I said. He continued to pound the dough.

"I liked that one," I said.

"It was not real good. I'm putting it away."

"You never do anything for very long, Gérard," his sister said. "Just make it better. I'm working now on my horse's mane. See?"

Gérard glanced at hers. "I like my mouse," he said.

"I will add my swimming dog and my galloping cow to your pile," I said to him.

"Thanks," he said, for that meant more cookies for later, and as Marie kept working, I helped her little brother gather his mat and mallet and put them in the cupboard.

We walked by the great chopping block in the center of the white-tiled kitchen. There lay three freshly killed rabbits, their pelts still on. The room now smelled of cognac and the seasonings in which Cook would marinate the joints of rabbit. Gérard was stroking one of them.

"Why are rabbits' ears so long?" he asked.

"So they can hear who is coming," I said.

"Can he hear us now?"

"No. He is not alive."

"Why is he looking at me, then?"

"He's not, really. Let's see what Cook is doing."

"Don't get in my way," Cook said. "Or you'll end up stuffed."

We watched her mince the smaller pieces that she was not marinating. She cut them with quick, even slices. She was so quick, I wondered how she did not cut off her own fingers. She then beat the minced pieces with the flat side of the butcher knife into the stuffing mixture. "This is for your dinner, Master Gérard." He smiled up at her, the soft fur of the ear in his small fingers.

Marie and Gérard dined early with Nurse. Their parents and I joined them for dessert, when the children each proudly offered their parents one of their Christmas cookies, with red silk ribbons tied around it, and made their parents guess which animal they had received as a gift. Marie gave her mother her horse with the flowing mane, which Marguerite had no problem in guessing, and she gave me another of her horses. Gérard had eaten his rabbit and my dog and cow, and he placed his last cookie in his father's hands. "This one's for you," he said. Paul looked a little bemused, so I said in his ear, "Something cats like to chase."

"It's a mouse," he said, "a splendid, fat, happy mouse, like ones we probably have at home, right now."

Since we had arrived at chez Dubourg, we had dined often with that affable couple (who themselves had no children), so we made it clear to them they were not abdicating their responsibilities as host if they accepted a recent invitation to dine with the vicomte and vicomtesse; an invitation that would be imprudent to refuse, from the standpoint of Orléans society. Thus it was just the adults from

Blois enjoying the second sitting of Cook's fine Christmas dinner, in a room wallpapered with cherry blossoms.

We had arrived now at everyone's favorite conversation topic: the royal family's aborted escape to Varennes last summer.

"They were so close to the border," said Maman. "They could have made it. Everyone agrees on that. I hate to think of it."

"If they had not had an escape party that could only fit in a *berline* and moved at a turtle's pace, and that conspicuous huge carriage also, because of its load, had not made the horses stumble and break a harness, they'd be across the border now, and we'd have a different world," Paul said.

"I think it was brilliant, the way they dressed as servants—the young prince in girl's clothing—and slipped out from under the nose of Lafayette and his National Guard," Angelique joined in.

Monsieur Vergez concentrated on his stuffed eels, and for once, I agreed with him. They were simmered in good wine with mushrooms and onions. I sipped the chilled white wine brought upriver from Vouvray, caught Marguerite's eye, and silently raised my glass to her. I had heard all this before. While I agreed with Maman that it was very unfortunate, I personally wondered why they hadn't just tried to go to Belgium instead of all the way to the German border—they would have made it easily. But with that thought I was guilty of the "What if . . ." conversation I was so tired of. So, like my stepfather, I enjoyed the dinner that was prepared with such care, and half-listened to the old litany.

"Oh, yes, it was all very brilliant," rejoined Paul. "They had to fit the Queen's friend the Marquise de Tourzel in, and Louis's sister, and the children's nurse, and two waiting women, as if they were going on a summer outing to Saint-Cloud."

"I love that they even adopted false names," said Angelique. "The King was Monsieur Durand, a valet; the Queen was the baronne de Korff, a delightful German name to explain her accent. And you must admit, Paul, it is impressive how they sneaked at different times out of the Tuileries, even if the Queen did get a little lost, and then went through side streets of Paris in a plain carriage driven by that handsome Swedish count."

"I will admit," said Paul, "that he—Count Fersen, no stranger to intrigues—was the only one among that crowd in the *berline* capable of taking charge if things went wrong, and *he* was not permitted to drive the coach past Paris because he was a Swedish officer and they wanted this to be a *French* escape."

"It could have worked," said Maman. "It was that silly man who recognized the King's profile from a stamp and rode to alert the National Guard—what a busybody—his own townspeople hated him."

"They did stop for soup, Maman," Angelique said.

"It wasn't that," said Etienne. "It was the inexperienced colonel leading the dragoons who were waiting to escort the King. He got nervous after two hours of waiting for the slow coach and, all on his own, decided that the escape was aborted and told his men to stand down."

The Dubourg's servants served white asparagus, then the rabbit, and poured Paul's cabernet franc in our second, waiting glass. Since the children had eaten earlier, I wasn't able to talk to Gérard about the rabbit we had seen being prepared. I looked at the others in the pause that always ensues for a moment between courses.

My family had dressed for the occasion: Marguerite and Angelique, one dark and one blonde, lovely in patterned silk dresses of *pelouse* green and duck-egg blue; I myself wore a *robe à l'anglaise* ; Marguerite's green silk mantle edged with net was draped over her arm and the back of her chair; Angelique was looking very modern, with a white sash that matched the bandeau in her hair. Maman had spent most of the day on her frizzed and curled coiffure of the eighties. The older gentlemen had on their powdered wigs; Etienne tied his long hair in a ribbon. This would be the last dinner in which all of us—minus Papa—were together.

"It's a pleasure to see everyone looking so charming," I said, and Monsieur Vergez looked up at me as he lifted a forkful of minced rabbit to his mouth.

"I love your *robe à l'anglaise*," Marguerite said.

"It matches the gentleman *anglais*, that foreigner, with whom she talked so long at the ball," Angelique said.

"Well, I noticed you wasted no time getting to know that bore from Bordeaux," I said.

"At least he can dance," said Angelique. "The Englishman doesn't even know how to participate in the most civilized of the arts."

"He's just received his degree from Cambridge University."

"What is his business here?" Monsieur Vergez said.

"He wants to learn our language better and become a gentleman's tour guide."

"It's hardly a time for that," Maman said.

"He likes to travel. He walked all the way from Calais to Lake Como and back."

"If he walks, he cannot afford to ride," Maman said.

"I think he seemed a very polite, if reserved, gentleman," Marguerite said.

"All English are reserved," said Angelique, "but he seemed to talk enough to Annette. Madame Dubourg told me his French was atrocious."

"It's not. It's just slow. Yesterday he told me all about—"

All the eyes turned toward me now. I'm afraid I blushed. "I accidentally met him when I was walking along the quai—"

"Marie-Ann," my mother said. She used my given name, which she knew I disliked, whenever she was upset with me. "I've told you not to go out walking alone. You insist, always, in disobeying me. What have I done to deserve this punishment? Your imprudence knows no bounds. You could have been seen and disgraced our hosts in *their* city—"

"Maman, I really don't think—" started Marguerite.

"There's only uncouth bargemen out on the quai," said my stepfather; "no one's going to see her there who *matters*."

I almost said, "Thank you."

"This foreigner, in these times, could be a spy," Maman said.

"Then he would be for the royalist cause," said Paul, "and hence, one of us."

"Far more likely he's a foreign agitator, come to swell the ranks of the revolutionaries," Monsieur Vergez said.

"In Paris," said Etienne, "English, German, Russian, American—

à la Franklin—they're thronging. They want to see what this Revolution is all about."

"That's as I said," Vergez said sternly.

I gave my little brother a look as if to say, *Et tu?*

"He's a *poet*," I said.

That seemed to silence everyone for a bit. No one knows how to respond to poetry. Then Angelique said helpfully, "François Villon was an outlaw *and* a poet."

Now the servants quietly removed our dinner plates and, starting with Maman, we passed the cheese plate, with the wedges of Vendôme and the *crémets* that went so well with Paul's wine.

"*Nunc est bibendum*," Paul said to me, and raised and drained his glass. That was the ancient phrase of the Wine Grower's Brotherhood, of which he was a member, and into which, he said, he had initiated our famous American visitor of long ago, Monsieur Jefferson. The phrase means, It's now time to drink.

"*Nunc est bibendum*," I said back to him and took a long sip. I was grateful to him for changing the subject. "Paul," I said, have you ever read Rabelais's satire on the Wine Grower's Brotherhood, when the hero goes on a quest for the Sacred Bottle?"

"Have I not?" Paul said. "The most important quest in literature."

"Satire," Maman said, "is not a proper conversation for a Christmas dinner."

"The sacred bottle," Etienne said, "I'd like to go on a quest for that."

"Tell us about the horses, Annette," Angelique said, "the *real* reason the flight to Varennes failed. It's so absurd."

"I'm tired of the flight to Varennes," I said.

"I don't know that story," Etienne said. "Does it have a sacred bottle in it?"

"This is your King you're joking about," Maman said.

"Not anymore," Paul said. "He may be imprisoned in a rotting palace, but he's still imprisoned."

"In the Tuileries," said Etienne, "if any of the royal family so much as show their face now, someone spits at them. Crowds gather outside just to have the chance to spit on a royal. It's quite a distinction in Paris."

Vergez threw his *crémet* against the wall. It landed on a blossoming branch of the wallpaper, like a fat white egg.

"We're not a pack of peasant rabble here," he boomed, "who delight in such gossip. Tell the story of the horses, Annette, and make it a tragedy; no irony, no satire, just tragedy."

"I'll try," I said. I noticed the servants quietly cleaning up the cheese on the floor and washing the stain on the wall. "Well, the royal family stopped at Varennes for fresh horses. But there were no horses anywhere to be found. The carriage driver and even the King himself knocked on doors in a panic. Meanwhile, the National Guard rode up. A retired soldier in the town who tried to defend the King raised his sword and was shot down before he could use it. They packed them all back in the *berline*, with a couple of National Assembly members to keep an eye on them, and drove them ignominiously back to Paris. All the while, at the other end of town, across the bridge, waited a groom with fresh horses."

"That has irony in it," said Vergez.

"It's hard to separate tragedy and irony," Paul said.

"I think it's tremendously sad," Maman said.

"No one," said Marguerite, "with all the vicious lies about the Queen, remembers that she is a mother. Think about her being a mother. A child on either side of her, soldiers out her window. Can you imagine it?"

"Ah, the poached pears and madeleines," Paul said, as the footman moved among us.

I don't think Paul said that last word in a particularly loud voice, but one of the tall doors suddenly opened a crack, and Gérard, who had been put to bed over an hour ago, poked his little head in beside the white petals on the spring boughs.

"May I have some madeleines?" he asked. His father motioned for him to enter, and Gérard scampered over the shiny parquet floor, soon followed by his nurse.

"I'm sorry, Monsieur Vincent," she said, "he couldn't sleep and said he wanted to come say good night."

"Quite right, too," said his father. "Here's a madeleine, my boy; here's two, and here's two for you not to forget to give your sister. I'll ask her tomorrow."

"She's asleep," Gérard said.

"Then you give them to her for breakfast," said Paul. "Now go and kiss your mother good night. Again." And Gérard ran around the long mahogany table to where his mother sat opposite his father and kissed her, my sister leaning her head down and her son rising on tiptoe, his cookies clutched in both hands. Nurse followed him out, silently enclosing us within the orchard of the Chinese emperors.

Then, just as Monsieur Dubourg's fruit liqueur was poured, and I had taken my first sip, we heard Gérard's voice again, sounding genuinely afraid. "I can't go," he said.

Marguerite started to rise, and I said, "No, I'll go." I wanted to escape from the political conversation, which Gérard could have overheard, standing outside the door. The boy stood beneath the stairway now, his feet rooted on the marble floor, with Nurse trying to pull him up the stairs with one hand; her other held a small brass candelabrum.

"He's being most unreasonable," she said. "I think he's just making up an excuse not to go to bed."

"What's the matter, Gérard?" I said.

"It's the demons," he said. "They're at the top of the stairs."

CHIMERA

We stood under the chandelier in the vestibule and looked up into the darkness. The servants were enjoying their own Christmas dinner and had not lit the sconces upstairs. "I'll go first," I said. "You and Nurse right behind." Then I thought of something. "Where's your hoop?"

"In my room," Gérard said in a small voice.

"We will put it by your bed, and nothing will get past it," I said.

"But it's upstairs."

We took our first steps. I could hear the branches of the poplar by the side of the house scraping the window at the top of the stairs, and even I felt a little frightened by the dark. Fear, like courage, is contagious, so I proceeded up the stairs, Nurse's candelabrum raised high behind us, in our soft moving sphere of light.

Then we heard a knock below us at the door. I turned and stood still. Then we heard it again. Three taps, then silence, then three more taps. Neither the Dubourgs nor we were expecting anyone, but why was I suddenly afraid? Had a four-year-old's mood infected mine? Nurse, perhaps thinking that it wasn't her duty to open doors, stood there, and Gérard followed me to the door. I opened it a few inches and saw Monsieur William standing there, a hat under his left arm.

"I wanted to wish you *Joyeux Noël*," he said. "I have brought you a little present."

"You should not come to chez Dubourg uninvited, but come in; it's cold." Monsieur William closed the big door behind him, and Gérard held on to my dress and looked up at the tall stranger. "Monsieur William, this is my nephew, Gérard. Gérard, Monsieur William is from England."

The foreigner bent over and said, "Do you know the game of hitting horse chestnuts against each other?"

Gérard shook his head no.

"It is done with string tied to the chestnut and a stick, and you swing the nuts against each other."

"Why?"

Monsieur William squatted so he could be at the same level as Gérard.

"To see which one is the stronger. The weaker one cracks. But one must find the right horse chestnut. I have seen some excellent ones near here."

"There is a chestnut tree at my house," said Gérard. "I have a secret hiding place near it. No one can ever find me there."

"Well, I am good at hide-and-seek. Perhaps I can play it with you there."

"*Could* play," I said. "You don't know if you'll ever go to Blois."

"Your wise aunt is helping me learn your beautiful language."

"You don't know how to talk?"

"Not very well. Often, others misunderstand me."

"Me too," said Gérard, and he reached into the pocket of his dressing gown. "Would you like a madeleine?"

"That is very kind of you." Monsieur William looked at me. "May I?" he asked me.

"If that is not one of his sister's."

"Hers are in my other pocket," Gérard said, in a somewhat insulted tone.

"I must give you something in return, then," Monsieur William said. He rummaged in the deep pocket of his English cloak. "Here." He held out his rock. "This is a stone that has a lot of stories to tell. I showed it to your aunt, but she . . . wasn't interested in it."

Gérard held it and examined it. "What kind of stories?"

"Do you know the word *imagination*?" Gérard nodded. "It's a big word for me too," Monsieur William said. "If you use your imagination, that rock can tell you stories about a new and better world."

"You will need lots of imagination," I added.

"I can do it," Gérard said, again rather offended at my words.

Nurse was looking down at the Englishman and her charge.

"Well, now that we have found that the darkness holds nothing dangerous, only Monsieur William, Nurse can take you back to your room. Remember to put the hoop by your bed."

"I think this is a magic rock," Gérard said. "I'll put it in the hoop to frighten the demons."

"It may bring more," I whispered to Monsieur William. "Good night, Gérard."

He turned and looked at us as Nurse led him up the stairs, his feet finding their own way, and he forgot about the darkness.

"You sacrificed your precious rock," I said to Monsieur William.

"It's for the future generation."

"You're really incorrigible. You do know this is a royalist household."

"I figured as much, as Monsieur du Vivier is of that persuasion. I apologize. I have a grave weakness for speaking my mind."

"The English must be a frank race."

"I hope I have not given offense."

"Not to me. I hate politics. And I love Gérard, and I'm glad you've given him a present that can help take his mind off the demons. Though I think the demons are caused by politics. That's one of the reasons I hate it. But my manners are terrible—would you like something to drink, Monsieur William?"

"No, thank you. I have just come to bring you something. I'm afraid I was a bit excited about it and wanted to give it to you straightaway. I am not a patient man. May I?"

I nodded, and he reached into an inner breast pocket of his cloak and pulled out a scroll, tied with a red cloth ribbon. He presented it to me with a slight bow. He looked excited, like a child himself. "Open it," he said.

I unscrolled it. It was a poem, in French, titled "By the Loire."

"Did you write this?"

"And translated it into French. I'm afraid my dictionary is weary of my company."

No one had ever written a poem for me before; or rather, translated one for me. "Thank you, Monsieur."

"You haven't read it yet."

"Was it what you were writing yesterday?"

"I started writing about Switzerland, and after talking to you, my thoughts moved to France."

"I hope I didn't disturb your muse."

"Read the poem, please."

And so I roamed where Loiret's waters glide
Through rustling aspens heard from side to side,
When from December clouds a milder light
Fell where the blue flood rippled into white.

"It's beautiful. The blue flood did ripple into white. Even though the aspens were across the river."

"I crossed the bridge and walked where you envisioned Joan of Arc defeating the English."

"This is as lovely as any description I read in *Romance of the Rose.*"

"You are very kind. But it's only four lines; the *Romance* is thousands."

"Was not translating your work an excellent lesson?"

"Mademoiselle Vallon, I have inquired of Monsieur du Vivier if he knew of a language tutor—"

Just then the tall doors to the dining room swung open, and Maman stood there, regarding us quizzically, then glided toward us, with a faint rustling of a silk underskirt.

"Maman, this is Monsieur William, who has come from England. He brought me a Christmas present." I realized I made it sound as if he had come all the way from England to deliver me a present. I felt like a little girl who couldn't get her words right.

"I am honored," Monsieur William said and bowed slightly.

"My pleasure, Monsieur." Maman nodded.

"He brought me this poem, Maman. He wrote it himself. And translated it into French." I showed it to her. She looked at the four small lines.

"That's very charming," she said.

Monsieur William twirled his hat in his hand.

"Would you take a drink, Monsieur?" I asked again, so Maman would get the idea. "Chez Dubourg is famous for its fruit liqueurs. Maman, Monsieur William has walked from—"

"Rue Royale," he said. "Above a hosier and hatter's shop."

"I wanted to stop at one of those shops on our way here," I said.

"Perhaps I would have met you earlier." I thought that that was also a stupid thing to say. I wanted Maman to invite him to stay.

"Thank you, I just came to give you this. I must leave before it starts to storm again."

Maman, as if suddenly remembering her manners, said sweetly, "Monsieur, perhaps you would like to sample one of our Christmas madeleines."

"May I have another madeleine?" we heard Gérard shout from his door at the top of the stairs. It was amazing how sharp his ears were when it came to delights, or terrors.

"That is very kind, but I already have one," Monsieur William said. Maman looked completely nonplussed. "I must go. Goodnight. *Joyeux Noël*."

And he was out the door in a gust of cold wind.

"Maman, how can you be so cold?"

"I invited him for dessert."

"Only when you knew he was going."

"What was he doing here unasked?" She spoke as if she were keeping the Revolution itself from her door.

"He is not so formal as we are, Maman."

"These are the changed times." She looked fiercely at me.

"I will invite him next time."

"You know nothing about him."

"I know a good deal."

"Marie-Ann . . . Annette, come here." She led me into the front salon.

She sat beneath the half-lit chandelier, and I perched on a nearby ottoman. I wanted now to be back in the dining room with the rest of the family.

"Annette, there is something I have been trying to tell you since you were sixteen, and you didn't understand it then, but with more maturity, you may grasp it now. I will try one last time, and I will make it brief."

"Maman, I know what you're going to say."

"Do you? Do you know that to live properly in the world, in any capacity, demands sacrifice, and of women are demanded the greatest sacrifices?"

"Of what sacrifice do you speak, Maman?"

"Even the most honorable of men know nothing of what love means to a woman. They feel pleasure, and that is their aim. A woman believes that love itself is her whole aim and pleasure merely one branch of a vast tree, deeply rooted in her heart. She believes it is her profound duty to care for this tree, nourish it each day, and give all of its fruits exclusively to one man and to her children. This in itself demands a sacrifice that men cannot comprehend."

She sounded like one of the righteous characters from *Les Liaisons dangereuses*, but all the same, I had never heard her talk like this.

Maman went on, "But believing in that tree of perfect love and happiness can be a chimera for unsuspecting women. Therefore I'll speak to you of another, even more virtuous sacrifice: the belief in that tree with its ever-blooming branches must in itself be sacrificed if prudence demands it. A woman gives happiness rather than delights in it, and if she must give it contrary to the direction she herself would choose, then her greater pleasure is in following that duty, since her own happiness was not her aim in the first place. Are you following me? It seems to me that you are still attached to the fancies of youth, that in your mind you have fallen prey to that chimera. But at twenty-two, there is no reason for you to be such a child.

"A man must be well-born, have a fortune and the advantage of birth. Do not scoff at these requirements; they are more necessary now than ever; life can be ruinous, and prudence dictates that above all, in times of misfortune we cling to the values that have always served us well and do not abandon them for the fallacious ones springing up; for instance, that one's station in life is not of consequence. Now to the point: a young man's character one can never be wholly sure of, but a foreigner's, even if he *is* well-educated? One who can only afford to live above a hosier and hatter's shop; one whose notion of self-advancement is to write *poetry*?"

I said nothing, and her tone was softer when she spoke again. "So I say to you, my dear, be careful of the belief in that tree that exists only in one's imagination; know that one can derive the purest happiness from sacrifice; and never allow the passing fancies of the heart to vanquish prudence, or you will be left with nothing." She sighed, and her tone changed back. "Now it is high time to return to our coffee." She rose from her chair.

"What about Papa?"

She slowly sat down and regarded me, then continued in her soft tone. "Your father, *ma chérie*, was an honorable man from a good family whose social level matched mine. He worked from a sense of social duty, not from necessity. We had a mutual respect, an affectionate regard that forms the basis of lasting happiness in marriage. You think, Annette, it is nothing to be without love. I tell you it is nothing to be without fortune or a good name. If it is nothing either way, you must make your choice."

She suddenly extended her hand out to me, and I grasped it. I don't think she had touched me for years.

"Don't be left with nothing, my girl."

I didn't want to disagree with her. I didn't know when the last time was that she had talked to me softly, and I didn't know when she would again.

THE SERPENT

When the vicomte and vicomtessee de Fresne d'Aguesseau invited the Dubourgs for an Epiphany soirée, they included—or should I say deigned to include—their guests from Blois. I had not seen their mansion for five years and was looking forward to sitting on a certain carved couch, embroidered with a scene of a white horse, the hooves of its back legs raised and in the act of kicking a wild boar, cowering beneath them. In a meadow behind it, another boar runs away.

Etienne had an appointment with a friend in Orléans from the Sorbonne, and Marguerite and Paul wished to spend Epiphany, the climax of the Christmas season, with their children, so Angelique and I joined Maman and Monsieur Vergez at the vicomte's soirée. Now I again sat across from my stepfather in our family carriage, and he opened his engraved silver box and took a pinch of snuff, and I glanced out the window at the huge triple doors of the Cathedral of the Holy Cross, rose windows above each door. The problem with a rose window, however, is that it needs light to make it truly beautiful. This was a particularly gloomy January evening; even though it was the day on which the Magi arrived at Bethlehem, no such bright star lit the glorious windows of the Holy Cross; the only light was in the corner of the square, where a group of beggars stood around a small fire.

Nor was there any star above the brick mansion of the vicomte, one of many across from a larger mansion in which kings have stayed on their visits to Orléans, before the current days when they were exiled from Versailles and confined to a dilapidated palace along the Seine. I noticed that, over the doorway, the ancient coat of arms of the Fresne d'Aguesseau family had been discreetly painted over.

Angelique and I passed through the vestibule behind Maman and Monsieur Vergez, surrounded by women's rustling silks, gold or silver braid glinting on gentlemen's culottes, knee-breeches, buckles shining on shoes. It had been years since I had seen so many beautiful people. And there was the short and jolly Monsieur Dubourg, gesticulating with the vicomte, a slim taciturn man in black and white silk, and Madame Dubourg, her height putting her on the level with the vicomtesse's old-fashioned tiered coiffure, leaning down and listening to the vicomtesse, in her royalist dress of white taffeta, the mode the Queen had made famous.

When we passed the dining room I glanced through the open gilded doors at the tapestry of Joan of Arc, sword in hand, light on her face, attacking the English where Monsieur William's aspens now whispered. We heard music playing from one of the salons and followed the sounds into a crowded room. Two elderly ladies with powdered hair and rouged cheeks sat rigidly on my couch of the stallion and the boar. I could see one of the white hind legs raised behind one of the tight blue bodices. The ladies looked brittle, as if should one of them fall off the couch, she would break.

The music sounded Italian, not French, perhaps that of Niccolò Piccinni, and in spite of the crowd, Angelique and I, arm in arm in our white muslin dresses with long tasseled waist sashes (hers gold, mine blue), promenaded around the edge of the room. I liked the new flat pumps that had come into style in rebellion from high heels and after Rousseau's statement that clothes should be useful, not luxurious. We looked at the beautiful people and nodded at a few ladies we had met in Orléans in previous years. They wore little jewelry now—and what they wore was clearly paste.

The National Assembly had issued an edict that all women were to give their jewelry to the government, as proof that their values had shifted from vanity to patriotism. It could then be used to help pay to build a new army. Of course, the men in the assembly who created the edict were not about to donate their silver snuff boxes. I was sure most of these women's jewels, though, did not go to make new cannon. They were probably hiding discreetly in the back of a drawer, waiting for a more felicitous time to dazzle the world once more.

Angelique and I each took a glass from a servant standing, still as a statue, by the wall, seated ourselves by a small tulip wood table, and sipped the chilled, sparkling Vouvray, which tasted fine in the warm, full room with a fire burning high in the huge hearth. I looked around the room for Monsieur William, thinking that his royalist landlord would invite the foreigner to see the best society in Orléans. But perhaps Monsieur William was not interested. He was probably writing in his room.

The music stopped, and it wasn't long before I saw a gilt-wood chair beside me pulled close to my own by a black silk arm, and suddenly it was not the frank face of the Englishman but the smiling facade of Monsieur Leforges, under a tightly curled wig, that looked into mine.

I almost gasped and caught myself. I wanted to leave immediately, but before I could say anything, he asked us courteously if he could join us. Angelique, who was only twelve six years ago and didn't know him at all, and who always appreciated the company of handsome and polite men, said, Yes, of course. He presented himself as Monsieur Leforges of Orléans, the conductor of the small orchestra we had just heard, and sat down.

He gave me a sardonic smile, lost on Angelique, patted my knee under the table, and rested his hand there until I pushed it off. His arrogance knew no bounds. I knew he was going to play a game now, in front of my sister, as if he and I had never met. He knew that I did not want to introduce him as my old *ami*.

I had often wondered, since I was sixteen, what would be my response if I should ever see Monsieur Leforges again. I had created a thousand clever and proud things to say, and now I could not remember one of them. Angelique gave her name and said we were from Blois, and when I failed to give my name, she looked strangely at me. She went on to say that the music was charming, and that it seemed that all the fashionable society of Orléans had come. He said that was always the case at a soirée chez Fresne d'Aguesseau. I could feel his eyes on me, and I wouldn't give him the pleasure of my looking at him, or of thinking he had made me uncomfortable.

I said, "Angelique, we go to many such soirées at the château de Beauregard, do we not?" Which wasn't true, for the count hadn't held any since my father died—or since the Revolution started, for those events happened at about the same time.

Angelique was silent, and our self-invited guest answered that he had once taught music and dancing in Blois, at which Angelique clapped her hands together. She said, "If you were at the château de Beauregard," she said, "perhaps for a moment, as you changed partners in a *contredanse*, you danced with Annette, or with my other older sister, Madame Vincent."

"Very unlikely," said Monsieur Leforges, "because I would have remembered anyone as charming as your sister here, and if your other sister had any resemblance to the two before me, well, I would have remembered her too." He then said that an unfortunate incident, however, forced him to retire from Blois and kept him from returning.

I realized I had neglected my Vouvray, but the silence at our small table, as we awaited Monsieur Leforge's explanation, made me place the glass soundlessly back on the veneered tulip wood.

"It actually had to do indirectly with your count," he said. "He may not be as kind a man as you may think. I won't go into the unpleasant details here, but suffice it to say that a rival instructor, in whose best interests it was to stop my growing success in that town, spread salacious rumors about me. The count, who prided himself on his noblesse oblige to the town, believed the slanders and publicized them, he thought, in his hasty judgment, to save other pupils from being 'ruined'—as he put it"—here Angelique gasped and waved her fan painted with butterflies—"so I lost my pupils, my reputation, and even had to leave Blois, a town of which, in my short time there, I had grown rather fond."

He had put his hand back on my knee. I tried surreptitiously to push it off, but through the fine fabric of the muslin, he pinched the flesh above my knee so hard I almost cried out.

"How horrible," my sister said.

"It was very humiliating," he said. He kept pinching hard. I had to bite my lip. "A certain young woman, it seems, out of jealousy of my attentions, purely professional of course, to another female pupil, was implicated in this crime to my honor. My rival instructor never used her name, naturally, but spread the rumor that I had ruined 'a certain young lady.'" He pinched extra hard, then let go. "You know how people are eager to listen to vile gossip, quick to believe it, and deaf to the voices of justice or reason."

"Yes," said my sister, "that's always the case."

"Well, I've built my reputation back here in Orléans: witness, I am invited to play at the best soirées local society has to offer. But next autumn I have been invited back to Blois to instruct a new generation, and, I tell you charming ladies, if I ever meet that man who slandered me or the lady who helped him, my revenge will be swift and sure."

"I'm afraid they would deserve it," Angelique said.

"I recall my humiliation in Blois only with extreme pain, and as it is indelicate to discuss such a matter with strangers and with ladies, I beg your forgiveness for my having made it a topic of conversation; it was only because your native town reminded me of memories I would rather forget."

I finally looked again at my lover of six years ago. He seemed older, with a few lines near his eyes. The smile that played about his lips seemed to be stretched tight, like a mask that is too small. "Monsieur Leforges," I said, "as it is not ours to judge, isn't it also not ours to exact revenge? Isn't the desire for revenge the most degrading of emotions; shouldn't you, as a conductor of sublime music, try to raise yourself above such pettiness?"

"Mademoiselle, you speak as one pure as divinity itself would speak, but alas, I am a mortal man and susceptible to all his weakness."

"What if one of his weaknesses, Monsieur," I said, "is to deceive others, to speak as guilefully as the serpent in the garden itself?"

"Then, Mademoiselle, a certain young lady would pluck and eat of a fruit she never should taste. And whose crime is that? Who must be punished for that? Not the serpent, surely."

"Your conversation has become entirely too metaphysical," said Angelique. "And I apologize, Monsieur; my sister is not in the best of humors tonight. May we return to the intriguing topic of supposed slanders?"

"I regret, Mesdemoiselles, that I must return instead to my orchestra, for our pause for refreshment is over."

And he vanished behind a lilac taffeta dress, and soon we heard the strains of his musicians again.

"Well, you were rude," my sister said.

I didn't say anything, and Angelique regarded me for a long time. "That was either very rude," said my sister, "or"—she let the silence hang there—"or . . . did you know him, Annette?"

Angelique was young and flirtatious but not stupid.

"He was my 'disgrace' that I'm sure the servants whispered about around the house years ago—or still do."

"Then he's just a big liar." She laughed a small, discreet, but delicious laugh. "And I just thought you were misanthropic or too proud where men were concerned. I am impressed."

"Angelique—"

"Well, I shall defend you in all things now, Annette. Now that I know how the world has mistreated you."

"It wasn't the *world*—"

"Excuse me, Mesdemoiselles, may I—?"

My sister nodded before I looked up to see a cavalry officer in his high-collared light blue jacket with gold lace, red cuffs, and red sash with gold cords and tassels, shining white trousers, saber, and black boots standing there in all his glory. He had under his arm a beautiful shako, a hat of blue cloth and black leather, with more gold cords and tassels—someone must do quite a business in them, I thought. My favorite item of all was a tall white plume. He was young, smiling, and fairly took both my sister's breath and mine away. I thought at that moment that soldiers should be purely for show; who would want to shoot at such a wonderful costume? We made our introductions to Captain Alivons, and he took the chair that Monsieur Leforges had left unoccupied, keeping his left hand on his shako. The plume nodded well above the table and looked, in this context, a bit ridiculous.

I asked him what one always asks an officer—to what regiment he belonged—but Captain Alivons was an anomaly. "My regiment,

Madamoiselle, is no more, as half of its officers have emigrated, and the more intelligent of the other half are about to emigrate. And that is the case with half of the regiments in the entire French army."

"With all of these halves leaving, do we have any regiments at all?" I asked.

"Soon, none of any consequence," said the captain. "At least none that can sit a horse. I shall reunite with my other officers soon, though, when I myself emigrate and join the grand émigré army."

"Are you going to England, then?" Angelique asked.

"Yes, to where they still respect monarchy and one's station in life. I'm lodging right now with an Englishman. Rather a strange fellow, though."

"A tall gentleman," I said, "from Cambridge?"

"Yes, that's right. How did you know?"

"A Monsieur William?"

"My sister knows a good deal about this foreigner," Angelique said.

"I did not know anybody did. He has an unpronounceable surname, so we just call him 'Guillaume.' He spends his time either outside, *walking*"—he pronounced the word with great distaste, in order, I assume, to remind us that *he*, Captain Alivons, was a *cavalry* officer— "or reading and writing in his room." All three of these occupations seemed beyond the good captain's ken. "He also has some strange ideas, but my fellow officers are working on him. Excuse me—" and the captain placed his shako on the table, dashed off in the direction of the statuelike servant, and, before Angelique and I could remark on him to each other, returned with three full glasses. My sister and I hadn't finished our first two.

"The émigré army is the only place to be now," Captain Alivons said. "With the King's own brothers, the comtes of Artois and of Provence, having fled, where does that leave the rest of us?"

"Well, I shall never leave Blois," Angelique said.

"You've left it now," the captain answered, and they laughed.

"Do you know that the *Journal de Paris*," he said, "daily advertises possessions the émigrés wish to sell before fleeing—carved couches, veneered desks, oak armoires—and for so little? It makes a fellow want to stay here and gather fine furniture."

"That's so sad," Angelique said.

"In Paris one sees in cab lines fine carriages with white clouds on their doors—and one knows that those were once the carriages of noble families, whose coats of arms have been painted over."

I caught the eye of a somewhat lost-looking gentleman at the door. Among all the ribbon-tied queues beautifully powdered, Monsieur William's hair looked windblown; his brown cloth coat seemed out of place, and his boots looked dirty.

"Monsieur Guillaume, do not tell me you walked all the way here?" the captain called out to him.

William hesitated, then strode up to our table. "Indeed," he said. "It enabled me to see Orion over the towers of the cathedral. And it's the same distance to the river, and I walk that every day." He glanced at me and smiled. Despite Maman's well-meant advice, through a series of happy accidents, I had met him almost every day since Christmas at the end of the Bridge Royal. I would have gone when it was storming, too, for I don't mind the weather, if walking out in driving rain were not behavior just too odd for my family or for the Dubourgs to accept. Monsieur William had even translated more lines for me, and I had corrected his French as we strolled. His most recent lines were from his trip to the Alps—about some Italian peasant girls with ringlets, sparkling eyes, and smiles, whom he had seen dancing. I wondered why he had chosen those lines to translate.

"You would be a credit to the infantry," the captain said. "So old Vivier procured you an invitation too, eh? He'll do anything to impress on you foreigners that not all the country is in the hands of lunatics."

"How do you know that there is not lunacy, also, here?" Monsieur William replied.

The captain introduced him to my sister, who managed to sneak me an unnecessarily knowing smile, then to me he said, "But I hear you met—"

"At chez Dubourg," I said.

"I *would* like to walk more," said Monsieur William. "That is the correct use of the conditional tense, Mademoiselle Vallon, is it not?"

"Your French is improving each day, Monsieur," I said, then realized I should not have said, "each day."

"—If Mademoiselle would care to walk briefly around the room with me?" he continued.

"I would very much like to promenade, Monsieur," I said.

Monsieur Leforge's music was actually very good to walk to. I did not take Monsieur William's arm, but just walked by his side, as we did by the river, the ebbing and flowing of dancers on either side of us. I fluttered my fan between us, for the room was stuffy. "Do you like to ride, Monsieur William?"

"I love it. I just cannot afford it. When I was a boy, though, we rented horses at an inn and went on expeditions to an abbey, more than twenty miles away, and back by nightfall."

"That's about the distance I've ridden from Blois to the château de Chambord and back."

"Is that the château where Rousseau stayed?"

"That was Chenonceaux. Do you like Rousseau?"

"A good deal better than most of our English philosophers. They recognize the importance of reason. Rousseau recognizes also the importance of sensibility, of simplicity, and of nature to an enlightened life."

"A lot of people do not like Rousseau. The King himself said that if so many people hadn't read Rousseau, then there never would have been a revolution."

I said the last word quietly, so as not to be guilty of bad manners. We were nearing the hearth, where a circle of men, including Monsieur Vergez, were gathered around the vicomte.

"That sounds typical of Louis's oversimplification of things," said Monsieur William, "but one can't underestimate the power of literature to change the world. 'Man is born free—,'" he started to quote from Rousseau.

"'And everywhere he is in chains,'" I finished. "And there are many types of chains, Monsieur, not all wrought by society, or one's form of government—the most binding chains being those of our own minds—as in Plato's *Myth of the Cave*. What is outside the cave, Monsieur? I assume, as a poet, you have been there."

He stopped, and a group of dancers almost bumped into him. I took his arm, and we went on. "The whole world," he said. "All of wild nature is outside that cave, and in Plato's story all the people are stuck back there in their chains, and they think *that* is reality. They're even comfortable in it and don't *want* to change. I don't know whether it makes me laugh or weep." He looked about the crowded, lively room. "There's something else," he said. "The sun is outside that cave. The blinding light of the sun. Plato calls it the Good. I simply call it a Presence. Something that runs through all things."

"And is in us," I said.

He looked excited, more even than when he had been talking about the four tasks of being a poet.

"I have never met anyone who has understood what I was just talking about—except, perhaps, my sister—when I . . . would come in from a walk at Cambridge, all ecstatic, my friends . . . would think I was crazy."

"They were still in the cave. Plato says the people in the cave never do understand one who has been outside to the light. They ridicule him."

"I feel as if I'm talking to myself. Where have *you* felt such a Presence?"

"While riding in the woods, or beside the river—or playing with my little niece and nephew."

"The child lives in it; we forget it as we grow older. Hence, the importance of Nature: she helps us remember it."

Now, passing by the orchestra, we had come full circle, back to our tulip wood table.

"You are a good companion on a promenade, Monsieur; you speak of things far more interesting than one usually encounters at a vicomte's soirée."

"The captain had to leave," Angelique said wistfully to me. "I suppose he's on his way to England."

"All dressed up with his plume," I said.

Then my sister whispered behind her fan, "You look excited. You're glowing."

"It was warm walking around the room."

Still whispering, she added, "You're not going to get yourself in trouble again, are you, Annette?"

Monsieur William asked if he could join us and sat quietly. Angelique sipped her wine. Our guest didn't have a drink, and I wanted to offer him some of mine. Instead I asked, "Have the 'four tasks' proved felicitous for you, Monsieur?"

"I'm working on a new poem," he said, "about a place called Windermere." I liked the sound of the name. He looked at me with an intensity in his blue eyes that made it impossible for me to look anywhere else. Angelique and the room itself fell away outside the radius of that glance.

"What's it about?" I said, from well within that radius.

"A packman I knew when I was a boy."

"A what?"

"Someone who packs goods on wagons or animals. There is quite an art to it. He packed things in like a puzzle. No one . . . could pack as much in a wagon as this man." I almost laughed again but smiled instead, and he continued. "He had the greatest stories. We roamed the hills together."

"What would you talk about?" I asked.

"He talked about his travels. He had seen everything. I wanted to be like him."

"Like a packman?" Angelique said.

"You would have loved him, Mesdemoiselles. Whenever I asked him to sing some of the old ballads he had learned on his travels, he"—Monsieur William searched for the right verb—"rolled them out as we walked along into the evening. He taught them to me, and I still sing them on my walks."

"I would like to hear them," I said. "What would you write about a packman?"

"About his true goodness." It was a quick answer. "He knew nothing of elegant society"—Monsieur William gestured to the room around him—"and everything about what does matter: honest speech, a few good books, absolute independence of character." Monsieur William was speaking deliberately, getting each word right.

"Pardon me, but who has 'absolute independence'?" We all looked up.

Monsieur Leforges suddenly hovered above us, like a bird of prey.

"Monsieur William is talking of a packman he knew as a boy," I said. I reluctantly made the introductions.

"A what?" Monsieur Leforges said.

"He packs things," I said.

"Oh, I am sorry," said Monsieur Leforges. "I thought he was talking about a saint."

"He admired his true goodness," Angelique said.

"I always mistrust people when they start to glorify the peasantry," said Monsieur Leforges. "They do not know what they are talking about."

"I knew this man quite well," Monsieur William said.

"Perhaps the vicomte has made a mistake in his invitations," Monsieur Leforges said.

"In what way?" Monsieur William asked.

"I tried talking to a handsome peasant who was packing Papa's wagons one time," said Angelique, "but he had nothing to say and wouldn't look at me."

"Perhaps they have more intelligent packmen in England," Monsieur Leforges said.

"Monsieur Leforges, perhaps in England they have not been made quite so afraid of their employers," Monsieur William said.

"It is not always wrong to employ fear," Monsieur Leforges said.

"And now who is afraid of whom?" Monsieur William said.

"I am not afraid of a pitiful revolution that doesn't even know who its leader is, if that is what you mean," Monsieur Leforges said.

"And your King?" Monsieur William said. "He isn't afraid?"

"How would you use the packman in your poem?" I asked.

"A poem for the uneducated. That is a very good idea," Monsieur Leforges said. They were raising their voices, and people near us were looking at us.

"This packman sang because he was not afraid," said Monsieur William. "And from him I learned the songs that are the very stuff of poetry. Even his simple way of speaking is poetry."

"Now the Revolution enters the arts." Monsieur Leforges would have continued, but at the mention of a certain word, more heads turned toward us. The conversations near us stilled. The vicomte himself suddenly walked over from the fireplace with a glass of deep red wine in his hand. He stood above Monsieur Leforges and said softly, "Either you talk about something polite or we settle the matter later."

"Pardon me, Vicomte, but this foreign gentleman has strange ideas."

"That is why he is a foreigner. Now be a French gentleman and talk with the ladies."

"I regret, Vicomte," the Englishman started, but the vicomte had already turned back to his bastion at the hearth. I wonder if Monsieur William had understood all that had passed.

Monsieur Leforges still loomed above us. "Many Frenchmen see foreigners as spies," he said. "As much we may find the present government disagreeable, it is still preferable to a foreign one. Be careful, Mesdemoiselles," and he lost himself among the other guests.

I wondered if his "Be careful" meant something else, along the lines of the revenge he was talking about. Would he denounce Monsieur William as an English spy just to have revenge on me? I didn't think so, but Monsieur Leforges disturbed me. Damn him for returning to my life after all these years.

Yet Monsieur Leforges was mostly words, after all. Words that didn't mean anything. Not like Monsieur William, for whom every word, even *packman*, had significance.

The soirée was breaking up. I had to change the subject, to free ourselves from Monsieur Leforges before we left. "Angelique, would you like to promenade with Monsieur William and me across the Bridge Royal to the quai des Tourelles tomorrow?" Monsieur William smiled. We usually met there fortuitously.

"I would like that very much," she said.

As we left, I heard Monsieur William apologizing to the vicomte at the hearth. The Englishman had courage. Many Frenchmen were too intimidated to address the vicomte directly, let alone apologize to him.

In the carriage on the way home we were all quiet, and the wheels were loud in the still night. We rumbled down deserted streets and took up almost their whole width. The glasses of Vouvray had made me feel that everything was fine after all, and I leaned my head back and closed my eyes. I could feel the carriage enter a smoother street, and I knew we were on the broad rue Royale, on which Monsieur William lived. But he would be walking home, far behind us.

I was enjoying the ride and the silence. I was thinking of Monsieur William's eyes in the noisy room and under the light of hundreds of tapers, how the rest of the room dropped away when he looked at me and how his eyes seemed now, in the memory of that glow, to be a strange and enchanted realm from which, once entered, one might never return.

Maman suddenly broke the silence. "Bernard has told me of the disturbance, Marie-Ann. It is regrettable that someone of our family was part of it. Especially when we are guests in this city. You shouldn't speak so long with foreigners, both of you."

"It's not Monsieur William or Annette's fault," said Angelique. "It was that—"

"I was there," said Monsieur Vergez. "This Monsieur William was talking about something he should not talk about. And at the home of the vicomte, of all people."

I returned from the possibilities of entering an enchanted land and said, "He was talking about a poem."

"What kind of poem?" said my stepfather. "I know about these new ideas from the universities. Etienne has enough of them."

"He was talking about a packman, Beau-père," said Angelique, "about how he admired him."

"He was glorifying a peasant, then," said Monsieur Vergez. "Rousseau started all that nonsense that has become dangerous now. Does Monsieur William not know politics is a forbidden topic in polite society?"

"He did not think this was political, Beau-père," I said. I hated calling him that. There was nothing *beautiful* about him.

"Marie-Ann," Maman said again.

"Maman, no one has called me that since I was a child."

"You are acting like a child if you can't see the ways of the world."

"I am twenty-two, and I am Annette."

"Marie-Ann, what Bernard is saying is that Monsieur William may not be one of us."

"He is an educated gentleman and we are going on a walking expedition to Les Tourelles tomorrow."

"With whom?"

"With Angelique."

I thought the silence would explode the windows. Angelique offered no more defenses for me. She had done nobly, but I had pushed it too far with the walking expedition. I just should have kept quiet. The Dubourgs' footman helped Maman, Angelique, and me out of the carriage. I was the last of the women to walk into the house, and when we were out of the footman's hearing, Monsieur Vergez turned to me.

"Do you know that Monsieur William keeps a piece of rubble from the Bastille in his room?"

"You have been in his room?"

"His landlord, Monsieur du Vivier, told me. Now what sort of souvenir is that, I ask you?"

"Quite a fascinating one, for a tourist."

"He is not just a tourist."

"What is he then?" I asked.

"At first I thought he was just an ignorant foreigner, a harmless poet and scholar."

"He is all those things."

"He is a Blue sympathizer."

"So are a lot of educated people."

"He is the worst of types, one who uses the privilege of his education to betray his own class."

"He does not believe in class distinctions in the first place."

"He is a dangerous man, and I forbid you to see him."

"What harm can he do?"

"He will fill you with treasonous ideas."

"Against whom?"

"Against your own people."

"This is not an argument against Monsieur William."

"I know his type. He thinks a glorious new age has dawned, but he knows nothing. He thinks the high price of bread was a plot of the wealthy, to starve the poor. He does not know it was because of the winter. Ideals do not know about winters. The Loire itself froze."

"Beau-père, this has nothing to do with Monsieur William."

"He will fill you with false ideals."

"I can take care of myself. And I do not care about politics."

"Then what *do* you care about?"

"People."

"You are a dangerous one."

"Why?"

"Because you do not take sides."

"I do not understand you men, with your all-important *sides*."

"Angelique understands about sides."

"She was agreeing with me."

"And do not pull Angelique into any more of your wild schemes. She is a good girl."

"And what am I?"

He shook his head and walked down the dim hall, lit only with sconces at this time of night. If one chose a side, one knew who was right and who was not. I slipped back out to the carriage entrance. The cold air felt good on my face. The trees showed the stars through their bare branches and I could make out Orion. It felt good to walk outside. Monsieur Vergez's was a small world. Out here, there were no sides.

I didn't know if I would ever see Monsieur William again. After Epiphany, traditionally, we made the return journey to Blois. This year, however, Monsieur Vergez had an important case and was the only one who insisted on returning right away. Paul had business to do with wine merchants in Orléans, and Maman wanted to visit more with Madame Dubourg. So it was decided that, for the sake of space in the carriages, my stepfather would return first with Marguerite and the children, and Paul would join Maman, Angelique, and me later.

But Marguerite cornered me and confessed she dreaded spending so long in a carriage with our jolly stepfather; she knew he was not naturally disposed to the company of children, so could I ride with them? There was room now, with Paul bringing some of the family baggage later. I couldn't easily say, even to Marguerite, "I'm happy to stay in Orléans longer so I can clandestinely meet Monsieur William," especially since she added that the children wanted my company, so I bid adieu to the Englishman in my mind, thinking, There are a thousand reasons why he is not for me, and moreover, I do not want to disturb my simple life of self-sufficient happiness. But I also thought I owed him a parting note, telling him that I had found his company agreeable and wishing him well with his travels and with his poetry. I wrote that I expected to hear of him in the future, and sent the letter via the Dubourgs' footman to the shops owned by Monsieur du Vivier on the rue Royale.

Early the next morning I said good-bye to my dear Etienne and, acting the role of the older sister, reminded him to be prudent in the company he kept in such a volatile and unpredictable place as Paris. He answered in the manner of an invincible young man that he and a friend had witnessed the riots on the Champ-de-Mars in July, and nothing had happened to him. When I told him fifty people had been killed in that riot, and accompanied it with a savage look, he promised that he would cloister himself most righteously and study like a monk for the rest of the year, and we kissed good-bye, but not before I added that I treasured his watch and thought of him every time I checked it, which was often, even though I had nowhere to go.

As I stepped into the carriage, a messenger hastened up to me, inquiring if I were Mademoiselle Vallon and presenting me with a note (Monsieur William must have described me to him—I wondered what words he chose?). I held it folded tightly in my hand as Monsieur Vergez settled himself on the horsehair cushions opposite, glaring at the excited children. I had determined to open the letter only after we left the city, but my fingers found their way beneath the seal before we left the thronging rue Royale.

I leaned toward the window for better light as we rode up the busy street, and as I read, I wondered if we could at that moment be passing beneath the window of the room above the hatter's and hosier's shop, where Monsieur William, in the same moment, might lift his eyes from his mountain verses and, in a happy accident, glance out the window as our carriage drove by. And neither of us would ever know that that moment took place.

He had told me that sometimes he spent the entire morning on one or two lines, but it would be worth it if he got them right. He was always happy when I met him in the afternoon after he had a good morning of writing. He said walking with me by the river was his reward for that work.

Now I looked at the cramped handwriting; he must have written swiftly. He wrote that he would treasure our time by the Loire, with the noisy bargemen coming and going, and that especially he liked talking with me about Plato's cave in the cave of the vicomte's grand salon! He wrote, Where else would I find such agreeable conversation? He had decided to enclose the last translation he had read for me. It was fitting, he wrote, because it had a tone of departure.

> *. . . Adieu*
> *To every charm, and chief to you,*
> *Ye lovely maidens that in noontide shade*
> *Rest near your little plots of wheaten glade;*

To all that binds the soul in powerless trance;
Lip-dewing song, and ringlet-tossing dance.

I considered his line about the soul bound *in powerless trance*, a
felicitous turn of phrase to receive, and one seemingly in great contrast with the courteous gentleman of our walks. What was the poet's
intensity that lay buried beneath polite convention? The ardor that
only found its way into the written word?

Monsieur Vergez and Gérard fell asleep; I played whist with Marguerite and Marie (I played two of the four hands, and no one minded
who won); then my sister rested and, while gray and brown and white
landscape rolled by, I read to Marie about the month of May from the
Romance of the Rose:

Hard is the heart that loveth not
In May when mirth calls from hillsides
And from each branch where birds sing clear,
In this season so delicious
When love wakes from slumber all things.

"Why do poets write so much about love?" Marie said.

"I don't know; I suppose because it's an emotion that excites them,
like the feeling of spring; the fellow in this poem is now going to get
his hounds and go out to the forest to greet the May."

"Have you ever been in love, Aunt Annette?"

"Yes, long ago, when you were a little girl. But it wasn't with the
right person. That's the tricky thing. On that depends all."

"How can you tell who the right one is?"

I could leave this unanswered and tell her she'd find out on her
own, but why not try to answer a child's sincere question? I thought.
Many adults don't answer children's questions simply because they've
never considered the answers fully enough themselves.

"I think the key is happiness. One makes the other happy; one is
made happy by the other. I think everything else is false. That doesn't
mean love is simple. That doesn't mean it's not without its obstacles
and trials. It means that making the other happy is the most important
thing for both. I myself thought I once knew this, but I was deceived.

That is why I have never married, why I prefer the company of you and your brother. I still believe that it exists. Your parents know it, I believe. Poets write about it. Poets know things others don't know, or rather, they, because of their unique vocation, are sensible of truths that others overlook. I would always believe the poets, even before I'd believe the philosophers."

Her little face regarded me with great seriousness and a little perplexity. "Here's another poem for you," I said.

And I read aloud Monsieur William's lines about the Italian maidens. "What's the main emotion you sense in these words?"

"Sorrow. And joy. More joy than sorrow."

"I think so too. It's the joy of that *ringlet-tossing dance*. Poets help us see what's important in life: perhaps it is the moment in spring when the world seems to be in love; perhaps it is the moment of departure from . . . loved ones; perhaps it is the moment of the dance."

"Who's that last poem by?"

"An Englishman. A friend of mine."

"You know a poet? Did he write that for you?"

"Just someone I met at Orléans. And no, he wrote it about someone else. But he gave it to me."

"I would like a poet to give lines to me sometime."

"That may happen. And if it does, make sure you write them in your journal. Even if the poet goes, his lines will remain. Now, would you like to help me make up a traveling story? I'll start: *There once was a hermit who lived in the snowy woods*—"

"You mean the woods outside Orléans where Papa says brigands live now, and no one can use that road?"

"No, this is a forest of the imagination. It is not near Orléans. It is far away, in the north of England, near a place called *Windermere*."

Since chez Dubourg insisted on providing us with servants, Claudette had enjoyed a holiday at chez Vallon, which was now called chez Vergez, but as I couldn't bring myself to call it that then, I shall not call it that now that I write about it. I looked forward to seeing Claudette again. There were things I wanted to talk to her about. I was surprised that it was not the solemn André, Monsieur Vergez's footman, but Benoît, the count's groom and the beau of Claudette, who opened the door of my childhood home. Monsieur Vergez hardly glanced at Benoît as he motioned for him to take his bags; he didn't care who it was, as long as he was a servant. Benoît gave me a sheepish grin, for he knew I knew of his relations with my maidservant. While the cat's away . . . , I thought.

"I'm giving old André a holiday," he said. "He needs one. The count is in Tours, visiting his wife and son."

"Don't his horses still need looking after?" I asked.

"I had my *assistant*"—he said the word very grandly—"help for a day or so. And the count said I should exercise his stallion, so I rode him here." He picked up Vergez's heavy bags. "The count is inviting your family to come to the Sunday-after-Epiphany dinner. He said he and your family had them together for many years. He said you don't need to reply; if no one can come, he'll just eat more."

"The roads were fine?" I asked him.

"You mean the mud?"

"They were safe?"

"Where is that blasted stable boy?" We heard Monsieur Vergez from upstairs.

"I'm a groom at a château, not a *stable boy*," Benoît said back, to me only. "The roads are always safe for me." He carried the bags up the stairs.

The invitation delighted me. Those were fine dinners, fine days. Setting off in the family carriage in the morning, I'd open my window and smell the winter woods on the way to the château de Beauregard. I'd hear an axe up an alley through the trees, see the smoke of a house.

We visited the count less and less now. Monsieur Vergez considered the roads risky with the occasional appearances of brigands, and the count wasn't *his* friend anyway. Sunday was in three days' time, still before Maman and Angelique were due home, and I thought I might just ride to the château myself.

I carried my valise up the stairs, and Claudette appeared in the hall, without her apron and with her hair down. "Mademoiselle is early returning. Did you have a fine time in Orléans?"

"Yes, and you in Blois?"

"It was very dull. Just the servants at chez Vergez, and they are not any fun. Until Benoît came." She smiled at me.

We were in my room now, and Claudette was unpacking my things. Benoît came in, built up the fire, and left.

"I saw that wink," I said. "Benoît is not very subtle. Are you going to leave me and become the wife of the groom of the château de Beauregard?"

"Not I, Mademoiselle. I have a much better position here." She pulled a bell rope, and Benoît appeared again at the door. "Have Cook prepare Mademoiselle a tisane and bring it up here." She closed the door. "You see, I have it immensely easy." She was helping me out of my traveling clothes and draping them on a chair. I pulled William's letter out of a pocket.

"Claudette, with all your time you must be a keen observer of life. Tell me what you think of this." And I showed her the poem about the Italian maidens.

"This is written to you?"

"Translated from the English, as a parting gift. I have others, all lovely descriptions of rivers or valleys."

I sat by the fire now, and she was brushing out my hair with one hand and reading the poem with the other. I waited.

"But this one is about a woman. Women, yes, but really about one. I wish Benoît would write me poems. He can hardly read. But how many grooms can even do that?"

"But what do you think of it, the poem?"

"Whoever wrote it may not admit it, to you or even to himself, but this, Mademoiselle, this is a declaration of love." She put the poem in my lap.

I valued Claudette's insight. I felt foolish enough to clap my hands. Instead I kept them calmly clasped on top of the poem and said, "Then it is a declaration at a safe distance. It was delivered to me upon our carriage leaving this morning. Notice the tone of departure."

"Perhaps it is an English declaration. The English are said to be rather reserved, no? One does not follow the words with action. Yet they are nice words. Mademoiselle is touched by them, no? All those boys and men ask for your hand and receive no quarter, and one foreign poet writes you lines, and you are taken by them. I always knew you were a romantic creature."

"I am not. I am very practical."

"Yet when one writes of a 'powerless trance,' it places you in that same trance, yes?"

I was staring at the fire and felt entranced by it, now. I heard a sudden snap in the flames and at the same time a knock at the door. The simultaneousness of the actions jolted me. "That must be Benoît with the tisane," she said. "Poor boy; he's used to grooming horses, not running up and down stairs. This tisane will calm you down now."

DIFFERENT

hen Sunday came, Maman and Vergez had not returned, and I made ready to ride to the count's to honor our old family tradition. I was in the dim world of the stables now. I spoke gently to Le Bleu, whom I rode sometimes to exercise him, but I'm sure he missed his master. He whinnied softly when he saw me saddle La Rouge, and I felt sorry for him. I told him I'd take him out when I got back.

A strip of light fell through the half-open door and made a line of light across the dark hay. The line grew wider, and I saw the door open slowly and the shape of a man outlined there in the high doorway. Because of the sharp light behind him, I could not see the face. It was not Jean, our groom; he was big and broad. I thought of what Marie had said about brigands in the woods near Orléans. I had heard rumors of them roaming the forest of Boulogne, south of Blois, and robbing homes in town. I gripped a whip that hung by the stalls. The shape looked in, and then turned to go. "Who is it?" I demanded.

"Mademoiselle Vallon?" It was the musical English accent of Monsieur William. What was he doing here? I walked out from La Rouge's stall and stood before him. I still could not see his face.

"Forgive me for startling you," he said. "You had a pleasant journey from Orléans?"

"What are you doing here?" I asked.

"I am preparing to be a gentleman's tour guide of the Loire Valley," he said, as if it was the most obvious thing in the world.

"I see. Well, this is a good place to start, then. It has a lot of history." I went closer to him. His face was still in shadow.

"There's so much history here," he said, "one doesn't know where to start."

I was a few inches from him now. He seemed taller close up.

"There's Charles d'Orléans," I said. "He was a poet."

"I just read about him," Monsieur William said. "He was imprisoned in England. Poetry helped him survive."

"Come here in the light," I said. "There, that's better." He was just as close, but the strip of light fell on half of his face. I could see his eyes, soft now. "Did you *walk* all the way here?"

"It's nothing," he said. "Try walking from Windermere to Keswick and back."

He said the place names in English and smiled. I saw the smile clearly. "Charles d'Orléans did come back," I said. "A quarter century later."

"I'm glad he returned," William said. "When I asked for you at the home of your stepfather, a nice servant girl asked me if I were English. When I said yes, she said I could find you in the stables, but I had to hurry. I thought I was too late."

"You are not too late. I am very glad that you have come." I put my hand out to him where I stood, right in front of him, and he took it and held it. "You will not be disappointed in Blois," I said. "There is much to see here."

We looked at each other in the half-light coming in through the door, with the close dark of the stable around us, and its warm smells entwining with the cold air blowing in.

I suddenly stood up on my toes, put my hands behind his neck, bent his head down, and kissed him quickly on the mouth before I dropped down again, out of reach.

Now I wanted that to seem like an everyday French greeting to a friend, although my heart was beating faster.

"Would you like to start your tour of the countryside today?"

"Would it include the pleasure of your company?"

"I am going to dine at a nearby château. He may be expecting more of my family than just me, so I'm sure you'll be welcome. He's a magnanimous fellow. He's a count."

William laughed. "You'll start me with the Blois aristocracy?"

"Certainly. If you're guiding English gentlemen, they need to know whom to meet. I was going to ride alone, for it is only six miles, but—would you be so kind as to be my escort?"

"I would be most honored."

"You said you liked to ride. My father's horse is a very fine animal. It is good you have long legs, for we won't have to adjust the stirrups much. I know you will treat him with kind hands." I entered Le Bleu's stall, who shook his head excitedly, and Monsieur William followed me.

The sky was stark blue with dark clouds massing to the west, and the air was fresh and cold. We rode slowly down the steep winding streets and passed the little church of Saint-Vincent. "You have procured lodging, then, Monsieur William?"

"Yesterday afternoon; a fine apartment at a good rate, and an interesting captain of a regiment stationed here in town as a fellow lodger."

"You know your display with that orchestra leader made you rather unpopular with my parents."

"That was not my fault."

"I know. I was there. Nevertheless, you are seen as a dread revolutionary and as a disturber of a young woman's mind."

"I would think your mind was already formed enough to listen to different opinions."

"You mean it's already disturbed enough?"

"Plato can disturb anyone."

We rode down to the bridge, where we picked our way through a tangle of slow carts and carriages and pedestrians. We began to trot as we crossed the bridge, the water below gleaming in the winter sun; then we were across, and the road was freer and the trees began.

"Have you written any new poems, Monsieur William?"

"I composed more lines of my Swiss adventure as I walked here."

I pictured him walking briskly from Orléans—he must have set out impulsively, almost as soon as we left. That was a wonderful thought.

"I translated some as I walked, just for practice," he said. "I thought I'd try something different. I am always interested in old folk stories of the people, and my landlord in Orléans told me one of an unfortunate couple—"

"A love story?"

"Yes, if you will. As I said, I wanted to try writing something new, for me. Obviously, the season had to be the spring—"

"Obviously."

"So it starts like this—

Earth lived in one great presence of the spring.
Life turn'd the meanest of her implements
Before his eyes to price above gold,
The house she dwelt in was a sainted shrine.

"That's all I have now."

"'Before his eyes'; I like so much that everything around him is transformed by his love. The presence is not just the spring, is it? Shall we try these horses out, 'Monsieur' William? Show me how an Englishman rides."

I urged La Rouge into a gallop and rejoiced at the gliding movement. I could hear the eight hooves beating in unison and see rider and horse just behind, at the edge of my vision, and the steam huffing out from Le Bleu's nostrils. He thrust his head closer, eager to lead, and I looked over and saw his eyes, alive, as at a hunt.

The thundering behind me quickened, and Monsieur William was beside me, smiling from under his cocked hat, his fair hair blowing behind him, his blue eyes catching mine for an instant. He was showing me how Englishmen can ride. He was also on one of the finest horses in the Loire Valley.

Monsieur William sped past and vanished around the bend before one comes to the village of Chalettes. I heard a shout, and when I rounded the curve, Monsieur William was on the grass on the side of the road, and the driver of a cart was cursing at him. The driver was standing up in his cart and had dropped the reins, the better to wave his arms about. I was mildly amused. Monsieur William was quiet, which enraged the driver more, and when the Englishman apologized in a foreign accent, this drew more curses. The driver could not tell whether Monsieur William was an irresponsible youth who should be whipped, a bourgeois who should keep off the road, or a foreign spy who should be arrested.

Le Bleu cropped the stiff, short winter grass. Monsieur William kept his silence and looked bemused. The cart rumbled on, and the driver gave a look that possibly included me in his list, as a witch, a woman who should not clutter public roads, and a prostitute. I was smiling as I drew La Rouge up beside her friend, the horses calm and familiar in each other's presence.

"I couldn't understand most of what he was saying. He was speaking so quickly," Monsieur William said.

"It's better. He enjoyed the cursing."

"I did not see him until I was right in front of him. He did not have to stop. I leaped immediately over the ditch at the side of the road, and that is when I fell."

"One must make allowances," I said, "for the unexpected around the bend."

Monsieur William mounted Le Bleu, and we were walking the horses. "Do all young women of the upper bourgeoisie ride horseback so well?"

"I'm not sure what classification I am, but I think most prefer carriages. I know my mother and sisters do. But even in a small open carriage, the man always drives, and this I do not care for."

"What else do you like to do that's different?"

"I like to hunt; no, that is not exactly true; I like to go hunting; I like the adventure."

Monsieur William laughed. The laugh seemed to resound in the empty forest.

"You have a sense of adventure as well as a keen eye and wit?"

"My father taught me to hunt and ride."

He grew serious again. "I would have liked to have met him. I am sorry he was lost so early to you. We have that in common."

"I want to show you something before we come to the château de Beauregard," I said. "Can you keep up with me?" And I dashed off the road, drawing in the sharp delicious smell of the pines, and followed a narrow trail, hardly noticeable under the forest duff. It had been years now since I had ridden here. The count had shut the lodge down. He still went hunting now and then, but after Papa died, he said he had lost the heart to have the old gatherings, the suppers in the lodge the night before, meeting in a circle outside in the frosty dawn. I could hear Monsieur William right behind me now, plunging deeper into the forest, following me blindly. We scrambled down one small ravine and up the other side, and there it was, blending perfectly with the woods.

"Why are we stopped here?"

"Look, through the trees. There."

"How strange! Such as I saw in Switzerland."

"It's the count's hunting lodge. Some of the best times of my youth were spent there, with my father and the count's friends. It's all shut now."

"Do you want to ride closer?"

"No, I'll leave it in the past. I just wanted to see it. There's a lovely meadow just beyond that stream. We can get back to the road that way."

The two horses recognized the meadow, even with the snowy patches. The sky seemed to lower itself above us, now, as if a storm were due. I led Monsieur William through the brush to the road, and we raced back along it to the count's tree-lined entryway, up the winding route where the peasants had led Etienne and me—all that tumult seemed a million miles away now—and to the Beauregard stables, a second home to the horses. I won by a length, but only because I knew the way.

We brushed down the horses and went along the side path to the great doors of the château. The impassive Edouard almost smiled when he saw me, and I smiled back. "He wasn't sure anyone would come," Edouard said softly to me. "Last year no one came." He took our coats and gloves. "The count occupies himself mostly in the library these days." We were passing the ground-floor arcades. At an inquisitive look from me, the valet ventured upon more information. "He is obliged to answer letters from his acquaintances in exile." Edouard announced us at the open door. The count was writing by the fire. I saw his sheepskin hat, such as Rousseau had on in his famous portrait, over the top of a high-backed chair. He had moved the Beauregard coat of arms down from the study upstairs, and the gold bells that had meant something to me on a night long ago flickered in the firelight above him. They were pinioned on deep azure and looked more stately in this larger room. When the count stood, he still had on his reading spectacles, and they made him look older. He took them off and lay them on the writing table.

"*Ma chère* Annette!" he said, and came toward me with his big arms outstretched and embraced me. "Are your *maman* and Angelique behind you?" He did not say, "Monsieur Vergez."

"They are still in Orléans. So I came myself."

His face fell a little, then he smiled all the way up to his eyes. "You're a true believer in tradition," he said.

"But I could not come alone. This is my escort, Count. A gentleman and a scholar from Cambridge, England, Monsieur William." My guest bowed his head.

The count faintly raised his eyebrows at me, as if to say, No chaperone; no stern Agnès, or even Benoît? And he immediately shrugged, as if again to say, You are twenty-two; the Revolution has changed so many things; who am I to say?—or at least that is how I interpreted his gestures.

"Monsieur William is also a poet," I added.

"I, myself, am unsure on that matter," the poet said. "A title is a difficult thing to bear."

The count laughed. "That is so true," he said. He extended his hand. "Welcome, scholar from England," he said. "I can't remember when we last had a poet here. We were mainly dancing or hunting, eh, Annette? By the by, you didn't . . . encounter anyone on the way here?"

"Whom do you mean? We met only a cart-man who was quite upset at Monsieur William."

"Oh, that's fine, then. . . . There's been some complaint about people on the road, that's all. I'll go rile up Cook; tell her we're having that dinner, after all. Show him around, Annette. Hope you like the improvements since the last time you were here," and he disappeared toward the kitchen.

I had only visited once since the looting, and that first Epiphany after father's death, before Maman remarried, the château was still bare. There were scarcely enough chairs and plates for those of us at table, just one new couch (not of the quality of the old ones), and the walls were still naked. Now in the front salon I saw that the Turkish couch had returned, even the firescreen with the little semi-nude Grecian figures. In the hall the old gilded clock sat on its place atop the ebony commode. In the second salon, the velvet couch embroidered with peacocks had taken up its former position. And in the dining room my favorite tapestry—the huntsman leaping over the log in a meadow of *mille-fleurs* and the white hart disappearing into the rabbit-filled forest—hung again, though the stag and hunter in the background had been raggedly cut out.

When the count returned, he was beaming. "How did you—?" I said.

"It was simple. I paid for it. Bought them all again. Most of those looters had lived here all their lives; some had even worked for my father. It was a bit of fun for them, the looting day. They went back to harvesting for me; I never said anything about it, then last year I sent an agent around to all the cottages to ask if they had anything they cared to sell, and I got much of my furniture back, even some porcelain plates and cups—a few are chipped, but what of that? No draperies, though—those are new—and no silverware. All that I got back I had cleaned—it was more filthy than you can imagine—and some of it's better than it was before. Come, sit down. New tablecloth."

Edouard glided in with three marcs. Another servant was building up the fire in the huge dining room hearth. This had been the main hall of the original château.

"I always felt time stood still here," I said, "and then the looting came, and I felt as if part of my own past had been ransacked along with the château. Now—"

"Beyond the reach of time, that's the château de Beauregard. I always deemed it symbolic that the coat of arms wasn't stolen—I suppose they had enough to loot down here without getting up to the ceiling," the count said.

"I understand many of the châteaux were burned, also," said Monsieur William. "You were lucky, then, Monsieur le Comte."

"Lucky. Yes, I suppose I was."

"You were not here that day, Monsieur William," I said.

"*You* were?"

"Yes, we made omelettes for them all, didn't we, Count?"

"For looters?" Monsieur William said.

The count laughed and proceeded to tell the story, filled with horror and humor, as if it had all happened to someone else.

He had got his *things* back, which he had said had no meaning in themselves, and yet, as I looked around, I felt it could never go back to the way it was, even if he ransomed every gilded and needle-pointed piece of furniture back, even if the missing hunter and stag were miraculously woven back into the tapestry. The man now leaping over the log was forever alone. Without my father the château de Beauregard can be dreadfully cold and dull, I thought, and now, with its *things* returned, it may miss him even more, for he is not here to enjoy them.

Then I realized it was I who had changed. The times that hovered outside the thick oak door, and which had burst through it once, had left me more uncertain; I felt no firm foundation to my life like the foundation of this château. Marguerite was right to fear that we would all end up like the Varaches, fleeing to foreign parts.

And yet there was something else too, and as I glanced over at Monsieur William, laughing at some silly joke of the count's, I perceived that the difference also lay right here, in this wonderfully odd foreigner, the sleeve of his plain brown frock coat on the gilded armrests, his long legs stretched out before him.

The château de Beauregard had never seen such a man. And he was so different than any man I had ever known: the way he broke out in sudden laughter—laughing, yes, I had often heard, even guffawing, but not a spontaneous peal that rang though a forest. And through his poems I saw an eye for nature that I had never encountered—that remembered blue patches in the icy water and kept details of faraway places pure and clear in his mind. Everything he did was frank and full of meaning—the opposite, for instance, of Monsieur Leforges's charm and guile—and he seemed to love the world, as I did, not *things*, not abstractions, but the world itself. I think that is why I had loved poetry—not just its romantic stories, but the way it took seriously the small things that people overlook.

> *I bathed my face in clear water,*
> *The bottom paved with shining stones*

"This is the vast forest of Boulogne," the count was saying; "from just riding here, you have no idea how far it stretches. There are wild places in this forest Annette herself doesn't know exist. This is the ancient hunting ground of the kings of France. You have just skirted along its edge."

Edouard entered and said something softly to his master. "Dinner will be ready in half an hour," said the count. "Would you like to see something of the gardens?" Monsieur William jumped up, and the count drew back the heavy curtains and opened the French doors onto the terrace, with its view of the manicured hedges and the crisp geometrical paths radiating out. We walked down the stone stairs toward the lawn. Mist wound through the alley of cyclamen. In the distance we could see the small lake, set like a pearl between lawn and forest. It was bitter cold now, but Monsieur William didn't seem to mind. It was probably much colder than this all the time in England.

"Those paths," said the count, holding his drink with his left hand, gesturing grandly with his right, "were laid out almost two centuries ago, as was that wing there, but the dining room, the front salon with the coat of arms—have I shown you the Beauregard coat of arms, Monsieur William?—they were built in the mid-sixteenth century, when Henri II hunted nearby with the great huntress Diane de Poitiers."

"The woods here still have much game, Monsieur le Comte?" William said.

"The most game-filled forest in France."

"Do you have much poaching, Monsieur? Especially since the Revolution?"

Monsieur William still had not learned about mentioning politics in polite society.

"I allow some."

"That is very generous of you, Monsieur. Landlords in England do not do that."

"It's best to overlook some things—certain people, fathers providing for families, for instance—even though I make certain, if they work for me, that their wages are fair and they always have enough bread. A band of brigands have been lurking round here off and on since the Revolution began. They're likely responsible for what happened at the château de Chambord and perhaps even instigated what happened here. Sometimes they drift down from their permanent residence in the forest near Orléans. If they want to take a deer, it is prudent that I do not alert the National Guard; the brigands would just hide out, then take their revenge on the château. And I have had one raid here. I will not tolerate another."

"You know of the existence of brigands, Monsieur le Comte, and the local National Guard does not?"

"It is a vast forest, as I said; it has room for a few villains tucked away under its branches."

"You are a tolerant man, Monsieur."

"No, only a cautious one. In all these changing times, I have one absolute: that which has stayed in my family for centuries, that which has seen intrigue and conspiracies come and go as kings came and went with their courts at Blois. My one object is this château. It will stand; I will repair every injury to it, and my son will inherit it."

"How is Philippe?" I asked.

"Your sister Angelique was visiting with him here, before you went to Orléans. Didn't she tell you?"

"No, she didn't," I said. "I suppose she's old enough to have her own little secrets."

"They spent the whole day together. Getting along famously." The count smiled. "I think she's very good for Philippe."

I thought, even my little sister has a beau.

Edouard appeared from nowhere and announced that the table was ready.

"You have not seen the portrait gallery of the kings," the count said.

Monsieur William raised his eyebrows.

"Another time. Come," said the count. "You will eat like the kings of old—like Henri II and Diane when they visited the château de Beauregard. And a grand Sunday-after-Epiphany dinner never hurt me." He patted his belly. He was as lean as ever. "Then I will skip supper, a boring meal."

The count kept to his word: we ate gray mullet from the Loire in butter, shallots, and vinegar; haunch of venison with chestnuts; braised green cabbage; a creamy Epoisses cheese, and little apple tarts with a fragile roof of burned sugar. The count had replenished his cellars: red wine from Chinon and white, of course from Vouvray, all served by two swift, silent servants whom I had never seen before.

The silver shone, but I put my finger on the chipped rim of my porcelain coffee cup.

Monsieur William asked us, I suppose to be polite and talk about French literature, what was our favorite play by Molière? I said, *The Misanthrope,* because it reminded me of my stepfather. The count laughed, though Monsieur William didn't get the joke. The count said he liked *The Bourgeois Gentleman,* for it was written right close by at Chambord, while the great Lully composed music for it to be performed for Louis XIV. "If it's culture and history you're after, Monsieur William," the count said, "the Loire Valley is the place for you. And much more . . . *quiet* than Paris." And throughout the conversation and the courses, Monsieur William and I would catch each other's eye for an instant, and one—or both—of us would smile, and the count and his swift servants would fade to the periphery of my awareness.

The drapes were closed again to keep in the warmth; a huge fire blazed; the hunter pursued the elusive hart; shadows strode across the carved oak of the walls, and I could almost believe that time was an illusion, but I got up and peeked out the curtains and saw that, during our long midday dinner, the short winter day had sunk into evening, hurried on by the clouds and a coming storm. I observed that, although it was only six miles, I had rather not do it in the dark or snow.

The Frenchman grasped the foreigner's shoulder as he shook his hand and said he was glad Monsieur William was riding Le Bleu; even if there were a blizzard, that horse could find his way. I was glad to see Monsieur William so accepted. The count had always been like an uncle to me, and now, with Monsieur Vergez's and Maman's marriage, I felt closer to him than to anyone else of my parents' generation.

DARK RAVINE

*T*he air smelled of snow coming. I thought of racing the horses home but wanted to delay the parting to come. We rode in silence, and I thought how comfortable I felt in Monsieur William's presence, even wordless, as if we had known each other all our lives.

"That was the best meal I have had in a very long time," he finally said. "And the count is a charming fellow. He doesn't seem too full of his superiority of class, as most of his kind would be in Britain, and perhaps here too, though I haven't met enough aristocrats to judge. I hope, as is the Duke of Orléans, he is working with, not against, the changes in society."

"You heard him. His concern is his château, not politics."

"He didn't expel from his service or have arrested the people who stole from him. Most extraordinary. Is that the main road there? I can hardly tell; the fog is so dense—it's like ghosts gliding through the trees."

"Maybe you can write a poem about it—the places you write about don't have to be just the glorious Alps—"

"What was that?"

I heard only leaves chafing each other in the limitless woods on either side of us.

"The wind sometimes sounds like a waterfall through these trees. I think it's the wind picking up the fallen leaves—your gliding ghosts." Then I noticed that the horses too were aware of some disturbance, ears perked forward, listening, alert. "Let's go," I said.

We commenced to canter, and the sound of agitated leaves continued under the trees. We could hardly see two horse-lengths in front of us in the fog. I didn't want to urge La Rouge blindly forward. Then I thought I glimpsed the bulky outline of a horse and rider passing on my right, between the trees, through veils of mist. Another shadow moved off of Monsieur William's side of the road. He looked over at me. I nodded. The horses' ears were still forward; Le Bleu snorted and tossed his head from side to side. The fog was bitter cold and cut through my coat and riding habit. "Faster," I said quietly.

We galloped into the fog and had not gone far before we had to rein in violently before two figures of horses and riders standing in front of us, not fifteen feet away: statues in cocked hats and capes, each pointing a pistol.

"Was it a passable dinner at the château de Beauregard?" said a voice on the right. "We saw you riding fast up the entryway at noon and figured you must be late for some feast. We had stale bread, didn't we, Antoine? Whatever happened to the days when Henri IV declared that every family should enjoy a chicken stew once a week?"

"I know what happened to them," a more uncouth voice said from the other figure. They looked indistinguishable in the fog. "Henri was stabbed to death." He sounded amused.

"What do you want?" said Monsieur William. "We have nothing."

"She does," said the rough one.

"Now, Antoine," said the other, "there are other things. And besides, this one is mine." He trotted his horse up beside me.

La Rouge twitched her ears nervously, and I laid a calming hand on her neck. I hoped Monsieur William practiced his reserve rather than his frankness and could react when I wanted him to.

"Your friend," he said to me, "from his accent, is obviously a foreign spy, Austrian, in league with the harlot queen. You are counter-revolutionaries, visiting the local aristocrat. We are patriots, here—"

"You are no patriot, Monsieur," said Monsieur William; "do not sully the word. You know nothing of it; you dress up your crimes in the cloak of righteousness. I tell you, we have nothing, and you will get nothing."

"What do you say to his pretty speech, Mademoiselle? Or should I say Madame, riding as you are in the evening with a foreign gentleman?"

"I say he is correct. He is no more a foreign spy than you are a patriot; we are friends with Count Thibaut, who will—"

"The count will not report us to the National Guard, if we do not harm his château. Our understanding is quite clear. What a fine chain—" He had reached his hand to my neck, where the gold chain that held the watch Etienne gave me was just visible. This was the closeness I had been waiting for. In an instant my riding crop sliced his cheek.

"Go!" I shouted to Monsieur William, and in that infinitesimal pause, as in the moment of a dance, I saw my victim's cheek run red; I heard his shocked cry of pain. I urged La Rouge like a plunging wave past him and into the woods, and I heard Le Bleu's hooves bite the earth on the other side of the road. I immediately heard a pursuer behind me and another to my right. His band must have surrounded us. I could not think of Monsieur William now, only of what I had to do. The forest whipped by, the fog sliced by low branches. I ducked down, parallel with La Rouge's mane, and heard a second cry from behind me. Then from my right I heard two shots. La Rouge knew she had to get away from these other horses.

I reined her from the more open chestnut trees into the pines. Boughs swished close over my bent head. My face was so close to Rouge's body, I could smell the earthy scent of her sweat beneath me, mixed with the smell of the pines rushing at me through the dim, fog-filled forest, the sound of hoofbeats behind me now muffled on the carpet of needles. I headed south, away from Blois, thinking my pursuers would naturally assume I would head toward town. I now only heard one pair of hooves following me. I rushed down a steep ravine, similar to the one at the bottom of which I had shot the boar, but wholly alien to me. As before, I almost stood in the saddle to compensate for the sharp descent, but this time, I allowed no decrease in La Rouge's speed. A branch snatched my hat off halfway down. Pebbles and earth slid with us. At the bottom a small stream ran through snow-covered rocks. It seemed colder down here; I heard no hooves now, above me.

I rode down the middle of the stream, splashing in the growing dark past roots as big as roof beams girding the banks above me. The walls of the ravine grew steep on either side. I stopped finally by a little sandy bank.

It was almost night here below. La Rouge stood quiet in the clear water, and I could hear my own heart thumping and the pulse beating in my throat, and I listened. My right hand lay on Rouge's neck. I felt as if my ears were being pulled upward, I was listening so carefully. I could hear the wind in the pines, far away. I heard distinct sounds of the stream: a small waterfall over roots, sliding over pebbles into a pool, rushing over rocks around a bend. I heard a bird suddenly cry as it soared through the deepening darkness. I believed I could hear anything in the forest for those moments. A branch clicked, and I started. La Rouge pricked up her ears. I heard no sounds of pursuit, no matter how hard I strained.

"You are a queen among horses," I said, and patted her. "Thank you. Thank you."

Now I looked around at the black, wet walls of rock, at the pines silhouetted on the ridge above me, at ice at the edge of the shallow stream, and realized I had no idea where I was. I didn't know how far I had gone south, or if I had kept to that direction, or in what direction I had now followed this ravine. After all our hunts, I thought, it seems I would know this part of the woods, but as the count said to Monsieur William, the forest of Boulogne is vast and full of wild places that I did not know. I worried about Monsieur William and whether he had escaped. I trusted Le Bleu, though, and I trusted the Englishman's riding and quick mind. The count had been glad Monsieur William was mounted on Le Bleu. How much of our danger had he anticipated?

Now that we had halted, I was growing frighteningly cold. What if this dark passage took me to where the brigands camped by a stream? Which direction should I now take? Thirsty, I dismounted, felt my legs a bit not my own, and knelt, took my glove off, reached my hand in the icy stream, and drank. I stayed, knees on a flat snow-covered stone, and prayed silently to my personal saint, Lucette. I drank again. The water was sweet as well as teeth-achingly cold. I hadn't realized how dry my mouth had become.

I stared up and could hardly tell the difference between the dark rock and a narrow strip of storm-clouded sky. Then, as La Rouge lowered her head again to drink the twisting water, for a moment a glowing sliver of a new moon appeared, alabaster against dusk blue; and Venus sparkled just at the edge of the gorge. When the moon is new, I thought, it sets almost as it shines; Venus is the eve-

ning star, drawing to the horizon by nightfall. Therefore I knew now
which direction was west, and consequently that this stream flowed,
roughly, north-south: I needed to go north to Blois, back in the direction whence I had come. Then clouds passed again over the top of the
canyon, devouring the moon. But I had felt its grace, and I mounted
La Rouge again and patted her. "We're going home," I said, and the
sound of her iron-shod hooves clattering in the stream blended with
the sound of water over rock that echoed up the steep walls as we
started into the cold night.

My wool riding habit, sodden with river water and the sweat that
comes from fear and exertion, clung to me under my cloak. I felt the
coldness of the night on my bare head. Rain began slapping against
the rocks and swiftly froze, causing La Rouge to stumble once on the
slick rocks of the stream. Then the sudden hush, as the first flakes
floated innocently down. I looked and saw them spinning randomly
through the still air. I usually liked this moment of the first rush of
snow; I liked its silence and its peace. But now it served only to make
me feel more alone in the vast maze of the forest. In spite of my high
collar, the snow slipped down my neck, and the cold seemed to grow
up from the ground, under my damp skirt. I swept the snow from
my head with my glove, but of course my hair was wet again in an
instant, and I tucked my head down like a sleeping bird and still felt
the cold burn my cheeks. I tried to hasten La Rouge along the stream,
but it was dark now, and boulders loomed, cascades tumbled, and I
didn't want her to trip again. She was doing her best. She didn't like
this either. She knew a rubdown, oats and alfalfa, and a warm barn
awaited her.

I heard her hooves snap the ice in shallow pools. I couldn't feel
my legs now. I let La Rouge lead the way. I had perfect confidence in
her; this ravine must end, Rouge would find our meadow, and thence
the familiar road to a warm barn. It is waiting for you, Rouge, I said
to her in my thoughts; Le Bleu is probably already there; Monsieur
William has a faster horse than those men, riding whatever broken
dobbin they could steal. Monsieur William spoke boldly to them,
didn't he? He leaped into the forest just when I wanted him to and just
in the right direction, opposite to me. How did he know to do that?
He must have known my thought. Then he must also know what I am

thinking. That I am coming, slowly, through a dark ravine; that I am
as cold as cold can be, that my face feels frozen under a hat of ice. No,
I don't want him to know those thoughts. He must know that I am on
my way to the meadow. He must be thinking that that is the best place
to meet me, away from the road. The old hunting lodge, that is far
enough. Blois is too far in the dark. Monsieur William, you are safe;
you are safe; you and Le Bleu are searching for your friends. Don't go
any farther. Stay in the meadow.

I felt like a statue now, my hand made of stone clutching the reins.
I closed my eyes and heard the stream sounds, distantly. In my own
darkness the world retreated; I suddenly no longer felt the cold. I
felt sleepy. I vaguely didn't want to fall out of the saddle. It would
be confusing for La Rouge. She would stay here in the dark and cold
and perhaps freeze to death herself, loyally, her sweet, small horse
brain telling her to stay by me. I've heard that freezing to death is
not uncomfortable. One feels wracked by cold, but now that is past,
I thought. One feels numb, then one feels sleepy; it's all rather comfortable after the cold is past.

I opened my eyes on the dark world of a fallen chestnut, its roots
lined with snow, and on its other side a steep slope. With a huge effort
I think I moved the reins a few inches to the right; I may have made
the old clicking sound with my tongue against my teeth. I may have
only thought to do that. But a horse such as La Rouge, sensitive to the
slightest nuance, knew my will. And she was glad to get out of the
water and push herself up the snowy hill.

At the top I recognized nothing but night in a forest with a sweeping wind that brought the snow into my eyes. I remembered racing
through pines with my father, but which grove was this? My world
went on uninterrupted by thought or sensation for I know not how
long. Something made me force my eyes open. The snow had ceased,
and there was only a thick mist. Perhaps it was my eyes. It seemed
hard to focus.

I heard a horse call out through the mist, and La Rouge answer. A
dim shape emerged from the nothingness and spoke. The words rang
senselessly in my ears. The figure coaxed the reins from my hand and
led La Rouge.

*M*onsieur William laid me down by a fire to remove my soaking cloak and gloves, soggy boots and stockings. I felt him rub my arms and my legs, then curse, low. I felt him peel away the jacket, then the vest, and felt his hands rub the stone statue of my chest under the thin linen shift.

At first I could only feel that the hands were warm, distantly warm; that they were the source of a warmth I no longer possessed. Then I felt them as part of each part of me that they touched. They passed that life on from themselves into me. The numbness grew into an uncomfortable tingling. Then I trembled uncontrollably. I heard my teeth click against each other. I opened my eyes to see my bare shoulder, not my own, shake violently, and the strong hand descend to chafe my arms as rapidly as they shook. He rubbed my legs now, up and down, fiercely, stopped to throw another log on the fire, and began again, feet to legs to chest to arms and shoulders.

I shivered and trembled again, then at last fell silent in my body and felt, for the first time, the warmth from the fire, the glowing from his hands. Sweat glistened in the firelight on his face. He said something in his language I could not grasp, and stood up, and the room and fear closed around me. Even though the fire was near, I felt it on my skin only, not penetrating within. I knew I would die before he returned. My chest felt as if a heavy weight lay on it.

Then he was back, lifting up my head, holding a glass to my lips and pouring burning liquid down my throat. I coughed, and he held a wooden cup of water to my mouth. "Drink, Mademoiselle Vallon," he said. "Drink and live. You got a bit cold, but you will be all right." And he placed a cushion under my head, laid me gently back down. I felt the fire's warmth beat into me, and I thought I heard him humming, or perhaps singing, low, one of his odd English songs, then I slept.

When I awoke, I saw the fire, low in a large rock hearth, and immediately realized I knew this room—it was the main hall of the count's lodge. He had heard my thought again. I saw all my clothes hanging on the firescreen, felt my nakedness beneath the blankets and a mixture of extreme embarrassment and gratitude. I raised my head and saw Monsieur William, in a high-backed chair, his legs up on a small table, regarding me quizzically. "They also serve who only stand and wait," he said, "or, in this case, sit and wait. How are you, Mademoiselle Vallon?"

"I hardly know."

"Move your toes. Can you feel your toes?"

"Yes."

"Are you still cold?"

"Not at this moment, I believe. Thank you, Monsieur William."

"Thank our horses, Mademoiselle. I'll never say anything again about them lacking reason. Those villains never had a chance with the horse you gave me. It knew its own way. And I think it talked to yours when yours was still far away, called her to the meadow. I willed you here, also. I thought that you would return to the place of your youth, for safety, if you could at all. I prayed also. The fire was ready for you, and by the grace of God you're here. Your clothes are dry now. I'm sorry, but you could have died with those wet garments clinging to you. I wrapped you in a blanket. I trust I did not impinge upon your modesty too much, but I know what cold can do. My own father—I'm sorry. I chatter on when you don't even understand how you arrived here. I've been sitting, watching. I'm so glad you're awake, feeling better. I was truly worried. I've seen people die of cold—I'll leave now so you can dress."

I leaned up on my elbow, pulling the blankets up to my chin. "Monsieur William, I have never heard you talk so much. I think my illness was good for your French."

"You tease me, Mademoiselle Vallon; you must be better. I will build up the fire so it is not cold for you when you dress."

And I laid my head back on the deerskin rug and watched him blow carefully at the logs and the flames mount and light his face. He squatted by the fire and held his palms out to it, then quickly turned and placed his palms on both my cheeks. They were radiantly warm.

"That's delicious," I said.

"Are you stronger? Do you think you can ride? I brushed the horses. They are fine in their shed. There was even hay left in there. Nothing in here, though, except an inch of old brandy I finally found in a cupboard. We'll need to eat soon."

"I want to rest just now, a little more. Monsieur William, am I mistaken, but did you not sing softly last night, as I was falling asleep?"

"Once I thought you were out of danger, I wanted you to sleep, but I wanted to keep myself awake, just in case you started trembling again—so I sang old border songs of Scotland and England."

"It was lovely. Could you sing one again?"

"In English?"

"The language doesn't matter."

"Well, that's probably a good thing, because they are all sad. You see, this fellow Gordon, Annachie Gordon, that's a Scottish name, loved this girl and she him." When I first awoke, he had been speaking excitedly, but now he spoke again in his quiet, slow, deliberate way. "But her father wanted her to marry a rich lord—it's an old story— so Gordon went out on a long sea voyage, and when he returned, her father had married her to the lord, and she, Jeannie, had died."

And in his sweet baritone he sang softly the long song, and I imagined the parted lovers, the one returning too late, and watched the fire leap up and Monsieur William sing as he gazed at the fire.

> *The day that Jeannie married was the day that Jeannie died*
> *And the day that young Annachie came home on the tide*
> *And down came her maidens all wringing of their hands*
> *Saying, oh it's been so long; you've been so long on the sands,*
> *So long on the sands, so long on the flood.*

And when it was over, he sat there, still staring at the fire for a long time. "Would you like some more water, Mademoiselle Vallon? I'm afraid that's all we have to offer here."

I nodded, for I did not trust my voice anymore, and he filled a

wooden cup from an earthenware jug and knelt by me and brought
the cup to my lips. I drank deeply, and when he had taken the cup
from my lips, I leaned back and held my arms out to him. He seemed
abashed. He did not know what to do. But I held my arms out, bare,
cold above the blankets. He put the cup down on the stones by the fire.
"Mademoiselle Vallon, I—"

My arms were still out, and he entered into them and kissed my
cheeks, then my lips, and I lifted the blanket, and he tried to speak
again, and I only kissed him.

Then he disengaged himself, and I watched him, still kneeling by
the fire, take off his boots, coat, and waistcoat. I watched him pause,
glance back at me, receive my smile, then remove his pantaloons. In
his long cotton underwear and linen shirt, he quickly climbed back
under the blanket. Just as our kisses became more urgent, our hands
more confident in caressing each other, Monsieur William said, "I
think, Mademoiselle, that you still need some warming from your
ordeal last night," and he sat up beside me and began slowly and
strongly again to knead my shoulders, my back, my arms. A delicious
warmth shot, then settled through my limbs. Feeling spoiled, I lazily
lifted a foot and let it dangle in the air. William received my message and began stroking it. Then I stuck my other foot up. A tingling
rippled down my legs from my toes and the balls of my feet. One of
William's hands departed from the ends of my body and gently made
its way up my leg and rested there.

I rolled over. His other hand skirted across my breasts, back and
forth. A current thrummed deep within me. My hips lifted and swayed
in a rhythm all their own. As the movements heightened, as a pitched
intensity drew us more and more as one body, suddenly all my limbs,
muscles, and thoughts lapsed into an exquisite stillness, luxuriant and
simple, united with William yet wholly myself.

We lay still now, and I felt again the warmth of the fire on my face.
Where had it gone, during our moments of passion? Where had
everything gone? I lay on my side, with his chest against my back,
with one of his arms over me, the other under my neck: his warmth
on one side, the fire's on the other, the only sound or movement the
hiss or snap or undulating dance of the flames.

The fire flickered on the high oak beams of the lodge. We were alone in all the world. There was no tomorrow, barely yesterday, and now the fire danced. Now I could hear his even breathing as he slept after he had watched me most of the night. He was a rare soul. I took our fugitive hour and held it close.

There lies my love,
My love lies on him and cannot remove
And I never will forget my love Annachie.

After the snow stopped, after the world was remade in white, the horses pranced in the powder with plumes of smoke rising from their nostrils. The earth glimmered at their hooves.

As we rode, Monsieur William asked me what I thought about the "understanding" that the brigands said they had with the count. "That understanding almost cost you your life, Mademoiselle," he said.

"Yes, but whatever understanding they *said* they have, I think it didn't include attacking innocent travelers on their way back to Blois."

"You're fond of that old fellow, aren't you?"

"I've known him all my life. In my mind, I suppose, he's like my father. They were such good friends."

"Your forgiveness is admirable. But the count was in the wrong to put the safety of his château over that of his fellow citizens. You're a loving soul, aren't you? I don't think you have a vengeful bone in your body."

"Not now, I don't Monsieur William. Not now."

Suddenly I felt curiously formal. "I would like you to meet my older sister and her family, Monsieur William. Will you ride with me there?"

I did not want him to return to his lodgings, and I to chez Vergez. And I wanted to share my newfound joy. I could trust Marguerite to be grateful for the way he had protected me. Maman, if she knew, would probably want him arrested for spending the night with me in an abandoned lodge.

"They are parents of the little Gérard?" he said. "I liked that child. A most delightful child," he said, "a most delightful child."

I agreed. The world was, briefly, a delightful place. It seemed odd that it was only yesterday that we had crossed the river. It was swollen now with the storm. For me it sang a panegyric on behalf of my personal saint, Lucette, who had lifted the moon from the passing clouds, who had led me to Monsieur William. I had almost died and had been delivered back to life. I had found a love that I had not thought possible. It was not the first time that I had felt that so much had changed in so short a time, but it was the first time I felt such joy.

As we rode along the quai Villebois, Monsieur William, too, was looking at the water. "The river glides by at its own sweet will," he said.

Once at chez Vincent, I asked Marguerite if a servant could deliver a note for me to chez Vergez. "Didn't you just come from there?" she asked.

"We rode from the château de Beauregard. I'll explain later." I didn't want to start off our visit with Marguerite worrying about brigands chasing Monsieur William and me through the forest.

She nodded, in her way of understanding and respect that Marguerite always has, and sent for old Pierre, who was slow but reliable. "You are always welcome here—you and any friend of yours. You must make yourselves at home and stay for dinner."

The note informed Claudette that I had dined late and had spent the night at the château de Beauregard and that we were now at chez Vincent.

Benoît then arrived. He had returned to the château that morning, and when he told the count that we had not returned to chez Vergez the previous night, Benoît had been sent immediately back, bearing a letter with the seal of the count on it addressed to the commanding officer of the local National Guard. But Benoît had first stopped at chez Vergez, and Claudette showed him the note. She sent him then to chez Vincent.

Benoît looked relieved to see that we were indeed safe. "The count was like a crazy man when I told him you had not returned to chez Vergez. He was crying and cursing himself and the walls of the château de Beauregard and calling to the ghost of someone named Jean-Paul."

"That would be my father," I said.

"He was like a crazy man," Benoît repeated. He looked curious, but said nothing more. I hastily wrote another note saying that we had been pursued, but our horses had proved their worth again, and that we were safe at chez Vincent. I gave it to Benoît with a big tip.

"Well, your holiday is over now," I said. "Please tell Claudette on your way back that there is nothing to worry about."

I would tell Marguerite after dinner, I decided.

Monsieur William tied chestnuts to strings, and he and Gérard swung and knocked the chestnuts together in a merry war until my sister gently chided them to come to the table.

I was happy to observe Monsieur William that evening with the Vincents. Paul was still in Orléans, and the Englishman was the gentleman of the table. To Marguerite he praised her casserole of chicken in white wine, saying dinners in the Loire Valley far outdid anything he was used to in England. He asked her to tell him a story of our childhood together, and she told him of our playing hide-and-seek in the crypt of the cathedral, a story the children had never heard, which widened their eyes and brought a laugh from our guest at the general unorthodoxy of the Vallon children, which was amusing because Marguerite herself sat there smiling placidly, the very picture of domesticity.

At Monsieur William's bidding, Marie played a Lully piece after dinner that I had taught her, and at her own instigation, she brought two drawings in from her room and laid them out before the fire, and they discussed the virtues of her different shades of green and blue in creating for the viewer the summer trees and river. Monsieur William said he tried to do in words what she was doing in painting. And I, I enjoyed them all liking him. This was my family, completed by Monsieur William.

I think they could tell that the Englishman and I liked each other very much. Marguerite asked him when he was thinking of returning to England, and he shrugged and said, "Not until my money runs out, and I am very frugal; not until I have finished a poem about my voyage to Switzerland, and it is very long." He looked at me and added, "Not until Mademoiselle Vallon has shown me all the best places to walk along the river, and she has said there are many." Then it was time for coffee and pastries, and for listening to Marie play. I thought how patient they had all been with Monsieur William's sometimes slow speech. I was proud of how willing he was to engage them in conversation in a language he was still learning, how frank his desire to please was, how he was utterly devoid of superficial charm, and how intelligent and warm a person they must think him.

After the children had retired, I gave a truncated version of events in the forest to Marguerite, who was shocked for our safety, and I had to assure her several times that we were fine. She said that she had heard rumors of brigands that had come down from the Sologne forest near Orléans and that, in addition to the count's letter, she would ask Paul to report our plight to the new Committee of Surveillance, though she had heard they reserved the use of the National Guard now mainly for locating and deporting priests who wouldn't take the new oath of patriotism. A bizarre definition of "crime," she said. Monsieur William said he would mention it to his new friend at his lodgings, who was a captain in a local regiment and whom he was sure would not look kindly on any anarchy in his demesne. "The captain will feel it is his duty to take care of the situation," he said.

During that conversation I felt a weight settle on my heart. I saw the soft look their eyes had all had during dinner harden. I was reminded of that world that I knew hovered just outside the door of the count's lodge. I felt it threaten to take what I had just found. Monsieur William went on about how the brigands had used the term *patriotism* in vain. He was growing angry. I decided, then, that I had to bring my friend back from brigands and Committees of Surveillance and regiments. I would lose him eventually, I knew, but I could not bear to lose him now. I picked up an orange from the bowl of fruit, cut it, and began to peel it with an ivory-handled knife. I felt a slight spray from it come up to my face.

"These people say they are *for* the Revolution. It's a travesty," Monsieur William said. The scent of the orange clung to my hands. My friend and my sister were outside its sweet range.

"Would you like some orange?" I said.

"Thank you," William said, and I passed him segments I had cut. He also chose a whole one from the bowl.

"Monsieur William," I said. "I was telling my sister that you are a poet, but she has only my word. Perhaps you could share some of the lines you've translated."

"Poems in translation are delicate grounds on which to draw conclusions," he said, perfectly peeling almost a whole orange in one cut. "But it's worth a try."

His eyes had their old light. His poems and he were *inseparable*; they were far more intimate to him even than his ideals of the Revolution. More intimate to him than I, but I had my place near them in his heart, I felt. It was to that place I had wanted him to repair. He put his orange on the porcelain plate painted with blue pagodas and willows and said, "You will not hear them as they are meant to be heard, but—" He paused. "I'll take another risk, Madame Vincent, and give you new lines even Mademoiselle Vallon has not heard. I was waiting to share them with her, but circumstances . . ."

He flushed and began. I had won my friend back, for now.

> *Once, Man entirely free, alone and wild,*
> *Was blest as free—for he was Nature's child:*
> *Confessed no law but what his reason taught,*
> *Did all he wished and wished but what he ought.*

"Those sound like the sentiments of Rousseau," my sister said, "the beautiful thought that we are all nature's children."

"Reflected upon from the vantage point of the pure and beautiful Alps, Madame," Monsieur William said, "in nature itself, where one pays proper homage to philosophy."

I did not want this fragile happiness to end, but at last I could not stifle my yawns. My sister clapped her hands and commanded us all to bed. She insisted that Monsieur William stay at chez Vincent rather than find his way to his lodging in Blois. He did not refuse.

We said good night before our rooms, and I kissed him on the cheek and shut the door behind me. I hoped he had waited to hear that the lock had not turned in its tumbler. I waited. I grew increasingly tired, feeling still the fatigue in my body from my travail in the forest the night before, and, wondering if the Englishman was concerned about his principles, or the principles of society, or if he loved me at all, I fell asleep.

I was woken some hours later by a gentle but persistent brushing of fingers against my door. I pulled back the bed curtains and stood before the door in the dim light from the low fire in the grate. "Enter," I called softly.

"Mademoiselle Vallon?"

I opened the door to Monsieur William, a silver candlestick in his hand, and quickly let him in, lest some hall porter was up who wanted to engender some gossip. "I was asleep from waiting," I said.

"Did you wait for me? I couldn't sleep, thinking of the liberties I didn't dare," he said. "I even took a short walk in the cold night air. I looked up at your room, with a soft glow coming from it, until my courage returned."

He stood with the candle in his hand and looked excited, boyish, almost. He had something he wanted to say. It could not wait until he sat down.

"I continued the story of those lovers," he said, "the one that I started reciting you lines from on our way to the château de Beauregard. I composed and translated them while I was walking. I looked up where I thought your window was." I was waiting for him to pull a slip of paper from his pocket. "Would you like to hear them?"

"By all means." I said. I took his hand, which was ice-cold, I presume, from walking outside for so long. "Sit here." I motioned to the bed and folded the silk coverlet over his legs. "Where's the poem?"

"I've memorized it," he said.

I placed his candlestick on the bedside table and got back under the covers and took both of his hands, and rubbed them between mine. "Here, I'm returning your favor of last night," I said, as I felt his hands warm. "Now, please, recite. If you are going to wake a lady up, you must have good reason. Could you please include the first four lines again, so I could hear them altogether?"

> *Earth lived in one great presence of the spring.*
> *Life turn'd the meanest of her implements*
> *Before his eyes to price above gold,*
> *The house she dwelt in was a sainted shrine . . .*

"Now here are the new lines, which it took walking outside to compose. Remember, this is about two lovers who are separated by—"

"I don't want to know how it ends; please continue."

Her chamber window did surpass in glory
The portals of the East, all paradise
Could by the simple opening of a door
Let itself in upon him . . .

"That's as far as I got, but I wanted to share it with you."

"'All paradise . . . by the simple opening of a door'?" I said. "I'm glad I opened it."

"I'm just telling a story that I heard—"

"It's beautiful. Thank you." And I leaned over and blew out his candle and drew him to me. "*Tout le paradis*, All paradise?" I said.

A few shadows intermingled on the ceiling. I had never bothered to close the bed curtains. He lay still now, with an arm enwrapping me, and I felt as if I had come home, after a long absence. He was so quiet, I thought he was asleep. Then he suddenly sat up, leaning on his left elbow beside me.

"Is this how it is regularly done in France?"

"How?"

"Without clothes."

"It's good to feel the skin, do you not agree? But you still have your long shirt on." I tugged at his linen sleeve, and he grabbed my wrist.

"I have never seen anyone more beautiful than you," he said.

"Before you have only seen clothes."

"No, even if . . . "

"What do you mean *anyone*?"

"Anyone."

"Where? Who?"

"In England."

"You have not known any French girls?"

He shrugged and said, "They laugh when I speak."

"I do not laugh when you speak, and I do not laugh when you do not speak." I pulled at his shirt. "Where in England?"

"Cambridge; I do not know."

"With clothes? And clumsy movements? What do you mean, *anyone*? Where else?" I was teasing him and loving to tease. I think he knew it did not matter what he said.

"At a country dance."

"This sounds more serious. During the dance?"

"No, afterward. You know how dances are."

"No."

"In the country. Everyone mingling."

"And where do you do it at the country dances, hidden in the hedgerows?"

"In England we do not talk of such things."

"And you wear clothes. The bodies must touch. From head to toe. It is no good touching clothes. You miss so much." I rolled over and started to pull his shirt over his shoulders. He pushed my arms down. Then I wrestled the shirt over his head.

"Now you are faceless. Flesh and facelessness."

"You are wicked."

I pulled the shirt over his head and threw it off the bed.

"See how beautiful you are. Just like a baby."

I swung myself over him.

"What are you doing?" he asked.

"Shhh," I said.

I moved slowly, and my face was close to his, then I sat up and could feel my spine very straight as I looked down at him. Then I slowly moved and kept looking at him and thinking how nice he was and that I should keep myself from falling in love with him, and my back straightened more. I felt taut like a bowstring pulled fully back, and everything was very still again. Then I let myself go, and I felt a heat beat in me, and I shook. Monsieur William held on to my hips as I was shaking. I finally let myself collapse on top of him.

"Is this good for us?" I asked.

"It's very good."

Then I raised myself slightly. His face was in shadow beneath me.

"Should I keep myself from falling in love with you?"

He looked at me in silence, then said, "I have already loved you more than I have ever loved anyone."

I collapsed back on him and kissed his neck.

"Have you ever known an *anyone*?" he said.

"Once, long ago, but I was mistaken, and he was a no one."

We paused, and I waited in the dark to hear Monsieur Williams's reaction.

"I said it," he said. "And I will say it again. I love you, Mademoiselle Vallon."

"You may use my Christian name now, and I love you, Monsieur William Englishman with the unpronounceable name."

"Besides, keeping oneself from loving someone would not be very healthy, would it?"

"That is good use of the conditional tense."

"You are a good teacher."

Then, "I must be going soon."

"No servants are up this early. You can stay a bit longer."

And I lay now curled at Monsieur William's side in the warm darkness of our world. "Give me those lines again," I said. "The ones about the shrine and the door." And he softly said them. "'All paradise,'" I said. "It's true," I said. "It's true."

I slept late that day, and found, slid under my door, a folded paper that contained the lines he had translated for me the night before, and a request that he might call on me that evening again at chez Vincent. At my breakfast, almost at the midday dinnertime, my sister said that Monsieur William was a very nice man. She liked him, the children liked him, and he was welcome any time at chez Vincent. "I am very happy for you, Annette. Are you happy?"

"I am."

"My only concern," she said, "is that he is foreign. It is bad enough, all the Frenchmen with different ideas and hating each other. God knows what could come of—having such a friendship with an Englishman. You could leave me like the Varaches, but your loss I could not accustom myself to. Ah, but I jump to conclusions. Please make him feel free to come here. You see, I have worried about you for so long. You have been too alone."

"You don't have to worry about me."

"I know. You're the independent one. But it's the independent ones that one worries about. What a pair you are. You like each other and don't care about what the world thinks. He comes to a foreign country in the midst of a revolution, all on his own, with only poems in his pockets. Yes, a fine pair, but I'm happy for you."

"You haven't heard him sing, Marguerite."

"He sings too?"

"Ancient ballads about separated lovers who die for love."

"Oh, my."

"He'll sing them in English, so no one knows how sad they are."

"Well, that's all right, then. Just don't you go learning English. It's a horrid language."

he next day Marguerite and I joined Monsieur William and his friend from his lodgings, Captain Beaupuy, dressed in his beautiful uniform, for a promenade by the river. I liked the captain. He was exactly like one of the men Maman always wanted me to marry—rich, charming, from an old aristocratic family; the only difference was that Captain Beaupuy had given up all his privilege to help usher in the glorious new age. He genuinely believed in that, and his and my friend's idealism together knew no bounds. Michel Beaupuy introduced Monsieur William to the Friends of the Constitution, the new patriotic club of Blois, where they spent hours together.

We had been walking by the bridge when Monsieur William softly said to me most extraordinary words: words that cannot be taken back and, once having been let loose, change one's life forever. "I've thought about this thoroughly," he said. "I have stayed up most of last night thinking about it. I have discussed it with the captain." He paused, and I could hear a wagon, coming fast, at our backs. I could hear the river rushing against the foundation of the bridge. "Would you join me, now," he said, "in the holy sacrament of marriage?" I'm afraid I laughed at first—what did he mean, *now*? Where? How? It was insane. But then I saw his face. He's in dead earnest, I thought.

"Yes," I said hastily. "Of course. But isn't the future tense usually used for such a proposal? I cannot marry you in the conditional tense."

He apologized and rephrased it. I again answered in the affirmative.

Marguerite stopped and turned her head. "What?" she said.

"Monsieur William asked me to marry him," I said. The captain was smiling.

"I heard him," my sister said. "When? Where? My God——"

"Monsieur William has thought about this thoroughly," I said, and waited. The wagon hastened by us with the creak of its wheels. We were beyond the bridge, on the quai Saint-Jean.

"Madame Vincent and Mademoiselle Vallon," my English lover said, "as you know, we live in changing times. I'm sure that you would agree that priests have become mere civil servants. I want the world and God to recognize our union. For the world, we have two honorable witnesses. For God, I ask you, where does He dwell? In a cathedral, which is now a function of the state? Does he not dwell where he has always dwelt, in nature?"

My sister and I had nothing to say. It seemed that Monsieur William had prepared a most sincere speech.

"Therefore, I ask you, what better place to perform the holy sacrament than by the river itself?"

"But Monsieur William, it would not be blessed unless it were performed by a priest," Marguerite said. She was taking him seriously too.

"I'm afraid, Madame," he said, "that Mademoiselle Vallon would not want to be married by a constitutional priest, and I cannot be married by a priest in any case, as I am not of your religion. But I believe in the sacrament. And I believe in the holiness of Almighty Nature."

"So do I," I said.

"Annette, is this what you want?" Marguerite said. "It's all too much like something out of Rousseau, but then it's you—"

I nodded. I believed in Monsieur William's sincerity.

My sister threw up her hands. "What would Maman say? Well, I suppose you're thinking she need never know. What would Papa say?" She saw my smile. "Ah, you think Papa would approve, do you? Well, I've said you're a pair. You're certainly a pair. I just hope you can find a proper priest, either in your religion or ours, Monsieur William, when these *changes*, as you call them, are over. Very well, then. And who will perform the holy sacrament in nature?"

"I will, Madame," Captain Beaupuy said. "I was an altar boy. I witnessed many weddings. I know the most important words, in Latin. And I am a *captain*." He smiled a disarming smile.

"And the holy vows are not a game, Captain?"

"No, indeed, Madame." He was not smiling now.

"Well, don't use all the words you know," Marguerite said. "It would probably be blasphemous. And you, Annette, getting married in your walking dress. We must all do this properly," she said again. "In good time."

"In good time," I said.

"Where are the rings?" she said, and sighed. "Here, you may use Grandmère's," she said to me. She was taking off the ring from her right hand and putting it in her pocket. "You can't get married without a ring."

My groom went dashing suddenly to the banks, where, amid the sand and slush of melting ice and snow, he plucked a long reed and braided it around his own finger, took it off, gave it to the captain, and said, Please hand this to me at the right moment.

We all walked down to the sand, now, where one could hear the river flowing, just a few feet from where we stood.

It was lovely. I am sorry I cannot present you with any grand cathedral wedding, with ancient bells tolling over the blue slate roofs and narrow, steep streets of Blois, but a river, still high from winter rain and snow, with sunlight glinting off patches of blue, and the air smelling cool and fresh and laden with the presence of the heavily moving water, and the music of lumbering carts and harness bells, and the litanies of cart drivers complaining to each other on the bridge nearby, and Marguerite and I getting the hems of our skirts muddy and finally laughing at our state, and Monsieur William all the time very serious, and the captain speaking in Latin and joining our hands: all of this natural and human beauty will have to do.

At that moment, just as we were finishing the ceremony, a heron flew by, its wings spread unbelievably wide and whitish blue as it skimmed the banks. Then it flew over the bridge and downriver and was gone.

Marguerite reached into the deep pockets of her skirt and gave the ring to me. Captain Beaupuy delicately took the twisted reed from his waistcoat pocket and handed it to my groom, and we slipped the rings on each other's fingers. Grandmère's ring, of course, only fit on his little finger, but that was no matter, as it was understood that everything, from our location to a kind of church we had built around us—not just the rings—was symbolic; but isn't a grand cathedral itself still only a symbol?

After we exchanged the rings, Monsieur William's fingers lay lightly on mine. Then he held both my hands by the fingers, lightly and firmly, and as he did so, all the sensations of sound and sight about us merged into an absolute stillness. I felt his firm, light touch, and nothing else. I could have wept, standing in the mud by the river, but I was beyond weeping. I was not even by the river, with the captain and Marguerite nearby, in that moment. We kissed before our witnesses. Marguerite and the captain softly applauded, and the world flooded gently back. "The river is so loud," I said in William's ear. "I've never heard it so loud."

"It's the longest river in France," William answered, "and we were married right beside it. I can put you in my pocket and take you back to England now. You can hear the Derwent River—"

"Don't," I said. "Don't." And now I began to weep.

"Don't what, my dear?"

"Don't make any more promises. This is enough for today."

Marguerite and I took the men's arms as they led us back to the quai, and people looked at us. Some even pointed to our skirts, and the captain bowed scornfully to them, his sword at his side, and silenced them. I had to say good-bye to William, as he and the captain departed to their lodgings. I would not see him now until dinner in two nights' time. As a foreigner, he did not want to be seen coming too often to chez Vincent. It could be imprudent for the Vincents. As the Austrians and Prussians were threatening France, and Great Britain was grumbling at her, foreigners were often looked on with suspicion.

He knelt and brushed the mud from the hem of my skirt, and that simple deed moved me so that I could not speak to tell him thank you or to say good-bye. He told me to wait, and took off down to the riverbank again. I saw him bending over the water, and when he returned, breathless, he had in his hand another reed, which he had already made into a circle. He gave Marguerite back Grandmère's ring and gave her the reed and nodded. On the quai, with a wagon of firewood passing, I placed the reed around his finger. "Now we're

equal," he said, "both bound to each other through the river itself."
He bowed and kissed my fingers. As he rose he looked astonished.
"What shall I call you now?" he said. "Between us, Mademoiselle
Vallon will no longer do."

"You are Monsieur William," I said. "You may call me Madame
Williams. You said once that is a real English name, is it not?"

"Welsh, actually, but that will do fine."

And I added softly, "And I am simply your Annette."

"Until tomorrow evening, Madame Williams," he said. "Until
tomorrow, Annette."

I liked him saying it. I liked hearing it. My husband vanished
behind a cart loaded with coal, and I could just see the top of his tall
head and Captain Beaupuy's black hat as they walked briskly away.

"Did you see that big bird?" I said to Marguerite.

"Yes, I saw it," she said, and smiled. "You don't usually see them
this far inland. It flew over just at the right time. It was a blessing, if
you choose to believe that."

"I choose," I said, and closed my right hand over my left and felt
on my finger the thin, tightly twined reed.

While the National Assembly ruled France, with the King as their puppet, two sinister developments stirred that winter: Committees of Surveillance, with virtually unlimited power to investigate and arrest anyone they thought was counterrevolutionary, and the rise of Maximilien de Robespierre and his friends, who, because they always sat on the highest benches of the assembly, were called the "Mountain Men." Among them were Georges Couthon, the crippled lawyer, Georges Jacques Danton, of the silver tongue and the oversize head, and Louis Antoine Saint-Just, who, long before the trial of the King was even discussed, demanded the execution of the King without a trial. Their ally was Jean-Paul Marat and his hysterical journalism: Marat of the yellow face and the skin disease; Marat who, through the virulent hatred expressed in his paper, earned the undying love of the people of Paris; Marat who, when he was later murdered in his bath by a young woman, trying to keep him from denouncing more innocent people, was called a god, his heart embalmed and hung in an urn from the rafters of his club. And Marat himself now looked up to Maximilien de Robespierre.

Robespierre was thought so absolute in his devotion to the Revolution, so pure in his lofty idealism, so above common human appetites, he was called *The Incorruptible*, though soon enough some used the title ironically, and I myself thought it was the human emotion of compassion that he was so icily above, from which he was so incorruptible.

But William at this time, and his newfound brother Michel Beaupuy, could not hear of anything but praise for the direction France was taking. They were always jolly.

"France is leading the world in the quest for freedom," the captain announced to me.

"What about the United States?" I asked.

"Well, they have slavery, don't they?" he said. "Even Britain, languishing with a tyrannical monarch, doesn't have slavery on its shores, does it, William?"

"It has a slavery of the mind," he said.

But that day the gentlemen had not come to discuss the world's movement toward freedom. William had convinced the captain that we must all go on an ice-skating expedition.

"They have nothing else to do up in the frozen north," the captain said.

"I cannot imagine a winter without ice-skating," William said. "It's immoral. And ice-skating is probably the most egalitarian sport there is."

"There you have it," said the captain to me. "Are you ready? Our foreign friend has spent all morning getting our boots shod with steel. But we need a second lady to balance our riding party. I've taken the liberty of asking your charming maidservant."

"Claudette?"

"The same," the captain said.

"Michel is nothing if not egalitarian," William said.

We were riding through the forest of Blois west of town, with wet oak and fir scent on the wintry air, and somewhere, far off in the woods, the blows of an axe. We were on our way to a pond near Molineuf. William was going to teach us all to ice-skate now. He said it was simple, and everyone did it where he was from. He carried the newly shod boots in a sack on his horse. The captain carried his sword, and Claudette carried dinner. I took spare stockings and skirts, for I was afraid that Claudette and I would get icily wet. But it wasn't about our expedition that the men were talking.

"Grégoire—that's the constitutional bishop of Blois, who served in the National Assembly—says it's the only direction things *can* take," William said.

"But you have a king *and* a parliament," I said. "Why can't we—"

"Madame Williams," said the captain, "monarchy in France is too used to absolute power. It will never abide the lessening of those powers. English kings have not held such power in hundreds of years—or if they have tried—"

"They were quickly dethroned," said William, "which is the inexorable end to which we are going."

"And what about the powers of your Assembly? How many Surveillance Committees does it need?" I said.

"They are protecting the people—," the captain started.

"I thought that was your job, captain," I said. "These committees can investigate anyone, anytime, under any pretext, under the broadest definition of possible treasons imaginable—and made up in their minds, mainly. Why, you, captain, could be investigated by them, if you were to say something disagreeable to them. William—well, a foreigner, he's automatically suspect and cannot speak for himself."

William laughed, and so did the captain. "I am a member of Les Amis de la Constitution club," William said. "The captain has introduced me to the most important patriots in the town."

"He has met the powerful Grégoire," the captain said.

"All I know," I said, "is that in the name of freedom from tyranny, we have set up new tyrants who have fewer restraints on them than ever before."

"The Austrians are threatening," the captain said.

"One can justify anything," I said.

"Is that the pond through those trees?" Claudette said.

It was amusing: William taking me by both hands on the ice and my legs going in opposite directions, the suave captain slipping and landing on his rear, Claudette spinning with William, falling and bringing him down. I came to enjoy gliding along, but was very bad at stopping and would make in increasing uncontrolled speed for an overhanging willow branch. Claudette and the brave captain soon surrendered and started on dinner, perched on a dry log and laughing at me.

I liked seeing them there, in their funny skates, one in his great blue cloak, the other in her long brown cape, his shining boots, her wooden clogs resting beside them. Claudette peered out from her hood with laughing eyes. The captain had a tricolor cockade on his hat. He poured wine into a wooden cup and handed it to her. This is how William and the captain envision the Revolution, I thought, the man of aristocratic birth and the woman of peasant origins, sharing a wooden cup of wine. But such a vision only comes from the eyes of the truly good. It doesn't take into account the hatred and ambitions of men.

William said the true skating experience must be at night, when the moon was reflected in the ice and one could hiss along, barely seeing the shadows of others, and fly through dark space like the stars through the heavens. I said I could fly into the willow tree no longer and joined the others on the log, while we all watched William perform curves with a grace and skill and speed that made him look, alone on a winter pond in the paling light, like some spirit from another world.

After cold roast chicken, bread, and wine, William further surprised us by taking a wooden flute from his pocket and sending haunting sounds through the forest. "I'm not very good," he explained; "we had a minstrel in our group at school, and we'd row him to a small island in a lake, and he would play from there and we'd hear it echo over the water."

William wants to help the world, I thought, but he's not a warrior, like the captain. He's not a politician, like their Grégoire. He's a poet who belongs in wild nature. He sits there like Pan himself, blowing on his flute and the forest listening.

"What brought you to France?" I suddenly said.

William put the flute down. The captain poured himself more wine. No one knew what William was doing here, except, now, staying in Blois to visit me, we three presumed.

"The Surveillance Committee could say you're a spy for England." The captain laughed. "They say England, not Austria, is behind all the counterrevolutionary movements. You'd better answer the lady."

"I am running away," said William. "Not from unjust governments or the law, just running away."

"From what?" I said.

"From nothing," he said. "Literally, nothing. I was doing nothing. There was nothing I *wanted* to do. My uncles wanted me to go into the church, my older brother to follow him into the law. I told them I was coming here to study the language, which was partly true. I told friends in London I wanted to observe a new republic being born, which was partially true. I had no home. I had restless legs. I have no parents. I am a dependent who must beg his uncles for money. So I am running away from the nothing that was my life in England."

"What have you found?" I said.

"Everything," he said. "Simply everything."

And he lifted his wooden flute, no larger than his hand, to his mouth, and a melody of some far-off realm, a border realm where starlight reflected on frozen lakes, filled the falling dusk.

Later, by myself, as the moon appeared above the treetops, I skated alone near the far end of the pond where a grove of bare chestnuts grew up to the bank. The forest seemed smaller with no leaves on the trees, as if one could see through it to the other side. I felt suddenly lonely then, by myself in the winter evening at the end of the pond. I felt as if William had already taken that inevitable ship back to England. What have I been thinking? I thought. In what an illusion have I been living? I skated back across the pond as fast as I could without falling. I thought every minute was precious now. I saw William cooking something over a little fire and headed straight for him. I took my eyes off him to look at my skates, to slow myself down, and when I looked up, he was gone.

Then I heard a whisper of skates behind me, felt his warm breath and a kiss on the back of my neck, felt his hand place something in my pocket and then saw his back, the tails of his frock coat flapping, as he skated smoothly away. I reached my hand in my pocket and pulled out hot chestnuts. I watched William sail over the ice, bearing in his gloved hands his gifts to the captain and Claudette.

The next time we were alone in the quiet dark of chez Vincent, with the shadows mingling on the ceiling, I asked him about his father and how he died. I had lost mine at age twenty, William at thirteen—his mother when he was eight. "I remember," he said, "hiding behind a low stone wall, away from a bitter wind. All I wanted to do was go home from Hawkshead School for Christmas. The horses that my brothers and I had sent for seemed to take forever to arrive. Meanwhile, my father's business duties had called him away from home, and he got lost in the mist on his journey back and spent a freezing night out of doors. He was burning up with fever by the time we got home and died before the new year. That is one reason, Annette, I was concerned about you and your night in the snow. I felt responsible, somehow. I felt that he got lost from hurrying through a stormy night to get home in time to greet us, returning from Hawkshead."

"I felt responsible too," I said. "I could have saved my father. I knew I could. I don't know how, but I would have. I still feel that."

"Sometimes it's not responsibility at all. Sometimes it's just the way of the world."

William kissed me on the cheek lazily, and I put my head on his chest. "You smell like an oak forest after the rain," I said. "Has anyone ever told you that?"

"No one," he said.

"The snow's melting," I said. "It's times like these you can hear the river, even from all the way up here."

"Impossible," he said. "The Loire is a quiet river."

It seemed very important to me, then, that we hear the river, that it not be impossible. I got out of bed, opened the curtains, the window, and threw the shutters back. The cold surged in. "What are you doing?" William asked.

"You'll see. You'll hear, I mean," I said.

"You look beautiful," he said.

"Hush, and listen," I said.

Clouds hurried toward the face of a large moon, illuminating the slate roofs of my town. Far off I could see the tower by Saint-Louis Cathedral and the bridge and the river. Then they slipped away when the clouds came. The sweet, rainwashed air rushed into the room, closed all winter.

"I don't hear anything," my husband said.

"Listen. You must listen hard." He sat up, leaning on his elbow. He was listening.

A deep, constant, low sound filled the night. It was the river flowing high against its banks.

"Once you hear it, it's unmistakable," he said.

"Then it's not impossible," I said. I started to close the shutters.

"No, leave them open," said William. "I like it like that."

And I got back into bed and warmed myself against him. There would be other, larger things that I could never prove to him were true just by opening a window. But I had no need to prove them now. I think we both thought, in that night in the late winter with the distant, unmistakable sound of the river coursing through the town, that our love was as permanent as the flow of all that water, season after season, through the land.

The cold, sweet air felt good. We left the window open the rest of the night.

During a pause in my conversation with Marguerite, I dipped bread in a bowl of hot chocolate, pondered again how long William could stay in France, with his meager means and with the suspicions of foreigners increasing, and at the same time noticed, outside in my sister's garden, the first daffodils of spring along the walkway. Once I saw them, I wondered why I hadn't also seen the quince just starting, and even a few blossoms on the plum and pear trees, their white petals against the branches still dark from the rain. Suddenly the boughs were lined with hundreds of tight, folded buds, ready to explode.

"Paul tells me the assembly has decreed that all émigrés are conspirators now, and their property is to be confiscated," Marguerite said. "Can you believe—the Varaches as conspirators? Little Sylvie, Marie's friend?"

"They think everyone is a conspirator," I said. "They even accuse each other."

"Is Monsieur William safe from being accused?"

"He's shut himself in his room lately, working on an essay, in French, mind you, in praise of the new constitution, which he will send to his acquaintance in the assembly, the mighty Brissot. It's called 'The French Constitution and the Dawn of a New Era: An Englishman's Perspective.'"

"Does he know . . . of what we were just talking?"

I shrugged and exhaled air and looked at the early efforts of the tree. Soon it would be its own white cloud.

"Will he want you to go to England?" my sister asked.

I shrugged again. I couldn't remember which bore fruit first, the plum or the pear tree. That the trees would be laden with fruit was the only thing that one could really be certain of, I thought.

"I am so sick of hearing of demands for war," Marguerite went on, "how all the émigrés gathering with the King's brothers in Germany mean to attack us and bring with them the armies of Prussia and Austria, so we should attack them first. Well, Grandmère Vallon said there never is a good time to bring a child into the world. They just come when they want to. And it's a good thing they do."

I smiled at her and patted her hand. "Yes, it's a good thing," I said.

"When Maman and Monsieur Vergez were here for dinner the other night, they looked happy together," she said. "It will be a bit complicated with Maman, won't it? I think you would be happier, staying here."

By that afternoon William had finished his essay and sent it to be read by *La Patriote Française*. We met when I was still on the last step on the Vincent stairway and he was standing in the hall below me. Without saying anything, we embraced there, and he said, someday we must have a house with a stairway, so I could always stand a step above him and we could embrace and be at the same height. I said, All right. He said, And a river running behind it too, and took from the inside pocket of his frock coat a long, slender box and handed it to me.

I knew what kind of box it was, and upon opening it, saw a delicate pink fan. I spread it out and beheld a line of people painted on it, with a wagon in their midst, drawing something. "It's the latest style of decoration for fans," said William. "It's the funeral procession of Voltaire. A great writer, and a great hero of the people."

"It's lovely," I said. Gone were the days when butterflies and flowers decorated a lady's fan. I was simply touched that William, with his little money, had bought me a present. I waved it and looked coquettishly over the top of it at him.

We were out on the terrace now, with the little fountain lapping. Gérard and Marie came out to greet Monsieur William, and he squatted to say hello to Gérard, then took Marie's hand, and we walked toward the blossoming trees. I showed Marie my fan.

"What are these people doing on the fan?" she said. "Where are the flowers?"

"This is the new style," I said. "It's the parade in Paris to honor Voltaire after he died," I said. "We'll read his *Candide* when you're a little older. He satirized the hypocrisy of governments and the absurdity of war. It's a historical fan."

"I prefer the flowers," she said. Gérard was skipping before us.

Marie ran ahead to join her brother. They were enjoying a wind that came up from the river valley. Marie held her arms out straight from her sides, and Gérard, looking at her, copied her. It was the first spring wind and felt noticeably different. This one carried with it, barely discernible, a scent of the new earth.

But it was still cool, and I shivered. "William," I said. "William, I have something to say to you."

He stopped. I looked over at the buds on the lean branches. "I am with child," I said. The enormity of that hit William stronger than any spring wind. He almost rocked in front of me.

He still asked the obvious question. "Are you sure?" he asked.

I nodded.

He opened his arms to me. I felt his arms around me and nudged my face into his shoulder. I felt him kiss the top of my head. "I'm so afraid and I love you so much," I said.

He pulled me closer. I could hear his heart. He didn't say anything. I could hear the children shouting something to each other. William was thinking. I knew he was thinking, with the spring wind ruffling his hair.

"It's a bad time," I said. "I know I would like a church wedding. Maman would want it, but the new priests are not real priests and— our ceremony by the river will do, for now. Marguerite says there are more frightening things happening every day. Grandmère Vallon says there never is a good time—"

He held me out from him, so he could see me. "I think," he said, "that I must return to England immediately. I will solicit my uncles for money. I will publish my long poem. I will secure a position as tutor, save enough to return, and—"

"William, I don't want you to leave. If you leave, too many forces could keep you from returning for a long time. Stay with me until the baby is born. Stay with me. Then go to England, if you must. You know I have a bequest from my father which I can draw on—"

He raised his hands in protest.

"My sister will let me stay here. I've already talked with her."

"I will stay with you if it is your wish," he said. "When is—"

"December. Sometime in December." I raised my fan and noticed the mob of little figures and the bier of Voltaire, then the spring sun pouring in through the pink color, as through the backs of petals. "I'm glad you will stay," I said.

"I had another present for you," he said, "but it seems small now, compared with what you have just told me. Here—" and he drew a folded paper from his waistcoat pocket. "I wrote some more about the story of the lovers."

I nodded. For some reason, I thought I would cry if he read me that poem.

"This follows," he said, "the opening of that door, if you remember, that let paradise in upon him." He paused. "Maybe you would like to read it."

It was better for me right now, reading it aloud, than hearing his voice say the words. How did he know that? I read,

> . . . *pathways, walks,*
> *Swarm'd with enchantment till his spirit sank*
> *Beneath the burthen, overbless'd for life.*
> *Not favour'd spots alone, but the whole earth*
> *The beauty wore of promise . . .*

"For life?" I said.

"Overblessed for life," William said. "There is enough in their short hours to last him more than a lifetime. The whole earth shares in the promise of their love and reflects it back to them. Look at the children," he said. "Running under the blossoms."

I leaned back into him and felt him pull me close. I held the poem in one hand. The children stopped shouting. "I think they're watching us," I said.

"That's good," he said. "That's as it should be. Let's join them."

And he took my arm, and I leaned my head against his shoulder. I folded the poem and put it in the pocket of my linen dress. Marie still stood with her arms outstretched to the current of the spring wind up the valley. Her eyes were closed. Gérard looked sheepishly up, his shoes and stockings wet. "That's a beautiful puddle," I said.

William's words shook me, and I reached my hand in my pocket and grasped the paper tight.

We returned to the house with Gérard's muddy shoes and Marie's messy hair and William's arm in mine. Paul was there, home from dealing with merchants in town. His face was tight. "Have you heard the news?" he said.

"What news?" I said. "We've been on a walk. Monsieur William has been shut in his room, writing."

"France has declared war on Austria."

"That is folly," William said. "Austria has a vast empire from which to draw resources. She also will ally herself with Prussia. Then they'll ask England to join the monarchies against the French Republic. This is pure folly."

"People are happy," Paul said. "They are singing, shouting, embracing each other. Why do people rejoice over going to war? It's unbelievable."

Marguerite bent down and spread her arms to her children. "I'm sorry about my stockings," said Gérard. "Is that why Papa is upset? Aunt Annette said it was a beautiful puddle." His mother merely kissed him on the cheek.

I felt a vise grip my stomach. What would I do now, an unwed mother in a nation at war with its neighbors, with William a member of an enemy nation? Would we have to leave? Would we all have to follow Monsieur William back to England? And how would we live there?

"What about Prussia?" said William. "I'm sure France will declare war against her too."

"No word yet," Paul said.

"And England?" I said. That William would be an enemy was my greatest fear.

"England will stay out of this, for now—this is a European affair," William said. "I'm surprised Russia is not involved."

I felt an immense sigh of relief.

"France is not ready for war," Paul said.

"My friend Captain Beaupuy will be leaving soon, then."

"When wars start," said Marguerite, "no one knows when they'll end. Remember what Maman said of her uncle Robert, Annette?

When he left to fight the English in America, he said he would be back in nine months, for Christmas, and six years later they heard he had died at Québec."

All I remember was that Robert was Maman's favorite uncle. She said he had died a hero. I felt the paper in my pocket, and its weight seemed so light in my hands.

"Well, it will take some time for France to muster its armies," Paul said.

I felt William's arm around me. "It will pass soon," he said quietly. "England will be cautious. France cannot afford a war for long. Austria just barks. It doesn't want a war in Europe. It's concerned with Turkey nipping at its borders. There are men who like to shout in this country, and there are always men like that. The constitution is stronger than they. The constitution is what France rests on. No one really wants to fight."

"Michel Beaupuy does," I said.

"My feet are cold," Gérard said.

"Does this mean we're going to England?" said Marie. "If so, can we live near Sylvie?" Her mother said, No, no, it doesn't mean that at all.

And as she said that, something eased within me. Fears had shaken me since Paul's news. But a mother's simple words of reassurance to her daughter had reminded me of something else: that France could become part of the Austrian Empire, and I'd still want to raise our child here, by the river, if I at all could. Oh, I would follow William to England if there were no other way, but it wasn't the time, not now.

And once I understood that, somehow, I felt stronger. It was crazy of me, but I even felt fortunate to be having this baby. Why not? The world could be falling down around me, yet I could still feel *overblessed*. I was having William's child. I would be strong for it, for us; I would not let anything harm it. For a moment I felt myself larger than my body. I was as big as the room. I had an urge to protect everyone in it. The child will need each one of them, I thought. I will be strong for all of us. I grasped William's hand. I looked out to the terrace and saw the first bird of this season dip itself into the fountain and shake its wings in the bright air.

BIRGHDAY

The young men of Europe began to kill each other by the thousands, and life grew within me.

Captain Beaupuy was all the time training his regiment for the front, and William was alone in the *Amis de la Constitution* club. He, a foreigner, was speaking out for France now to keep to its constitution, even in times of war and fear of counterrevolution at home. The constitution would limit the power of one seeking to curb all possible counterrevolution in the quickest possible ways.

It was my birthday in June, and we had stayed off politics for the day. I was turning twenty-three; William had turned twenty-two in April. He had caught and fried two trout from the river this afternoon, and we were eating our supper now along the banks. The trout was flaky and crisp, and I licked my fingers. William had made a present of four new lines that he had translated, which, he said, spoke "of a peace felt high in the mountains, a peace not usually found in the world," but that preface itself implied what we were avoiding.

> And sure there is a secret Power that reigns
> Here, where no trace of man the spot profanes.
> How still! No irreligious sound or sight
> Rouses the soul from her serene delight.

All the while the river flowed by us, just lapping a bit on the banks.

"I've never felt such ease before with anyone," he said. "With my sister I could feel contentment, but she'd be writing in her notebook," he said and laughed, "trying to get it all down. With you—we can just listen to the river—that's all." He stretched out on the bank with his head in my lap, and I stroked his forehead. "How can anyone deserve this much happiness?"

"We do," I said. But even as I said it, I thought of him leaving. A part of me wanted this pregnancy to last and last, for after it I knew William would have to go. I tried to hold on to each passing moment that slipped quickly by us like the water at our feet.

"Do you see that spiderweb there, between those branches?" I pointed to it.

"I would have missed that," he said, "I would have missed the shining. What is that from?"

"From the spray of the river, landing on the web and catching the light."

"No one sees things as you do."

"You do," I said.

William was washing the pan now with the fine gravel on the banks. "Did you hear about General Dillon?" he said. Had he forgotten that we were going to try to keep away from politics, just for today?

"What about him?" I said.

"What the troops of the glorious Patriot Army did to him."

I had just heard that the army had panicked and run at its first encounter with the Austrians. When I didn't answer, William continued.

"In the Austrian Netherlands," he said. He was rubbing gravel hard against the pan. "When the army withdrew, they hanged their own general. Then—pardon me—they took parts of him and paraded them through the streets and burned them on a bonfire. What kind of savages do that?"

I felt slightly ill. The water glittered in the shallows at William's feet, and he had to squint to look at me. "There's something wrong, Annette," he said. "There's something going wrong with the Revolution. One can even feel it at the Friends of the Constitution club. Our name has become ironic. The Mountain Men, or the Jacobins, as they are also called, are gaining far too much power. Robespierre's ambition is boundless. The power the Jacobins want goes against the constitution, so they simply dissolved the Constitutional Guard, which checks abuses. They said it was polluted by having too many ex-aristocrats on it. Yet the Jacobins have ex-aristocrats among them." He was rinsing out the pan, which had been clean for several minutes now. "And they've started deporting priests again who won't swear allegiance to the new government—refractory priests, they're called. I'm no priest lover, but—leave them alone." He put the pan in the rucksack.

"What about that friend of yours in the Assembly—Brissot?"

"The Jacobins don't like him," William said, "him and his friends—called the Girondins, for they're mostly from Bordeaux and the Gironde. The Jacobins think the Girondins are too moderate, even accuse them of being on the side of the counterrevolution. It's ridiculous. The Jacobins just want all the power. And they're willing to do anything for it. And they do it all in the name of national security. There is no more brotherhood in Paris, no more embracing each other as brothers in freedom."

William packed the pan in the rucksack, gave me his hand, and we began our walk back up the hill. "That's why I wrote that essay," he said, "to support the constitution against the Jacobins' abuses. We can't give up." He stopped, gripped my hand, and looked at me hard, his blue eyes fierce. "We can't give up on anything, Annette."

That was my twenty-third birthday. We couldn't keep off politics if we tried. It was all around us, and the world was being changed by it. One could hate politics, but one couldn't ignore it.

IS IT STILL YESTERDAY?

At Maman's and Vergez's last dinner visit, I let her know that, to be more readily available to tutor Gérard and Marie, I was staying indefinitely at chez Vincent. Maman said, Well, if you're not going to have a family of your own, at least you can help others who have. You'll save Marguerite money on tutors. I think Monsieur Vergez liked the idea of me not being in the house.

Etienne was home now from the university, and he and Angelique came to visit us at chez Vincent. I saw him from the doorway of the salon, hair grown long, neckcloth carelessly tied, English jockey boots unpolished, striped waistcoat and blue frock coat looking as if they had not been pressed in a year, a glass of wine in his hand. I wanted to embrace him, but even with my loose gown I was beginning to show, and I wanted somehow to explain things first. I had not seen Angelique since the last dinner with Maman, and she didn't know either. I entered the room and sat behind a writing desk near the door. The Vincents' old family servant, Pierre, brought me a glass of water. He knew that is what I preferred. "There she is," Etienne said. "There's the recalcitrant sister."

Angelique sat by his side on the sofa with the gilt lion's feet. She had on a white linen summer gown, as I had, but wore a pale blue sash around her waist and a blue scarf knotted in the form of a cap on her blond curls. She looked fresh and cool, and she, too, had a glass. They had been laughing about something when I came in. "Maman says she has not seen you in over a month," Etienne went on. "And Angelique said she herself did not see you even for your birthday. It's now the end of June. What have you to say for yourself, Mademoiselle l'Abbesse?"

"Hardly," I said, "Mademoiselle l'Abbesse."

"She's been playing with and tutoring your niece and nephew every day," Marguerite said, and shifted a bowl of fruit in front of her.

"And walking with that Englishman," said Angelique. "Your friend Isabelle's mother came to visit and said she saw you, Marguerite, a stranger, and an army captain walking by the bridge. You can't fool us. Etienne and I know you're staying here because Marguerite has a soft spot for you, and you can visit your Englishman. You told me at Easter he had followed you here from Orléans. I think it's quite exciting. Vergez says he forbade you to see the foreigner. So good for you, I say. Etienne and I are proud of you."

"Well, after that speech I have some interesting news for you two," I said. "*That Englishman* and I are to be wed." That produced gasps from Angelique and silence from Etienne. But before they could say anything, I said, "And I trust you find being an aunt and an uncle charming, for—" I stood up. I put my hand on my belly. "This is in the strictest confidence, for I trust you as friends, not just as brother and sister. Maman—and certainly Vergez—are not to know. I'll choose my own time about that—"

Etienne coughed on his wine. Angelique ran up to me. "You horrid person," she said, "for not letting me know." And she turned on Marguerite. "Why am I always left in the dark?" Then she kissed me. She took my hand and led me to their couch. "I told you in Orléans," she said, "that I would support you against the world that misunderstands you—"

"No world misunderstands me," I said. "But thank you."

"Maman, though," Angelique said, "And Vergez. You'll know what they'll want. They'll feel that you have irretrievably shamed the family and for you to see out your confinement out of Blois— somewhere convenient like Orléans. What are you going to do? Hide out here until—"

"December," I said.

"Or is the Englishman taking you away from us?" Etienne said. "Are you going to become an English wife?"

"Monsieur William is going first," I said, "after the baby is born— then . . . well, perhaps we can stay here, I hope. William will secure means, and—"

"Foreigners aren't exactly the most popular people in France, now," he said.

"He's sent an essay to *La Patriote Française*," I said. "He has friends."

"But are they the right friends?" Etienne said. "Among certain powerful people, like Robespierre, Brissot and his paper are about as popular as foreigners."

"Will you go to England?" Angelique said.

I was between them on the sofa. They were right to barrage me with questions. I should not have kept them in the dark so long. They were right to be alarmed. It was hardly the best of situations.

"He's a poet," Etienne said. "That's a respectable profession—for a gentleman. His family has means, then—" My little brother was worried about me.

"He has uncles who have means," I said, "and a lord who owns much of the north of England who owes his family money—"

"Well, he can't count on that," Etienne said.

"I think you've got yourself in a mess again, Annette, but we love you," Angelique said.

"Again?" Etienne said.

Angelique ignored that. "We just have to keep our mother, stepfather, Robespierre and the Jacobins, surveillance committees, and poverty away from your door, and everything will be fine," she said.

"Everything will be fine," Marguerite said, with chastisement in her tone, to Angelique. "You don't know what a respectable man Monsieur William is—"

"You're going to be Madame William?" Etienne said. "That is such an un-French name; can't you at least be Madame Guillaume? 'De Monsieur William' is actually the name of a type of pear tree," he added. "Well, I think it's a funny coincidence."

"Monsieur William is marvelous with the children," Marguerite said. "And Annette will stay here as long as she likes. No one is sending her anywhere."

"Well, I guess Maman isn't coming to chez Vincent for dinner," Angelique said. "You know we don't want you to go to England."

"We could be at war with England soon," Etienne said.

I felt like I was going to cry. "Don't you think I've thought of all those things?" I said. "Don't you think I've thought of them over and over? That they have no real answers? That I really don't know what I'm going to do? That I know Marguerite is saving me from disgrace and—why don't you ask me about how Monsieur William and I love each other? No one has asked me that."

"You're such a child of nature," Angelique said. "We didn't ask you that because we know you—that only true love could lead you into such a mess," and she laughed. Then I laughed, a little.

"My big sister, like Julie of *Héloïse*," Etienne said. "She became a national literary heroine for becoming pregnant out of wedlock."

"Just get him to become a famous and wealthy poet here," Angelique said. "I'm telling you, we don't want you to go off to that cold island. Do you want a boy or girl?" she added.

"A girl, so she will never have to go to war," I said immediately. I had also thought about that.

"Ah," Etienne said, "Especially not to war against her father's nation."

"What do you mean?" I said.

"Don't you know England is threatening to join the coalition of Prussia and Austria?"

"Paul has not mentioned that," Marguerite said.

"In Paris one hears things before anyone else does," said my brother. "Have you heard of the Liberty Tree incident and the invasion of the Tuileries?"

We hadn't. "Well, it was only two days ago. You're so isolated down here," Etienne said. "Do you want to hear what happened? Paul will be surprised. I'll have to repeat it for him at dinner. I'll just wait till then."

"Oh, tell it," said Angelique. "I know you want to. We look to you for enlightenment."

"You are our sole representative of knowledge of the outside world," I said.

"Since you acknowledge," he said, "my august role in this matter, I will."

I was glad the conversation had shifted away from me, but I didn't know what new ill tidings my brother brought from the capital. It's said, How Paris goes, France goes.

He looked at us all individually in the eye, then began: "You know the King is in virtual house arrest in the Tuileries—a woebegone palace, if you could see it. Now, on June 20, the anniversary of the royal family's escape attempt last summer, a Jacobin mob of thousands enters the grounds of the Tuileries, on the pretext of planting a 'Liberty Tree'—a bare pole with tricolor ribbons. The National Guard lets them right in. Imagine this: it's a hot day; these people are sweating; their clothes are dirty anyway; their odor wafts up to the King and his family at the open windows of the Tuileries. So the mob sticks their ridiculous tree in the ground, does a little dance, then—they invade the palace. They're carrying hatchets, mind you, pikes, all decked with tricolor ribbons. This is their party. One has a miniature lamppost, a filthy doll hanging from it, with 'Marie Antoinette' written on a placard beneath it."

I felt faintly nauseated.

"A butcher bears the King a fresh bull's heart on a plate," Etienne went on, "and places it before him, with another placard that reads 'The Heart of Louis XVI.'"

"Stop," Marguerite exclaimed. "You're making Annette ill."

"Sorry," said Etienne, "I didn't know—"

"No, finish your story," I said. "We've heard worse. I'm just thirsty." I drank the rest of the glass of water.

"That's the worst part," Etienne said. "Now imagine the King, looking rather kingly in his embroidered silk suit and the *cordon bleu* sash across his broad belly, and the butcher presents to him, on the edge of a pike, a red woolen bonnet—a 'cap of liberty,' they call it—and forces him to put it on over his powdered wig. They make him drink toasts to the Revolution."

"How humiliating," Angelique said.

"They finally make him sit there, in his silly red bonnet, and listen to speeches on what a beast he is. I personally think the king is sunk so deep in melancholy, nothing will shake him out of it—and nothing will shake him. He asked the butcher to feel his heart, to see if it were beating faster, and it wasn't. The butcher was impressed."

We were quiet now, each probably picturing the scene in our own ways. I always found dolls disconcerting myself.

"Well, it's inevitable now," Etienne said. "The government is going to change again. And this time, there won't be a constitution that will have a place for a king."

"I wish they had escaped last year," Marguerite said. "It must be so hard on their children."

"Yes," Etienne said, "they knocked down the little prince's door with a hatchet, pulled him into the King's apartment, and put a red cap on him that was so big it almost covered his face. He couldn't say anything, just clung to the Queen. It's reported that all the next day he kept asking, 'Is it still yesterday?' The mob had shouted death threats against his mother, whose lady-in-waiting then sneaked her out through a secret exit behind a panel while they lectured the King."

"My God," Marguerite said.

"The mayor finally arrived and bade the invaders retire—but he's a Jacobin, like them, so he had done nothing to stop them entering the palace. The mob left laughing and singing. It was good fun for them. Couldn't have been much fun for the King."

"He could have been killed," Angelique said. "They killed his guards two years ago, paraded their heads on pikes all the way to Paris from Versailles."

"Yes, he could have," my little brother said.

"Well, you be careful, living in Paris," I said.

"It can be a dangerous place, but it's an exciting place," he said. "And still has the best university in the world. I'm going back early in August, to get a jump on the next term. I'll be a doctor in a year. I'll be back here all the time, then."

"We've missed you," I said. "Stay a bit longer."

"We can't go riding together this summer, dear sister, in your interesting condition. What reason is there to stay, then? Ah, we'll play cards after dinner," he said. "We'll play cards all night."

THE SOURD

The Prussian army had joined the Austrians now. There were two fronts, one along the Rhine and one in Flanders. The Allied commander had sent a manifesto to Paris, saying that if the Tuileries were invaded or the least outrage done to the King and his family, all of Paris would pay for it through total destruction. The assembly had officially declared *la patrie,* the nation, in danger, and Captain Beaupuy's Thirty-second Bassigny Regiment had now left for the Rhineland front. William missed his good friend.

He was visiting chez Vincent even more now, and he and Etienne had taken an instant liking to each other. They talked politics together. We played cards, and William always lost. We even played charades and laughed at each other's absurdities.

In our charades of the night before, William had acted out the word *Enragés*—"the Madmen"—a group of Jacobins who had recently smashed one of the Girondin presses of William's friend Brissot. William had been quoting Brissot's statement in *La Patriote Française* about the Enragés. It was a serious topic, but we laughed to see the poet pretend to tear his hair, gnash his teeth, and howl on all fours. Etienne finally guessed it, only because he had recently read the article or heard about it. They were talking about it now, as we walked above the Vincent vineyard.

"He has also called Robespierre a false friend of the people and an enemy of the constitution," said my brother. "Brissot has courage but not prudence. Soon all the old Friends of the Constitution will be seen as traitors, if Robespierre gets his way."

"Just one good man can still save the Revolution from tyranny," William said.

"And who is that, Monsieur? Brissot? He lacks the cunning of Robespierre. His friend Louvet? He's a novelist, not a politician."

"I will write another essay," William said. "I will write of Brissot as a friend of the people and of the constitution, and against the Enragés. A foreign voice can be seen as more impartial."

"Or more traitorous," my brother said. "Anyone can be seen as counterrevolutionary, as having 'impure blood.' Have you heard of the song of the *fédérés*, the united National Guard of the provinces? After killing counterrevolutionaries and burning royalist villages along the way, these *fédérés*—thousands of them—marched from Marseille to Paris singing a bloody song.

Let's march! Let's march!
To soak our soil
In impure blood.

I'm afraid it's rather a stirring melody, though," he said.

We stood then overlooking the valley. The setting sun lay in bars across the steep green vineyards descending to the river, and streaked the pale blue water with red ribbons. Clouds in the west obscured the sun itself. We heard the sound of the *sourd*, the insect that sings a melancholy song every summer evening along the Loire. It reminded me of recent lines of William's.

"Etienne, you should hear some of Monsieur William's new work. You should hear it before you go back to the land of bloody songs," I said. "It's in my pocket. May I read it?"

"I should love to hear it," Etienne said. "It will be an edifying contrast to the political slogans or songs I'm used to now."

I pulled several poems out of my pocket at once and tried to find the most recent one.

"It appears, Monsieur," Etienne said, "that you are filling my sister's head with verse. Well, it can use something in it besides horses and hunting and dance steps."

I looked crossly at my brother. "I wanted to share this with you, Monsieur-Man-of-the-World from Paris," I said. "Listen—

And oh, fair France! For now the traveller sees
Thy three-striped banner fluctuate on the breeze,
And martial songs have banished songs of love,

And nightingales desert the village grove,
Scared by the fife and rumbling drum's alarms
And the short thunder, and the flash of arms,
That cease not till night falls, when far and nigh,
Sole sound: the Sourd prolongs his mournful cry."

"'Martial songs'" Etienne said.

"'Have banished songs of love,'" I said.

"Not a good trade-off," he said. "I'd rather people be drunk on love or nature than on war. It's a very sorrowful poem, Monsieur. That little insect is crying."

"Monsieur William told me that its name is pronounced 'sword' in English, which means 'saber'—"

"So even nature is overcome by the presence of war," Etienne said.

"Nature may reflect the sadness of humanity," William said, "but I don't think she is ever, truly, overcome by it. Witness the river."

And we regarded it, blue in the pale sunlight between golden sandbanks. It looked very peaceful.

"It makes me want not to go back to Paris," Etienne said. "It makes me want not to go back to where drunken men sing at night in the streets of soaking the soil with blood."

THEY'VE FALLEN EARLY THIS YEAR

On the days William and I didn't see each other, we wrote to each other. The man seemed to live on nothing at all. I was concerned about how little he seemed to eat, until I realized he really got along fine with eating very little and with walking quite a lot. Some strange northern constitution, I thought. Still, Marguerite and I tried to get him to have as many dinners as possible at chez Vincent and to take bread with him when he left. He lived so frugally. He said it was his custom, and he was sure he had enough money to last through the year.

Etienne left on the first of August with the count, who had some business in Paris and was happy to have my brother accompany him there. Etienne would spend the voyage in the comfort of an elegant carriage rather than feel the jolts of the *diligence*, though the count had taken the precaution of painting over his coat of arms—it would be just another carriage in Paris. Benoît, Claudette's *ami*, was going as coachman, groom, and valet. The count was traveling light.

Ten days later, at about one o'clock in the morning, I had just finished writing to William. I was brushing my hair out by an open window, and in between strokes taking sips of a tisane of peppermint leaves that Claudette had prepared for me. I heard the little fountain lapping below. Marguerite had some jasmine planted a year ago by the doors to the terrace, and I could smell it now in the warm night.

Claudette and I must have been the only ones awake in the house, for when I heard loud knocking on the door, the ancient Pierre did not answer it, nor did Françoise, Marguerite's maid. My room was closer to the front of the house than Paul and Marguerite's. I asked Claudette to see who it was and, wrapped in my dressing gown, followed her to the vestibule. She opened the door, and I was shocked to see Benoît and my brother holding up a disheveled and coatless count, who stood between them and leaned on Etienne. I thought the count was drunk. But what were they doing here?

"Excuse us," the count said. "There has been some unpleasantness in Paris. You'll hear about it tomorrow. Could I prevail upon you to give me a room for a night? Didn't want to go the extra miles to Beauregard—"

"Come in quickly," I said, as I ushered them in and Claudette closed the door.

"He's been wounded," Etienne whispered as he half-dragged the count to a settee.

"Tell me what I can do," I said.

"Help me get him to a spare room. Benoît is driving the carriage round to the stable." We had the count between us now, going down the hall. "It was bad, very bad," Etienne said. "We got him out before it got any worse. If we had waited till the afternoon, Benoît would have had a hard time driving over the dead bodies of Swiss Guards in the streets."

I opened the door of the room across from mine, where William had stayed, and we laid the count on the bed. Now old Pierre appeared, a lamp in his trembling hand, and Claudette carried in a candelabrum and put it on the dresser. Paul entered now, taking it all in. "What's happened?" he said.

"The count's hurt," Etienne said. "I cleaned and stitched his wound quickly before we left Paris, and once, when we stopped at Orléans, I procured fresh linen and changed his dressings. I will need to do that again now, then he can rest." Claudette and I fetched the necessary items, the linen, the hot water, and a sponge. My brother retrieved a bag from the carriage and asked us to wait in the salon.

When Etienne returned, Paul handed him a brandy, and we sat in the salon together. "I thought it better to let Marguerite sleep," Paul said. "She'll find out everything tomorrow. I had Pierre ready a room up for you," he said to Etienne. "You'll need to get your rest." Etienne gulped his brandy.

"The count will be fine. He will recover," he said. "He just needs his dressings to be changed three times a day." I felt proud of my brother's confident manner as the young doctor. He suddenly reminded me of Papa. Etienne paused. "I'd like to tell you something about what happened, if I could, if you're not too tired. I'm not ready for sleep, myself. And who knows what rumors you'll hear tomorrow. Benoît's the one who needs to sleep right away, driving hard for thirteen hours or more."

I had my water. Paul also had brandy. Pierre had only lit the candles on the table, and the room around us remained in shadows. My brother's face came in and out of the light as he leaned forward or back in his chair. "In short," he said, "so you can go back to your rest, it's this: the King has now taken refuge in the National Assembly, and they are debating his fate. The royal family fled there when it seemed imminent that the Tuileries would be attacked by thousands of *fédérés*—perhaps ten thousand—plus a Parisian mob.

"As soon as I returned to Paris, I noticed the tension in the air. The city was just waiting for something to happen. I myself felt that I was in some fiction—a chapter from *Candide*, perhaps, when some senseless conflict is about to explode—the quotidian seemed so unreal. But it was exciting, somehow. More *fédérés* kept coming in every day. Oh, they wanted to fight. I thought, if they have to fight someone, let them stay in the Rhineland and fight the Prussians. But they hate the King and Queen and counterrevolutionaries more than they hate the Prussians. This morning we heard the shots start, around nine o'clock.

"All the rest I tell you I heard from the count, in our journey down here. It appears that an old friend of the count's—I believe he said the Vicomte de Maillé—had written him from Paris, saying that the Tuileries were going to be attacked any day, that they needed loyal aristocrats to boost the numbers of the Swiss Guard, since they couldn't trust the National Guard, which was supposed to protect the King. (Imagine! The King had gone to inspect his own troops, and they had jeered at him.) I think the count, beneath his pragmatic mien, is a romantic at heart, and he couldn't refuse a call on his honor, even such a quixotic one.

"The Queen—I suppose in a gesture of gratitude for their courage—ordered all the remaining troops protecting the palace be given a round of brandy. The King and Queen wanted to stay, but Louis Roederer, the new man the Assembly put in charge of the protection of the Tuileries (the Marquis de Mandat, the King's man, had been shot to death the day before when he visited the City Hall), convinced them that they had to escape to the Assembly nearby, which hates the King and Queen, for the safety of their children.

"The count was near a formal garden at the west of the palace and saw them flee silently, surrounded by Swiss Guards, through the garden. He said the Queen was crying. One tall guard carried the little prince on his shoulders, to make better time. The count heard the King remark calmly on the amount of leaves already on the ground in the Tuileries. 'They've fallen early this year,' he said. The count said he will remember that statement all his life: that is, he said, if he is to live much longer. He will, if he only stays out of trouble.

"About a thousand of the Swiss Guard, perhaps the most highly trained troops in the world, and who for generations have protected the kings of France, stood like a wall outside the palace and on the grand staircase, within, still guarding the entrance to the chambers of the royal family. Of course the irony in all this is that by now the family had just escaped—the *fédérés* had lost their reason to attack—but perhaps they had never had much reason anyway. The count thinks the *fédérés* knew the royals had left. So was it because they were frustrated to lose them? Because they had planned and were primed for an attack? Because of their blind hatred? Who knows? They rushed the palace.

"Now the count said the Swiss are forbidden to attack, that they can only respond with force to force. They had four hundred loyal National Guard and about four hundred aristocrats with them. The Swiss were as silent as could be.

When the fixed bayonets came at them, the Swiss probably fired the first shot. But tomorrow you'll probably hear that the King had ordered his guard to fire on the innocent *fédérés*. In any case, the Swiss, far more professional than the *fédérés*, held them off for most of the morning. The count thought the *fédérés* might withdraw. The mob itself was waiting in the rear, outside of the action. But the Swiss ran out of ammunition. The count told me the firing was so fierce, he had run out by mid-morning and was using theirs.

"Soon thousands of *fédérés* were at them, hand to hand, and had penetrated the palace—that's when the mob charged in too. And that, said the count, is when a bayonet thrust entered his right shoulder. He said he had fallen to the ground, with others around him, when he saw limbs of the fallen being struck off by some eager victors with swords and hatchets. He crawled into the garden, then ran toward Louis XV Square. He shed his coat and waistcoat, even his shoes with silver buckles. He had already witnessed the mob stripping, even mutilating, the bodies of the Swiss and the aristocrats, and now the disheveled count could have passed, perhaps, as a wounded tradesman, part of the mob.

"He was losing a great deal of blood. He skirted the side of the square, where *fédérés* on horseback were running down any fleeing troops from the Tuileries, where he saw a pike festooned with an arm of a Swiss Guard, waving as in a parade. And in the attention fixed on that arm raised on high, and the cheers and shouts that went with it, the count got by the edge of the square, across the bridge that runs into it, and somewhere in the alleys of the Latin Quarter, as he dripped blood in the gutters, the idea came to him that he was nearing where he had left me, a week earlier.

"Now, I had stayed indoors at the first sound of shots. That is what one does in Paris if one is at all prudent. The shots have now lessened; I am thinking, whatever new revolution has happened is over for now, and I'll find out about it later, when I hear someone slowly hauling themselves up my stairs and pounding on my door."

I couldn't believe that this was my brother telling me all this, and that it was the count, whom I had known most of my life, who had just been stabbed with a bayonet by another Frenchman and had shed his coat and shoes so as not to be caught and mutilated. It *was* like something out of *Candide*. It was unreal. Things like this happened in fiction or to people you didn't know on faraway battlefields. Not to us.

I looked at Paul, and he seemed not to believe it either. He was leaning forward with a look of horror on his face, sometimes shaking his head.

"The count practically fell in, when I opened the door," Etienne continued. "I closed and locked the door, took care of his wound then and there—my first live patient; I had only practiced on cadavers! I felt the count had to be evacuated because of the seriousness of his injuries—and who knows what else could happen to him, waiting to heal in Paris. I bid him rest, and as I now heard shots closer by, in the faubourg Saint-Germain, I had to go in that direction, to the marquis's residence on rue de l'Université, where Benoît and the carriage were. In the street I lifted up a fallen, bloody pike myself and ran along, cheering, in order to fit in. I couldn't have been more grim, on the inside. It is not wise to wear knee-breeches in most sections of Paris now, and in working man's trousers I could appear as one of the sans-culottes, the breechless ones, as they call themselves. I stepped over bodies of the Swiss Guard, naked and missing limbs, in the gutters." Here Etienne stopped and took a long drink of brandy. This is my little brother, I thought, whom I used to protect. I wanted to run a poker through any sans-culottes who threatened him, as I had once used a poker to pin against a wall his thirteen-year-old friend, whom I had caught cheating Etienne at cards so long ago.

My brother put the glass back on the table. "I found Benoît at the house of the marquis," he said. "He hitched up the carriage, and I directed him through narrow backstreets. Together we carried the count down the stairs and into the carriage, and the fighting was still going on as we left. I do not doubt that it went on the rest of the afternoon, until all the Swiss were dead and the palace had been ransacked.

"I gave Benoît directions through more side streets, past the church of Saint-Sulpice and the Luxembourg Gardens into the Val-de-Grâce quarter, and past the Observatory to the Porte d'Orléans. He drove fast and sure. Everyone was still too busy with the carnage along both banks of the river to worry about a carriage lumbering through streets barely wide enough for it to pass. It's good we left when we did, though. I'm sure soon they were stopping all traffic leaving Paris, to make sure some stray Swiss Guard—or some old aristocrat—did not leave intact. The count revived near Orléans, where we stopped for water for him, soup for Benoît and me. Benoît deserves a lot of praise. He kept his sangfroid."

"So did you," said Paul. "Few men could have done as well. The count owes you his life. Your father would be proud of you. So are we all."

Etienne stood up, and they embraced. "Now rest well in chez Vincent," the older man said. "Let Paris stay in Paris."

I embraced my brother. "I wish I had been there to help you," I said. "Somehow, in some way—"

"My big sister. I could have used you, if only for company in the long voyage with a wounded man who told grisly stories and then passed out. Annette, it's good to see you. It's good just to be here."

"Don't go back," I said. "Not just yet."

"Not just yet," he said.

The candlelight behind him cast his face in shadow. "I'm finally tired," he said. "I can sleep."

But I didn't know if I could. I knew when I closed my eyes I would see the images he described again and imagine cries to go along with them. I would lie awake worrying about Etienne in Paris, worrying about us all.

I wish this chapter I had read in a book and not lived through. You'll hear different stories—justifications or attempts at reasons—for the first part of what happened; but as there was no reason for the *fédérés* to attack the Tuileries, as my brother said, just blind hatred, the only reason for the prison massacres was blind fear. The patriot army had had steady losses at the front. A fortress had surrendered. Now the Austrians were on French soil. More and more people had been indiscriminately arrested—anyone whom anyone else *thought* was a counterrevolutionary. And the prisons were full, overcrowded. Someone had the thought, What if the Austrians arrive in Paris, and the prisoners get free and join them? Then Paris would truly be laid waste.

You can see, I am making the same attempt to reason that I indicated was a fallacy—for there was no reason. Someone got word, William told me later, that Jacobins who had been wrongfully arrested were to be released, and they were. That implied, said William, that the Jacobins were behind what happened. They knew the massacres were coming.

In any case, they—*sans-culottes*, men who considered themselves great patriots, I don't know—quickly set up tribunals, as they called them, in halls in Paris prisons, and held sudden judgments on whether someone was such a threat to national security that he should be immediately killed, or whether he was a minor threat or—rare enough—a mistaken threat, and could be merely imprisoned longer or perhaps even let go. I heard one English writer whom William knew had been arrested as a royalist, but he was a revolutionary writer. They had arrested him because all Englishmen were thought to be royalists, since *they* had a king. Someone spoke up for this famous writer at the last minute, and his judges were instantly his friends—clapping him on the back, calling him "Citizen"—but it could just as easily have gone the other way. And most of the time it did.

I heard that people passing the prisons heard the cries, and kept on going. I heard they were told that dangerous counterrevolutionaries were being dealt with. Well, one thinks, that's all right, it's for the good of the nation. It only became a scandal later. And it was only a scandal because the Girondins blamed the Jacobins for the massacres. If the Girondins hadn't made a case of it, perhaps no one would have heard much about it at all. Then of course the Jacobins blamed the Girondins for *using* the massacres politically. No one really knew who was to blame. I think it was fear, and the great license that was given and was to be given to anything that was done in the name of the security of *la patrie*.

William, informed by his friends in Paris, told me that as soon as the outcome of each swift trial was decided, doors were flung open, and the victim was thrown to a group of patriots, who weren't executioners—no black masked professional, no soldiers doing their duty, just common drapers, carpenters, butchers, carried away by an extreme sense of national duty combined with the excitement of spilling blood. Perhaps one was the butcher who had offered the King a bull's heart in June. I don't know. But they didn't have an executioner's axe or a soldier's firing squad to do the deed. Like a firing squad, though, no one person was responsible. I think they didn't have an officer, either, or any one person who gave the order. Their cue was only the opening of the door, the flinging of the enemy of the state into the small enclosed courtyard, or even the anteroom of the tribunal chamber—and the convict was dealt with efficiently by all, with whatever means they had on hand. A knife, a hatchet, a pike. Muskets were very rare—this was no military matter, but a citizens' tribunal, a citizens' cause, and a citizens' execution.

Once these tribunals started, they spread rapidly through one prison and another. The prisoners didn't know if they were to be called before the tribunals or not. Apparently the tribunal started with a list but didn't always keep to it, or improvised upon it. Each killing justified the last and led to the next, for the great fear required that bloodshed call for more bloodshed. There wasn't time to call witnesses or listen to attorneys. The citizens decided, and they acted with an absolute and infallible sense of justice, for everything was for the greater cause. If there were some mistakes, well, Paris was going to be invaded. The citizens were not to blame. Their intentions were right.

The September massacres, as they came to be called, spread to Orléans. No one knows what goes on behind prison walls, but, as I said, people heard. And some people spoke, who had been released, or who had witnessed the bizarre rites. After about a week, the Girondins finally put a stop to it by daily denouncing the massacres as Jacobin-inspired anarchy. The tribunals that were to come later would be conducted with a greater semblance of law and protocol, not by citizens in red caps—although the lawyers and politicians who were later to design what we would afterward call the Terror might just as well have been butchers or carpenters, with silk neckcloths instead of red woolen caps. I heard some three thousand were killed in the prison massacres in Paris alone—and disposed of with lime and a quick burial. They did not keep meticulous records.

The pear tree was brilliant gold now in the September sun. The leaves fell in the wind onto the gravel paths of Marguerite's garden. It wasn't a good time to be carrying a child, but anything that threatened her would have to threaten me first. I didn't know how, but I would keep it from our door. But William—I couldn't come between the world and him so easily. He courted the world and its dangers with his writing and his speaking up at his club. He believed in Plato's Good more than anyone I ever knew, and I was especially worried for him now.

In that atmosphere of fear and even hysteria of the autumn of 1792, I met Monsieur Leforges once again. Marguerite and I were returning from the château de Beauregard, where we had been visiting the convalescing count. But now we were stuck in cart traffic on the bridge into Blois, with the river moving slowly below us, and Monsieur Leforges sat on horseback beside my window, peering down at me. I would have done anything for the carriage to move on, but with carts and carriages stopped before and behind us, we were immovable, next to a smiling man for whom there was no difference between charm and malice.

He had traded his black silk coat and breeches, his bamboo cane and powdered wig for blue-and-white-striped trousers, a red-and-white-striped waistcoat, and a blue coat with a tricolor cockade on it. He doffed his black hat, which also had a cockade on it, and bowed.

"My dear Mademoiselle Vallon. I would have recognized you anywhere. Still the most beautiful bourgeoise one could imagine. Do you still prefer the decadent Austrian music? Do you still sing foolish Mozart duets? Have you heard news of the music master of Blois? It turns out he was a dangerous counterrevolutionary. His mother was German; he came from Metz, near the Prussian frontier. You can't always tell. His name was French. He seemed a nice man. But there he was, plotting away with the aristocrats and the bourgeoisie in their salons. I hear even some of his students, some of the homes that invited him in, are now suspect. It's a great service to our town and nation that he was imprisoned last month."

"What do you mean, 'our town'?" I said. I was drawn into his net, despite myself.

"Oh, I live here now. I am the new music master. I only go to the homes of patriots, where we learn French songs. Don't you think that's better?"

I peered out the window, toward the front of the carriage. The line of traffic was still unmoving.

"Oh, I'm afraid we'll be here awhile. There's a cart overturned up ahead. Horses down, harnesses broken. You haven't introduced me to the lovely lady at your side."

"Monsieur Leforges, this is Marguerite Vincent, my sister," I said coldly. She nodded but did not say anything.

"Ah, the wife of the proprietor of a vineyard. You see, I know the people of Blois already. In fact, Mademoiselle Vallon, I have even heard that you are often seen in the company of an Englishman, a frequent guest at chez Vincent."

"Monsieur Leforges, do you ever tire of inquiring into other people's business?"

"Ah, many things are a citizen's business that were mere gossip before. Now—"

"Since when have your politics so radically changed? Why, just in January, at Orléans—"

"One must adopt the disguise of an aristocrat when one is in their company," he said. "Just as they adopt a number of disguises in ours. For instance, a poet. A poet, a scholar, is a very convenient disguise. One can enter the most patriotic clubs, saying one is a scholar doing research on the new constitution. One could write an essay about the constitution, publish it in a traitorous Girondin newspaper, and be extolled as a patriot, when really one is an English royalist."

I laughed. "If you're referring to Monsieur William, he hates the monarchy in England. He's no royalist—"

"People are not what they seem. Why would a foreigner be in France at this time, unless he were a spy?"

I felt my sister squeeze my hand, warning me to be quiet.

"Monsieur Leforges, you are ridiculous."

"And he has friends who are now challenged in the Assembly as being secret monarchists. They are trying to preserve the monarchy when all of France is ready to throw it off."

"The Girondins hold the Jacobins responsible for the prison massacres, and for that they are called traitors?"

"Annette," my sister whispered behind me, "say no more."

"You had best exercise your own prudence, Mademoiselle. Consorting with a foreign royalist, a Girondin supporter, a writer of monarchist articles—yes, he supported a constitution that had a place for a king; his later article clearly was an attack on Citizen Robespierre and puts your foreign friend under suspicion of counterrevolutionary activities."

I felt a cold fury gripping me. "Monsieur Leforges, I am tired of listening to you. Go back to your martial music. Just go away."

"Mademoiselle Vallon, you misunderstand me. It is not I who must go away. It is your friend. I have seen the order for his arrest. It is being drawn up now at the Committee of Surveillance, by the subcommittee that oversees the activities of foreigners. Do you forget how your family has wronged me?"

"Monsieur Leforges, you jest clumsily. You are not on any Committee of Surveillance."

"Oh, but I am. How do you think that music master was denounced? I knew the good man in Orléans. We were *colleagues*, after all. We shared all sorts of personal information. His mother *was* German— Metz, his hometown, even has a German-sounding name."

He suddenly doffed his hat again. The traffic was breaking up. "It's a pity," he said, "he has peculiar talents. But he should have stayed in England. He should have stayed away from the woman who is the object of my revenge in this town. You know what Laclos says, *Revenge will prosper sooner than love*. Laclos is an officer in the patriot army, now, by the way. He knows on which side his bread is buttered." Monsieur Leforges rode through the throng toward the end of the bridge. He wasn't a very good rider.

*M*onsieur Leforges did not threaten idly. When I asked Paul at chez Vincent, he said, Yes, he had heard that the previous music master was arrested as a counter-revolutionary. He was either still in prison, or had been killed in the massacres in the prison in Orléans. "Monsieur William has to leave tonight," he said. "He no longer has Captain Beaupuy to speak for him. You yourself said others at the Friends of the Constitution have lost their membership because they were Girondin sympathizers, and the club is now Jacobin and has even changed its name to the Patriot Club. These are not times to hesitate. I must ride to his lodgings tonight."

"He won't come," I said. "He'll think he can protest his innocence and loyalty and talk his way out."

"He'll come," Paul said.

I'm not sure of all that Paul said to Monsieur William. He would have tried to avoid telling him who denounced me and why and just impress upon William the urgency of the situation. While I waited for them, I knew that William, though, would be leaving. I knew he would return as soon as possible. But what if that "as soon as possible" was months, or even years, from now? What if the rumors of England joining the Allies were true? What if England wouldn't let him leave, or France wouldn't let him return?

So Monsieur William, against his will, appeared at the door of chez Vincent in his battered tricorne, with nothing but a rucksack, the same one he had carried the frying pan and the bread in for my birthday dinner a few months ago. "I'll be back soon," he said to me, alone in my room, after a quick supper. "I have friends in Paris. I am not going all the way to England, as you suppose. I am going to Paris to sort this out, get new papers with the help of Brissot—"

"The Jacobins hate him now—"

"Brissot is still powerful. The madmen are in the minority. You'll see. I'll return," William said. "I'll get a sealed and signed letter from the National Assembly that a thousand Committees of Surveillance couldn't contest." He shouldered his rucksack. "I like walking in the autumn night," he said.

William was ready to walk, but Paul suggested that he would be safer if he were driven inconspicuously in a wagon up to Vendôme; then William could go on from there, avoiding the more obvious route from Blois to Paris, through Orléans.

"I walk fast," William said.

"A wagon at night can make better time," Paul replied. "We'll load it with vine clippings, as if we're bringing some vines to be planted near Vendôme tomorrow. It's near *vendange*, the harvest time. Nothing will look amiss with vines in a wagon in September. Save your legs, Monsieur William. Drink a last brandy; I'll explain it to Jean. He's always saying life was too dull here."

And William, who had appreciated so much of the Vincent hospitality over the months, did not gainsay his host of the summer, the good man who risked his own standing to warn him of his danger.

I told William I had to retire to my chamber for a moment and left him talking with Marguerite in the drawing room. I used this time to change into my riding boots, put on a woolen cape, and tell Claudette to let Monsieur William know I would say good-bye to him down at the stables. I found Jean harnessing Paul's gelding to the wagon.

"La Rouge loves to pull a cart," I said to him. "She's been doing it since she was two. She'll yield to a wagon. Let me harness La Rouge." As I did so, and quietly apologized to La Rouge for this indignity, I saw William come down from the house. I could tell by his gait he was reluctant. He didn't like running away. He didn't like giving in to the Committee of Surveillance. If it weren't for me, for the child, he would have stayed for certain—and yet, I told myself, if it weren't for me and my past friendship with Monsieur Leforges, William would not be in trouble. But that way of thinking also became ridiculous. If it weren't for me, William would not be in Blois.

"Monsieur William," I said, more formal because of Jean, "I do not believe in good-byes. And, as you said, this is not a farewell. I just want to ride to the edge of the vineyard with you. Please help me up, Jean. I can drive." And Jean helped me onto the seat. I saw Paul had hastily cut some vines and tossed them in the wagon. I also saw a small basket on the seat. "What's this?" I asked Jean.

"Cook gave it to me. She said Madame Vincent had told her to put some bread and cheese and water in a basket. Cook said she added cold chicken and a flask of wine."

William hopped up, and before Jean could get on also, I said *"Allons-y"* to La Rouge, and we drove out of the stables. I looked back at Jean and waved. "Tell my sister I'll be back by tomorrow," I called.

William stared at me. That September night was clear over the vineyard. "I'm your guide to Vendôme, Monsieur," I said. "I will get you there by daybreak and be home myself by noon. You need someone to recite poetry to you on the voyage, for I have memorized yours, in French. You need someone with whom to discuss names of children, for we haven't decided that, and what if you are stuck in Paris, waiting for your papers? A baby needs a name when it enters the world. And you need someone who cares for you to make sure you get at least to Vendôme and no *sans-culotte* or Committee of Surveillance patriot gets to you first. Not that they would send riders out in the night after a lone English royalist Girondin counterrevolutionary spy."

"You're a marvel," he said, "a crazy, reckless, lunatic marvel. But now I fear for *you*. Alone, I only have myself to worry about, and I can take care of myself. If you were caught aiding me——"

"No one will be after you until the morning, and by then you'll be past Vendôme, well on your way to Chartres—without me."

We were through the north edge of the vineyard now, and turning onto the quai Villebois, then across the bridge, through town and north to Vendôme. William took the reins from me. "I've told you before, there is no one like you in England, and probably no one like you in France."

"I hope not," I said. "I don't want you finding two of me."

"Actually, there are many of you. All within yourself. You contradict yourself. For instance, your sister and brother-in-law, whom you

love, you have just now distressed. The woman who is so concerned
for her child has just subjected herself to a wagon ride at night with a
Committee of Surveillance behind her."

"And to those people, one must add another," I said, "the woman
who is in love with a foreign spy and must get him safely out of the
country."

"You have lost all reason," he said. "But I love you for it."

"Let me give you the latest line I memorized," I said. "It will be
short, for I will try to give it to you in your own language,

Faint wail of eagle melting into blue / Beneath the cliffs

"I'm sorry; it must sound dreadful. It's hard to get my mouth
around all those *l*'s."

"I like it," he said.

"That's like us," I said. "We're the eagle melting into the blue of
the night, melting out of sight."

"Eagles mate for life," he said.

"Our nest is in the clouds," I said. "Out of sight."

"I like walking by myself, Annette," he said. "I like walking on
autumn nights. I wouldn't mind outwalking any Committee of Surveillance. But I'm glad you're here. I'm glad you came."

After midnight William offered me some bread and cheese.

"That's yours for the trip," I said. "You'll need to keep your
strength if you're walking to Paris. You don't know what you will
meet on your way. But I'll have some water."

William drove on, and I glanced up at the night sky and drew again
from my recent hoard of his words, words to be hoarded all my life. I
spoke, this time in French,

Where daylight lingers on perpetual snow;
Glitter the stars above, and all is black below.

"It *is* rather black below," said William. "All the precious ideals of
the Revolution turning into tyranny. The stars," he said. "The stars
come from another realm."

The night was clear, and the stars stretched out along the road to Vendôme. A waxing moon was three-quarters full, and the road lay white, the woods huddled in darkness, and the fields and passing apple orchards an overlapping of black and white. You felt that you could see for a hundred miles on such a night, and such a feeling also made me nervous. I listened for hooves behind us, for some pursuing member of a Committee of Surveillance, but only heard the wind through poplars along the side of the road.

Then I heard something stirring, in and out of the trees. "Something, there," I whispered. La Rouge snorted, and William hastened her along.

Then a horse stepped out from the trees and looked at us—simply stood beside us as we passed and regarded us. La Rouge whinnied softly. The horse answered.

"Wait a minute," I said. "It must have got away from somewhere," I said. "Stop. I need to stretch my legs anyway. Look." We had stopped in the middle of the deserted road, and William helped me down from the wagon. I walked toward the horse. It was grazing on the dewy grass beside the road. It looked up at me, then bent its head and went on eating. "Perhaps it was requisitioned for the cavalry and it escaped," I said. "Perhaps it belonged to someone, and it's trying to get back." I stroked its mane, combed it with my fingers and untangled some knots. "It's a lovely gray mare," I said. Now William rubbed between her eyes.

"I wish I could take her home," I said. "Just tie her to the back of the wagon, or give her to you for your journey. Someone's bound to catch her here."

"She might make it home," William said. "Better leave her that opportunity."

And we left her there, grazing beside the road in the moonlight. I looked back as we started again, and she suddenly snorted and took off. I heard hooves on the other side of the trees.

"William," I said. "She's following us."

The gray now grew bolder and trotted just a few yards off.

"She likes La Rouge," William said, "and she's escaping too. At least we're not alone."

I looked to my right and caught the eye of the mare, who then tossed her head and trotted before us, as if she were leading. Rouge quickened her pace.

"She feels secure just being with us," I said. "I'd like to be like her, William. I *could* be like her, keeping alongside you, all the way to Paris. We don't know what's going to happen to us, any more than that horse knows what will happen to her. I want to go with you to Paris, get your name cleared, then back home, or to England if you must—"

I grew silent and listened to the sound of hooves on leaves and watched the silhouette of the horse moving now in front of the white and black orchards.

"Of course I'd like you to come," William said. "I ache for you to come with me. But now's not the time, not with Committees of Surveillance and the uncertainty. Any possible danger I want you to avoid. And when you accompany me to England, I want everything to be as comfortable for you as it could be. And the baby—"

"The baby," I said. "We haven't decided on a name. I know you're right. We've talked it through before. It's just—for a moment I thought it could be different."

And I lay my head in his lap, tucked my legs up, and pulled my cape over them. William sang softly one of his border songs, a mournful, haunting melody with words unknown to me. And with that, and with the gentle jostling of the wagon, I slipped into sleep and the horse merged with my dreams. I heard her now as in a forest, trotting through thick autumn leaves, snapping twigs underfoot. Through it all I heard William's voice softly singing, and I waited in the pause between hoofbeats for the horses to land, for the hoofbeats to continue. And they did, with the creaking of the wagon, all through the night.

I woke up, startled by the noise of a cart passing, going in the other direction. Lying on my side, I saw deep pink streaks in the east.

I sat up. "Where is she?" I said. "Where is the horse?"

"Sometime just before dawn I didn't hear her anymore," William said. "She just wasn't there anymore. I don't know why."

"Maybe she was just a dream," I said. "Maybe she was some strange dream we both shared."

"Then it was a good dream," William said, "one we can have in memory, together."

"Any sign of a rider from Blois?" I said.

"Not a sign," William said. "I suspect he wouldn't leave till daylight. No one's been up this road. No one in Vendôme knows that I am a spy." He smiled, then looked ahead and nodded. "The towers of Vendôme?"

"The tallest is the bell tower," I said, "of the old abbey. People made pilgrimages to Vendôme for centuries, up until a few years ago."

"What's there?" he said.

"A tear," I said, "a single tear, wept by Christ on the tomb of Lazarus, a tear said to have healing properties. A knight of Vendôme brought it back in a vial, all the way from the Crusades—"

"It didn't dry up?"

"How could it? It had already lasted a thousand years. William, you, of all people, must leave room for the mysterious, for that which reason or science finds unaccountable."

"Forgive my skepticism. It was merely curiosity."

"In any case, pilgrims came to see the Holy Tear. My own father, a practical doctor, went there with me when he had eye trouble, and after that he never had to wear a monocle."

"We should visit it. We could use it."

"The local Committee of Surveillance, I heard, stopped all pilgrimages—considered them counterrevolutionary. We must only worship Reason now."

"Reason alone misses many things," William said. "Now look at that humble and beautiful cottage. We could live in such a cottage," he said.

It was just ahead, to the right of the road. Wisteria wound its way up the chimney and along the side of the cottage. A little fence encircled it, and, as we spoke, puffs of smoke started forth from the chimney.

"Yes, we could have such a cottage," I said. "We'd have to pick lots of apples." Behind the cottage an orchard stretched, and, even from here, you could see the boughs, heavy with apples, bending toward the ground.

"I'd have a writing room upstairs, also," William said. "And you could keep La Rouge in that barn."

A big barn was below us now, and a broad chestnut tree, on a little rise, stood between the barn and us.

"Let's stop here," I said, "give La Rouge a rest."

William stopped the wagon beneath the low chestnut branches, as under a green and yellow tent, and helped me down. I took Rouge's harness off, leaving on the halter and lead rope, and let her graze free on the grass beside the road. William opened the basket and passed me the loaf of bread and the jug of water. He took a drink from the wine flask.

"I've seen cottages like that on the edge of Blois," I said. "With my bequest from my father I could find one and buy it. It couldn't be very expensive. I'll write you when you go to England and tell you to meet me in our cottage. We'll have roses as well as wisteria. And a Monsieur William pear." I laughed. "We'll bottle our own eau-de-vie."

A small thunder of hooves smothered my words, and six National Guardsmen rode from the direction of Vendôme, dusting the bending boughs of the apple trees. One dismounted and pounded on the door of the cottage. A man in shirtsleeves appeared: he towered over the soldier who had pounded on his door. I heard a raised voice from the soldier, and the tall man shrugged, a big shrug with both arms spread out wide to either side. The soldier strode to the barn down the slight hill and beat on its broad doors. They didn't open. Even though I was sure word could not have reached Vendôme yet of William's flight, I was afraid, and I'm sure William was too, for he silently took my hand—or I took his. We stood still, hardly breathing, beneath the overhanging chestnut leaves, in earshot but, I hoped, hidden from obvious view by the branches.

The soldier now ordered his men to dismount. They hit the butts of their muskets against the planks of the door, which must have been shut with a crossbar; one even shot his musket at it, and the report echoed through the quiet valley. Finally, the door splintered and gave way. In a few minutes they dragged out a woebegone priest, in dirty robes, as if he had been in hiding for some time.

As soon as they stood him before the officer, one soldier hit the priest in the stomach with the butt of his musket. Then another did the same.

Their officer looked on. They had free license to beat a priest. One took his musket to the priest's head, as if it were the barn door. Then another followed him, too. Now the priest was down. You could not see him, only the soldiers' backs and their muskets going up and down. Now and then we heard a moan or a cry that was silenced by the next falling musket. We saw spurts of dust where his legs kicked.

"They'll kill him," I said.

"This is intolerable," William said.

We saw the muskets go up and down again, not in unison, but like some weird water wheel.

What few people understand about William now, as a famous poet, is that he is—or at least *was*—a rash and passionate man. And he acted spontaneously because he always trusted his feelings. He looked at me under those leaves, each muffled cry of the priest louder in our ears than the one before, each rising and falling of a musket more impossible to watch, and each dull thud wrenching our own insides. It was one of those split-second looks that determine lifetimes. I nodded—I don't know now why I nodded. I think I was a fool for nodding. But I think I felt the same as William, that it was inhuman to stand so close to this suffering man and do nothing, just *watch*.

So with no words passed between us, both thinking that the National Guard could not have heard about William yet, he emerged from under the branches of the chestnut tree and shouted for them to cease. With gaping mouths they held the bloody butts of their muskets still; the priest curled himself around his injuries and lay still in the dust below. All were silent. The officer stared at William.

"Who are you?" he said.

"Monsieur Guillaume," my husband said. He, too, was much taller than the officer. "I am a member of the patriot club of Blois, the Friends of the Constitution."

"Are you?" the officer said. "And on what authority do you give my men an order?"

"On no authority, Citizen"—William looked at the man's insignia—"Citizen Lieutenant. I ask it in the name of humanity, in the name of *fraternité*, of brotherhood." The lieutenant then snatched a musket from the soldier on his right and shoved its butt, with great strength, into my beloved's chest. William couldn't breathe. He

doubled over, and I ran out from under the branches also. I fear I
screamed. The lieutenant ignored me.

"No one," he said, "tells my men what to do or not to do but
myself." He raised the musket again, and I moved in front of William.

"You've beaten two unarmed men this morning, Lieutenant. Will
you start now on a patriot's wife?" I wondered if he noticed my state,
partially hidden as it was by the cape.

The lieutenant lowered the musket and handed it back to his soldier. "Madame, I commend you for your bravery. But I'm afraid I will
have to arrest your husband."

"On what charge?" I said.

"For interfering with my arrest. I have orders to bring in that
priest." He said the word with disgust. "Perhaps you and your husband are royalist friends of refractory priests. I notice your husband
has an accent. Is he Austrian? That would be quite a find, to bring in
a priest *and* an Austrian spy."

"He's English," I said.

William reached in his pocket now and handed the lieutenant his
papers. Everyone nowadays carried their papers on their person, as
soon as they left their house.

"These don't prove you're not a spy," the lieutenant said. "Many,
most, spies have perfect papers. Yours, Madame?" He kept William's.

I fumbled in my pocket, pulled out a poem, then another poem,
then reached in another pocket, pulled out a poem and my papers.
I handed the papers to the officer. "Rather a lot of writing there,"
he said. "And some of it, I see, is in a foreign tongue." I had William write out all his translations also in the original, so I could try to
sound out the lines.

"My husband is a poet," I said. "An English poet who loves
France."

He gave my papers back to me. "What do you have in that cart?"

"Vines," I said. "We are transporting vines, of the cabernet franc
variety, from Vienne to Vendôme. Our employer intends to start
growing his grapes there, too."

"A poet hauling vines at dawn. A foreign poet who loves priests. I'm afraid, Madame, that this matter is decided."

William, though held by two soldiers, struggled to step in front of the officer. "I have friends in the National Assembly," he said. "I know Citizen Brissot. I have a letter signed and sealed by Brissot."

"And you're transporting vines," the lieutenant said.

"A poet must eat somehow, Lieutenant," William said, and almost smiled.

"I would like to see that letter," the officer said. No one wanted to offend someone in the National Assembly.

"It's in my rucksack, in the wagon," William said.

"Go with him." The officer ordered one of the soldiers.

The three of us walked up the little hill, and I prayed to Sainte Lucette that this letter would convince the lieutenant to leave William alone. The other National Guardsmen stayed with their prisoner. A soldier stood him up and roughly tied the hands of the priest behind him. The priest swayed as if he were drunk. Blood ran from the top of his head in several lines down his face and onto his robes. La Rouge looked up as we approached, then continued nibbling the grass on the verge of the road.

William told the soldier he had to get in the wagon, and as he brushed past me, he gave me another look. Almost a smile, almost a twinkle in the eye, accompanied the look. I put a hand on La Rouge's side to alert her. I thought I heard him whisper, "Vendôme." He was standing on the seat of the wagon, going through his rucksack. Quickly he leaped onto La Rouge's back. I said "Allons-y." William grasped the lead rope and kicked her sides, and they rushed off through the apple orchard.

It was all confusion for the soldiers. They didn't know whether to stay with the priest or mount their horses and pursue their new suspect. The officer cursed the soldier who ran back down the hill from the wagon, then ordered two of his men to follow the Englishman. He himself stayed with his charge. He and his three soldiers mounted their horses, and the priest, attached to the last soldier by his rope, came behind. I saw La Rouge far away in the orchard and the other two horses running under the boughs bent with fruit. Dust rose there into the morning air. The lieutenant walked his horse up the hill to the main road.

"You've lost your husband," he said.

"You've lost your prisoner," I said.

"I have got mine," he said. "My orders were for this one," and he jerked his head back toward the priest, following them up the hill. "You've also lost your horse." He laughed. "It's a long walk to Vienne." He gestured for one of the soldiers to ride to the farmhouse. "That farmer may have had nothing to do with the hiding of the priest," the officer said, "but now he and his neighbors will learn it is wrong just to have a counterrevolutionary on one's property. He won't have much strength left to help with his harvest. The same could go for you. I don't know why I'm not arresting you along with this priest and your fleeing husband. Associating with counterrevolutionaries is a crime. Maybe I believe his story of Citizen Brissot. Maybe I've fulfilled my duty and am feeling magnanimous. Maybe I've noticed your state and for some reason don't want you to think we are monsters. I don't know, Madame, but it's a lucky day for you. Think of my mercy on your long walk home," and he commenced his horse into a trot and resumed his place before his soldiers and the tottering priest.

I contemplated the lieutenant's words and silently thanked Sainte Lucette, then prayed again for William.

I myself didn't know what to do. I stood there for several minutes, staring in the direction of the orchard and now seeing nothing, nothing at all. I sat down on the grass at the side of the road. I looked at La Rouge's hoofprints in the grass. After a while I got up, climbed into the wagon, and retrieved William's rucksack and the basket of food and water.

If I were correct and he had whispered "Vendôme," he would need his rucksack and his food. There were poems in the rucksack, a notebook full of notes for the long one he had been working on he was calling simply "Descriptive Sketches." He would definitely need the rucksack, or I, too, needed to eat. I'd have to leave the wagon.

I drank from the jug. I looked toward Vendôme. It was not too far to walk. I would find a *diligence* there that could take me back to Blois. I had some coins in my pocket, under the poems. I could pray all the way to the gates of Vendôme that Lucette would guide La Rouge as she had before. How could any National Guard horse hope to catch her? With what audacity they attempted it! And William looked fine riding bareback on La Rouge, leaning forward over her withers, his legs holding fast, his long hair flying. He looked fine jumping onto Rouge's back. That was a good spontaneous decision. I laughed a little, there by myself, walking along the dusty road carrying a basket and with a rucksack on my back. He surprised me, I said to myself.

I sat down by the side of the road and held my head in my hands for a minute. *Would* I see him in Vendôme? What would become of us? Could he ever get this all worked out with his friend in the Assembly whom the Jacobins hated? It was all impossible to think about. I wouldn't think about it. I would walk to Vendôme. That was enough for now.

I got up, adjusted the rucksack and started walking again. The bell tower of the Abbaye de la Trinité glinted above the city. The road, white with dust, stretched out toward the bright spire of the tower. Now a morning line came to me,

> *The tall sun, pausing on an Alpine spire,*
> *Flings o'er the wilderness a stream of fire.*

The morning sun paused on the bell tower and flung out in my direction a stream of fire. I made for that tower. The road seemed longer than it looked. I had to stop several times before I arrived at the gates of the city.

THE HOLY TEAR

I crossed the bridge into Vendôme and stared back at the gargoyles that lined it, protecting the town from dangerous intruders like me, or English heretics like William, and paused, leaning on one leering face, to look at the light gleaming on the Loire, which divides here into several different streams, each with its bridge, so it seems that one is always recrossing the river and never really gets across.

I arrived at the Porte Saint-Georges as the bell tower tolled ten, dust coating my skirt and flouring my face and fatigue weighing down my body. Beyond the town, on La Montagne, the steep hillside, was the old château, the sun from the east on its ancient earthen walls. How could they make something out of earth to last for so long? I thought.

I waited by the huge towers of the *porte*, as an old gendarme stared at my papers and at me, until I grew uncomfortable and afraid that the National Guard officer had included me in their reports after all. He finally gave my papers back and nodded. I was free to proceed into Vendôme with my basket of food and rucksack of poems.

I proceeded to the center of town, thinking that's where the stage relay might be, and walked along rue de l'Abbaye past Trinity Abbey, which still housed the Holy Tear, perhaps waiting for happier times that would produce more innocent hearts that once again could believe in mysteries and miracles. I stopped before the bell tower, which had been the destination of my own recent pilgrimage here. I liked it better from far away, though, for here more gargoyles stared down at me silently, like the old gendarme at the *porte*, the stone masks and monkeys forming their own mute, ancient Committee of Surveillance.

I finally asked directions of a strawberry vendor, who, noting my state, put a few berries in a twist of newspaper and gave them to me.

I learned that the depot lay across another bridge, in the Place de la Liberté. I carried my burdens through the rest of the town and vaguely remembered riding down that street in the family carriage with my father, after he had visited the Holy Tear. He had been very jolly, I remembered. He took his monocle off and pointed out Ronsard's house. "You should read his sonnets to Cassandra," he said. "Yes, I think you're old enough for that." I finally entered the Place de la Liberté and remembered it as the Place de Geoffroy Martel, the knight who brought back the Holy Tear. Everything had a new name now.

I saw two *diligences* being prepared, and I was so tired and disoriented that when I spoke to the driver, it seemed that he himself spoke as if in a dream, his words and gestures not quite matching his lips and voice. I scolded myself to concentrate: one *diligence* was leaving immediately for Chartres and on to Paris, and one would be leaving for Blois and on to Tours, at noon. I had time to wait for William. That is what mattered.

I counted my money and bought my ticket. It is amazing the things one can do when one is not really there, I thought. The world does not know, nor does the world care. How many other people were walking around like me, numb but operable?

Everything seemed normal. The drivers of the diligences were changing horses, a man was weighing a sack of flour at a nearby booth, and a vendor was calling out about his low prices for used hats. The old hats made me think of William. He needed a new hat of a more modern shape, even if it were a used one.

A man walking past me was saying in a loud, grating voice to his friend how, in the battle at the Tuileries in August, the Swiss Guard had invited the *fédérés* into the courtyard, fraternized with them, then opened fire on the innocent patriots. "The King's to blame," his friend said, who stared over at me, alone, with protruding belly, walking like a pilgrim with my bundle.

I wanted to be away from people, not to be obliged to talk to anyone, and also not to be gawked at myself, and remembered a public garden that my father had taken me to years ago, and crossed another, more narrow bridge of gray stone and found a bench by some towering hydrangeas. An old man, kneeling in the dirt, was pulling weeds.

He wore a battered straw hat, looked up at me briefly as I sat down, then went back to his work. He had probably been here when I visited before, I thought, the eternal gardener, working the soil, making things grow independent of history, like the Holy Tear in its vial.

I rested on the bench and looked at the deep blues of the huge hydrangeas and took some small bites of the bread I was saving for William. I drank some of the water, closed my eyes, and felt the sunlight on my shut lids. It seemed no time had passed when I heard the belfry toll eleven-thirty. I shouldered the rucksack again, picked up the basket, and thanked the old man as I passed for his beautiful garden. He looked up, surprised, and grinned a gap-toothed grin.

Standing in the shade under an arcade on the square, I heard the driver call for the *diligence* to Blois and Tours. Another coach had just arrived and was in the process of changing its horses. Horses were being led across the square. At the edge of the relay station I saw a sorrel mare, standing alone with its halter on.

I left the protection of my arcade and walked straight over to it, and it whinnied softly. I took La Rouge's muzzle in my arm, and tears were in my eyes as I stroked her. "Where is your rider?" I said softly. "Did you save him as you did me? I didn't know if I would ever see you again."

"Here," I heard an English accent say, and I looked over La Rouge's back to see William's face smiling under the eaves of the relay station. It was as though I saw him through a cut of clear sunlight in the haze between the world and me.

"Do you have anything in that basket? I am a bit hungry," he said.

I walked over to him and stood there, looking at his face. I wanted to throw my arms around him but feared attracting any attention.

He took my hand. "I had quite a ride. La Rouge never could be caught, could she? I thought this is where you would be finding your way to Blois, without a horse. I said I'd meet you in Vendôme."

I couldn't say anything but took his arm.

"You have my rucksack," he said excitedly. "You *are* a marvel." And he took it from me and placed it on his back.

"Don't talk here," I finally said. "Your accent could arouse suspicions."

"I have a perfectly good accent," he whispered.

He held the halter of La Rouge, and I led him back to my shady place, away from glaring sun and curious eyes or ears.

"May I talk now?" William whispered.

"Aren't there soldiers looking for you?"

"I had to see you before I left. Could we open that basket?"

There was nowhere to sit, and I handed the basket to him and took La Rouge's lead, and William drank and tore off a hunk of the bread.

"You must have the chicken for your long walk," I said. I thought, that was a ridiculously banal thing to say—but aren't one's last minutes before parting with a loved one often taken up in such trivialities? As he finished his bread and took another drink of the water, I took the basket, gave him La Rouge's rope, moved behind him, and opened the rucksack. I packed the items from the basket on top of his thick, leather-bound notebook, a clean shirt, and a pair of stockings. "Thank you," I said as I worked. He gave me the water jug. "Thank you for the mare. Thank you for coming into Vendôme when you didn't have to." I tied up the rucksack tight. "Just be careful," I said. "Don't come back to Blois if it's dangerous." I moved in front of him and took La Rouge's rope. "Tell me about something we'll do in England when you take me there."

"First, you will need a good English tutor." He laughed, and I smiled with him.

"He will take you to the great English theater to reward you for learning so quickly. You will see Shakespeare, perhaps a play by Sheridan, but it is silly stuff, after Shakespeare."

"I like silly stuff."

My eyes were watering, in spite of myself. I looked down at the basket, empty except for some knitting wool and needles of mine. William looked out at the square. The driver of the *diligence* called out for everyone to board the coach for Blois. William stepped out of the arcade.

"No, don't go," I said. "The driver will make one last call. Don't move. I just want to see you there. I want to memorize you, with that half-light on your face." La Rouge snorted behind me, and I brought her up beside us and stroked her neck. William patted her shoulder.

"Thank you, La Rouge," he said. "Thanks, girl."

I leaned my head against her and cried silently in her silken mane.

The driver made his final shout for the diligence to Blois. The bell tower was striking twelve. William led La Rouge to the coach, and I asked the driver if she could be hitched behind. He looked at me as if that were an odd request. I explained to him that because of my condition I couldn't ride her. He secured her rope and asked me if I had any luggage and looked at me strangely again when I said the basket was all. William and I stood near the door of the *diligence* as people were getting on.

"I didn't tell you," I said. "I'm knitting a cap for our child. It's in the basket. I can work on it now. On the way back."

"Let me see it," he said.

I opened the basket and lifted up a scant half-inch of soft wool. I shrugged.

"It's pink," he said. I shrugged again.

He took my hand and held the scrap of fabric briefly to his lips.

"Just in case," he said. "Now I've touched something that will touch her."

"You already have," I said. "You already have."

William was looking at me, and I could see some water forming in his eyes. I was in control of myself now.

"William." He stared at me and said nothing. I think he was afraid to speak. It was bad there, with all the people around. The driver was looking at us, and the people in the coach were looking at us through their open windows, waiting for me to get on. I had forgotten what I was going to say. "Cher William, we never decided on a name," I took his hand and led him a little way from the coach.

"Madame, everyone aboard," the driver said.

"You decide on a name," William said. "It will be beautiful."

I kissed him on the cheek. I whispered, "I'm so glad you came to Blois."

"So am I," he said softly, and his chin trembled.

He helped me into the coach and I sat on the seat facing straight ahead, in the middle, between an older, wealthy-looking man and a plump middle-aged woman with a fat yellow cat on her lap. I don't know who was sitting across from us. I never looked at them the whole trip.

I leaned forward to see William standing alone, watching, in the middle of the square. I wanted him to get back under the arcade, lest someone recognize him. But I waved to him from the window as I leaned over the man. The man made a sound of disapproval as my body touched him, and I could feel him looking at me as I waved, then felt him surreptitiously pat my behind.

I turned to see the plump lady slapping him on the hand and saying, "She is saying good-bye to her *ami*. Have some decency."

I watched until the coach turned down a side street, and suddenly I was staring at a stone wall. William was just gone, and that was it. There was an old half-timbered house, with geraniums in a window box, then a studded door of a medieval church. And Monsieur William, who had filled my days since Christmas, was simply gone, replaced by a wall, a window box, and a closed church door. He had vanished with the flick of a coachman's whip, with the clopping of hooves on cobblestone and the turning of a coach into a narrow street. I feared that I would never see him again. I sat back and put my hands on top of the basket and studied them.

"Your husband?" said the woman next to me, who smelled of expensive perfume. She was stroking the cat with her plump hand, and the smell of the perfume seemed to be on the cat too. The cat was beginning to purr.

"Yes, my husband."

"Is he going to the wars?"

"Yes."

"It is not easy. You have a child coming?"

"Yes."

"There is never a perfect time. There is always something. It is good to have the child. Even if you do not see him again, which I know you will, you will have the child."

"Yes."

The cat nudged the side of the basket. "Any food in there for Egalité?" the woman asked. "Egalité has a nose for duck liver paté. That is a clever name for a cat, isn't it? Cats are the original aristocrats. The irony is luscious. Cats would never grant equality to anyone." She laughed.

"There's no food left, I am sorry. Only a cap."

"What sort of cap?"

"I'm knitting a cap for my child-to-be."

"Oh, may I see it?"

"It's not much, yet." I opened the basket and showed her. The other people in the coach were looking at it too. No one seemed very impressed.

"But what if it is a boy?" the woman asked, laughing again.

I appreciated that the woman was trying to be nice, but if she were really trying to be nice, she would let me be, I thought. I wished I were alone in this coach. I should be back in my own room, or in my room at chez Vincent, and be able freely to cry. I should sob properly, shake the coach with sobs. Holding back was worse than the sorrow, and the anger from it made me forget William, for a time. My shoulders and neck felt stiff from the effort, and my hands, folded on the basket, started to blur.

All the others in the coach spoke of who was in charge of Paris now. Was it the Jacobins, or were the Girondins still prominent? Or would Austria march in and restore the monarchy? The haze was back between the world and me.

I had wanted to get him a new hat, even if it were a used hat. I should have given William something. I leaned my head back. I thought of William coming in from the cold rain on Christmas night with a gift of a poem and how rude my mother had been. I smiled slightly with my eyes closed. That seemed a very long time ago. Why couldn't I make noise and cry like a widow?

I felt the plump soft hand of the woman next to me rest on mine, for a moment, then it was gone.

BOOK III

October–December 1792

IRREVOCABLE STEPS

I cannot tell you how tired I was, after the *diligence* had stopped in Saint-Louis Square, in front of the cathedral, after I had crossed the long stone bridge with its many arches over the river, and after I had climbed the hill, all the time leading La Rouge, and sighted the gray facade of chez Vincent. All I wanted to do was to have a hot bath and a cup of Claudette's tisane, go to bed, and sleep a hundred years. Maybe after that century was over William would return, and we'd raise a family with no war and no Committee of Surveillance. But mainly, I just wanted to sleep. I didn't want to think or to act. I felt as if I had done too much of both, and felt the baby kicking—I was now over seven months along, and a comfortable bed was all I wanted.

I was greeted at the door not by old Pierre but by little Gérard, who had never opened the door before to anyone. He wasn't even allowed. He took my hand and said, "Papa is gone to Bordeaux to look at grapes. That's a long way away. Do you think he will be back in time for my birthday? He must be back for my birthday." His birthday was October 11, in three days. I didn't know why Paul had left so suddenly and at this time.

"I suspect your father will arrive just in time," I said.

"Maman has been crying. She hurt herself in the garden. Marie won't play with me and only wants to draw pictures. I'm glad you're back."

"Goodness, I've only been gone two days." Then I saw my sister coming slowly down the stairs. She noticed me and flew down the rest of them.

"Nurse is looking for you, Gérard. Into your room for a nap. Come now," and she lifted the boy and carried him back up the stairs, depositing him in the hall. "We have things to discuss about your birthday. Go rest now." And she ran down the stairs again and into my arms, where she cried. "I'm so glad you're safe," she said into my neck. Then she pulled back and looked at me. "You poor thing. How are you?"

"Tired."

"How's—"

Claudette came down the hall now. I was always glad to see her happy face, and now it was tight. I embraced my old friend as well as maidservant. "Monsieur William, he's—"

"Yes, he's safe now, on his way to Paris," I said. "He's walking in the open air, so he's happy."

"Well, that's a blessing, at least," she said.

"What's going on here?" I asked. "Will someone tell me what has happened here? Why is Paul in Bordeaux?"

"I will make you a tisane," she said. "And boil some water for a bath. Madame would like a hot bath?"

"Very much, but I want to know why everyone is acting so strangely. What has happened? Is Maman all right? Why was Gérard left to answer the door?"

Claudette left, and Marguerite took my hand and led me into the drawing room, and we sat on the silk couch with the gilt lion paws. She looked composed now.

"I didn't want to tell you until after you had rested," she said. "I know what it's like to be pregnant and tired, but not pregnant and running away with one's beloved from Committees of Surveillance." She took my hand, and her eyes watered. "Oh, Annette," she said, "They've taken Paul. They've taken him," and she started to cry again. She stopped and gathered herself when Claudette entered with a tray. There were two cups on it, and jam.

"It's the apple and apricot jam," Claudette said. "The specialty of late apricots and early apples. Annette is back, Madame," she said to my sister. "Everything will be all right now. She is the first for the Fates to return to us. Now the rest will follow," and she curtsied slightly and left.

"I wish I had her confidence," Marguerite said, "in the Fates."

"Tell me," I said. I had taken the first sip of tea, and it warmed me. Just its sweet familiar scent of mint and lavender, rising in its steam, helped me. I had to be strong. Going to bed now and waking up a hundred years later was not one of my options.

"First they came here, early this morning, looking for Monsieur William. Someone had told them he often stayed here. They questioned Paul, still in his dressing gown, and he said he had no knowledge of the Englishman being a spy or an Austrian sympathizer. He just thought the foreigner was a scholar and a poet and was entertaining him as such. They asked did he know the penalty for entertaining a counterrevolutionary? He said he was not aware that it was against the law to have a guest for dinner. They finally left and said Paul would now be under surveillance."

"I am sorry," I said. "This is all my fault."

"No, listen," Marguerite said. "Paul himself rode to Monsieur William's lodging and told him, in no uncertain terms, to come here. It was Paul's choice. Now listen." I had no appetite for Claudette's wonderful jam and sipped my tea. "Paul had just concluded some business at a wine merchant's office in town. He said he was signing the papers when he heard from the street outside, 'Monsieur Vincent! Help, Monsieur Vincent!' It was old Pierre, who was waiting for Paul by the carriage. Paul ran outside and saw three *fédérés*, whose regiment had recently come into town, hitting Pierre, Pierre falling, and them kicking him on the ground. Paul immmediately shoved them away, and a fight ensued. Paul was arrested for physically attacking government troops, which puts him in the category of an enemy, of a royalist counterrevolutionary. Pierre was arrested too. It seems that the *fédérés* said something disparaging to Pierre, something about him being an aristocrat's dog, and Pierre said something back."

"Surely the charges will be dismissed. They'll see Paul was just trying to help an old servant."

"That's of no consequence. The fact remains, he physically assaulted government soldiers. They've had individual soldiers or small groups of them attacked throughout the provinces. They can never find who does it. Now that they've got one, they want to make a lesson out of him. That's what Monsieur Duclos, Paul's lawyer, says. He's talked with the prefect of police, with the Committee of Surveillance, even with a judge of the peace, an old friend of Duclos. They all said the same thing, what I've told you, except the judge said he was sure Paul was innocent, but his, the judge's, hands were tied. They added that, since Paul was already under surveillance, this action against the *fédérés* assures his guilt. They're sending him on to Orléans for trial. I'm afraid of what that means. What am I to do? I've told the children the Bordeaux story, but Marie suspects the truth, I think, especially after the Committee was here."

"When are they sending him to Orléans?" I said.

"In two days, with many others. They have to walk all the way."

"I want to visit him, and Monsieur Duclos. Where is Paul being held?"

"They had too many in the old Beauvoir Tower, and in the cellar of the new Town Hall, so they made a makeshift prison out of the abbey behind the church of Saint-Nicholas. I visited Paul there last night. It's a wretched place, now. He hadn't any treatment for his wounds. Oh, Annette, his poor face. He said not to worry, that he had a witness, the wine merchant in the shop, but Duclos said the merchant is afraid to speak against the Committee and the *fédérés*, lest he himself be accused of being counterrevolutionary. Duclos has even recommended that his agent withdraw money for us, that we prepare to leave the country, as others have done. He says that if the trial goes wrong, we will lose chez Vincent, and it will be much harder, if not impossible, to get our money and to leave. He's actually got me thinking about emigrating. Can you believe that? Can you believe I would act like the Varaches and flee, and without my husband? What strange dream are we in?"

"I will talk to them tomorrow. There must be something—"

"You will need to get a pass from Duclos. Only one person is allowed to see Paul at a time. I must do business with the agent. Please bring him some bread. Be sure to bring him good bread and water. I don't know what they give him there, if anything. That will be a relief, to know he has good bread. I was in such a hurry, I left with nothing. I washed his face with the hem of my dress and with some foul water they had there."

Marie entered the room then. She embraced me, holding her drawing paper in one hand. "I'm so glad you're back, Aunt Annette. Would you like to see my new drawing?"

I nodded, and she held it up for me, all orange and red leaves against a black night sky. "It is as if the tree is on fire," she said.

"Yes, it is," I said. "It certainly is."

I believe Claudette put some herb she had secret knowledge of in my bedtime tisane, or else the bath and my physical exhaustion took their toll, for, in spite of my worries, I slept soundly and woke fresh to visit the prison.

In the small carriage used for everyday business, Jean—the old groom of chez Vallon, whom Paul had now hired—took me first to the offices of Monsieur Duclos. I listened to the lawyer's pragmatic cynicism. It is a tragedy, he said, but what does one do in such a circumstance? One makes inquiries, one argues one's position to the proper authorities, one seeks out the most powerful and entreats them for support. All these he had done, he said, and to no avail. So what does one do? As unpleasant as it may be, one must look at the possible outcome of events.

And for Monsieur Duclos, then, it was a matter of logic that one must accept that one's client of many years, the son of one's former client, would be a prisoner of the state unless a miracle occurred in Orléans. And they do occur, daily, in the randomness of the present state of affairs, he said. It's just that one cannot count on them. When tragedy strikes, it's best to be practical and not emotional; that is why he was counseling Madame Vincent to prepare for possible exile. One must pray and then prepare for the worst. It is not logical to count on miracles, he said, and smiled patronizingly. We were women who needed to be protected and to be told what to do. If there were nothing that he, Duclos, could do, with all his worldly wisdom and connections, there was certainly nothing we could do. I nodded in resignation and thanked him.

If one could not count on miracles, I thought, then one must provide them for oneself.

The anger, the outrage, that I had felt on William being denounced to the Committe of Surveillance by Monsieur Leforges, I had deferred on account of the necessity of removing William from Blois, then deferred again in the fear of his capture and in the unwieldy sorrow that I had felt on his leaving.

But now, upon the arrest of Paul and the resignation of his lawyer, I felt it all explode. I would not let these people, who had killed my father in their delirious rage, who had sent my beloved away in their delusional fear, and who had now arrested an honest and loving *père de famille* out of their petty hysteria, rule our lives. It was anger that drove me by the graceful Louis XII fountain, which for three centuries had shimmered in the morning light. It was anger that led me into the small court that for half a millennium had been the entrance of the Benedictine Abbey of Saint-Laumer. And it was anger that made me snatch my pass back from a guard who seemed to sneer at me, as a visitor to a counterrevolutionary, and who, I thought, had no business being there himself, in front of gates that should lead one to a secluded world of the devoted and now ushered me into a common den of thieves. The new order, as I understood it, was none other than an excuse for brutes or the brutish-minded to bully the world. But it was a white-hot, controlled anger that carried me down the simple arcades between plain stone buildings—no sculpted arches and cloisters here; these Benedictines had renounced even beautiful architecture.

The irony of seeing an abbey used as a barracks for the National Guard and one of its buildings as a holding pen for prisoners seemed to crystallize for me all the priorities of the new order: military might and the politics of fear. Now that the patriot army had finally won a victory in Valmy, it had changed everything: we were now a world power, to be reckoned with. It made me sick. Where had all the quiet monks gone, who had once blessed these halls with meditation, work, and prayer? "Freed," a young officer glibly told me, as he escorted me to a guard, who was to take me along another corridor. "The monks," the officer enlightened me, "are now liberated from the torments of their lifelong vows."

"That was altruistic of you to do so," I said.

"You'll find, Citizeness," he said, "that many people, sometimes whole nations, have been left in the dark so much and for so long they do not know what is good for them. It is up to the more enlightened to show them the way."

"And that would be you, Monsieur?"

"That would be this whole nation. And we will do that now with Austria, you will see, and with Prussia. And then, perhaps, with the rest of Europe."

"You're on your own crusade, then."

"To lead Europe out of the Dark Ages. And you could say it begins here, with this abbey, with that bell—" He pointed to a cracked bell, probably used to call the monks for matins and vespers, lying in the corner of the courtyard. "We leave it there as a symbol of the lost age of superstition."

"It could be said, sir, that you have merely substituted a new religion for the old. That you yourself are a zealot to reform people who may, themselves, have a right to remain unreformed."

"Just because you are *enceinte*, with child, doesn't mean you are beyond suspicion, yourself. I now know why you are friends with a counterrevolutionary."

"I am just engaging in logical discourse, Monsieur. You do still do that—"

"You are an insolent aristocrat, Citizeness, and your day is long over." And he handed me over to another guard, who, after saluting the officer, without looking at me, led me along a corridor to a third guard, with keys at his waist.

The third guard had a large mustache and stroked it as he glanced at my pass, then longer at me. We didn't move; he just looked down at me and lovingly stroked his mustache. Then he finally gestured for me to walk in front of him. I thought of him stroking his mustache and looking at me still. We went down an arcade, with the dried-up remains of an herb and vegetable garden in a court on my right and a long stone building on my left. The guard finally grunted for me to stop before a large wooden door. He stood beside me now, and his hand brushed my thigh as he drew a key from the ring at his waist. Now he stroked his mustache again as the key turned. "You'll come to me," he said. "I can help you much more than your bourgeois lawyer." And I hated him, much more than I hated the self-righteousness of the officer.

He closed the door, and I entered a stench of crowded unwashed bodies and open buckets of human excrement in one large room that had never known an open window or door. This must have been some meeting or dining hall for the monks. I nearly gagged and put my hand over my mouth. I called "Monsieur Vincent! Paul Vincent!" but no one seemed to notice me. I was just another unlucky prisoner. Then an elderly gentleman, with tattered lace at his cuffs, a dirty silk neckcloth, and even a blue velvet hat, doffed his hat for me, bowed, and said, "May I help you Madame?"

I started to speak and almost retched. The man immediately drew an embroidered handkerchief from his sleeve and handed it to me. "Hold it over your mouth, my dear. It was, at one time, scented with vanilla. There might still be a residue. It has helped ladies before."

With the scarf to my mouth, I managed to tell him whom I was looking for. "You mean you are not one of us, a prisoner? The world has not deserted you." And he bellowed out, in a voice that belied his age, Paul's name and politely maneuvered us through the throng of men and women, languishing on a thin layer of straw on the floor or standing in small groups. The only other sounds than his voice were low conversations or the constant hacking of someone coughing, and soon Paul strode up to us. "Annette, you're not—" he began.

"No, I'm visiting, as Marguerite did."

"Thank God. How is Monsieur William?"

Other prisoners moved away to give us our privacy. The old gentleman bowed, and I thanked him. I never saw him again. Such are *the unremembered acts of kindness and of love, which are the better part of a good man's life*, as William was to write later. But I remember that man and thank him again now. In the world of anger into which I had succumbed, I remember his simple act of compassion.

"Monsieur William is on his way to join his powerful friends in Paris and rectify his situation. Oh, Paul, look at your poor face, that's what Marguerite called it." I lifted my hand to it and realized I still had the gentleman's handkerchief. I looked after him, but he was lost in the many dim figures in half-light.

"It's an awful face but glad to see yours. Come, sit on my little handful of straw." And he helped me down. I put the handkerchief back to my face.

"You shouldn't have come, though, Annette. This is no place for—"

"A woman in my condition? No, neither is riding a wagon to Vendôme and walking throughout that city. I think we all need the Holy Tear, Paul."

"Ah, yes, that would be a boon."

"Here," and I opened a cloth sack. "The guard at the gate was very interested in this bread and this jug of water. Even this cheese, which you can't smell in this place. Marguerite insisted that you have the bread, especially."

"You are good to me. How's—"

"Marie's making beautiful drawings of autumn leaves. Gérard's waiting for your return from Bordeaux. He's concerned about his birthday."

"I'm afraid he's going to have to wait a long time." He winced when he said that, as if the words had caused the bruises on his face new pain.

"Marguerite is strong. She says she doesn't know why she hasn't fallen down and died, and I said she hasn't because she can't. She's being strong for the children. That bread makes you feel civilized, doesn't it? Just the taste of it."

"It does," Paul said, with his mouth full. "Excuse me." Then he added, "How is Pierre?"

"Monsieur Duclos's arguments prevailed there. Pierre's being released tomorrow because he is old and, they said, not right in the head anyway. They said you, on the other hand, were quite sane."

"I don't know about that. Well, I'm glad for Pierre. All this would be too hard on him. He wouldn't have made the march to Orléans."

"Paul, are you ever allowed out into the courtyard, for some fresh air?"

"Once each morning, a few others and I have been given the honor of carrying two buckets each out of this stinking place. It's hardly enough. But it's an attempt at being civilized, as you would say."

"Where do you empty it?" I asked.

"It is of no concern. It does not affect my health."

"Your health is my concern. If you are sent on to Orléans, it could truly suffer."

He paused with a bite of bread between his teeth and looked sharply at me. Then he spoke softly.

"In the latrine. There is always an armed guard right behind me."

"Where is the latrine?"

"At the end of the courtyard, near the wall."

"Where near the wall?"

"What do you mean?"

"The north end of the wall? The south?"

"About halfway."

"Does the guard ever leave you?"

"Only when I enter the latrine. He says that is not his job, to follow me in there."

"Is there a window in the latrine?"

"At one end."

"Where is the guard in relation to the window?"

"He is at the door, and the window is at the other end."

"Not facing the courtyard?"

"Not facing the main courtyard, but the remaining area between the latrine and the wall." He looked down at his straw. "The wall is very high, Annette."

"Can you arrange to be by the wall tomorrow?"

"Annette—"

"At what time are you sent to empty the bucket?"

"Seven in the morning."

"The same each day?"

"I hear the bell tower strike." He touched his face. "Marguerite washed my face and did not say anything about it being all one bruise."

"It will look better in daylight, tomorrow morning," I said.

"Does Marguerite know of this?"

"Not yet. I wanted to talk with you."

He paused.

"It's not worth it, Annette, to endanger—"

I put my hand on his hand and shook my head. He looked at me, then down to the straw, and was silent. When I rose to leave, he helped me up and met my eyes and said, "Thank you." Then he escorted me to the door, pounded twice on it, and yelled, "Visitor leaving." The mustachioed guard opened it a crack, saw my face, and let me out. I had no time to look back at Paul before the guard slammed the door.

He didn't start down the arcade but stood still and stared at me again. I realized I still had the handerchief over my nose. I left it there.

"You like your friend?" the guard said.

"My brother-in-law," I said.

"You stay with me," the guard said. "One night, and I will see that he walks out a free man." I wanted to slap his mustache and the hand on it. "I don't mind that you are going to be a mother. I like them better like that," he said.

I spoke through the handkerchief. "That is very kind," I said, "but my brother-in-law is innocent and will be released."

"This is your last chance," he said. "You should take it. I do not ask again."

"It is not necessary," I said, and he motioned for me to walk in front of him again, and I felt him staring at me from behind.

I lay in my bed that night wondering if I were a fool, a brash fool endangering her dear brother-in-law, who might, after all, be released in Orléans. I could be ruining the happiness of my sister and of her children, and needlessly endangering myself and William's unborn child as well. What right had I to do that? What right had I to think I could help? What hubris, for which I would be punished? And now they were trusting in me. What had I gone and done? And if I were caught? I had heard they didn't guillotine pregnant women. They waited until they delivered their babies in prison, then guillotined them. And if William's child was then raised by the state? Would I go to hell for making that baby an orphan, for bringing Paul to the scaffold?

I prayed to Sainte Lucette that I would successfully help Paul and his family. She had helped me twice before. And it was really such a simple plan. I had not told Paul or Marguerite what it was, for it was so simple they could doubt it, and it probably left out a thousand variables. I went over it again, pictured it all in my mind, step by step, even imagined things that could go wrong and dealt with them. Yet I still felt afraid.

Marguerite had the children ready now. They thought they were going on a trip, although I think Marie knew. When I played the scenes over and over, I always stopped when we all got in the family carriage, waiting in the road that wound through the vineyard, the carriage that would then go east on country roads, avoiding the bridge at Blois and crossing the river at Beaugency, then north on other side roads to the Channel. Paul would hire a boat from there. We just had first to get to that carriage in the dusty autumn vineyard.

I said good-bye to La Rouge in my mind. She would not understand. In a letter to Angelique, I had given my younger sister care of Rouge. Tomorrow Jean would bring Rouge and Le Bleu back to chez Vergez. Then other thoughts deluged me: William, I thought, would not want me to put myself in danger. Yet William was not a predictable man, and he was fond of Paul. No, no one could say what Monsieur William would think. I wanted Claudette to come, but the carriage was full. In a letter that Claudette would bring to my mother, Marguerite asked that Claudette, Jean, and old Pierre work at chez Vergez. Claudette and Angelique liked each other, and it would be a felicitous arrangement until I could send for Claudette, as soon as—

Sleep was useless. I pushed back the bed curtains, wrapped my old dressing gown around me, and lighted a single candle from the night-light on the wall. As I opened my door, I saw the sack behind it that held the length of rope I had bought that day, the receipt carefully left with it. I knocked on my sister's door, heard her wide-awake response, and soon we were sitting, side by side, covered in a wool blanket, on her balcony on a soft October night, the same moon that had lit the horse, escaping to it knew not where, shining on the rows and rows of vines descending steeply to the river.

"They don't grow grapes in England," Marguerite said.

"I believe they're beer drinkers," I said.

"That's unfortunate," she said. "I'm all knotted up inside. Other people do this kind of thing. Dramas happen to *other* people. You don't think they will happen to you. Why? What did we do? Monsieur Duclos is hopeless, now. Polite and very helpful—he stayed up all last night, and he had his agent get the money, but he's hopeless. I don't want anything to happen to the children. But Annette, if we stayed here and did nothing, it's likely that, if Paul, well, if he were convicted in Orléans, the state would confiscate chez Vincent anyway, and the children would lose both a father and a home."

"That's likely," I said.

"My God, what did Paul do? Help an old servant, who had been with his family since before Paul was born. Wouldn't any self-respecting man do the same? And to be put in jail, to be called a traitor, for *that*. For keeping bullies off an old man. I never knew there was so much hate in the world."

"There's enough love for us to be sitting here, trying to get away together."

Then my sister's tone turned suddenly light, even playful. "What if, Annette—what if we made it to England, and Monsieur William lived down the road, and we all ate horrible English food under the same roof?"

"That would be a delight," I said. "But I wish we could fit Cook in the carriage. Monsieur William said her sauces were always a miracle and a mystery to him. She could set up a restaurant, and all the English would think she was mysterious and miraculous, and she'd become famous and we would be her servants. Now that's a revolutionary turn that I could like."

"What about Maman, though?" Marguerite said. "She'll never forgive us for leaving. And poor Angelique. She always said we didn't include her in our games."

"I don't think she would want to be included in this one."

"And sweet Etienne. He'd want to come."

"He'll probably follow us."

"I just—," started Marguerite, "I just can't let anything happen to the children. If they stop the carriage, they wouldn't arrest the children—"

"They would only want Paul and me. Don't—"

"Why are you doing this, Annette? I love you so, for your courage, but you don't have to. You don't have to do it."

"We only have a short period of time. As you said, Duclos is no help. And I'm the one who thought up the stupid plan."

She laughed a little. "How do soldiers ever sleep the night before a battle?"

"I don't think they do. I think they lie awake and talk around their campfires or stare into the flames."

"What do they talk about?"

"Home. Loved ones. Not the next day."

"Do you remember, Annette, when we used to lie under a blanket, like this, and talk away summer nights, talk till dawn about boys, or some prince—"

"You were always going to some castle."

"Chez Vincent is my château on the hill," she said. "I got all I wanted." I held her hand under the blanket. "Gérard's fifth birthday is coming up," she added. "He was asking me about it today, and I almost burst out crying, right in front of him, talking about his birthday."

"He's always wanted to see the Channel. He's heard about it. Huge waves and ships. It will be exciting."

"It will be that."

I felt all right now. As I sat and talked with my sister about it, somehow my fear and self-doubt had dropped away, and a peculiar calmness had taken their place. Everything looked clearer than I had ever seen it, as if I had suddenly awoken from a long slumber and was seeing my sister's face in the moonlight, the river in the distance, for the first time. "Look at the moon, Annette," Marguerite said. "Look at the moon on the vineyard of chez Vincent." And it lay now, as it sunk westward, in a sheen over the vines and on the river.

"Doesn't the sheen look solid on the river?" I said. "Like ice, as if one could just walk right across. Why not?"

We held hands silently and looked over that land that was still hers. "Thank you, Annette," she said. "Thank you for what you are doing for us."

"Roses," I said. "The English are fond of roses, and so is Marie. I think she will become a great painter of English roses. Gérard will become a sailor, an admiral of the British fleet."

"Oh, no. Let's not get involved in any more wars," she said, and leaned her head against my shoulder. "Jean's a good driver, yes?"

"He's very reliable."

"It's just so irrevocable. That's all," she said. "So irrevocable— like a death, a marriage, a birth. The church should have ceremonies for leaving a home and leaving one's country, as they do for the other irrevocable steps of life."

"I'm afraid such ceremonies would be called counterrevolutionary," I said.

"Well, I'd do them anyway," Marguerite said, sleepily. I didn't say anything, and soon heard her regular breathing beside me. I looked a bit longer at the moon dipping into clouds above the river, and when the moon had gone fully into them, I led my sister, sleepwalking and not really awake, to her bed, and I went back to my room, dressed, lay on my own bed and noticed all my doubts and fears still playing about my mind, yet underneath feeling calm and ready.

MERCY

I thought, I should turn back right now, before I do anything truly foolish. Marguerite would understand. So would Paul. Nothing would be lost if I turned back right now. Yet I knew I would do nothing of the sort. I wouldn't knock on the ceiling of the carriage to tell Jean to stop. It was all in motion, after all. And it was, of course, foolish. But sometimes wild, foolish plans work.

We were across the bridge now and going along the quai Abbé, lively with early-morning business: wagons filled with grain and barrels of wine, carts loaded with sacks of sugar and coffee, just upriver from Nantes; bargemen calling and carrying and hauling. We must have seemed incongruous in this traffic. Farmers unloaded hay bales and herded livestock onto *sapines*, broad fir-planked barges with no sails, headed downriver. Two large *gabares* with their beautiful tall sails were docked on their way to Orléans. I thought briefly of the quai at Orléans, where I had walked with William. Where was William now? Then I saw the road we would turn on to drive by the abbey.

It was suddenly silent and deserted. We passed by guards in a small court at the south entrance of the abbey. I could feel them staring at us, even in our small, plain carriage. Any carriage now, betokening aristocracy, raised suspicions. I thought one of the guards caught my eye. He looked young, about Etienne's age. But they were at their posts and could not see the carriage once it was past the courtyard.

The abbey had a thirteenth-century wall, built to keep intruders out rather than the devout in. Its thick, chipped limestone, about ten feet high, followed the monastic buildings. The ancient wall was on our left. We were the only vehicle on the road, and the crunching of the wheels on the gravel was louder than I had anticipated. I thought one could hear it all the way back to the château de Blois.

About halfway between the south and north entrances, we stopped as planned, and I leaned out of the window and asked Jean what was the matter. I wondered if the guards had heard the stopping of the carriage, this far down the road. Jean said that Gascony, the lead horse, appeared to have picked up a stone in its hoof, and I said I wanted to see. Jean helped me out of the carriage, the basket over my arm. I checked my clock, and it was five minutes until seven. I looked up and down the road. Two empty wagons, heading toward the quai, trundled well ahead of us. Jean cradled the back hoof of Gascony in his large callused hand for me to examine; Gascony looked around at us, swiveling his ears in curiosity, wondering what we were about. The problem with plans, simple or complex, is that something always happens to interrupt them. We were out of sight of the guards, but apparently not out of hearing.

Out from the court, walking quickly, came one of the guards. He shouted, "Is something wrong?" I saw that it was the young one, who had caught my eye. "I heard your carriage stop," he said. "May I aid you in some way?"

"That is good of you, but it is nothing. My coachman can take care of it."

He looked disappointed. He knelt by the horse and looked at the shoe, then the ankle, and he looked up at me. "But I can see nothing wrong," he said, in a tone more surprised than suspicious. Perhaps he *was* suspicious, but he didn't want to admit it, even to himself. He wanted to help.

"It is probably nothing, then, as I thought," I said.

He straightened up. It must be seven by now. "Then you will be all right. Let me help you back into the carriage." He looked at the basket. "You are going to market? So early?" The clock tower was striking seven.

"The best vegetables are to be had early."

"That is true. But a lady like you does the buying for the house?"

"We are all citizens now."

"That is true." He stood there looking at me with his eager face.

Just then the other guard appeared around the corner. "Arnaut! You imbecile! You leave your post, and you will lose your head."

"My friend, he always exaggerates," Arnaut said.

"You have been very kind."

I allowed him to help me back into the carriage, then he ran down the road and turned into the court. Jean helped me step out again. In the basket, underneath a baby's pink knit hat and my ivory needles, a white cloth covered the rope. I took the rope out and quickly threw it over the wall, but my arm was not strong enough, and it fell in coils at my feet. I threw it again, and it glanced off the top of the wall. I did not think this was going to be so difficult. I had to ask Jean. Jean looked down and thought about it.

"Please, Jean, we don't have time to think."

In my anger, I heaved the rope over the top. Then I grabbed my end and gave it to Jean. He stood there with it in his hands.

"Tie it to the luggage railing. As we practiced." When I had asked Jean to help and told him it would be dangerous, he had been eager for the adventure. He had always been dependable. Now he seemed frozen with fear. "Do it!" I said, as loudly as I dared.

Suddenly he woke out of his trance and tied the rope quickly to the railing above my head. I saw the rope suddenly grow taut, heard shoes scrabbling against the stones on the other side, then the rope went slack again, and a weight dropped to the ground. I looked up the street, and there was a flower woman, on the other side, carrying two baskets of violets and roses and broad lilies toward Louis XII Square. A voice shouted roughly, "Hurry up. Your time is up in there."

Then I saw the rope tighten. It stayed taut, the shoes clicked again against the wall, I heard some labored breathing, then I saw the top of Paul's head above the wall. I looked at the flower woman, who had passed the carriage, and she was looking straight ahead. Paul's shoulders appeared, then, with a mammoth effort, he pulled himself up and over the wall and slid down the rope. He held out his shaking hands; the rope had skinned his palms.

"Untie it!" I hissed at Jean, for the railing was out of my reach. Jean did so, and we left the rope dangling there. Paul gave me his raw hand to help me into the carriage.

He looked at me briefly: it was a look I was later to become familiar with in others, one of resoluteness, in spite of fear. Even with his bruises, his face seemed as white as could be. But his eyes were steady, and he managed a slight smile. It was a smile of a minor victory, of the success of a first assault. He said softly, Thank you, and I handed him a spare set of Jean's clothes, including worn boots and hat, and turned to the window.

I could see Louis XII Square just ahead, and as we got closer, I saw the sun catching the ornate fountain on the far side. The square was already filling up now with carts and even a few carriages entering it, shop people setting up their wares and others intent on doing the early, best marketing.

Paul handed me his clothes and shrugged. Though he and Jean were about the same height, Paul was much more slender and swam in the breeches and shirt. I smiled and curled Paul's old clothes into a ball and dropped them out the window and under the wheels of a cart behind us. I glanced at my watch; we were doing well. I tapped on the ceiling, and Jean pulled to the side of the road and stopped. I told Paul he was obliged to drive now, and he nodded, got out quickly and climbed up to the driver's seat as Jean jumped off and mixed immediately with the others going into market. He'd walk home unnoticed up the hill to chez Vergez. Paul snapped the reins over the back of the horses, and we rode on.

We were about to enter the square, and I could see from here a gleaming mound of red tomatoes, greens of cabbage and lettuce and courgettes piled high, plump yellow squash, pears and apples, and the shining silver of fresh fish laid out in rows. Bright silk and cloth ribbons for sale swung in the breeze, and the smell of fresh bread reached me. The man selling used coats and gowns of those who had emigrated or been imprisoned called out the glories of their silk and lace and velvet and their cheap prices. If we could just enter all that teeming life, I thought, and I could even buy some bread for the trip to make our presence credible, then we could be out the other side by the fountain, across the bridge, and on our way.

Just then four horsemen in the blue-and-white uniform of the National Guard, swords rattling at their sides and hooves pounding between crowded carts, tore into the Wednesday-morning life of the square. Soon came the tramp of about twenty soldiers marching up from the abbey. They cut a swath through the marketers, some setting up position at the end of the square, near the fountain, and others poking carts and investigating wagons already in the square. Even disguised as my driver, I didn't want Paul scrutinized; perhaps one of the prison guards who knew him was among those troops.

I shouted up to Paul, "Jean, take us around by Saint-Nicolas. Now. I want to pray." And Paul turned on rue Saint-Lubin, and we headed back toward the church, on the other side of the abbey.

We passed outside the long nave of the ancient church, and I breathed deeply and thought that, somehow, I had got along without breathing much since I had first tried to throw the rope over the wall. About six National Guardsmen stood at the intersection of our road and the entrance into the courtyard in front of the church. An officer looked at Paul, with Jean's hat pulled down over his eyes, and motioned for him to stop. The officer came up to my window. "What is your business?"

"I am on my way to the church."

"On what business?" he repeated.

"To pray."

He grunted and said, "I need to look inside."

I opened the door for the officer, and he looked in at the small, empty interior. He patted both seats and even knocked on the wood beneath them. Then his eyes fell on the basket. "Open it."

I lifted it to him, and he drew away the white cloth. "A cap I am knitting for my unborn child. I am going to pray for the child now. I have not been well." The officer glanced down at my protruding belly and motioned for us to pass.

"On to the church, Jean," I said, for I was not sure if Paul had heard the conversation. Then, before we could leave, the officer stopped us again.

His face was at my window. He looked tired and bored, idly curious. "Your coachman, he has a bruised face."

"So would you if you had a wife like mine," said Paul, in a coarse voice. The officer stepped back and gazed at him.

"She is a cat. She could smell another woman on me and took a candlestick to me."

"Why don't you join the army?" said the officer. "Go and fight the Austrians."

He motioned us on again, and we drove into the court before the church and stopped. Paul came around to help me out.

"I want you to come in with me," I said.

He went before me and opened the great four-hundred-year-old door, then followed me in. It was cool and dim, and I noticed for the first time that my mouth was very dry. I felt as if I was suffocating. I tried to swallow, but could not. I turned back and walked down the long south aisle of the nave to the font of holy water near the entrance, dipped my palm in, and lifted it to my mouth. No one saw this blasphemy except Paul, and I repeated it twice.

A few bent heads turned my way, then bowed once more. I chose one of the many radiating chapels of the chevet, and entered its small enclosed silence. I knelt on the cold stone, and Paul knelt behind me.

I did not know what we were going to do here, nor how long we would stay. We could not leave the carriage unattended for too long. But I wanted to wait until the search had subsided somewhat, and the market in Louis XII Square was thronged. I extended my arm behind me, and Paul took my hand and squeezed it for a moment, then let go. When I drew my hand back, I noticed there was blood on it.

I could not pray. I felt like a statue with a racing mind. The sunlight was bright in the little chapel, and I felt suddenly like the chapel was a prison, and we would never leave it. I bowed my head and thanked Lucette for our safety thus far.

Boots rang out on the stone floor far behind us, coming quickly down the nave. They were not reverent boots. I felt Paul stiffen behind me. For something to do, I opened my watch and looked at the time. It was twenty-five minutes past seven. Incredible. I felt two and a half hours must have passed. The steps were now in the transept. They paused. Two soldiers, perhaps three, but they sounded like more in the echoing vault of the church. The boots entered the chancel. They were definitely looking for something. I heard them come toward the apse and pause. The owner of one of the pairs of boots said, "We should check the chapels." His voice snapped out in the stillness their boots had already fragmented.

I cast my eyes wildly about. The chapel offered a place of concealment, but not the altar, which seemed too obvious. I could not see Paul's eye, under the wreck of Jean's hat, but his face looked badly marked. I bowed my head again, and he did the same.

Then the older voice said, "He is probably far away from Blois by now, on his way to join counterrevolutionaries in the Vendée. We are always too late. And it is not our fault. We were minding our posts. It is the fault of guards inside. You check the rest of these chapels. I will look in the transept chapels, and then we will go."

The boots paused before each of the radiating chapels, and the voice called out, "Nothing . . . Nothing . . . Nothing . . . ," until it came to ours.

"Excuse me, Madame, for interrupting your prayer." I looked up from my hands, which were knotted, rather than folded, in prayer; it was Arnaut, the young guard from outside the prison.

His eyes flicked toward Paul.

"But you were going the other way, to the market, to buy your vegetables early. Who is this man?" he added. He seemed on the verge of calling the other guard, which I knew would be fatal.

"He is my coachman. I wanted to pray here first. This is a place of significance, Monsieur. I feel reassured here. And lately, I am needing much reassurance. It is a dangerous time to bring a child into the world."

"Dangerous indeed, Madame. Your coachman, he accompanies you to the chapel?"

"We consider him part of the family. We are all citizens, now, as I have said."

"A prisoner has escaped. He went over the wall near where your carriage had stopped. And now your carriage sits in the square, empty."

"Surely, with the National Guardsmen about, the carriage is safe while its occupants pray in the cathedral?"

I was still kneeling, but I turned toward him now. I knew he didn't want to arrest us. "The burden of motherhood sometimes frightens me, but I am praying for grace, for a Providence that protects one from danger. Will you join us, Monsieur? The more people that pray, the more powerful the prayer."

"That is an old superstition, Madame. You can do nothing against the dangers that are around you."

"I can put myself in the hands of the tenet behind all these candles lit in these various chapels, behind the very structure of this ancient church—mercy."

The morning light was full on Arnaut's young face, and he looked at me, then at Paul, silently kneeling, then back at me. "This coachman has yellow hair. Your other one had black hair."

"I am praying, Arnaut, for my family. You had asked me if there was anything you could do to help."

"I am not a traitor."

"And you also know what is right."

"I know what I ought to do."

"Don't do it."

"I cannot help it, Madame."

He put his hand out toward Paul, and it was trembling. "You," he said, "come with me."

"You don't have to do it," I persisted. "He wronged no one. What good will killing him do? We are leaving. We are fleeing France and will not return."

Arnaut moved toward me, and I could see the sweat on his forehead. "You are not special," he said. "But you are beautiful. And you are brave. I care nothing for this one, bruised and filthy like a criminal, but for you I would lie. I don't know why. I'm a fool. Now go, after I leave. But if someone recognizes the prisoner, I will say where I saw your carriage, and it will not go well for you. You are, perhaps, more of a fool, than I." He pivoted, and his boots clicked toward the transept chapels.

"Nothing, again," Arnaut said crisply.

"It took you long enough. Saying a paternoster for your dead mother?"

"My mother is not dead."

"For your girl to lie with you?"

"I have no girl. Let us go, I do not like churches."

I heard their boots echo back down the long nave, and I loved that boy, and wished that he would not get killed in the war and that I would never see him again.

I stood up and leaned on the altar, and Paul put his arms around me, and I buried my head in his coat. Suddenly, I thought he looked so absurd in this coat that was too big for him that I started to laugh;

trying to muffle my giggles. I realized how close we had come. "Not now," Paul chided softly. When the fit subsided, I brushed the laughter-tears from my eyes and looked down at my hands in Paul's wounded ones.

"Your poor hands," I said, then it seemed ridiculous that I should feel sorry for hands, when everything had been at stake, and I put my face into Jean's old coat again and held on to Paul. Then it stopped as suddenly as it had come, and I felt a great need to relieve myself.

I asked Paul to go check on the carriage, as it should not be left unattended for so long, and said I would meet him there. When I heard his footsteps far down the nave, I rushed into the next chapel. I did not want to use this one; it had protected us. I went behind the altar, said a brief prayer for forgiveness, knowing that I would be given understanding, and relieved myself. I felt the sound of water on stone could surely be heard out in the transept, but no one came. Before I left, I took off one of my petticoats and mopped it up and left the petticoat rolled up behind the altar. When I left, I looked above the entrance of the little chapel and saw that it was the private chapel of the mayor of Blois and his family.

There was still so much that I wished were over. I did not want to risk going through the square, nor going along the quai near the abbey, where they would probably also be looking, so we would have to go out of our way, up the hill, around the huge château de Blois, and back to the bridge that way.

I wanted to skip over time and have us all traveling north in the carriage on peaceful country roads and hear Gérard ask if he could ride up front with his father. Marguerite would say no. I walked back down the nave, dipped my fingers in the holy water, and walked out into the brightness of a still early morning.

A NARROW LEDGE

*W*hen we drove by the officer at the intersection, I
nodded my head politely to him. Now we took the
narrow road around the château. I glanced up. If things went right,
it would perhaps be the last time I would see the crazy asymmetry
of those windows and balconies of old François I, looking like some
eastern palace, not like the abandoned château it was, now barracks
for the military. I had always liked it. It was the château of my city
and it was unlike any other, with its different wings built in different
centuries. And I liked the winding, sculpted stone staircase in which
Marguerite and I had once, in another life, chased each other around
and around, and stood on the balconies and imagined the torchlit carriages of guests stopping below. Even then it had been abandoned.

The château de Blois had seen murders of dukes and cardinals,
the poison collection of Catherine de Medici. My little intrigue was
laughable in comparison. I pulled out Etienne's watch from a pocket
in my dress. We were almost thirty minutes behind the schedule I
had made. I imagined the ghost of Catherine de Médicis, the witch
queen from Florence, cackling at me from the window of her ransacked room.

I prayed to Sainte Lucette that we make good time, that we get back
to chez Vincent well before the inevitable arrival of the National Guard.
I finally felt the roll of the carriage down the hill toward the bridge.

Guards at the bridge stopped us, and it was the same as at the intersection. Paul seemed to pass as a coachman. Perhaps it would have
been that way in the market square too, and I had made a wrong decision, but I had been afraid at the square. We were among the traffic
of the bridge, and the blue water moved lazily beneath us. I could see
the vineyards on the slopes of chez Vincent now. Paul had made good
time. We had only lost an hour, going into the church and taking the
long way back by the château.

I closed my eyes and realized how tired I was. Marguerite and the children would get in the carriage, and then I would sleep, even with Gérard chattering. Paul must be tired, but he was a man who had to protect his family, and he would not let himself be tired for a long time yet. I wanted it all to be over now. A dim fog floated behind my eyes. Then I opened them.

Paul jumped down, and Marguerite came running out of the house, with the children following, and embraced her husband.

"Are you ready?" Paul asked her.

"We've been ready for an hour. When I heard your carriage, I prayed that it was you and not the National Guardsmen."

Paul hugged Marie and kissed her cheeks, then squatted down and took Gérard by the shoulders.

"Are you ready to take a trip to England?" he asked.

"Papa, your face is hurt."

"It's fine. I fell from a friend's horse. We will have good riding in England. Come, help me put the bags on."

In a matter of minutes all the bags were on top of the carriage and roped down, and I put one small bag and a basket of food inside. Cook had prepared a last meal before she and Françoise left for the house of Isabelle, an old friend of Marguerite's and mine.

"Come, let me wash your face before we start," Marguerite said to Paul.

"We don't have the time," he said. "Quick now, everyone in the carriage." Paul stood beside the door and helped each of us in. He kept looking back toward the road.

We commenced along the side of the house and into the vineyard. Across from me were the children, each with their favorite pillow, and I could smell the sausage and cheese in the basket. For the first time that day, I thought I could eat. I leaned out the window, took a last look at chez Vincent, and saw the dust rising from about six horses rapidly approaching the front of the house. I could make out the blue jackets and black hats. And at this short distance I knew we could not outrun them. I shouted up to Paul to stop. "National Guard," I said to him.

He stopped the horses. "What's wrong?" Gérard said.

"Hush," Marie said. "Bad people are here."

"You can drive, Annette," Paul said. "It's me they want. Come, now," and he jumped down and opened the door to help me out.

"Papa, I know a place to hide," Gérard said.

"Gérard, we can't hide," his father said gently. "This is not a game. You ride on, and I'll meet you later."

"No," started Marguerite, and a look from Paul stopped her.

"It *is* a good place," Gérard insisted. "No one ever finds me. It's my secret place."

"Is it the one on the other side of the terrace?" I asked.

"Yes, that one. Come."

"It's a good place, but a dangerous one. It's a narrow ledge, hidden from view from above. They would still follow us, Paul, if I drove. It is worth a try. What can it harm? If they find us there, things are no different."

"Let's go," Paul said.

We left the carriage at the edge of the vineyard and almost ran back up to the terrace. I held Gérard's hand as he proudly ushered us behind the chestnut tree. "Down there," he said, and pointed over the low wall to a little path just on the other side that descended to the left, then stopped suddenly on a narrow rock ledge, directly below the terrace, where, a lifetime ago, Gérard had shouted, "Find me!" then froze with fear. Now we were all afraid.

"I don't like his place," Marie said.

"Show us, Gérard," his father commanded.

First, we climbed over the low terrace wall, then I could feel Gérard's little hand enclosed in mine as he led us carefully down to his secret place. His fifth birthday was in two days. Then I let go of his hand before the path got too narrow to pass, and leaned back against the cliff wall so the family could go in front of me. I wanted them to be together. Paul held Marie's hand. On one side was the cliff wall that turned into the terrace wall above us; on the other was a sheer drop into a ravine, then the vineyards sloping down toward the river. It was a good place. You could not see us unless you were hanging over the terrace balustrade, and then only if you looked straight down.

They all quietly passed me, and for a moment I looked down at Marie's lambskin slippers, then beyond them to the drop. When I was rescuing Gérard, I had been too intent to notice it. Now I knew why he had frozen. All I could think of was falling, my body breaking on the rocks.

I felt bad in my stomach, then my head began to spin. The vineyard swayed beneath me, and the cliff swung down toward the valley. I lurched, and Marie gave a shriek of fear. I knew I had to get away from the cliff. I would endanger them all. Right now I didn't care about the National Guardsmen as long as they didn't find the others; and it wasn't me they wanted. Someone shouted from above me that he had heard a cry. I stepped back off the cliff and gave a look to Paul and Marguerite. I didn't know when I would see them again. Paul's eyes were questioning, but my sister's broke my heart. She knew. I waved to them and pointed from them down to the carriage in the vineyard, so they would have no doubt as to my meaning: I wanted them to escape, and this wasn't my time.

Then I half ran back up behind the chestnut tree and leaned against it, gasping.

A guardsman grabbed me roughly by my upper arm; he stank of fresh sweat and old sweat in an unwashed uniform. "Here's one," he shouted. They assembled about me.

"Where is Monsieur Vincent?" one said.

"I am pregnant. I am sick. Let me sit down."

I started to sit on the stone bench below the tree, then thought better of it. "I must go sit inside. You frightened me, and I'm afraid I will get sick," I added, which was half true. There was a blur of blue coats and black pointed hats around me, and I didn't care. I opened the French doors myself and sat on the couch in front of the fireplace. I leaned my head down.

"Get her something to drink," a commanding tone said. "Where are they?" A hand emerging from a scarlet cuff lay heavy on my shoulder, and I shook it off.

"Keep looking upstairs. In the stable," the voice connected to the hand said.

The Vincents' brandy decanter was held in front of me. "Drink."

But I didn't want to drink. I shook my head, and they took the decanter away. My nausea was real. The room I knew so well blurred into a dream, and the guardsman stood above me, with his scarlet

collar and cuffs, shiny sword hilt, snow-white trousers, and deep
blue coat, his carefully curled mustache, his face showing a growth
of whiskers, his hazel eyes that were not evil, but impatient. I was a
task, unpleasant and frustrating, that he wanted to get over with. The
escape of Paul Vincent had got in the way of his well-planned day,
and he resented it.

"They have already left," I said.

Another guardsman entered the drawing room and stood where
Marie liked to lie on the floor and work on her drawings. He saluted.
"We have found their carriage, Captain. It is ready for travel, but no
one is inside."

"If they have already left," the captain said, in a smooth, almost
cordial tone to me, "then why is their carriage still here?"

I had to think through the fog. I said what seemed logical to me. "I
was going to follow them and bring them their luggage. They wanted
to leave, immediately. They left on horseback over an hour ago. They
can all ride."

"Why were you hiding?"

"Wouldn't you hide if you were a woman alone and soldiers
rode up?"

He ignored that. "Where were you going to meet the Vincents? At
one of the counterrevolutionary strongholds in Normandy?"

"They are not counterrevolutionaries. This has all been a hideous
mistake. Monsieur Vincent was merely protecting an old servant
when he was arrested."

"They're aristocrats and counterrevolutionaries."

The captain had foul breath, and when he spoke, I involuntarily
turned away. He also smelled of sweat under the gold braid on his
uniform, the uniforms in which men feel so important.

"Look at me," he said, and his hazel eyes and stinking breath and
pressed uniform and smelling body and shiny boots and violence
coiled up in an arm that would strike me if I were a man; and all of
this made me see my dream of so long ago, my nightmare of the men
with their weapons. Suddenly I was in it. The captain grabbed my
arm, and I screamed.

"You, a woman ill and expecting, were going to drive that carriage
alone?"

"I am a good horsewoman," I said. "My father taught me to hunt—and to drive a carriage and a wagon. We were an egalitarian family. We didn't leave everything for the servants."

"Where are the servants? I want to question them."

"They were sent away. There is no one here but me."

A guard entered the drawing room and reported that no one was upstairs. Another came in from the stable and announced that it was empty except for a large carriage.

"If they had left in a carriage," I said, "they would have taken that one. See for yourself. They have left. Search outside. Search all the Loire Valley. Which town will you choose? Aren't there more important concerns? Farmers hiding priests in the Vendée? Armed brigands attacking ripe crops? Austrians and Prussians at the frontier? Your nation is in need of you, Captain. One harmless winegrower, who could have furnished France with excellent vintages, and his small family are surely as important a threat as all these other things. So go search for them. But they are not here."

He slapped me with the back of his hand. The slap stung, but it helped with the dizziness. My eyes swung into focus. And it seemed to be the officer's last effort at communicating with me. Then someone else entered the room. He looked as though he had just arrived.

A guardsman entered and saluted his superior, but seemed to be addressing me, in tones of dripping sarcasm. "Sir, as you ordered, we have inquired in the shops in town, and one merchant does remember selling such a rope as was used in the escape. His bill of sale is written out to a woman who resides here, the home of the escaped prisoner. Is that not a coincidence? This woman, named Madame Williams, is furthermore married to an Englishman, a suspected counterrevolutionary, who fled Blois. The merchant described her, and his description matches you. Are you not Madame Williams, born M. A. Vallon?"

I looked up at him. "Yes, I am Madame Williams." I enjoyed saying it. "That merchant did sell me a rope. But it is unused, Captain," I said. "Just send a man upstairs. It's behind my door, third room down the hall on the left."

"No need, Madame," he said. "You just admitted the merchant sold you the rope."

I thought, this man needs an arrest. It is a point of honor, especially if his main prey has escaped. But I tried once more.

"It's there," I said. "I'm telling you, it's there." It was hard to keep the tone of desperation from my voice. I had been too naïve to think my "evidence" would make any difference.

The captain poured himself a glass from the Vincents' brandy decanter, gulped it down, looked at me for a moment, and said calmly, "Oh, we'll find Paul Vincent. Rest assured that we will find Paul Vincent. But now, if we can't arrest the traitor, we can take his accomplice. You think this is just fun, don't you? Another sport, like hunting? You enjoy the danger when you corner the boar, but it is at a safe distance. You like to race, to see how fast you can ride before you fall off, but you will only bruise your thigh. But now you have misjudged the danger. You aristocrats are all the same. You're just bored. It's not a sense of loyalty to a fallen king that you respond to, just a sense of boredom. Arrest her. Let her be bored in prison."

"You have no evidence."

"We have the word of a clerk, and the rope you left dangling on the prison wall. You will lose your head, Madame, pregnant or no. It will save the world from more like you. Married to an English spy." He paused. "That is good."

Then he put his face close to mine and held my chin between his thumb and forefinger. I turned away, but he jerked my face toward his. The smell of his breath and his body mixed into an odor that surrounded and trapped me. I stared at his bright scarlet collar. "It's a nice head, though," he said, "a very nice head."

Then he straightened up and motioned for the others to take me. I was glad it was over, that I could breathe freely. The family must be exhausted with fear, clinging silently to that ledge. How long can one stand on a ledge? About one second, for me.

I was the prize of the National Guards now. The officer could resume the duties that Paul and I had interrupted, for he had something to show for his work. One counterrevolutionary brought to justice. I was not afraid, it sounds strange to say. I was tired and dazed and relieved that some decision had been made. I had a soldier at my arm, as if I were being led to dance. Angelique would like this, I thought; she likes soldiers.

Two guardsmen remained behind, stationed at the front of the house. I did not think they would be able to hear from there a small carriage slowly rolling out through the vineyards below.

They tied my hands behind me and put me on the crop of one of the saddles, and I rode like a girl with her lover, sitting in front of a soldier on his horse, down the hill, across the bridge, and through the streets of my childhood.

I was expecting them to take me back to the abbey prison, but they took me to the old Beauvoir Tower instead. This was the oldest prison in Blois, used since the counts of Blois bought it from the lords of Beauvoir five hundred years ago. Many centuries of woe had gone into the stones of that massive square tower. At first I was with prisoners who had been there since before the Revolution and knew nothing of the changes outside. Their hair and beards were matted, their faces covered with sores, and it was with some relief that a few hours later I was led up a flight of narrow stone stairs and locked in a room, covered in a thin layer of straw and only half filled with other recent arrests, most of them women and some children. One named Madame Pellegrin took one look at me and said Divine Providence had blessed her with five children and that this was no place for me—how cruel could the National Guard be? She led me to her corner of straw and gave me most of her bowl of broth, and I fell asleep with my head in her lap as she stroked my forehead. No one had done that since my good nurse, Madame Bonnet, who died before my fourteenth birthday. She was the true confidante and guardian of my childhood.

When I woke, I saw a dirty stone floor and smelled the hay and was lost, for a moment. Then I saw the back of Madame Pellegrin, curled asleep next to me, saw the prostrate bodies of others, a couple stirring in the dim light, one sitting on a bucket in a corner, and remembered. I looked up at the dark wall and the thin slit that was its only window. Light was slanting through the slit in a tiny line and touching the edge of the hay near my face.

I held my palm up in the tiny slant and watched my hand fill with golden light, as if the light were a liquid thing. Darkness fell sharply away from the edge of my illuminated hand. I gazed at my palm now as if it were an isolated detail of a Renaissance painting, a hand with fingers longer than mine, not surrounded by shadow, but resting on the folds of an azure skirt rippling with light. Thus I spent my day, dreaming of paintings or of tapestries I had seen in the châteaux of my childhood. I noticed how in the morning the shaft fell also over the top of Madame Pellegrin's head, across her soft features and onto her arms as she cradled her four-year-old son. She should be the model for a modern Madonna and child, I thought, but there are no painters in prison, and the only art done now is in praise of the Revolution.

She had told me that we were the lucky ones; there weren't many of us. We were all going to be tried before the city magistrate and not sent all the way to Orléans. They probably thought we were not fit, she said, and it would look bad for the revolutionary government to be sending women and children on a long march.

"Grace," she said, "takes many forms." Her husband and older son were walking with the others the forty miles to Orléans. She cried for them at night, after her younger son was asleep. They had fed and hid a refractory priest in the Vendée for months before being informed on. Her three daughters had escaped.

I thought my mother would be notified and would, perhaps, visit me, but no one came. When, after about a week, Madame Pellegrin and her son left, I felt impossibly alone. I withdrew more and didn't talk to the other prisoners, who left me alone. I thought of the Vincent family, hoped that they had made it safe to the Channel, somehow, and worried that Marguerite and Paul worried about me. Then I couldn't imagine or think of them, except that my sister's face reappeared regularly in my mind, as if she were checking on me. I asked Lucette to protect my sister and my baby and thought of how the name Lucette means light or bringer of light. Yet I didn't notice the strip of light anymore after Madame Pellegrin left.

I saw again in my mind moments that I had lived with William, some that I have told you about, and some not. These moments became more real than my reality. Then one day it was suddenly impossible to imagine anything outside of the darkness and odors and coldness of my walls, and I curled up in a ball on the straw and dozed or slept most of the day. I would feel the baby kick and think that I was a bad mother, having taken these risks and now provided such poor nourishment for her growing body—just the meager, bricklike, wormy biscuits and stale water—then I thought, also, if I had not this precious gift within me, *then* I would truly be alone.

The beige muslin dress, short brown wool jacket, wool stockings, and cotton underskirts that I had worn that morning for travel grew increasingly filthy, and my hair became as matted as that of the old prisoners I had seen on my first day. I tried to comb my hair with my fingers. No wonder, I thought, it is easy to think the accused guilty, for by the time they come before the judge they look desperate enough to have done anything. When my name was finally called, I had no time to wash my face with dirty water. Nine others and I had our hands tied behind our backs, were led out to an open cart, and made to stand as we drove in the rain through Blois. It was as if it were someone else's city. Or as if this was all happening to someone else. Things like this, Marguerite said, happen to other people, not to us. We drove past Saint-Louis Cathedral and stopped at the Town Hall.

In spite of the cold and the rain, I found I was now extremely thirsty. We stood in a small courtyard, perhaps once used to receive goods for the Bishop's Palace. We were to stand and not move. It had stopped raining, and we stood in puddles in the old court of the Bishop's Palace.

Two National Guardsmen walked by us to receive a carriage. The horses looked overworked and uncared for, but one black one could have been fine, and could be once again. The guardsmen looked tired, as if they had been on duty all night.

Out of the carriage stepped a citizen in a white silk cravat, a loose gray jacket with wide lapels, yellow leather pantaloons, and a round hat trimmed with a feather. He had a lackey behind him who carried a bulging leather satchel. The lackey ordered two of the guards to fetch boxes out of the carriage. The guards walked by us, carrying boxes filled with papers into the Town Hall. One of the guards returned to the court, went over to a barrel in the corner, took its lid off, and poured water from a dipper into his mouth. It looked like an act reserved for the gods.

My own thirst now became unbearable. All I wanted was a cup of that barrel water. I asked one of our own guards, a big man with a fixed bayonet who stood just to my right, if he could please ask one of the others to bring the prisoners a dipper full of water. He did not look at me.

"I'm very thirsty," I added. My voice was husky from lack of use. He continued looking straight ahead. "You're a very good soldier and will be promoted soon. I know that. But it would not hurt your chances if you asked one of those men to get us a drink of water from that barrel. It will show the sympathy and the reason of the new order if you were to offer a pregnant woman and other prisoners some water. You must agree that one of the worst things about the old regime was its unjust treatment of prisoners. The Bastille was chosen as the site to start the Revolution for precisely that reason."

He looked at me. "If you talk, you will become more thirsty."

"Monsieur, do you have a lover?"

"I will not engage in conversation with you."

"I just wondered if you had a lover."

He stared straight ahead. He was right; it was none of my business.

"I just wondered if you had a lover, because if you did, you would know what it is like to do things for someone to make them happy."

Someone called out from the building to send the prisoners in, and my guard led our pathetic band, with me first, hands tied, a big guard before and after us. We walked invisible through the high halls of the old palace. Well-dressed citizens mixed with National Guardsmen, even some *fédérés*, in dress uniform. They all walked briskly by us, intent on some bureaucratic task. I glimpsed through a half-open door a tapestry somehow left from the days of the bishops, angels carrying a cross down the sky to a hill strewn with soldiers. We were taken into a large room with cherubs painted on the ceiling, their puffy cheeks emerging out of rosy clouds. The guard who had refused me the water told us to sit on a bench. An older man in a powdered wig, whom I vaguely recognized, and a younger man, the one with the gray wide-lapeled coat and the yellow pantaloons, sat in the middle of a long table, facing us. The magistrate and the young lawyer, I assumed. The fashionable lawyer's lackey sat next to him and shuffled through papers and spoke softly to his superior.

The magistrate told my guard to untie all our hands. The sudden freedom was delicious. I rubbed my arms and then my hands. The skin of my wrists was raw where the rope had chafed against them.

The younger man stated the charges, and after a few words from the prisoners, and asking for witnesses, of which so far there were none, the older man gave the verdict. Occasionally he dismissed the charges, almost at random, it seemed to me. Most of my fellows were sent back to the Beauvoir Tower, with terms of three months to a year. We were all weak from hunger and looked wretched, I am sure.

The young lawyer called, "Madame Williams, born M. A. Vallon," and I stood up, more than ever feeling the dryness of my throat. He started listing my crimes, and the older man looked up from his list, regarding me, as if trying to place me.

"I knew a Dr. Jean-Paul Vallon," he interrupted. "He was a credit to this city."

"That would be my father, Monsieur," I said.

"Then this is a personal tragedy to me," he said.

"May I continue?" the man with the yellow pantaloons said.

"I knew a little girl who sometimes would accompany her father on his rounds."

"That would have been me, Monsieur."

"Your father would not have betrayed his nation."

"No, his nation betrayed him. He was killed in a grain riot, while attending one of the rioters who was hurt."

"Enough," said the lawyer in the yellow pantaloons. "These are her charges . . ." And besides consorting with counterrevolutionaries, helping a foreign spy flee the city, and arranging a prisoner's escape, there were a few others of which I was unaware.

"You are accused, Madame Williams, of being a traitor," the magistrate said. "What more disgrace could a family have?"

"I submit to you, Monsieur, that these charges are all hearsay and slander. My husband is an Englishman, but he was a member of the Friends of the Constitution club, the intimate friend of Captain Michel Beaupuy, who would speak for him except that the captain is now defending his nation on the Austrian frontier. My husband is also the friend of Citizen Brissot, and is at this time meeting with that powerful member of the Assembly, who was not himself afraid to speak up against the excesses of the September massacres, and perhaps that is why I am having a trial now, and not a summary execcution by Parisian sans-culottes. The prisoner who escaped is my brother-in-law, Monsieur, and is no counterrevolutionary, but merely acted out of loyalty to an aged servant who was being mercilessly beaten by recalcitrant *fédérés* for their own amusement. Whoever freed him only freed him from injustice."

"She just confessed, Citizen," Yellow Pantaloons said to the magistrate. "This trial has gone on long enough. There are others—"

"Let us hear all the evidence," the magistrate said.

"After her confession, there is no need—"

"She did not confess. Oblige me."

"Very well," Yellow Pantaloons said. "We have a witness."

And the shop owner, a little man who had been sitting at the back of the room, was brought forward and asked about the rope and to produce the bill of sale, which he did.

"What have you to say, Madame," said the magistrate, "to the serious charge of the rope used in the escape of Paul Vincent, and of the testimony of the clerk?"

"That if you check my room at chez Vincent, you will find that rope the clerk sold to me. It will not have been used."

The lackey looked up at this.

"The evidence against me is circumstantial. Find that rope, and you will know I am innocent," I said. "What *woman* of sound mind would attempt to help a prisoner escape, especially when she is carrying a child? It is absurd."

"More absurd things have been done, by fanatical counterrevolutionaries," the young lawyer said.

"I am no fanatic. In fact, I have very little feeling about politics. I believe in the Declaration of the Rights of Man, as you do, but I am just a woman and want to raise my child in a world where people are not indiscriminately arrested. That is one of the ideals of the Revolution, that no one should be arrested and sentenced without due process of law, is it not? No one can be sentenced on merely the word of another?

"My father raised me to feel that politics and law are a man's concern; therefore I ask you, Monsieur Magistrate, to relieve me of this weary thinking and speaking, for I am very thirsty and hungry and would like to sit down, and please to consider my assertion that the rope the clerk speaks of is still in my room and has never been used."

"Bring her a cup of water," the magistrate said to my guard. Then to me, "And what were you going to do with this length of rope?"

"I was going to use it in training horses. Anyone who knows my family in Blois knows that I am a horsewoman. I used to hunt with my father, and I was going to help train horses for Monsieur Vincent."

"In your state?"

"They are yearlings and only ready for ground training."

"You may sit down." I told him the location of my room, and he sent two guardsmen to chez Vincent.

"Meanwhile, you are a prisoner of the state," the young man said. "If no rope is found, or if one is found that is of a different description than the one the clerk reports having sold you, I will personally see that you will be sent to Orléans for further trial or locked in the dungeons of the Beauvoir Tower."

The guard I had spoken to earlier entered with a wooden cup and handed it to me. I looked at him and thanked him, and his eyes were flat.

"If you please, Monsieur Magistrate," I said. "I cannot drink this unless my fellow prisoners, who are just as thirsty as I, may also be granted the same boon. The water in the Beauvoir Tower is not—"

"Yes, yes. Guard," the magistrate said, "show mercy and bring them all water."

"Thank you, Monsieur," I said, and my guard departed.

The drink was paradise. First, I took a sip and felt my raw mouth moisten and my throat open. I wanted to savor this cup. Then I took a deeper drink and let it stay on my tongue and felt it deliciously cool against my teeth and the roof of my mouth. I closed my eyes, to block out the room and taste the water.

When I sat down, I found my knees were trembling. Now they were still trembling, and my legs were stiff, as if all my fear and effort to talk well had gone into my legs. I wished for William and his gentle, intelligent hands. I could think of him now, because I felt it was going to be all right.

An hour later, I had listened to the young lawyer and the magistrate mete out justice in three more cases. One was sent on to Orléans;

one was sent back to the Beauvoir Tower, and one was dismissed. It almost seemed a pattern.

When the two guards returned, one carrying the rope, and testified, with some disappointment it seemed to me, that it had tallied with the measurement of the clerk and appeared unused, I suddenly felt lightheaded. The magistrate told me to stand. I felt my knees could give way any second, and felt the reassurance of the bench behind my ankles.

"The State chooses to be merciful in the case of one Madame Williams and to dismiss your charges, though with a stern warning to be extremely circumspect with those with whom you consort, young woman."

"I give you my word, Monsieur."

"You are free to go." In my filthy dress, I curtsied as befitting a magistrate. I turned to leave, then paused. "May I ask, Monsieur Magistrate, how is your gout? It was for that, I remember now, my father called on you. He often told you our hunting stories."

"My God, you're the girl who shot the boar."

I curtsied again, and Yellow Pantaloons threw up his arms, and I left the room of the cherubic clouds.

I couldn't believe my freedom. I went again down the busy halls, now with no escort, and again no one noticed me. The door to the tapestry room was now closed. I stepped past sentries at the door, and outside the sun slanted down through spent rain clouds and danced around on the puddles in the square. Everyone who is not in prison, I thought, ought to be happy simply because they are not in prison. This thought seemed profound and logical to me at the time, but I daresay no one will understand it unless they have had my experience. People will continue to be unhappy when they can actually walk where they want and drink water when they want.

I had a new problem, though. Where to go? I only had one answer, and in spite of what I was afraid would be my mother's reaction to my pregnancy and to her favorite daughter's leaving and to my arrest, I wanted to see her. And I wanted to see Angelique and Claudette. And La Rouge was home, too—La Rouge, who always understood. So I walked up the long hill.

A TRIPLE DISGRACE

My looks did not inspire confidence. Claudette, who answered the door, immediately thanked Mary and Joseph that I had indeed arrived there, then really looked at me and said, "My God," before quietly ushering me up the stairs, where—let this be said with no exaggeration and with utter seriousness in my chronicle of these years—I took the most blissful bath of my life. Claudette scented it with lavender, and the steam enveloped me, and the Beauvoir Tower I scrubbed forever off me.

I dressed in a plain chemise gown and cotton kerchief, while Claudette prepared the others for my presence. I descended in time for supper. Angelique embraced me and cried about Marguerite. Maman, whom I had never told of my pregnancy because I was waiting for the right time, now took in the sight of me. I kissed her and said, "I am going to follow Marguerite to England and marry Monsieur William. It is all arranged. Do not worry."

She shook her head. "There is a lot to worry about, Marie-Ann," she said. "Don't be naïve. But for now, I am glad they let you out of—" and she couldn't say the word. I kissed her again and thought that her mother's heart had got the better of her. I also felt terribly sorry for her about Marguerite, whom I knew she dearly loved.

Angelique had a hundred questions for me during dinner, about the Vincents and about Monsieur William. Monsieur Vergez looked sullen over his stuffed bream and said nothing, not even *bonjour*, to me. He murmured some words to Maman. Then she said quietly, "I had that letter from Marguerite, and it broke my heart. I still don't know why they had to go. Since Paul was innocent—"

"That didn't matter, Maman," I said.

"Then Madame Tristant came to visit her," Monsieur Vergez added. I didn't see the connection. "*And* her daughter."

"Isabelle, my friend from convent school?" I said.

"Yes," Maman said. "Isabelle, a well-brought-up girl. As tractable as can be, and very pretty. Never concerns herself with politics. Has suitors who are both republicans and royalists. What's it to her? As long as they are from good families. Well, Madame Tristant is one of those women who always knows everything. She informed me over coffee and apple tart that Paul had been arrested. Can you imagine? I couldn't say a thing. She also said that rumor had it that you were regularly seeing an Englishman, who now had been implicated in a counterrevolutionary plot, something about Britain's interest in gathering an émigré army on her shores. Then she said the Committee of Surveillance had learned of his spying, and the man had to flee. Think of it! All in a few minutes, as I myself put sugar in my coffee and complimented Isabelle on her matching sash and bandeau.

"I couldn't eat a bite of my own tart, but they devoured theirs. I told them she must be mistaken, her sources must have meant *another* Monsieur Vincent, and that I had warned you about the Englishman and that you had taken my advice. That from your short acquaintance with the man, you had gleaned the true lesson that one can never trust foreigners. Madame Tristant confirmed that that is indeed an important lesson, and we went on to discuss how the elaborately curled hairstyles of our youth are unfashionable now and how hard it is to keep up, but the damage had been done."

"I am sorry it was all so distressing for you, Maman," I said, "but you must know that *both* Paul and Monsieur William are no counterrevolutionaries. As for Monsieur William, he is rather the contrary, which I thought was your complaint against him. I am a bit confused."

"To be counterrevolutionary now is to be against the law," she said, "and, as Bernard is a lawyer of some recognition in this city, it is important that, whatever the new laws are, we follow them with the respect due from peaceable citizens."

"Then you ignore your past convictions, and those of my father, for the sake of expediency?"

Monsieur Vergez placed his glass a little too vehemently on the table, and some drops spilled out, which his servant André wiped clean before his master even glanced at his presence.

"I think it is a time of rejoicing," Angelique said. "Annette is here, and she is safe. And Paul is not in prison, and—well, I'm glad their family escaped—at least, I hope they did. We should all give thanks. Annette's by my side. At least one of my sisters is." And she started to sniff again.

"I give thanks for this lovely dinner," I said. "It is heaven."

I couldn't believe that in one day I had gone from a worm-filled biscuit in the Beauvoir Tower to fresh asparagus and stuffed bream. I was used to eating so little, though, that I could not finish my portion.

Then over the poached pears Maman said, "Madame Tristant came again the next day, and I admit that, though it was my visiting hour, I was not keen on receiving her. This time she came without her sweet daughter, which I took as not a good sign. By now I had received Marguerite's letter, which, as I said, was a great blow. You were included in the letter as escaping with them. Madame Tristant proceeded, after she had finished the Tours pastry, a recipe that your little Claudette brought with her, to say wasn't it a great shame that my first daughter had now fled from Blois and my second daughter had been arrested.

"I nearly collapsed this time, but I held on to the arm of my chair and didn't give Madame Tristant any pleasure that she had shocked me. I said, 'Things like that happen in these unfortunate times. We must trust in Providence.' Madame Tristant had the temerity to correct me: 'In the Supreme Being,' she said. It's all from knowing that Englishman, I say to you now, Marie-Ann. Bernard and I knew it from the start, but you didn't listen. Now my sweet Marguerite is gone. And my grandchildren. And Madame Tristant said that you were taken to the Beauvoir. That's where the worst people go. My own daughter, whom I held next to my breast as a child. It's unimaginable."

"I was hoping someone would visit me," I said. "I don't even know how long I was there."

"I wanted to go, Annette," Angelique said, "but I couldn't go alone—"

"I wouldn't let any of them go," Monsieur Vergez finally spoke to me. "It's a triple disgrace. A daughter fled. Another one arrested."

He held up a finger with each disgrace. He kept the two poised above his wineglass. I was waiting for the third. "Now I am about to be elected to the Trade Commission of this city," he said. "One must be *elected* now by city officials, not appointed. Do you know what that means? What they will say? 'He married into a family of counter-revolutionaries,' they'll say, and"—he held up the third finger now for his *coup de grâce*—"of women of low morals. 'The decadency of the old upper bourgeoisie,' they'll say, and they'll be right."

"But no one knows—," I started.

"Madame Tristant heard *that* from Françoise, Marguerite's maid-servant," he said. "Your mother couldn't sleep that night. Her own unmarried daughter with child, and from a man accused of being a spy. I know responsible citizens on the Committee of Surveillance. There *are* those who are plotting to destroy us and give us over to the great empires of England or Austria. Don't be so naïve. But most of all"—and he slammed his fist on the table as the bowls of pears and their attendant spoons hopped up and down—"don't disgrace my table again by striding in here as if you have done nothing wrong and by eating my food, when a woman of any decency left in her would be living in shame and confinement. But you have no decency. I give you two days—that's ample time—to gather your things, and I'll pay for the family carriage to take you to chez Dubourg in Orléans—your mother has already written to them. That is more than generous of me. Another man might throw you out—"

"I'm going too, then, Monsieur Vergez," said Angelique, and threw her embroidered napkin on her bowl. "I'm going, Maman, if Annette has to go. It's not right. *She's* our family—"

"This is chez Vergez now," her stepfather calmly reminded her. "Your sister knows that women like her are usually sent away, so as not to disgrace the family. Usually to a convent, where they never see the world again. Well, convents are now state property, so *that's* a little harder to do. And chez Dubourg is cheaper. So, *Madame Williams*—" He said the term so disparagingly, the term that was so sacred to me, that I stood up and ran out of the room. This was my homecoming from the Beauvoir Tower.

Maman came running after me and caught me below the stairs. I jerked away from her hand on my arm.

"You must see, Marie-Ann—"

"I see," I said.

"Bernard said it poorly, but he is only—"

"Let me go," I said.

"It's not that simple, Annette. You can't just go. You'll be paying for this all your life."

"Yes, paying through love for a child from a man I love."

"No, paying and paying for a mistake. I know he may never return. Probably will not. Our nations are close to war. You'll then have a child of the enemy."

I pulled free and started up the stairs.

"Annette," Maman said. "I understand. I do."

"How can you?"

"Like many others, I've been guilty of my own small weaknesses in my youth. Not having a child as you are, but weaknesses, nonetheless. So I understand. But I was saved because of my discretion. Just be discreet, my dear. The Dubourgs can help you find a place for your child."

"Is that what you wrote them? This child is mine for all my life, Maman, as you said. You are guilty of weakness again, but of a different sort."

And I went up the stairs to my old room and lay on my bed and listened to the rain. It was falling again—a fine autumn rain over the vineyards of chez Vincent, over the gray river and over the Channel and over England. I missed my older sister.

And the rain was falling over the streets of Paris. How would William find me now?

After Monsieur Vergez had excoriated me so, I *wanted* to leave in two days, or earlier. I wanted not to talk with or even to see Vergez or Maman. In fact, I saw Maman not at all until she embraced me and wished me well on my parting; perhaps in those two days she had avoided me as much as I had her. We both murmured respectful platitudes, and it was best to leave without anger or rancor. I myself wondered how she could not have the desire to see her grandchild as soon as it was born. Perhaps she did, and it was one of the many sacrifices she thought it prudent to practice. I saw Vergez only once: he was directing several men how to move Papa's old desk out of the library and into a wagon. They were working well and ignoring him.

I asked Jean to take La Rouge and Le Bleu to the château de Beauregard. I didn't trust Monsieur Vergez with their keeping. He could sell them to the army. And the count liked the horses and would ride them. That night—*our* last night, for Angelique was indeed accompanying me—we supped in my room. Then, late, when I was sure Maman and Vergez had gone to bed, I took a lantern and went to see my old friend. As soon as I opened the big door and entered the stable, I heard her soft whinny. She knew it was I.

I stroked her soft mane and told her that I would be back. Then, either I would take her with me to England with Monsieur William, or, with the use of my father's bequest, I would purchase a small cottage across the river in Vienne. It would have wisteria growing along it, like the one William and I had seen near Vendôme. There, La Rouge would not have a nice stable like this one, and she'd have to share a barn with chickens and goats, but we would be together. My child would learn to sit on a horse as soon as she could sit at table, and once again Rouge and I would ride the paths through the woods.

Then I asked her if she remembered herself giving birth. I recalled to her the story as I brushed her by lantern light: In the middle of a cold night in early spring I could not sleep because I knew you were close to labor, I said. I went out to the stable, and when I entered your stall, the water was two inches deep. All your straw was wet. I led you to a dry stall and put more dry straw around you, but it did not seem to help your nervousness.

I didn't want to go wake Jean, for, since your water had broken, I didn't want to leave you alone, I said. You kept lying down and standing up, lying down and standing up. You had never seen another horse give birth, and you did not know what was causing you this pain. So I had you lie down with your head in my lap, and I stroked your neck and talked to you, as I am talking to you now. Do you remember that, I said.

Finally, it started to come out. First, the small nose, the size of a teacup, then the long neck, then the whole body came slithering out, and water gushing with it. Some of the sac was still clinging to its face and I pulled it off, so your foal could breathe.

You did not know what this strange thing was, I said, except that it had been causing you great pain. It was dark and wet and trying to stand. You backed away and snorted at it and stamped your hooves on the floor, as if you were confronting a snake, or an angry dog. The poor little one was still trying to rise, and would fall when you snorted at it. I went to you and led you slowly, talking to you all the way, over to the dark wet thing. You sniffed it and still backed away, snorting and stamping. Then I led you again, and you sniffed again, and this time something started to take over. You licked once, then twice, then several times the strange new body in your stall. I held the foal on its weak legs and led it to your teats. I caressed a teat so the milk would flow and placed it into the foal's soft mouth.

You proved a fine mother, Rouge, and I the horses' midwife of chez Vallon. Even the count called me to the château de Beauregard, and we rode through the rain to help with one of his mares. Now it is my turn, I said. I rubbed her forehead, and she snorted softly. The lantern light flickered over her russet flanks. Her intelligent eyes stared into mine.

Jean drove us to Orléans, and before he started his return trip, I asked him to make friends with André, Monsieur Vergez's servant who usually fetched the mail, and offer to help him with that chore, so that if there were any letters forwarded from chez Vincent to us, Jean could intercept them and send them on to Orléans. I was greatly worried about William having no address for me. I offered to pay Jean in advance for this favor, and he refused and said he would do it for the sake of my father, whom he thought was on Marguerite's and my side.

The Dubourgs were happy to see us again. They were solicitous and accepting of me, and Madame Dubourg, whom I had often thought of as a bit haughty, said I had to understand my mother's position in Blois, but she, Madame Dubourg, could give me all the attention my own mother, because of protocol, could not. They were still best friends, although there were now political differences between them. The Dubourgs remained fierce royalists.

Madame Dubourg, who had no children of her own, was now excited at the prospect of having a baby in the house. It was as if she were the grandmother. Angelique, Claudette, and I took walks in the town, and even along the quai where William and I had walked, until Madame Dubourg found out I was promenading in my increasingly visible state, and admonished me only to stroll about the rooms of chez Dubourg, which I did, arm in arm with my sister in our satin slippers, and we daily awaited the arrival of the mail, and daily were disappointed.

Until this missive from England, forwarded by Jean:

My Dear Sister—

I pray to your Lucette and to my Bernadette that the National Guard did not hold you because they had no evidence—you told me about the rope. Because of your courage and your sacrifice, we are ensconced now safely in England. Paul has friends that he has found among the émigrés, who have been kind to us and invited us for dinner. It is rather sad, though. They seem to be pretending that they are still in France, and the France of former times. Paul does not want to suffer in that illusion and has been learning

*English rapidly and meeting with wine merchants here, who daily
do business with Bordeaux and need a Frenchman to help with their
negotiations.*

*But can you believe it? I have met Sylvie Varache! She has
English roses in her garden and Marie is so glad she has Claire to
play with again. They will have a tutor who knows both French and
English. Gérard asks daily when you're coming, and I start to cry
every time he does. Now you know our address, here in the busy port
of Southampton, so tell us when you will arrive. Will Monsieur
William be accompanying you? Has he cleared his name? I'm supposing you're not wanting to travel now and will wait until after the
baby is born. How exciting for Marie and Gérard to have a little
cousin. Just don't wait too long for them to see her. How is sweet
Angelique? Everyone should join us now, except poor Maman, stuck
with old Vergez.*

*I will not bore you with the vicissitudes of our flight to the coast,
but suffice it to say that it was a miracle: not once were we stopped.
The National Guard of Blois seemed content with you. Paul found
passage for us in Saint-Valéry—there were a few other émigrés on
our boat, and Gérard was thrilled with the wind and the spray of the
Channel, and I was quite ill, both with the sea and with the thought
of what had become of you—with the tragic irony that the person
to whom we owed our safe departure was herself unable to depart.
Annette, we owe you everything.*

*Now Paul is saying that, when he gets his position secure with
the British Bordeaux company, we'll get an English cottage, with
our own roses. I, though, am waiting for the French government to
change again and don't want to put down roots here. The English
papers, however, say the King is going to trial. Everyone here thinks
France is a most barbarous land now, taken over by criminals. They
may be right, but it's still the most beautiful land on earth. I don't
think I shall ever learn the harsh language of the British, but they
are polite to us. They have the reserved nature of your Monsieur
William, with, as far as I can see, none of his passion or sensibility.
He is unique, I'm sure, even among his own people. I must go and
fetch Marie now from the hotel where the Varaches are living, for
now. Marie has drawn a beautiful picture of the Loire and of you*

standing on a cliff above it, looking down at the river. Your hair is down and the wind is blowing it back. She showed it to me and it made me cry. Gérard misses his good friend so, as do I,

your loving and most grateful sister, Marguerite.

When I wrote back, I didn't mention my imprisonment. I said Monsieur Vergez had been a bit testy, so Angelique, Claudette, and I were staying for now with the Dubourgs. That was a very comfortable arrangement, I said. I congratulated Marie on her paintings and told Gérard not to forget to make Christmas cookies for me. I had to stop writing at that point, for I suddenly started to cry. When I went back to the letter, I told Paul that I was sure he would make a fine British businessman. It was so easy to be cheery about everything in a letter. I missed them so. I wrote that too, as my last sentence. I added their address in Southampton, and it felt strange to be writing to England.

In late November, when we had been in Orléans for three weeks and I was over eight months pregnant, Jean brought another letter to me. He said it had taken him a while to get Vergez's servant to warm to him and to entrust Jean with picking up the mail regularly. Jean was afraid we might have missed some letters. This one was, itself, about a week old:

My Dearest Friend—

With the disorganized state of affairs in France, did my letters not get through to thee? Though I have waited impatiently for the post each day, I have received no word. I have sent some half a dozen letters, since the first day I arrived here, but my chances seem to be no better than if I had placed them in a bottle upon the high seas. Is the Committee of Surveillance holding them? Do they check every letter to Blois? Therefore I grow increasingly anxious about you and the baby, as well as impatient as to when I can procure the necessary papers to proceed safely back to you. So I have decided to return to Blois tomorrow, with or without papers.

I must write, then, as if you will receive this letter: Every interesting hour I spend in the company of the Girondins, I am aware, is less compelling because I cannot share it with my dear Companion. I long constantly to be telling you this thing and that thing, about what I see and hear. Your dislike for politics would be mitigated by the sheer drama of the moment. Citizen Brissot told the Jacobins again that they must take the blame for the September massacres. He even accused them of turning the revolutionary government into their own dictatorship. And in return they call Brissot unpatriotic. The script of the National Assembly could have been written by Sophocles. Brissot has no lack of courage or conviction, but his speeches have not hastened the process of obtaining my new papers—my only real reason for being here—for no one knows whether they should do him a favor or not. Power shifts every day.

Everything now in Paris is either the conflict between the Girondins and the Jacobins—a conflict that will decide the fate of the Revolution—or the coming trial of the King. I myself have written in support of Brissot and his uncompromising patriotism and am working with the journalist Antoine Gorsas, who has become disillusioned with the Jacobins and is writing for Brissot's paper. These Girondins are the most dedicated and articulate men I have ever met. Their tragedy is that the world cannot keep up with their ideals. I wrote last night:

—ALL CANNOT BE: THE PROMISE IS TOO FAIR
FOR CREATURES DOOMED TO BREATHE TERRESTRIAL AIR.

I longed for your company at their dinners at the Reunion Club with Brissot, Roland, Vergniaud, and the novelist Louvet, who stood up before the Assembly and denounced Robespierre, the master of the Jacobins' slander, trickery, and vying for power. You, who see through all hypocrisy and pretense, would have appreciated the sincerity of these Girondins. The future of perhaps all of Europe now hangs on what will happen here in the next months. Meanwhile, my Beloved is about to bring into this glorious and frightening world a new soul, straight from the lap of heaven. I pray that I, in some small way, may make the world a better place for her arrival, that you are indeed safe and well, and that our love triumphs with ease *over the petty powers that work to separate us. I will be at chez Vincent in several days—*

adieu most tenderly thy dearest Friend, William.

I wrote to William immediately in Paris—his address was in care of the journalist Gorsas—just in case he had been held up and didn't leave for several days. I told him how glad I was that he had arrived safely in Paris and to come to Orléans, not all the way to Blois, but I knew my letter would go east as he went west. I added a hasty message on the Vincents' flight and how it had been caused by Paul's protection of Pierre, but said nothing of my own imprisonment. I said how Monsieur Vergez must have kept or destroyed any of William's letters that found their way to his address—for the name Vallon in Blois still meant chez Vallon, the house he occupied. But I said how nice it was to be here, now, in Orléans with the Dubourgs, to walk again where he and I had walked along the quai, and where he had written beautiful verses about the river. I said I was in the city where we had fallen in love, that Orléans would always be special in my mind because of that. If he were here, I added, he could feel the baby kick and see my ignominious progress on the pink cap.

But when I put the pen down, I was overtaken with worry that William would make the trip without papers and be arrested along the way, or be picked up by the Committee of Surveillance if he called at chez Vincent or was recognized in Blois. He knew many people there from the old Friends of the Constitution club. What if he had asked one of them and been denounced as a spy or for associating with counterrevolutionaries? Poor William did not know what had become of the reputation of Paul Vincent.

I hoped his work for the Girondins was too exciting for him to leave, but I knew William's resolution—once he decided to do something, whether it were to walk from the Channel across the Alps to Lake Como and back, or to write a long poem that would take him a year to complete, or to come to France by himself in the midst of revolution and against the wishes of his family, nothing would stop him.

I had no appetite and could only drink Claudette's tisane and eat some boiled potatoes. I wanted my child to have a father who was not in prison—and who was alive. I had no desire to walk about the room anymore. The letter that I had been waiting so long for had left my mind as agitated as the November wind that shook the shutters now, so the Dubourgs' servants had to close them all tight against the first real winter storm. William could be out in it, I thought, or, if we are unlucky, languishing in the cold dampness of the Beauvoir.

The Dubourgs, Claudette, and Angelique all worried about me. They said, This is not the time for you to distress yourself over something you can do nothing about. Your baby needs you to be calm, to rest. So I drank the tea and read *Héloïse* again, to be amused, but it did not amuse me. It made me think about distressed lovers.

A single candle stretched its flame across my page. Writing was the only thing that calmed the thoughts that unflaggingly paced through my mind. This time, however, I was not recording or reflecting in my diary, but starting a prose version of my favorite poem, the medieval epic *The Romance of the Rose*. I thought more people would read it now if it were in prose. But I suppose I really did it for myself.

I went from the writing table to my bed, blew out the candle, closed the bed curtains, and fell asleep as I listened to the wind in the shutters. In my dream Claudette knocked softly on the door and opened it, a candle in her hand illuminating her happy face. "Madame," she said. "He is here. *Monsieur la Valeur des Mots*." I had made a joke about his name once when I had translated its meaning to her, "the worth of words," but I had never actually called him that. Now, in the dream, it was his regular name. "*Monsieur les Mots* is outside in the rain," Claudette said. There was a panic in the dream about him being stuck outside. I went to the window and opened the shutters. I thought I could feel the cold rain blowing into my face. William stood below me, and he was singing. In my dream I recognized the melody of the Annachie Gordon song, about the sailor who came back too late and his lady had died. Then I saw a big black dog in the rain. It was behind William, coming out of some alley. I didn't like the look of the dog. I called to William, but he didn't hear me. He just lifted up his voice in the rain and finished his song. The dog crouched right behind him, as if ready to pounce.

Then my eyes opened suddenly. Thunder shook the shutters. In my mind I still heard William singing. I almost went to the window and looked out.

That afternoon this letter came, forwarded by Jean:

My Dearest Friend:

I walked to chez Vincent in search of thee and found a bevy of National Guard. I went to chez Vergez, hid in the stable, and noticed La Rouge was not there. I knew something had gone dreadfully wrong. I will leave this note in the post for chez Vergez and hope, somehow, it will find you. I am leaving for Paris now. I pray to your Lucette and to the Almighty Protector that you and the baby are safe.

I will find you, even if it takes years.

Adieu most tenderly thy dearest Friend,
William.

Perhaps he's walking through Orléans right now, I thought. I madly wanted to run out to the rue de Bourgogne. Perhaps he would pass along that old Roman road, going east. I convinced Claudette it was logical, and we stood there for an hour in the rain, carts splashing mud on our skirts and coats, Claudette holding an umbrella and I scouting every tall pedestrian. "It *is* possible," I said. "What if he came through Orléans, right near my door, and we both of us didn't even know?"

"What if he went through Chartres, Madame? I heard Mademoiselle Angelique say *that* is the more logical route, the one you yourself said he took when he left Vendôme. Lovers," Claudette said, "are not the most logical people."

"I am always logical," I said.

Claudette shrugged, made a sound like *poof* as she exhaled, and continued, as I scanned the gray street. People stared at us as they passed. "When I had to leave Benoît," she said, "to come here, he was not logical. He said he would leave the count's service and get a position in Orléans. That might not be so easy, I told him, and what about when we return, after Madame Annette's baby is born, I said, and you, Benoît, are still stuck in Orléans, polishing a harness in some dim barn by a noisy street. Then, working in the count's service, in his grand château with fresh game to eat, will sound very desirable to you, Monsieur Benoît the Groom of the château de Beauregard. That is what I told him, so he stayed with the count."

"Your story is not at all like my situation, Claudette."

"It is the same principle," she said. "A woman, with a belly as big as a house, will stand in the rain, when it is not logical or good for the baby. Monsieur William—*Monsieur les Mots*, as you called him once—"

"What did you say?"

"You made a joke once about his name and called him—"

"Yes, but what made you think of that?"

"I was only trying to make a joke, to enliven our dull hour, waiting on this street for no purpose."

"Claudette, have you seen a black dog?"

"Madame?"

"A big, black dog in the rain."

"I think we should go in, Madame."

"It was in a dream, Claudette. A dream I had last night about Monsieur William, and you called him that funny name in my dream also."

"I do not know about the name, Madame," she said, "but I do know—it is just an old superstition—but where I am from in the country, a big black dog in a dream is not a good sign. I think we should go in. Have some soup. Put your feet up on the settee. Work on your long story. Monsieur William, I was going to say, he can take care of himself. He is a resourceful Englishman. Rain does not bother him. Walking long distances is nothing to him. And he loves you. He will find a way, as he said in the letter."

"Even if it takes years," I added, and we left the old road in the rain on which Joan had once entered in triumph.

Two weeks later I received another letter forwarded from Jean.

My Dearest Friend,

I just received your dear letter from Orléans! I rejoice that you are safe and well.

On my return from Blois, Citizen Brissot succeeded in obtaining my new papers and a travel pass for me. The pass, however, is only good for two weeks. Brissot added that, since the antiforeign sentiment continues to be strong with the constant threat from the Austrians, if I cared for my safety I should not wait to depart. It is not my safety, right now, for which I primarily care.

One Englishman, however, has just immigrated here because of the tyranny of the British government. I would have liked, my darling, for you to have met last night the writer Tom Paine. I thought, Annette would like this fellow; she could see that I am not the only Francophile in England. But Brissot said to me that it may not be safe for Monsieur Paine to stay here, either. He is a hero today, he said, but—and he shrugged.

In any case, I am almost penniless and cannot afford to stay any longer. It wrenches my heart to leave at this, of all times! I gave you my word, and now I must be leaving on the morrow. Forgive me. I will keep to our original plan: somehow to procure support from my uncle—a fierce endeavor sprung from Necessity but calling upon Sacrifice to carry it out—, publish a book of poems—I am almost finished with the long one which I have shared with you throughout my sojourn—and, thereby, as soon as is humanly possible, gain the means by which I may either return to thee or a situation which will allow me to send for thee.

The longings of absence are intolerable, but they are mitigated when I think toward the bliss of our reunion. By then I will have so many things to say to you, from each hour of each day, that the burden of those thousands of words in my memory will quite overwhelm my mind and I will have nothing at all to say, only embraces to give you. And so you see, sweet love, how dearly I should wish to be alone with you again, and that, forsooth, you may have the pleasure of being right after all: revolutions, it turns out, no longer hold the position of my highest esteem in life because they do not partake of the higher and more lasting values: they come and go;

but love remains. Revolutions can call us to Duty, but never to love, and that, Darling, will always be their failure. I leave in sorrow, but dream of seeing my Beloved again in joy, when the light from the eyes of our child will exceed and extinguish any darkness we will have known from our separation. Then, let us not be parted again!

Adieu most tenderly thy dearest Friend, William.

So that look I had of him in Vendôme, beside the carriage, standing alone in the middle of the square, would be the last look I would have for a long time.

My labor started late that afternoon. The letter was on the bedside table, and Claudette read it to me from time to time when I was in a fit state to listen. There were certain passages that I liked hearing again and again. The baby was born the next morning, on the fifteenth of December, 1792. With the Dubourgs present as godparents, she was baptized Anne Caroline Wordsworth, though the curate couldn't understand the strange foreign name and wrote it *Woodswodsth*. I didn't catch this mistake until I read the birth certificate later, and then I couldn't do anything about it.

BOOK IV

1793–1802

My Dearest Friend,

Are you well, and is our child in your arms?

My arrival in my native land was not a cause for rejoicing. I stood on the boat and gazed back to France. Everything I loved I was leaving. The coastline would not show itself for the driving mist.

I am on to London now, to speak with my stern uncle, who will not, I know, approve of you or of me, but I must move him to compassion. I have made it through the dangers of the Committee of Surveillance—my uncle cannot be as formidable.

I pray that I leave thee and our child in health.

I remain yours in exile, William.

I wanted to write to him immediately but had no address. William had posted the note as soon as he had landed in England.

All the news in the papers at that time was of the King's trial. People read, or had read to them, every detail reported of a trial the likes Europe had never seen. William's friends, the Girondins, at the end had voted against the verdict of death, but the rest of the Assembly had disagreed with them. The King's lawyer, the great Malesherbes, went without sleep preparing a brilliant last defense, portraying the King as a victim of calumny and circumstance. The King himself had wept when they asserted that he had shed French blood at the Tuileries. I know Papa had thought Louis rather a ninny, but one couldn't help but feel sorry for a man trying so desperately to keep a vestige of his dignity when he was treated so callously by those around him, sneering accusations at him, calling him Capet instead of Louis, the mob eating ices in the balcony as he stood on trial for his life. His lawyer was not allowed to sit down for fourteen hours and cried when he heard the verdict. I did not read the papers then and only heard from the Dubourgs about Louis's speech that cold January day on the scaffold, when he, in his new role as martyr, forgave everyone, and they didn't care because they were so drunk with glee at the prospect of a king's death right in front of them. His dangling head would solve everything. His head paraded on a pike would make the world a better place.

I preferred to look at my daughter in the light that fell through the gray day onto her face. I had never known anyone as beautiful as she. I was glad William was safe in England. The world had turned upside down. Who would rule France now? Citizen Robespierre? One of William's friends? General Dumouriez, who had won that victory in Valmy? No one seemed to care at this moment, for Louis's lonely head was the prize of the century. I felt for his family, locked in that cold tower now and unable to see even each other. I sang my happier version of the Annachie Gordon song to Caroline, who knew nothing of kings or the fall of kings, and I didn't let the fire in my grate go out that winter night.

Then I heard from William in London.

My dearest Friend,

We have heard here about the King, an outcome I knew was inevitable. I myself have been on trial, so to speak, before my uncle, and have not fared much better than your erstwhile king. In short, my guardian is not kindly disposed. It is so humiliating to be judged by him and to be in his miserly mercy. He does not see fit to give me or us a penny. My dear sister, who in spite of her disapproval of my actions, of her own gentle lecture to me, and of her scruples on the matter, is going to take up my cause and intercede for us. She can be very persuasive, arguing, as she always does, from a firm moral stance. This is a very courageous position for her to take, and I am deeply in her debt. Her name is Dorothy, and I am sure you will grow to respect and love her also.

Meanwhile, I have also been unsuccessful in publishing my book of poems and am actively engaged upon rewriting their many imperfections. I have consulted newspapers and feel I may be able to procure some means of livelihood there, so I may send for thee.

*But I would have done far better as a gentleman's tour guide, with
headquarters at a certain charming town on the Loire, had not the
world and its troubles interfered.*

*I write this in haste so it can go out with the morning post and you
can receive my London address. I long to hear from you. You and our
child, who is perhaps slumbering by your side as you read this, are
never out of my thoughts. Dear Annette, I love thee with a passion
that, were it known, would stun this meager world.*

Yours in exile, William.

In spite of William's vision of us, every time I laid Caroline down,
she awoke. I was dying to write to him. I sang her the Annachie
Gordon song a hundred times, it seemed. Then I laid her down and
hummed softly as I wrote:

*Monsieur William Wordsworth
Staple Inn No. 11
London
Angleterre*

My dearest Friend,
*The cap I started working on when I last saw you is almost fin-
ished now. You can place it on your daughter's head yourself, when
you return. I tell her that her father has put it to his own lips! It will
keep her very warm. When I look at her I see your eyes; when I read
your letters I hear your voice; you are in the room . . . Good-bye, my
friend . . . always love your little daughter and your Annette, who
kisses you a thousand times on the mouth, on the eyes . . . Good-bye,
I love you for life.*

There was more that I wrote, both in this letter and in others, but
the word *Angleterre* in the address, it turns out, alerted the Committee
of Surveillance, who impounded the letters on the spot. Once one did
get through, for William exclaimed how ecstatic he was to hear from
me and that the baby and I were well. But mostly I heard of how dis-

traught he was that I wasn't writing, or that something ill had befallen the baby or me.

I continued to write to William, whether he received my letters or not, and even though, after a few weeks when war was declared between our nations, I received none at all myself. I told him of the pink cap, how Caroline now wore it. I wrote of many other things, but it is sad for me to think of them, even now, as an old woman, for none of those words ever reached him.

LA BOUCHERIE

I remember sitting with Caroline many, many hours, late, early, a small fire in the grate, her crib set next to my bed, so often I was not sitting, but lying with her by my side, nursing her while I myself was half asleep, hearing dimly the rain outside, then feeling her going back to sleep, her tiny back rising and falling with her breath, and the bedcovers over us both, and when Claudette would come in with the tisane in the morning, she'd find us both asleep, side by side.

I was fascinated by Caroline's small but complete body—the miniature ears with whorls like seashells, the palms deeply lined like an ancient soul. I made up songs—what did she care about lyrics? I fancied that she knew my voice from the day she was born and that her eyes turned in my direction when I spoke.

When Caroline was about two months old, I had a letter from my mother that she was sending a nurse to help me out. Now, Claudette and I were quite capable of doing everything, but still, one more pair of hands could not hurt, and I was pleased with the gesture from Maman—it was a long trip on winter roads to Orléans, and she herself had still not come to visit her granddaughter, even though I had written her several times of Caroline's health and beauty.

When the nurse arrived, I was not impressed. She was tall and thin as a stick, had a stern demeanor, and said I should let Caroline cry instead of picking her up and soothing her. "How else will she learn that in this world you cannot always get whatever you want?" she said. I told her that was a heartless and impractical notion—the baby was telling me something in the only way she knew how, and it was my job to listen to her. I let the nurse help then only by cleaning and watching Caroline while she slept, so I would be free to leave the room and occasionally even walk, whether about the house or even on the street. It was still cold, but I longed sometimes to be out in the fresh air and to see the liveliness of the world outside our walls.

One clear morning in late February Claudette and I walked down the busy rue de Bourgogne all the way to the quai, and, even with the fewer boats and barges of the winter, after months of being inside it was like a tonic to hear the coarse shouting of the bargemen and the noise of the carts on the cobbles, the smell of the river and the cold sunlight glinting on it, and the men carrying loads on their shoulders for whom we stepped aside to make way. I knew when Caroline's nap would be most likely over, and we returned to chez Dubourg about that time. I was exhausted but happy—I hadn't walked that far in a long time.

I went to the room that Caroline and I shared, but she wasn't there. I asked one of Madame Dubourg's servants, and she said the nurse herself had taken Caroline, all bundled up, out for some fresh air. This seemed incongruous with the nurse's character; I myself had only taken Caroline out once, in an afternoon of sudden sunlight, and had come back in ten minutes.

But we waited. Ten minutes turned into an hour, and by then I was near panic. I went out with Claudette again, up and down rue de Bourgogne, asking anyone if they had seen a tall woman carrying a baby. No one had seen a thing. I thought when we returned to chez Dubourg, Caroline and the wayward nurse, whom I would now discharge, would be there. But they were not. A maid thought she had seen a carriage briefly pull up to the front of the house about the time the nurse had left with the baby, but she had taken no notice, as she had chores to do.

It was Angelique, with a sad and shocked expression, who approached me down the stairs with a letter dangling from her hand. "I was in your room, looking for any indication of where Nurse had gone, when I saw this, sticking out from under the pillow in Caroline's crib. Nurse must have left it there. Oh, Annette, I'm so sorry. I don't know what to say."

With my heart racing and my stomach tight, I stood at the foot of the stairs and read the letter.

Dear Annette,

Do not distress yourself about the safety of your child. Her little life is secure and well provided for. I knew I would never be able to convince you by logical argument, so Bernard and I took matters into our own hands. Forgive us. We are doing what is best for you and for the family.

You don't want your reputation forever tarnished in Blois, to which you will want to return, for it is your home, and you will want to marry well here, eventually, whether you admit it to yourself now or not. I myself, you see, do not have the confidence you have in your elusive Englishman—I have seen too much of men in my time and can guess the tenor of itinerant foreigners, especially these days.

Furthermore, a client of Bernard's, who was recently in Orléans and has an associate who does business with Monsieur Dubourg, heard from this associate's valet that an unmarried Vallon girl, living with the Dubourgs, had a newborn child. This client, just on that hearsay, has stopped his business with your stepfather, for, as the client said, it is not good to be seen to have dealings now with the old upper bourgeoisie if they have not conformed to the moral ways of the new order. The client, an ardent revolutionary, said Citizen Robespierre himself, who is called the Incorruptible, has even given speeches in the National Assembly that, revolution or no, if we can't improve the moral rectitude of our people we will not improve the nation. Lack of moral rectitude is a serious charge to lay against a man or his family.

Therefore, in your best interests as well as that of your family, we have chosen the traditional solution—that of putting the child out to nurse with a fine, caring mother whom you can visit regularly. When any hint of scandal is blown over, you even may be able to return the baby to your bosom and say, perhaps, that the husband was a patriot killed in the wars, but for now we believe it the most prudent approach to let the baby live with this kind woman, who will care for her as her own, for she recently lost the infant that God gave her. We also thought it best if you did not know—at least until the baby is secure in its new surroundings—of the address of this noble woman. But rest assured, we will let you know in a short time.

Pity your mother, too, for this difficult decision which she has made. It is a cruel world, and we all must pay the consequences of our actions as is our due. I have faith that you will see, sometime in the future, the prudence of this choice, and will, if you are unable to forgive, at least understand, why this course was taken. Have courage, my dear. We are born to suffer. Resignation is the wisest path.

With unreserved affection for you and for Angelique, who must witness this, your Maman.

I sat on the bottom stair and wept. As in a dream I felt Claudette on one side, Angelique on the other, lead me to a couch. I felt a hot cup of Claudette's tisane put in my hand. I smelled its mixture of mint and hibiscus. I took a sip and felt its warmth flow into a body I did not own. No one tried to say anything to me. I finally slept late that night and had a dream of children drowning in the river and of myself fighting to save them, and of little hands slipping away under the cold, dark water. When I awoke I was convinced that I would not let my baby be taken from me; somehow, as I had tried to do in the dream, I would fight to save her. But unlike the dream, I would succeed. I was living without my husband. I could not also live without my child.

My plan was simple, as usual. Claudette, Angelique, and I would visit the churches in Orléans, ask the curates if we could see the baptism registry—no baby, even in these secular times, went unbaptized, for some old "superstitions" died hard, and the new government approved of meticulous records of its populace, by any means. We would also see if any of these babies had recently died in this cold winter, leaving a mother still able to nurse. (It would have been impractical to have taken an infant all the way to Blois, and Maman did mention that I would be able to visit her, so she must be in Orléans, I reasoned.) We would say we were looking for an illegitimate child of an unfortunate woman in our family whom we couldn't name, and we wanted to let the mother know she wasn't deserted by her family and that we would help provide for her. In case these curates needed

encouragement, we piled together coins we had brought with us from
Blois—not the new, worthless *assignat* paper money—Angelique put
it all in her purse. It would have to do.

My mind was clear now, not clouded by any trace of emotion
except the drive to succeed in my enterprise. Angelique said I frightened her a little. I said I hoped I frightened the curates into comply-
ing, the pseudo mother into submitting. We walked first to the ancient
Saint-Pierre-le-Puellier; the curate was amenable but his information
was less forthcoming. Then, with Monsieur Dubourg now concerned
for me—his wife, having allegiance to my mother, would not side
with me, even though she herself was distraught with the loss of the
first infant ever in her house—he loaned us the use of his carriage and
of his groom, Alain, with the instructions that he also be our chaperone. Alain drove us to Saint-Donatien, then across the rue Royale
to Notre-Dame-de-Recouvrance. At these two churches the curates
informed us that a constitutional priest from Blois had been there, just
several days ago, asking the same question. It must be a very important family, he said. That priest must have been sent by Maman and
Vergez to find a likely nursing mother. We were on the right path.

I felt a little like a medieval pilgrim, visiting all the holy shrines
of the city. We had not had to use any of our savings, but all these
mothers, their names written faithfully in the ledgers, had been fortunate and not lost an infant in the last week or so. We thought we
would have better luck at the Cathedral of the Holy Cross, with its
larger registry, but I had a feeling Vergez, if he had a choice, would
prefer a mother of the classes who baptized their children in the local
church of an old quarter. She would be less likely to mix with society. The Dubourgs and I had used the cathedral for Caroline, and I
also didn't want to be recognized. So we entered the little church of
Notre-Dame-de-Miracles. There we found that one Catherine Mora
had lost a child last week. The visiting priest had also noticed her
name. She lived just a short distance away.

We passed down a street of brick and half-timbered houses. On
our right was an archway to a square. Angelique said softly, Isn't that
the house where Joan of Arc stayed? Papa told me that once, she said.
I nodded. In an alley behind Joan's old house was the address that
Madame Mora had given. It was a *boucherie*. She must have married

the butcher. I wondered if he were going to give us a hard time. We had come prepared to pay.

The ancient half-timbered houses here seemed to be leaning over us. Alain stopped the carriage right along one of the walls, so he would not block the entire alley. Women, children, and older men crowded around us. It must be a strange sight, I thought, a carriage stopping in their alley. It was a bit of a show for them. Alain pushed through foul-smelling people, and we followed in his wake into the small shop that smelled of fresh meat. Alain went back to stay with the carriage. Now Angelique had a plan, to be used flexibly in whatever establishment we might need to look for Caroline. She said she and Claudette had rehearsed it early that morning, while I slept.

A trail of interested persons stayed near the door, and a big woman behind the counter stared at us. Her hair was cut in bangs straight across her forehead; her face was square and red, and when she wiped her hands on the dried blood on her apron and asked us what we ladies wanted, her voice was more intimidating than her looks.

"We hear this is an excellent *boucherie* for veal," Claudette said.

"Yes, it is, what cut do you want?" the woman asked, as though she were accusing us of something.

Then Angelique screamed, threw her arms in the air, and fell, caught by Claudette. The catching was perfectly timed.

"Is there some place where she can lie down?" Claudette asked. "This is serious. She is ill. She is having an attack."

"I don't want any attacks in my shop. This is a healthy *boucherie*. Get her out. I don't want attacks in my shop."

But Claudette had loosened Angelique's blouse, and Angelique's knees were up and her arms flailing and her tongue sticking out to one side. The people who had followed behind us were staring at her and blocking the door.

"Have mercy, Madame," Claudette said. "She needs to lie with her knees and head up, without people staring at her, until it passes. It's not good for your business to have her here on the floor either, and we cannot take her through all the people to the carriage. Do you have a room she can be in, just until it passes?"

"Take her in the back room and do not come out until it has left her. Over there." She pointed.

I looked at Claudette, and we each took one of Angelique's arms and dragged her, moaning and kicking, across the dirty floor. The citizens who had followed us continued to stare at her, and at her legs and petticoats as she kicked.

The *bouchère* lectured us as she walked beside us. "They used to say people like her were possessed. I say she is possessed by weak blood. I can tell she is upper bourgeoisie, or aristocrat. Look at those petticoats and underthings; who else could afford those? And she has no shame, showing them like that. Nothing like this has ever happened in my shop. Now I am like the parlor of a brothel, the way those people are staring at her. Pull her dress down. Put her there, on those sacks. Never come back in my shop, ever, and leave as soon as the spirits or whatever it is have left her. You know it is because you all have weak blood. You have intermarried and ruined yourselves. Your children, if you can have any, should marry strong people from the citizenry. That alone will save your kind." With one last glance at Angelique, whose eyes were rolled back and whose tongue was still sticking out, *la femme de la boucherie* left and slammed the door behind her.

Angelique was lying on a pile of brown paper sacks and soiled aprons, streaked with dried blood. In the middle of the room stood a table, also stained, with a butcher knife lying on it. Carcasses of rabbits, chickens, and geese, their legs tied together, were hanging upside down from hooks in the ceiling and blankly staring at us. A half-skinned pig dangled from an enormous hook in the corner by a canvas bag full of ducks. A dark wing with a velvet strip of green protruded from the bag. Beside the pig carcass, an open door led to narrow stairs, winding upward. We heard the *bouchère* yelling at people in her shop to leave unless they were going to buy something.

"I'm going up those stairs," I said.

"I'll talk to the chickens," Angelique said.

She sat up and brushed herself off, and Claudette and I went up the stairs. It was dark, and we had to turn three times, my shoulders brushing the narrow walls as I raced up. At the top there was a little kitchen on our left, and a sitting room just before us, with the shutters open and cold February light coming in. A small fire licked the grate. To our right was an open door into a dark, shuttered room. I blindly rushed into it, hitting my leg on a table. Now I could make out a crib in the corner and, I thought, some color there in the dim room. I ran around a bed and leaned over the crib and caught my breath. The pink cap as if glowed out of the shadows of the room. I snatched her into my arms. I was crying and kissing her and talking to the waking Caroline as we quickly pattered down the narrow stairs. I had no plan but holding her tight.

Then we were in the small back room of the *boucherie*, with the audience of dead animals, and Angelique brightly coming up to me and kissing me, delighted by the success of her scheme. Claudette murmured, "I'll look for a back way out."

"No," I said, "I want to talk with that woman."

"Don't do that, *chérie*," said Angelique, "it will accomplish nothing; let us leave, now."

"That would be wrong," I said. "I don't want to do to her what Maman and Vergez did to me."

"She will not listen to you," Angelique said.

But I was out of the room and into the shop. Before I could say anything the woman saw me and screamed, "What are you doing with my baby?"

She lunged at me and tried to seize Caroline, but my arms were locked. The woman pulled at my arms with her strong hands and screamed, "You deceiving aristocrats! You think everything is yours for the taking. I show you mercy, and you pay me back by stealing my baby because you cannot have any." Her strong arms wrung at me, and I do not know how I kept my arms bound around Caroline. "*Au secours!* Help!" the woman shouted in Caroline's little shell ears. "They are stealing my baby!"

Caroline began to wail, and people rushed back in from outside the shop. "Arrest the aristocrats!" one shouted; "The kidnappers!"

"Make your own children," one yelled in my face as she joined Madame Mora in trying to pry my arms apart.

"She is mine!" I was shouting back, but no one attended to me in the tumult. Someone tore at my clothes. I did not think I could keep my arms together any longer. Caroline was screaming, now, and I saw Alain's large, frowning face at the door of the shop. He was pushing aside the mob to get to us.

"Give her to me," Madame Mora yelled, "Give me back my baby. She's mine."

"She's mine," I screamed through my tears. Caroline was slipping away from my grasp, red-faced and choking from her sobs. Then Claudette was behind Madame Mora, holding the butcher knife from the back room at the woman's throat. All was suddenly quiet except for the wailing of Caroline.

"Now you will listen to me," I said, "since you will not listen any other way. It is I who should say, 'Give me back my baby,' for you know she is not yours. How much is Monsieur Vergez paying you? How much?"

"It is a lie."

"How much?"

Caroline's screams had called milk from my breasts, and I could see, just above her red-stained apron, tied high on her waist, the woman's cotton blouse was damp in the same place.

"I need to nurse my baby; may I sit down?" I said.

The mistress of the *boucherie* looked at me hard with the big knife under her big chin, which did not tremble, and she waved at the people in the shop, "Everyone out. I will talk with this deceiver. I do not need you; out."

They left slowly, muttering and sullen, and Claudette withdrew the knife. I nodded to Alain, and he left too, but stood guard outside.

"I need to nurse her," I said and was unbuttoning my blouse.

"I can do it," Madame Boucher said, and again tried to grab at Caroline's little pleated linen dress, but I quickly put Caroline to my breast. The woman's red hands rested on her tiny head a moment, and when the woman looked at me again, her eyes were wet. I sat on the sawdust floor, leaned my back against the wall, and continued nursing.

"She is mine, too," the woman said, standing above me. She had suddenly become gentle in her bigness, and her voice had changed also. I liked her now and felt sorry for her as she loomed above me like a ship. "Her name is Marie-Louise," the woman continued. "It is a beautiful name. I bore her and birthed her and then one morning she did not wake up. I screamed at her, then at God to help us, but she did not wake, and God did not seem to hear. They say now God is just an idea, but I was not raised that way. A priest had pity on me, and through him, God supplied me with a new child, before my breasts dried up. The priest said she was the illegitimate child of an aristocrat who was putting it out to nurse and who would pay me for my pains of keeping her. It was only fair and moral. I would give Marie-Louise a good home. You cannot keep her; she would cause you scandal. It is your pay for having an illegitimate child. A payment of the decadent aristocracy to the citizenry."

"I am not of the aristocracy," I said. "My family has no title. My father was a doctor."

But the woman's voice was changing again. I felt unafraid, sitting there against the wall with the baby at my breast, as if Caroline were feeding me strength, not I her. Her eyes were closed.

"I have a husband," the woman was saying. "He is away, in the army at the frontier. He must not know his child died. That would be too horrible, coming back from these terrible wars and finding his child died. He would blame me. You must give her back, now. See, my breasts are ready for her and are asking for her. I carried a child and deserve her. God brought me this one. He took it away from you and gave it to me."

"My stepfather, Monsieur Vergez, and not God, had my Caroline taken away from me and given to that priest. But I must have my child. You know that. I am truly sorry you lost your child, but you cannot make up for it with mine. You cannot do to me what fate has done to you. You would not wish that upon another woman, would you?"

The woman's eyes were watery, but she was looking straight at me. "She was mine. God brought her back to me." She reached out her hand, and I thought she was going to kneel and stroke the baby, nursing while she slept, and the woman's big hand looked as if it could be very soft. Then her eyes turned angry, and her hand turned into a finger pointing at me. "Then you, spoiled aristocrat who has liaisons and never pays for what she does, must pay me. You must pay me double, to take my Marie-Louise away. I will make you pay," and she brushed her eyes with the heel of her hard hand.

My eyes met Angelique, leaning against the meat counter, and she pulled the purse from her skirt and said, "Let's talk, Madame."

After they had arranged the finances, dickering with some satisfaction as if they were settling on the price of a joint of beef, the woman stopped me as I was leaving her shop and rested her hand on Caroline's head. "Good-bye, my poor child," she said, then walked, without looking back at us, behind the counter, defiantly standing above the raw meats.

A few Orléans folk still milled around outside, hungry for more drama. One shouted "Kidnappers! You think you can buy anything. Not anymore," but it was with less enthusiasm than before. I hardly noticed them as Alain helped me back into the carriage and closed the door behind us. I had Caroline. I felt the carriage lurch forward down the alley, and the taunting voices were like a nightmare receding.

The three of us were quiet at first, a bit stunned, I think; then crossing rue Royale seemed to set Angelique and Claudette's tongues free. They chattered madly. They must have been as scared as I. Now they were laughing and complimenting each other. Then they moved on to the topic of their sweethearts: Angelique's Philippe, the count's son, and Claudette's Benoît, his footman. They exclaimed with delight how they might both end up living at the château de Beauregard. This thought had never occured to them before.

I gazed into Caroline's face, smoothed of its grief. I still feared the reach and influence of Monsieur Vergez's malice. I would never return to chez Vergez. They continued in their giddiness, oblivious.

"You're a marvellous actress, Mademoiselle Angelique. You should go on the stage."

"You're a wild citizeness, Claudette Valcroix. You should join the men at the wars."

Once Caroline was asleep in my room, exhaustion filled my limbs with a heaviness they had never known before. But when I lay down on my bed, rage drove out fatigue. I could not sleep for composing a letter answering the one I had received the day before.

Maman, this is our tête-à-tête: how can I say it plainly and clearly? Prudence dictates that I banish you for life from your grandchild. Your act, so opposed to true maternal solicitude, should incite in you a fear of burning in the afterlife, if it were not that your over-

whelming self-righteousness prorogues such a fear to the time when you must account for your actions. This child shall receive my blessing to the end of my days, a gift I cannot fully claim I received from my own mother. What depths of vanity could allow you to place reputation and Vergeʒ's career before the promptings of your own mother's heart? What blind belief in propaganda could make you invoke the name of Citiʒen Robespierre as a paragon of moral rectitude? What rectitude is there in silencing compassion? You asked me to pity you, and I do. Yes, it's a cruel world, and yes, we must all pay the consequences of our actions. But I don't believe we are born to suffer. We may be born to alleviate the suffering of others, never to increase it. Did you ever read Rousseau's Emile, *and his simple exhortation to the child: the most important lesson for every time of life—is this: "Never hurt anybody."*

Though it may hurt you, Maman, to know that Caroline's smile is a thing you will never see.

I got up from my bed, wrapped a shawl around me, lit a candle, and wrote it all down so I could sleep. Alain posted it the next day.

*T*he house was asleep, and my own eyes were heavy. I had been up with Caroline late at night and now had just finished brewing a tisane of *tilleul* leaves. I sat at the servant's table in the kitchen and listened to the March wind and rain howl in the eaves of the house and in the two poplars that grew beside it. A small candelabrum lit the steam rising from my cup. Then I heard a knock. I thought it was just the wind against the shutters, but I heard it again. It was at the scullery door. Perhaps the footman had gone out to do one last chore and had locked himself out. I picked up the candelabrum, the knocking growing more insistent; it was not the knocking of a servant. Could it be William? I thought, irrationally. I put the candelabrum down on the cutting block and opened the door a crack. In the uncertain light, with water dripping from his hat and cape, I saw the lined but still handsome face of Count Thibaut. He smiled and said simply, "May I come in?"

He stood in the kitchen, hat in hand. "I saw you through the window," he said, "and thought that my prayers had been answered. I only wanted to talk to you. I trust you. I want no one else to know I'm here."

"My, all this mystery, Count," I said. "If you're going to be so full of intrigue, let us discuss it in the drawing room. No one is up, don't worry."

He placed his tricorne hat on the table and his cape over a high-backed chair. I fed him some brandy for having been out in the cold and left the decanter at his disposal. He took a long sip. "I thought," he said, "for a moment, just for a moment, that twenty-five years hadn't passed and that it was your mother there, sitting in the halo of the candlelight. You know she was called 'the beauty of Blois.' You get more lovely every time I see you, Annette."

"Intrigue seems to have brought out your old flattery, Count."

I could not say the same for him. I had not seen him since Marguerite and I had visited him last September, when he was convalescing from his wound from the Tuileries massacre, and he had dark pouches now under his eyes. He said nothing and looked at his brandy, then around at the gilding of the fine carved paneling, catching the flicker of the candlelight.

"Much has changed, but not this room," he finally said, as if to himself. "I attended many of the old fêtes at chez Dubourg." Then he turned to me and gently said, "I hear you have a beautiful baby girl—"

"Where did you—"

"How is your Englishman?"

"Safe back in England."

"That is good. It's not a time for foreigners. It's not a time for many of us." And he laughed, a little.

"I heard that it was that old music teacher of yours who denounced him. Revenge twists men's hearts, if he had a heart to twist. And what did he have to complain about? We merely made it uncomfortable for him to stay in Blois. Well, now he's back preening himself with the most zealous of the Jacobins. He doesn't care a sou for you or anyone. I should not have kept your father from running him through. How is your mother?"

"She's busy being the wife of an important lawyer about to be elected to the trade tribunal. They've adjusted to the new order."

"I was happy to see her well remarried. I was one of her only old friends who would come."

"Yes."

"You know my son has been seeing much of your sister."

"Yes."

"I believe he is very fond of her. Do you know if the feeling is mutual?"

"From what I know, yes."

He looked down at his brandy. The glass was empty. "I'm afraid it must be obvious to you that I have not come here to discuss my son's future plans," he said and poured himself another brandy. "You know, if Angelique marries my son, she will have a title. That will please your mother. Not that titles are so important nowadays. In fact, they can get you in trouble. Which is why I dropped by chez Dubourg at this inopportune hour."

He was becoming more like his old self, with the brandy. He twirled his sodden hat on the table. "Denouncing has become a prudent business, Annette. It serves two purposes. One gets a reward and, even more important, one looks like a patriot in the eyes of the Committee—an increasingly important reward in itself. It turns out your old friend, the dancing instructor, finished his steps by finding out from the erstwhile maidservant of the Vincents that I had been involved in the battle at the Tuileries—and on the wrong side. Like your Englishman, I was warned, by an old friend who has managed to keep his position as city magistrate—he invited me back, by the way, when this blows over, and he's sure it will; he says everything changes every three weeks now—and when I return, he wants me to take over his situation; he has had enough of it. He says the town needs an old respected name on the bench, and he can put me there, vouch for my patriotism. I just have to disappear for a while."

I must have looked surprised. "Didn't you know, being the second son, I studied law before my brother died in the American war? I was not *meant* to be a count."

"I never knew that," I said. "All my life you were simply 'the count.' How could you be anything else?"

He took a long sip of brandy. "But my past and my dubious future aside," he said, "in short, like Monsieur William, I have to flee, and like him, I need your help."

"I can make a guest room."

"You know they have dismantled the Committees of Surveillance," he said. "It's a grand thing for civilization. The Girondins made such a fuss that the Jacobins were using those committees to set up their own dictatorship that the Assembly voted to disband them."

"That's great news, then—"

"No, my dear," he said. "The Jacobins merely reformed them a month later under a different name. They are now part of the Committee of Public Safety, which is part of the Committee of General Security—those committees will soon control all of France. You see, one doesn't need a king. One just needs a committee with a good name. Just say the words 'patriot' or 'security,' and everyone will follow you."

"I'll find you that room—"

"I can't stay in a guest room—or the servants' quarters. No one must know I am here."

He looked at my face and laughed. "I will not bother you or the baby. I hear you not only aided the Englishman but helped Paul Vincent escape from prison, and his family from France."

"Those are just stories, and stories abound now. It is a time for intrigue."

"Yes, it is a time for intrigue, and I ask you, Annette, to help me now. It will be as nothing, if you have done these dangerous things, and if you have not, it is still nothing."

"Where would you like to stay?"

"Annette, I must be concealed in the secret room."

I laughed. "I thought you knew this house. We have no such room."

"It is behind the mirror, in the upstairs hall. I'll show you." He draped his cape over his left arm, held his hat and his glass easily in his left hand, and picked up the candelabrum in the other. He apparently didn't want me to carry anything for him.

He walked before me up the stairs. We paused outside the floor-length mirror in the hall. The nearest room was unoccupied now. It had always been my mother's since she visited Madame Dubourg as a girl and had been left as she liked it. The count moved as quietly and as gracefully as a cat. In front of the mirror stood a small inlaid marble table, a pale green porcelain vase on it. Beside the mirror stood the grand clock of veneered violet wood, mounted in gilded bronze.

"It has been a long time," the count said.

The candlelight was reflected dully in the mirror, as were the count, the table, and I. The clock next to it said ten minutes past three. The count placed the candelabrum on the table. With the cape hanging like a black wing over his arm and the hat and glass poised in his hand, I watched in wonderment as he reached up behind the two bronze figures, clad only at the waist, who perched above the clock. The woman figure leaned over the man, dangling a bunch of grapes. The count ran his hands behind the gilded man about to enjoy a grape. His brow furrowed.

Perhaps his secret room has lost its entrance, I thought. Perhaps he's thinking of another house. He's getting old. He's been under heavy burdens since the Tuileries massacre. He cursed under his breath. "My God, doesn't anyone dust behind clocks anymore?" he whispered. Then his fingers caressed the back of the bronze woman's thighs. I saw a smile appear on the count's face. "How silly of me to forget," he said. "It's behind the woman, of course." He pressed a hidden lever, and the mirror swiveled inward to reveal a small chamber with a double mirror framed in curling bronze vine leaves, a carved oak armoire, a vanity table with another mirror, a triple tray table, veneered with ebony, and a carved and gilt wood bed *à la Turque*—that is, with cushioned borders on three sides. All had a thick layer of dust on them. An arched door stood on the other side of the bed. The purpose of the room seemed obvious.

The count moved the marble table aside, bowed, and gestured for me to enter. "We must be discreet," he whispered, and he reached up and pushed the button again, and the mirror swung back. He deftly picked up the candelabrum from the table before the room closed us in. The candle flames now flickered in the shadowy, doubled mirors. Twining roses covered the arched door and the unmirrored walls. The count smiled with satisfaction. "It is a lovely room," he said, and shivered. "But would you be so kind, Annette, as to do me one more favor—I'll open the mirror from this side—could you please bring me a scuttle of coal? Just tap on the mirror."

A horrible thought was troubling me. "Count—"

"We need to rest now," he said. "It's been a long day and night for me, and I assume for you too, my dear. Thank you so much. I am forever in your debt."

"How did you know about this room?"

"Many of the old houses had secret rooms built into them, as the grand houses had *petite maisons* on their grounds. We used to play in here. This room is far older than I."

"Whom did you play with here?"

"Card games among friends. A late meal on that amazing table—the middle tray slides out or can be raised or lowered. Here, watch—"

And he put his glass and hat on the top tray and slid the middle one out. A cloud of dust blew in his face.

"Now one can bring a dish to the card table, for instance." He slid the tray back.

"Were you having a liaison with Madame Dubourg?"

"Madame Dubourg? My dear, look at her. A giraffe eating leaves in the Jardin des Plantes." Then I saw instantly by his face that he knew the mistake he had made. He placed the candelabrum on the vanity table, and it shone back from the mirror.

"I am tired," he said. "I speak nonsense. It's just a room where we had private fêtes after a more public one. Those were jolly times. We were all young." His sunken eyes looked deeper as he stood outside the immediate glow of the candlelight.

"Doesn't that door," I said with difficulty, "lead to Maman's room?"

The count sighed and opened his mouth to speak. I didn't give him time.

"You were friends with my father since your youth."

"At university. He studied medicine, I law. We roamed Paris together."

"Maman was girlhood friends with Madame Dubourg. She stayed here weeks at a time. And she married when she was sixteen. You wouldn't have—before then—that means—"

"Annette, you don't understand—"

"What don't I understand? A definition of friendship that includes treachery?"

"My dear, sit down."

"On that bed? I'd rather stand."

"I am sorry you had to come to this conclusion."

"Did you think I would be so stupid as not to guess? Or were you just thinking of yourself? As when you didn't warn William and me about the brigands—"

"The deal was that the brigands stayed in the south end of the forest—"

"You make deals with the devil." The count started to raise the glass to his lips but stopped.

I held my arms straight out from my sides, palms upward, as if I were going to dance, with a gentleman on either side. "This is such a lovely room," I said, lightly. "So *discreet*. So *prudent*—Maman's favorite words, you know. Card playing among friends. A late-night meal—on this wonderful table." I pulled out the middle tray and threw it on the dusty floor. "Self-righteous, deceitful, lying hypocrites, the both of you! Oh, I should have not let you in and instead let the Committee wave your head high on a rusty pike. I will fetch you no coal, Monsieur Count. You can lie on your old dusty Turkish bed and freeze—"

Suddenly I started to cry and sat down on the bed in spite of myself. The count held his half-filled brandy glass in front of me, and I finished it, and coughed.

"You are quite right, my dear," he said. "Everything you say is true. As far as your father goes, I told him, when we were out in the forest on a ride. I asked his forgiveness and said I would end it immediately, which I did. He rode away, without saying a word. He didn't talk to me for a month. When hunting season resumed, I wondered if he would be there. He rode up to me in the dawn and said simply, 'Hatred is a waste of anyone's time. My wife and I will have a family. You and I will hunt the stags, and the world will go on.' That was a long time ago, Annette. Your father was an eminently worthy man, unlike myself. He intimated to me once that he had had some kind of vision in the forest."

"He said something of that once to me—that two people he loved had hurt him, and he rode deep into the forest and—something appeared to him."

"Do not blame your *maman*, Annette, if you know anything about love that grips you in your youth, about indiscretion. . . . She and I knew each other *before* she met your papa, but it was my duty to marry a woman who had a title, and she . . . she preferred your father to me, it's just . . . we were each other's first passion. Love is not prudent. I think your *maman* has tried to give you the wisdom of her experience—though, from her lesson, she may err on the side of duty and authority rather than on that of natural feeling. If you could have known her at sixteen, at seventeen, her laughter, the look in her eye when she turned her head in a dance—"

I stared at the empty glass. I saw where my hand had made a print in the dust on the bed. A hundred candles flickered in the mirrors, reflecting each other indefinitely on in the distance, the shadowy figures of the count and me repeated manifold.

"You can see yourself a lot in this room," I said.

"Yes, it's regrettable," he said.

"I'll get you that coal. Your clothes are still wet. Stay here. Just let me out, please."

When I returned, carrying a brass coal shuttle, I also brought with me a jug of water, a loaf of bread, and some cheese, and more candles. "I thought you might be hungry," I said.

"You are your father's daughter," he said.

"My mother's too," I said. "Good night, Count."

The next afternoon, five armed members from the Committee of Public Safety arrived at the door of chez Dubourg. They said that Count Thibaut of the château de Beauregard had last been seen in Orléans, and they were checking places in town where they knew he had friends. Before Monsieur Dubourg could say anything, I told them that no one here was a friend of the count's; my parents had been. Nevertheless, they searched the house thoroughly, knocking over the green porcelain vase outside the gilded mirror, then left without saying anything.

The count stayed five days, and the Committee never returned. I brought him *Les Liaisons dangereueses* and Montaigne's essays for him to read in his lonely room, which I only visited late at night. Then he left on a journey to Tours, where his estranged wife lived. He did not want to burden us.

INTRIGUERS

Caroline was over three months old and smiled regularly. Those are, perhaps, the most beautiful smiles of a person's life: innocence beyond an adult's comprehension. Later, William would write that a child entered the world *trailing clouds of glory*. That certainly seemed true of Caroline. She had just laughed at some expression I had unwittingly made, and now I was making the same expression purposefully and getting the same reaction—blissful belly laughs that made me laugh in turn. When Claudette knocked, I singingly told her to enter, then looked up and saw her face.

"My parents," she said. She looked shocked and frightened. "They're here, in the stable."

"All the way from near Tours? What—? Tell them to come in; I'm sure Monsieur and Madame Dubourg won't mind."

"They're hiding, Madame."

"What have they to hide from? They are not aristocrats, like the count."

"My father would not let my two brothers be taken by the *levée en masse*. He hid them when the men from Paris came. They want *all* unmarried men, between eighteen and twenty-five, Madame. There are others like my parents, many others. They are tired of their priests being taken, now their sons and husbands too. It's happening throughout the Vendée, my parents say, and in Normandy, Brittany. The Committee of Public Safety will soon have a civil war on their hands. I have brought my parents food, but—they need a place to stay, and I am afraid for chez Dubourg if we shelter them here. It is not my decision."

"We will tell no one—except Angelique," I said. "No servants; they might talk. Tell Angelique to help you fetch fresh sheets—several pairs—and extra blankets, and meet me by the clock down the hall in a few minutes." I tried to put Caroline down, but she was not sleepy and was insulted at the gesture, so I carried her.

It was with some pleasure that I reached up on tiptoe behind the gilded couple and glanced back at my two conspirators with wide eyes, then dropped jaws, as the mirror swung open. I quickly ushered them in and closed it again. "Angelique, please cover those mirrors with the extra sheets. Claudette and I will change these sheets and make up the bed."

"But how—," Angelique began.

I didn't like lying to them, but it wasn't the time to explain the history of Maman and the count—I might never tell Angelique—nor was it the time to reveal that the count had recently stayed here. As much as I loved Angelique, she wasn't the most discreet person.

"I'm sorry I never told you," I said. "It was one of Marguerite's and my secrets—the mean older sisters. She found out about this room when we were children. It was built long ago for parties, and no one ever used it anymore. That is why you and Etienne could never find us when we played hide-and-seek. This is where we were."

"You scheming girls. To keep a room like this from me! We could have had our own parties. This is wondrous! I would like—well, never mind what I would like."

"It's a strange room, if you ask me, Madame," Claudette said. "I don't think my parents will feel comfortable here. It has a flavor of ancient liaisons."

"That's why we're covering up the mirrors."

"I want to look in that armoire," Angelique said. "What kind of gowns are in there?" She finished hanging up the sheets and opened it. I had never looked inside when I brought meals to the count. Caroline was lying on the bed, and we had to work around her. I kept glancing over at Angelique, at the open door of the armoire.

"Look at this," she said. "Look at this nightdress. It's lovely." She held it up to her. "It just fits, even if it is old. But how can *négligés* go out of fashion? It suggests everything but actually reveals little. It would be quite comfortable. What a shame it's the only one in here. What parties they must have had in the old days. Why couldn't I have been born then? Did you and Marguerite ever try this on when you hid in here? Tell me the truth."

"I've never looked in that armoire. That's the truth."

"You prude."

"I think," Claudette said, "that you should leave that old gown alone. There's something very strange about his room. I would like to put some painting of the Virgin in here for my parents—but I've never seen any paintings like that at chez Dubourg. And it's strange," she said, looking around, "that the layers of dust are not even. And," she said, squatting by the grate, "that these ashes are not old."

"Perhaps some of the servants know about this room and had their own parties," I said.

"Well, it must be a secret now," Claudette said. "No one must know my parents are here."

"This room is cut off from the world," I said.

The spring weather we had waited so long for had not arrived, and late that night Claudette led her parents in through the never-ending rain. "I do not like this," her father said softly in the kitchen. "We should have permission of the master of the house."

"Madame Annette has invited you."

"But she is not the master," he said. "I want to see the *monsieur* and ask him. I am not a criminal."

He stood there, defiant. The candelabrum I held flickered over his broad face and weather-beaten cheeks, and the black hair coursing down over his forehead. He was tall and broad and straight-backed. His long wool coat had patches at the elbows, and his brown trousers were tucked into working boots. "You best take those boots off here, Monsieur Valcroix. We must not let Monsieur Dubourg know you are here to protect him, not to hide information from him. That is a sacrifice to one's honor that one must make in these days."

He grunted and sat down at the kitchen table and took his boots off. His wife wore a long cloak with big pockets and the hood still up. Underneath that she had scarves around her head, and I couldn't see her face clearly. She was small, about my height. But I noticed her kind eyes, under the dimness of the hood and her scarves. "Thank you, Madame," she said. "Claudette has always told us how happy she is in your service."

"I am mainly in her service, Madame. I could not live without her." It was true.

They followed me quietly up the stairs, but I heard them behind me as the mirror opened. Claudette's mother gasped, and her father invoked the Virgin.

"This is an unholy room," he said when he walked in.

"It will have to do, Papa," Claudette said. "If you're going to defy the Committee you'll just have to sleep where you can. It's a very nice bed. It has fresh sheets for you. A fire is in the grate. A pitcher of water is on the top tray. Cold mutton is on the second tray, which slides out. Bread, cheese, and apples are on the bottom tray. You will be very comfortable here. You will live like kings."

"There are no kings," her father said. "They have killed him."

"Well, dukes then," his daughter said and threw up her arms. "Good night, Papa, Maman; I will visit you tomorrow."

We started to leave. I was about to press the lever, nestled in the center of a wallpaper rose, that swung the mirror open from this side.

"Your brothers," Claudette's father said. "I am sorry, but your brothers are pursued. I told them to come here too. Your mother said that you, *ma petite*, always said that Madame Annette could do anything. We had nowhere to go. There are those in Normandy who can help if we can get there. We are really very grateful. We will not stay long. We will find our way to those Norman houses, and we will work there. I do not like not working. Your brothers will come in a few days. After we leave. Then they can go on to Normandy and work again too. They are good lads. They did not want to fight for the Parisian government. Do you know the men from Paris came and took the bell from our church? After they arrested our priest. Then they wanted our boys to fight their wars. Who are these people?"

"I don't know," I said. "But we will keep your sons safe."

"They burned our barn where the boys were hiding," Claudette's mother said, "took our animals, destroyed our crops. The land that your grandfather worked on—"

Claudette embraced her mother and told her to rest now, that it was time for sleep, that she should fear nothing now.

It was a long way from Tours, in bad weather, on foot. A network of resistance had already started, and they had been shunted from barn to barn, living with fear and hunger and fatigue. Claudette kissed her father on the brow, and we closed them in the secret room.

A few days later, just before they moved on to a location in Normandy, Claudette's father came up to me. "That bell," he said. "That is what I miss, more than my land, my animals—it was as if that bell rang beneath my window, though it was all the way in town. The wind would bring it to my window."

After Claudette's parents left, we did help her brothers, and after them, somehow, the word had gone out that there was some safe haven in Orléans, if one went late at night and only a few at a time. The Vendée was already beginning to get bad. The Committee of Public Safety was sending additional troops. It was ironic. Now the royalists were called "the rebels." Claudette, Angelique, and I went to market to buy supplies for the hungry refugees who would discreetly wait in the stable and send one person to stand in the shadows near the kitchen door, which we regularly checked now after the house was asleep. Once the footman woke up at the sound of voices in the kitchen, and I bribed him to keep silent, though I think he wouldn't have talked anyway. The servants were loyal to chez Dubourg, and chez Dubourg was quietly a royalist house. Monsieur or Madame Dubourg may even have known, but thought it prudent to pretend that they didn't.

I loved helping those who came. They became fond of Caroline, and some would even arrive already knowing her name. Claudette told me they called me "the Mother of Orléans," as a play on the maid of Orléans, Joan of Arc, but I never heard them call me that. They all only stayed for a few days and had destinations to walk on to. But they hadn't slept indoors, in a room with a bed, for who knows how long.

General Dumouriez, head of the Revolutionary Army, had won a series of victories since Valmy last September. But by the spring of 1793 it became clear to him that he had been winning them only so

Robespierre and his committees could gain and maintain more power. They had now declared war on Spain as well as Austria, Prussia, and Great Britain. The general closed the Jacobin clubs, declared himself in open opposition to Robespierre, and planned to march on Paris himself and establish a more moderate government. But his troops refused to move against France, even if it were against an extremist regime that rarely paid them and overstretched their limits in the field, keeping them constantly at war against the increasing numbers of allies. The general had no choice but to defect, leaving Robespierre and his committees now to run the government virtually unchecked.

Now it was the Jacobins' time to act against the Girondins who had spoken out against them so articulately, courageously, and unwisely for so long. First the Jacobins smashed the rest of the Girondin printing presses, their voice of opposition, for which William had written. Then the Jacobins put their own man, Hanriot, in charge of the National Guard, who, on a fine spring day, surrounded the National Assembly with cannon and fixed bayonets and demanded the arrest of the Girondins, on the grounds that they were all intriguers, or counterrevolutionaries. Some managed to escape later, but went into hiding throughout France. One was found at the bottom of a well in the Dordogne Valley near Bordeaux. A farmer and his wife had been bringing him food for a week. The Jacobin control was now complete. I thought how sad William would be—the ideals he believed in sacrificed for power for a few and for the illusion of security for the many. And these Girondins, in prison now or in hiding, were his friends, his comrades. Once again, for his own sake, I was glad he wasn't here.

By my birthday on the fifteenth of June, when I became twenty-four and Caroline six months, I had become increasingly afraid of chez Dubourg getting visited by the Committee of Public Safety. It was time, I thought, to move back to Blois. And Claudette wanted to see Benoît; Angelique, Philippe. She had written to Philippe and told him of my idea about the cottage, and since there are many of that description in the Loire, he and his father had found Claudette and me just such a home in Vienne, across the river from Blois, not far from where chez Vincent once was. But Angelique would not move there with us. She would rather live in a fine home than in a crowded cottage. "It's easy to avoid Vergez," she said; "it's a big house." Monsieur and Madame Dubourg loaned us their family carriage for the voyage.

If there wasn't wisteria growing on the chimney, I would plant some, I thought. No one could get across the Channel either way now, but William could live with us there, when the war was over. A humble cottage would be just the right place for him to work.

*I*t had a blue slate roof, like the houses in the city, plaster-covered walls of flint and stone, a huge oven for baking bread attached to the south wall, and a stairway that curved by the oven up to the bedrooms. A rambling rose, rather than wisteria, meagerly bedecked the front of the cottage, facing the rising sun. It had a small barn in the back, where Claudette and I planned to keep chickens, rabbits, a pig, and of course, La Rouge. We would plant a kitchen garden in the space between the cottage and the barn. Two walnut trees and a chestnut grew beside the cottage, as did a pear, an apple, and an apricot tree, which all bore green leaves of summer in the breeze that blew softly in from the river, just to the north. We could see the spires and towers of Blois across the river. Jean had brought some of my old things in a cart from what was once chez Vallon. All that was missing was William, working on his poems in an upstairs bedroom or out under the chestnut tree, or working with us in the garden. Claudette, raised on a farm, was buying rabbits and chickens today at the market. Jean had loaned me Vergez's cart horse, and I rode it now to visit the count, to retrieve La Rouge.

At the château de Beauregard, Edouard, as silent as the flight of an owl and dignified as only a valet born and bred into service of a count can be, served his master and me white wine from the old cellars. "I'll be drinking cider now," I said to the count. "It's cheaper. It was very strange, though, when I went to pay the agent, he said the cottage was already paid for."

"You'll need all of your father's money, now, believe me."

"That was very kind of you, Count. You'll have to come to a dinner of rabbit with onions and mushrooms from our garden," I said. He nodded. "But how is it—just over three months since I saw you?—and you're comfortably back at the château de Beauregard. Why isn't the Committee of Public Safety pounding on your door?"

"The dance instructor," the count said, "the smiling serpent, has, in the present dearth of officers and his position with all the right people, got himself a commission as lieutenant in the Revolutionary Army. He just might get himself blown up, although the world seems denied such luck nowadays. I suspect he was really after the uniform—he'll look more impressive that way when he teaches the wives of the Jacobins how to dance like ladies. With Monsieur Leforge's strident and persistant voice gone, my old friend the magistrate found me in Tours, invited me back, and, as I said he would, he has handed his position over to me."

I gasped.

"Yes, Madame, respectability has come to the new regime, and the new regime has come to the count. And it's a lot safer for me that way, to be playing their game. There's a lot of old aristocrats among them, even in the National Assembly—they just have to make their sympathies clear—"

"But you'll have to support all the unjust new laws."

"Ah, but I will temper justice with mercy. And besides, they are right—it is time we aristocrats did an honest day's work—not that being involved in law is necessarily *that*. My old friend said he had some interesting cases in which he was able to help some innocent people—one, he said, was that girl who shot the boar. I'm supposing there is only one of those in all of France, but I also suspect that's another story . . . "

"Count, besides thanking you for finding—and now for buying—the cottage for me, and for keeping La Rouge—"

"Benoît exercised her when I was away, but he had to be careful of the National Guard—she's a pretty horse for a cavalry officer to requisition—you'll want to keep her hidden in the barn and be chary where you ride her—"

"I will. There's another thing—I used the room—"

He burst out laughing, a deep resounding laugh such as I hadn't heard since William. "No one laughs like that anymore," I said.

"More's the pity."

"And I didn't use the room in the way you think—"

"That was not ribald laughter; it was laughter of delicious irony."

"Well, the irony stops there. I probably shouldn't be telling you this, now, with your new *situation*—but I used the room to hide refugees from the Vendée—Claudette's family, others who have lost everything—the type of wonderful cases you'll get—"

"I knew your heart could not let such a valuable piece of information as that room go without using it for some good—even if only a place for Caroline to nap in peace. So all went well—no one is under surveillance?"

"I believe we kept it all discreet—that's the key thing about that room, yes?"

"Yes, my dear."

"And there's one other thing."

"Yes?"

"I liked doing it. I liked seeing the expression on their faces grow from fear and helplessness to some calm and hope."

"I always said you have a noble soul."

"There's one more thing."

"How did you fare in mathematics in that convent school? I think we must be up to three or four things by now."

"They're all the one thing." The count waited, sipped his wine, looked out his windows at his lawn.

"The hedges never came back after my absence," he said. "That will be a failure of the new order—no one will keep well-clipped or shaped hedges anymore."

"I would like, please, the use of the old hunting lodge to help protect more refugees. When I left Orléans, they asked me, was there a way I could continue to aid in their plight? There are more of them coming every day. It's just getting worse there."

"Helping others, my dear, has a beginning but no end. It's a dangerous business to get into. Especially nowadays. Why don't you stop with your success with the room, transforming its . . . purpose."

"I can't, though, not just yet. I will, soon, when the trouble in the Vendée has subsided—"

"Trouble will only continue now. Look at who's running the government—the Committee of General Security; that can only bring danger. Oh, my, look at your face. Anyone would think you were denied an apple pastry for dessert. I'll have to talk with Edouard about that. Come, have lunch with me of a simple casserole of chicken in a cream sauce—what you need is a goat, to provide you with milk and cheese. I'll buy you a goat for looking so pretty and being so sweet and stubborn, when all the world is ugly and mean and easily compromised, like myself. We'll do anything for security; you'll risk anything for—"

"Oh, hush, you old flatterer—will you let me use the lodge or not?"

"Use it, my dear—no one has for a long time. Just be chary, as I said before, only late at night—no one shall know; I myself have already forgotten. If you come before my bench, I will spank you and send myself to the guillotine for being so indulgent to your childish whims. Now, lunch? You didn't have to kill this bird out in your barn. You couldn't do such a thing, could you? And all those fluffy rabbits?"

"Claudette said it's all in the wrist motion, at least the chickens are," I said. "Count, I don't want the world my daughter just entered to be the world she grows up in."

"I understand. You just frighten me, that's all."

The bridge into town had sentries now, especially curious at night, but the location of my new cottage eliminated the problem of crossing it to get home—the cottage was already on the other side, on the way toward the château de Beauregard and the lodge. I walked La Rouge with very little trotting, leading Vergez's cart horse, and it was dark when I saw the cottage, its windows lighted.

With the help of a few discreet words from Claudette at the market to a woman who sold pigs to a woman who sold cotton scarves, the resistance network had already passed on that the Mother of Orléans (or Madame Williams, as Claudette said I was called) was now arranging a safe place for more refugees from the Vendée, that this place would house more—maybe twelve at a time—and that the meadow near the lodge was the meeting place. The lodge itself was isolated, and the meadow well set off from even the quiet road that went through the forest.

At chez Dubourg I had sometimes leafed through the *Journal of Style and Taste*—that is, before the Jacobins shut their presses down in the spring. And that bastion of French fashion had recommended a *costume Catholique* to show sympathy with the priests who would not take the government oath. So to make sure the refugees recognized me as a friend, I wore part of that costume: pinned to my hair, a bonnet of black satin trimmed with a white-and-gold ribbon and a white-feathered aigrette. Among the things that Jean brought down in the cart from my old room was the hunting pistol that my father had given me long ago, and it was now safely tucked in the pocket of my coat.

I kissed the sleeping Caroline on the forehead and told Claudette not to worry and that I would be back before dawn.

"Oh, I'll not worry," she said. "I'll just think about thousands of soldiers and my mistress dodging them all."

"I do have La Rouge back." I smiled.

"As if one horse can protect you from all the National Guard. A secret room was one thing. You didn't have to leave the house. You're courting danger now."

"Claudette, I'm doing this for your region, for people perhaps from your old village."

"*We* are your village now, Caroline and me."

"Yes, you're my family. And these people I don't know are also my family. I can't explain it. I don't really understand it."

"Just don't die and leave me alone with this baby."

"I have to go," and I kissed her on the cheek and quickly left.

I was glad that Jean had agreed to be my escort, and he was happy to be away from chez Vergez. The pines and chestnuts made long and shifting shadows across the road in the moonlight. The wind rushed through the tops of the trees. I was out again on La Rouge, going toward the old forest where I had hunted with my father. Deep-throated frogs sung out from the darkness. Our saddlebags were bursting with potatoes, carrots, onions, and mushrooms for a stew we would make at the old lodge for the refugees. William would enjoy this adventure, I thought, but I didn't want to be anywhere else in the world, right now. An owl on silent wings suddenly emerged from the dark trees and passed over my head, the moonlight just catching his white feathers.

I didn't know how many there would be waiting for us, but I thought about a dozen. We were off the road now, past the lodge, on the narrow track at the edge of the meadow. I was in the lead, and the hooting of an owl made me slow La Rouge. I heard it again and stopped.

Suddenly, out from under the trees I saw in the moonlight a man's bearded face under the low brim of his hat, then another face, which appeared to have only one eye, though this could be the trick of the shadows. The bearded man took the bridle of Jean's horse; One-Eye took La Rouge, who snorted and stepped back. I checked her. More shapes of men appeared behind these two, and I saw distinctly two muskets, their owners in darkness, pointed at us.

"Madame Williams?" said One-Eye.

"Yes."

With one hand still holding Rouge, he stepped directly to the side of my saddle, where my leg was tucked, and stared at me. I hoped he was taking in my white aigrette. He slowly raised his arm, and as he did so, dark heads and shoulders appeared out of the silver grasses. My new escort led me into the meadow now, where I saw gathered about fifty people. "But——"

"Something wrong, Madame?"

"It will just be a bit crowded in the lodge."

He grunted. "We have been sleeping in ditches, among cattle, even in trees; what is a crowded house?"

"May I show it to you? We're going in the wrong direction."

He gestured for me to be silent and led me to the center of the meadow.

Someone had lighted a torch, and I could clearly see the crowd around us now—as many women as men, and most of the women had one or two children with them. They were all waiting for something.

Then the one-eyed man took a stole from his pocket, unfolded it, kissed it, and put it around his neck. With a sudden soft swish, the people knelt in the grass.

"I am going to perform mass now," the man said. "Ever since they passed a law forbidding outdoor worship, I do it every night. Would you care to join us?"

"Let one of your sentries come. I'll ride over to the road and keep watch."

"As you wish," and he whispered words to the bearded man, who departed into the darkness.

"Forgive me," I said. "Are you a priest?"

"I'm a cobbler," he said. "They killed our priest." And in the torchlight he smiled a rather eerie smile, with missing teeth and sunken cheeks and, clearly, one eye.

I told Jean to unlock the lodge, find the cooking pot, and prepare the biggest pot of soup he could manage with the supplies we had brought. I would join him soon. I glanced at the bowed heads, the torchlight flickering over their ragged breeches, coarse woolen dresses, and tired faces, young and old, and felt embarrassed in my satin and ribboned bonnet. I dismounted and walked Rouge softly out to a vantage point at the edge of the wood where I could look down on the road and back at the meadow, at the flitting shadows of the mass of the cobbler priest. It went on in silence.

Then I heard the unmistakable sound of hundreds of marching feet. I held my hand over Rouge's muzzle so she would not call to the officers' horses. I hooted like an owl twice, heard my call answered, and immediately the torches were out and the meadow lay silent and still except for the breeze in the grass.

It seemed to take the soldiers a long time to round the bend in the woods and come into sight. The clomping of boots echoed up the timbered hillsides and surrounded me so that I couldn't tell from which direction they were coming. Then I saw a glint of moonlight on bayonets to the south. They were marching toward Blois.

Finally a column of men came into view, black on the white road, curling around the bend like an undulating snake. They kept coming and coming; one cry of a child, one whinny from Rouge or from Jean's horse, would betray us all. I couldn't see any faces—just a dark blur with the outlines of hats and muskets, faintly moving legs, light catching on the white breeches of the National Guard; officers on horseback alongside, the constant rustling and jiggling of the packs on their backs and ammunition at their waists and the earth tremor of their boots—as if they were all one entity, let loose on the forest at night; then the last of them was gone: their sound faded and the forest swallowed up their noise and movement into its own silence, as if they had never been.

Then I heard crickets again, and the stream at the edge of the meadow. I gave the owl call and saw shadows moving in the grass.

I mounted Rouge and rode fast back to the lodge. Jean would need help with that soup. He had already gathered buckets of water from the stream and fortunately hadn't lit the fire before the soldiers came. The cobbler priest had found the path to the lodge, and now women were slicing fast, throwing handfuls into the huge kettle under two torches, set in the rafters of the lodge. I gathered sprigs of thyme and rosemary from my saddlebags, and Jean tossed salt and dried pork into the brew. I rummaged through dusty cupboards and found about eight porcelain bowls and some pewter mugs, and soon I was standing by the steaming kettle, ladling out soup to a quiet procession of very hungry, if not starving, people. The families came first. Some brought their own bowls; others waited patiently for the bowls and mugs of those who had gone first. Each one of them thanked me.

I saw one girl of seven or eight, sitting in the shadows by herself; and I brought her a bowl and placed it in her hands and placed my hands around hers. I could feel the warmth of the bowl through both our hands. She looked up at me and said in a shy voice, "Are you the Mother of Orléans?" I nodded. I felt I could put bowls of steaming soup in the hands of hungry little girls for the rest of my life and be happy, just doing that.

"They grow on you, Madame."

I turned and saw a young man, of about Etienne's age, smiling. I hadn't noticed him among the crowd, but he was well dressed, although his clothes were shabby too. He wore a cloth frock coat with a faded velvet collar and large buttons, with dirty lace at the sleeves, a silk waistcoat, leather knee breeches with silver buckles and jockey boots. He doffed his worn bicorne hat and bowed, saying, "Chevalier de Montivault at your service, Madame." I curtsied, in the appropriate manner for a chevalier. He smiled again. "It is a good thing you do here. Not many would do it. These people have so little hope. Ah, it is my turn for soup. Would you care to join me?"

"No, thank you, Chevalier."

"Then pardon me."

He ladled himself some broth from the bottom of the kettle and shrugged. "Families must eat first," he said. He looked around. There was nowhere to sit.

"Would you care to step outside? I live out-of-doors, these days." I followed him, and we stood near the entrance, above the clearing where we had gathered in a circle before the hunt.

"This is your land?" he said, and sipped from his bowl.

"It belongs to a friend of my family. I knew it in a happier time."

"Ah, the happier time," he said. "These people"—he motioned to the lodge—"they remember a time too when they were free and could hunt where they wanted and raise their crops, before the army from Paris came and took their men off to war and imprisoned their priests. But a good thing has come from all of this." He took a long drink from his broth and delicately fingered out a soggy potato and ate it. "Some of these villagers," he said, "didn't even talk to each other—had some old feud and didn't know why—and now they would die for each other. And they would never have cause to talk to me nor I to them—and now we walk side by side. Fate and danger have made us all like old friends—even those we have just met." He bowed slightly, and there was a sudden awkwardness about him, after the expression of such sentiment.

I looked toward the meadow that glimmered in the moonlight through the trees.

"What will become of these people?" I said.

"Most of them will cross the Loire, look for work in farms and villages in Normandy and Brittany. They have friends, like you, who risk their lives to help them. They have nothing to go back to but civil war and destroyed villages; all their livestock and property have been confiscated."

"And what about you?"

"I? I am bound for England, to join the émigré army."

"Ah, England. It is a popular destination."

"You want to go too, Madame?"

"Maybe later. I have an infant. And work to do here."

He gestured to the lodge. "They are all fed and will sleep soundly tonight, for once. Thank you, Madame, so much," he said. "May we meet again"—he paused—"in happier times." He bowed again, and we returned to the lodge, where most of the people were already asleep, curled up on the floor and in nooks. Jean and I prepared to ride home, well behind the column of National Guard.

From that night on, we rode out to the lodge about once a week throughout the summer. One night Angelique caught Jean coming in late and asked him, By any chance are you helping Annette in some intrigue again, as you helped her deliver Monsieur Vincent from prison? (I told her about that when we stayed in Orléans and asked her never to repeat it—that was my mistake.) Jean, an honest old fellow, gave in, and the next week we had Angelique riding beside us.

That was the night we heard a patrol of National Guard coming in our direction. We rode into the brush, muzzling our horses, hoping the patrol hadn't heard us leave the road quickly and couldn't now see us through the trees. Angelique said the whole time she just wanted to be home safe and warm in her bed, and that risking one's life to serve stew to a lot of dirty refugees wasn't her idea of fun. She vowed to keep quiet, and Jean and I could keep our intrigues to ourselves. Besides, she said, I never did like horseback riding, especially at night. I was glad, because I did not want Angelique to run the risks I did—and she wasn't as discreet in a dangerous situation or in her daily conversations as I would like.

One night I asked Claudette to ride out with me, while Angelique watched Caroline. Claudette was in tears as she herself placed the bowls of mere broth—shortages in the market now limited the supplies we could bring—into the hands of people like her parents, who had fled her region. After that night, she never again opposed any of my "intrigues." She even had me put in writing that, should anything happen to me, and until Monsieur William returned or sent for his daughter, she, Claudette, would take full responsibility for the raising of Caroline. We both signed it.

That night I lay awake, Caroline asleep in her crib across the small room. I recalled her laughing that afternoon—the eighth-month-old-child laughter that dares the world that anything be wrong. I had carved a small wooden horse that looked more like a duck, painted it red, and attached to it a leather string. Every time Caroline pulled the ducklike horse to her and it touched her bare feet, there in the shade of the pear tree, she laughed. Hard green fruit hung from the branches above her. She stared at the light through the leaves with the same innocent and intense gaze as her father, and suddenly I wept that he could not hear that laugh, nor see that gaze. Now, as I lay in the dark, I felt a double loss engulf me: that I had signed that form, and that I was alone. I had got the cottage, tended the garden: Where was William?

THE TITUS CUT

That summer my brother and his friend from university, Jean-Claude Marché, became our first guests in our new home. For a housewarming present, they brought candles and soap, increasingly hard to come by. Etienne and his friend mirrored each other; they were the young men from Paris—tailcoats, high-crowned hats, English jockey boots, and canes—except Etienne wore beige breeches and cropped hair, his friend green breeches and hair that fell to his shoulders.

"What happened to your hair?" I asked my brother.

"You don't know much about what goes in the world, do you? This is the Titus cut: from that Roman play by Voltaire. A week after it opened, all the young men cut their hair to look like the character Titus. Really they did it because the ladies love the actor who played the role, but then everything is political now, so all Paris says it's manly and revolutionary to have your hair cropped, and effeminate and counterrevolutionary to grow your hair. What do you think, Annette?"

"I think it is wise for you to appear like a Republican," I said. "And what about Monsieur Marché?"

Etienne's friend cut himself a slice of bread and said, "But I am not wise, Madame."

Etienne laughed and said, "Jean-Claude is a bold one. You won't see me wearing royalist green or growing my hair. He has had to use his stick more than once for protection against sans-culottes who tell him to cut his hair like a good Republican."

Jean-Claude shrugged.

"I draw the line at wearing dirty shirts, though, Annette." He pointed to his white neckcloth. "It's almost treasonous to appear in public in a clean shirt"—and he laughed again. "You think it probably wasn't *wise* to attend the demonstration in May—we joined the

Girondin supporters and shouted, 'Down with anarchy! To the devil with Robespierre, Marat!' Not that it did any good."

The gentlemen poured themselves cups of water from the porcelain jug that had stood atop my dresser at chez Vallon.

Claudette had gained knowledge of cooking from her years of friendship with the cook of chez Vallon, and this afternoon my wise maidservant and friend had already combined shallots and thyme with stems of parsley and tarragon, added walnut oil and lemon juice—all ingredients grown on our own property—and poured the mixture over a large pike that she had bought at market. The pike had been marinating for six hours, and she was now frying it.

My job was to work on the sauce, which was to chop twenty-five walnuts, plus parsley and tarragon leaves, and add them to some precious melted butter, it being a scarce commodity now too. I had never cooked before and wasn't very good at it, but I liked it. Claudette and I would talk as I helped her, sometimes with Caroline tucked under my left arm.

Because we had no drawing room, the men now sat at table on hard wood chairs in what we called the dining room, which was really just an extension of the kitchen. Etienne's manner was the same as if he were at the large mahogany table at chez Vallon. He continued to talk about the politics of Paris, of which he said we were woefully uninformed. He was the authority, and he would enlighten his big sister. I loved to hear him talk, and I wanted to hear more because it was what William would be interested in too—in a way, we were also talking about him.

"The Girondins' biggest mistake," he said, "wasn't just that they voted against the verdict of death for the King—they wanted the *people* to decide his fate, not just the National Convention—the mistake was when they tried to arrest the madman Marat, whom the Parisians love. The Jacobins, in turn, printed pamphlets with absurd accusations that the Girondins had really created the whole revolution to destroy France and have it taken over by England. It is amazing that people tend to believe what they read in the papers. Jean-Claude and I were actually in the crowd behind the National Guard when they pointed their cannon at the National Assembly and drew their swords to arrest the Girondins. No one knew what was going to happen. I tell you, Paris is the most exciting place in the world to live."

I served Jean-Claude dinner and said, "And what do you think, Monsieur Marché?"

He smiled. "I think your brother is right, as always, since he is the *wise* one. But whether Paris is or is not the most exciting place to live is really of no concern to me. I leave in September to join my parents and younger brother and sister, who emigrated to England two years ago. Etienne hasn't told you. They're suppressing the university. The spreaders of propaganda need hysteria, not science, to bolster them. The last thing they want is for people to *think*. But I've finished my studies. Etienne the Wise has another year."

"What are you going to do?" I asked.

"You started before me," my brother said to his friend, ignoring me. "There are still medical schools," he said to me. "But the most prominent ones in this country now are in the field, that is, the battle-field."

"You could have finished," said Jean-Claude. "But you are always so slow and careful."

I served my brother now. "What are you going to do?" I asked him again.

"I'm not slow and careful," he said to Jean-Claude. "Just prudent, like my sister Annette."

"Not always prudent." I gestured in the direction of Caroline, sleeping upstairs. Etienne understood.

"Ah, but you refer to *love*, dear sister," he said. "One has a duty in love not to be prudent, or one loses the love." The gentlemen now stood as Claudette and I took our seats, then they sat again. I asked Etienne to say grace, and he mumbled something.

"And what do you know of love?" I asked.

"I've been to the opera."

"Well, the opera will explain everything," I said.

After a pause for serious eating, Etienne said to the table at large, "So when are we going?"

"Where are we going?" Claudette asked.

I thought he was referring to some local opera.

"Despite this fresh and excellent food, which one can only pro-cure in the French provinces," said Jean-Claude, and bowed to Claudette and me, "I'm afraid Etienne is referring to the *levée en masse* of 300,000 in the spring, which, as students, we managed to avoid; but now, as I said, they are suppressing the university. There is talk now of another *levée*, a larger one, which no able-bodied unmarried man under twenty-five will be able to avoid, and while Etienne is so knowledgeable about love, I don't think he has plans to marry, and I certainly do not intend to cut my hair. And your brother must complete his studies—"

"Etienne," I said, "you, too? After Marguerite and—"

"And you, too, dear sister. And Caroline—she's half English. And you, Claudette. And Angelique, if she wants to flirt with cold-blooded Englishmen—sorry," he said to me, "not all Englishmen are cold-blooded—isn't yours waiting in London?"

"I believe so—"

"Then it's settled," Etienne said. "Two gentlemen full of the latest French medical science, two lovely young ladies, one with an English fiancé—what more could the waiting British public ask?"

"Dessert?" I asked. "An apricot tart made from apricots from our own tree?"

"We're not leaving till September," Etienne said. "You have the whole summer to think about it."

"You and your prudence," I said. "Where are you going to get the papers?"

"There are means," Etienne said.

"People get arrested all the time for traveling with false papers," I said. "I don't want to hear another word about it."

"I'll write to you from England," said Etienne. "Until then, may I help you with the tart?"

The rest of the evening passed agreeably, with Etienne even bringing out some cards, for old times' sake, until Caroline woke up, and that was the gentlemen's signal to part. I didn't want Etienne to leave. I wanted him to spend the summer here, picking apricots and making jam with me in the day. But there were other things I needed to do now—things that I didn't want him to know anything about. He was still my little brother, and I didn't want him to go near any danger.

He kissed me good-bye. "You have a loving home," he said,

"worthy of your excellent heart," and he pulled out his watch I gave him and popped it open to my likeness.

"I don't look like that anymore," I said.

"Then you'll have to supply me with a new one," he said. "And I check the time quite often."

And the men were out our little gate, and I heard my brother's steps recede into the dark.

AN OMEN

I liked working in my kitchen garden. It was a new experience for me, to have my knees on an old cushion and my
hands in the soil, weeding, as now, or, in the late spring after we had
moved in, planting squash, aubergine, courgettes, tomatoes, potatoes,
beets, cabbage, and herbs—including lavender for a sweet smell that
lingered over the whole garden. Caroline lay on her blankets in the
shade of one of our three fruit trees, and her wide eyes watched the
stream glistening and falling from the watering can as I stepped gingerly from one young plant to another. I liked the magic and mystery
of the garden—suddenly, as if overnight, a spear of green courgette
would appear under its wide leaf and splendid orange blossom, or a
plump purple aubergine would bulge out from its hiding place.

I sang to Caroline as I worked, mainly just to keep her quiet,
spontaneous lyrics about the names of the plants and their colors. I
gave her a big squash blossom to play with (although these were also
delicious sautéed lightly, and rolled up as crêpes), and glanced at her
under my wide-brimmed straw hat, and moved her, as my work and
the morning progressed, from pear to apple to apricot tree. Caroline
also liked to watch me feed the rabbits (she was too young to pet
them), and Claudette milk Emilie, the goat, and Caroline looked out
from a sling around my neck as I talked to the chickens and spread
feed for them as they bobbed and clucked at my ankles.

It was also good to work in the garden after riding out to the count's
lodge the night before, for, despite their victories in July against the
army from Paris, many people of the Vendée still fled the region, and
after their defeat at Luçon in mid-August, some still managed to come
this far east to avoid capture. There was a regular network set up
now; one only knew the next station to send people, and the Mother
of Orléans, with her white feather in her black bonnet, her green
riding cloak, and her fast sorrel mare, was definitely part of that net-

work. The trick, for now, was never to use the lodge more than once a week and never to have more than twenty people at a time. These were conditions I sent on to the network itself, which now was calling itself the Chouans—after the call of the owl, *chat-houant,* which we used in the woods at night. Their leader, whom I heard was an ex-salt smuggler, had even taken the pseudonym Jean Chouan.

I myself was aware that I was developing—and thought it would be prudent to cultivate it more—a double identity. I was at once an ex-upper-bourgeoise, now a simple citizen and hardworking young widow, who lived with her one servant and her infant daughter—and who had already brought apricots, summer squash, goat cheese, and rabbits to sell at market—and the secret member of the Chouans, who rode out at night with a white aigrette in her hat. These two identities were only contradictory to others, whom I wanted to deceive. To me they were both true, but different, aspects of myself, just as I kept secret a third identity that slumbered beneath the other two: that of a lover of a poet, whose nation was an enemy to mine.

A little before noon I was weeding around an aubergine plant, with its tiny, deep purple blossoms, when I saw the garden before me darken as a cloud drew across the sun. Then Claudette came running from the house. "Look, Madame!" She was pointing to the sky. It was cloudless, yet a sudden evening had fallen over the world. "Look at the sun," Claudette said.

"Shield your eyes," I said, for the glare was sharp, though a dirty brown gauze was being drawn, or was drawing itself, over the sun's disk. The yellow was rapidly being eaten up. Noon became twilight.

"It is like the end of the world," Claudette said.

"They used to think so," I said. "It is an eclipse of the sun. The moon has moved between the sun and the earth, that is all."

"That is not all, Madame. It is an omen."

"That is indeed what even the wise Romans thought," I said. I didn't want to admit it, but I agreed with Claudette and the Romans. Rational explanations are all very fine, but they cannot replace the feeling one has when the source of life is taken from you before your very eyes. I heard screams from other houses. Science can be true, and myth also. Why not? Everything was a great mystery—how my aubergine grew, how Caroline lifted her tiny hand and grasped the squash blossom tightly; how La Rouge's alfalfa transformed itself into thundering strength. I knew William would agree. He had called the mystery "Presences" in nature and said one of his goals was to reveal their power and life in his poetry. These unknown Presences were now showing us that the source of light and warmth could be drawn suddenly from us, without warning. Hadn't we seen that in the last several years? Hadn't I felt it with the sudden death of my father? And now, if one followed the indications, more of it was to come.

I knew the men in Paris who sent the armies of shopkeepers to plunder and terrorize the provinces—the men who decided that ideas were more important than individuals; who manipulated people's fears to further their own ambition and rid themselves of their own enemies by proclaiming that these enemies were dread "destroyers of national security"—these men, I was sure, would look at the twilight skies over a Paris noon and laugh at what fools the Romans and the medieval peasants were. The irony was that they themselves otherwise tried to emulate the Romans in all things, from their style of government to their dress. And that they did not know that they, too, were standing beneath this same sun—they too were unknown characters in the tales that were to unfold from its untoward vanishing—they too, as confident as they were in their hubris, would be victims of the disappearance of light.

This day, the fifth of September, was the day that a delegation of Jacobins in the National Convention righteously exhorted that all the legislators place "Terror on the order of the day." This was the day that brought so much darkness for the next year.

It was also the day that finally brought me news of William. That afternoon after the eclipse I walked past the cloisters of Saint-Saturnin to the little tobacconist shop that also served as the post office, and the general center of gossip. I always brought Caroline because she was popular with the man who ran the shop and his wife, and with anyone else who was standing around talking with them, and Caroline also deflected interest away from my asking for mail. I often bought something there, for it was a type of general store—leaves for tisane, paper and ink for writing—to make my visit seem more credible. They always said, "Oh, nothing for the little mother again today. Oh, look how the baby's grown." But today they were all in a dither when I came in. First it was about the eclipse, then, "There's something for you, Madame, forwarded from Orléans. Two—*two* letters from England. They must let the mail through twice a year. Whom do you know in England, dear?" "Oh, my father's brother," I said, "who married an English lady and moved there years ago." And they put two letters in William's handwriting in my hand. I tried to keep my agitation to myself and left the shop. "Don't you want any of that tisane?" I heard behind me.

Where was I going to open them? To walk all the way back home past the somber cloisters was unthinkable. The quai was right here. I sat on a low stone wall facing the river and propped Caroline in my lap. "These are letters from your papa," I said. "Now let me read, and be a good girl." I ripped open the seal of the earlier letter. Caroline started to grab it, and I took off Etienne's watch and chain from around my neck and gave it to her to play with.

My Dearest Friend,

I cannot express to you my regret at leaving you or the privation of my separation from you. I have not heard a word from you since war was declared. All I hear are stories of horror from France. How can I be in comfort in England when you and sweet Caroline are exposed to heaven knows what dangers?

I had to leave London. Its many people and buildings were bearing down upon me. I decided I could no longer live with such uncertainty as to what had befallen you.

Therefore, I am travelling now with William Calvert, a friend of mine from my school days at Hawkshead. He has taken an interest in my plight, has money and a desire for adventure. We are visiting the Isle of Wight, and my friend, through discreet inquiries at the market, was directed to a heavily bearded Irishman, who never gave us his name, who sold at his booth lace from Belgium, miniature portraits of fine French ladies, and porcelain teapots. This odd fellow, it seems, smuggles common goods—butter, soap, candles, coffee—which I hear France is in need of, to her shores, and brings back sundry items, probably plundered from châteaux. From him Calvert purchased passage for us across the Channel. This Irishman assures me he has often, in his laden fishing boat, outmaneuvered the British blockade—and the French National Guard at ports. He will let us off on the Normandy coast, and we will then walk to Orléans—or Blois—to wherever you are.

My sufferings are intolerable. In London I even followed women in the streets who resembled you, thinking, perhaps, that you had somehow fled to English shores and were seeking me. This was especially true when I saw a woman with a small child. My sister and friends feared for my sanity and urged the remedy of fresh air and open spaces. But they did not know truly my feelings.

Thou lovest me; I doubt it not, but the certainty of seeing thee must drive away the doubts of thy safety that assail me. And of course, I must see before me the face of my child. Please do not worry for me. I like walking and sleeping in the outdoors; it is my custom.

yours in exile
17 July, 1793

That was almost two months ago, I thought. What had happened? The second letter was also from England, not Normandy. I rapidly tore its seal and unfolded it.

My Dearest Friend,
I was happy to set off with the Irishman to find you, happy as I had not been for a long time. With the gulls and the waves slapping his small boat, some splashing over the bow and drenching me, I felt alive again. I was going back to France.

It was at night when we left the Irishman's cave on the Isle of Wight, with only the slip of a moon, and we were well out in the Channel before we saw any vessel. A ship of the British blockade loomed before us in the dark. It was so sudden, coming out of a low fog, we almost hit her. The Irishman turned his small boat west, and we were not seen. But by the time we were back on course, we had lost valuable time, he said.

We saw nothing but the choppy sea until hills on the French coast hung in the distance, like a charcoal cloud on the horizon. There was little difference between sea, sky, and land. Then the hills began to take shape, the one before us a little like a giant, with trees and outcroppings like wild hair and arms outraised. It reminded me of a mountain near a lake of my youth, a mountain that seemed to be following me once; I may have told you of that story.

We made for a small bay in Normandy, our smuggler's appointed meeting place with the Frenchmen on the black market. We could see one or two small lights on the shore, and the Irishman said these were the lanterns of the men who were meeting him. We entered the mouth of the small bay. France was just yards away now. As we bobbed near shore, a figure raced into the water, waving his arms. Then we heard the explosions of muskets and saw their sudden fire and smoke in the dawn. The man who had been running cried, "It's a trap. Take me with you," and swam toward us in a panic.

I recognized the uniforms of the French National Guard now, as they took aim in the shallows and fired a volley at us. We three lay flat on the deck. I thought of diving overboard and swimming for the other side of the bay, but then noticed more National Guard running down the steep hill there and forming themselves on the beach. We were surrounded.

The swimmer reached us now, and I held my hand out to him. In the pale light I could see dark blood running from his sleeve. Calvert and I, while lying down, each had one of his arms and were just raising him on deck when the next volley came. The man simply moaned softly and went limp in our arms. We let him slide back into the water, & I turned & saw the Irishman lying under the mainsail & maneuvering it with one raised arm. By the time the third volley came, we were out of range & just saw spurts of fire on the shore. "What a waste of merchandise," the Irishman said, and we headed back toward England.

The cliffs on the Isle of Wight rose through shrouds of fog, and we heard the welcome cries of English gulls over the waves when we came again up to a British ship of the line. It looked like a floating fort, from where we were, like a piece of kindling, on the water. This *time we had been seen. I half-expected the Irishman to start bailing his cargo overboard, but he simply said, "She's a slow monster."*

Our captain, while filling the air with Irish curses against the British, took us right across the bow of His Majesty's ship, and so a broadside missed us. Only when we were safely hidden in the fog again did a random cannonball lodge itself in our stern. Calvert and I bailed buckets of water overboard as more filled the deck from below, and the Irishman managed to take us into his watery cave that we had left with such high hopes.

He told us that even when he had finally repaired his boat, no amount of money from my friend could induce him to take us across the Channel again, for we were decidedly bad luck. Calvert, though, in any case, had had enough of adventure, and I felt very bad that I had got him into that danger. We parted on Salisbury Plain after he drove the one-horse carriage that he rented into a ditch. He said our whole expedition was folly of the highest order, and, indeed, not suffering for love himself, how could he possibly know what desperateness had driven me to such folly?

You, my love, more prudent than I, are probably happy that I am safe in England. I, however, despite this disastrous expedition, would far rather confront any Committee of Surveillance than this desolation I now feel at my destroyed hopes of seeing you, a desolation agitated further by my anxiety for you & for dear Caroline.

Last night I took bleak shelter at Stonehenge as hailstones the size of rocks pelted the plains. I closed my eyes and imagined the wailing of wind to be voices of ancient races, raised in cries of war or of human sacrifice—and indeed how different are we now, than then?

The cries of war now have made an insurmountable barrier out of a narrow strip of choppy sea. What remains for me now? Shall I sacrifice prudence again and undertake another expedition of folly? I do not have the money or means, and will, at any rate, yield to what I believe your wishes to be—that I remain safe, though to see you for a moment, to hear your voice say one word, would be enough for me to try that folly again.

But for now I will walk to North Wales and visit my friend Robert Jones, whom I told you about, with whom I traversed the continent

three years ago. In the woods and mountains of that country I will
seek the solace of Nature. If I find thee again during this war, it
will be there.

> *Adieu most tenderly thy dearest Friend, William.*
> *Bath, England*
> *27 July, 1793*

I raised my eyes and gazed for some time at the September haze on the river. I could hear Caroline, as if far away in my lap, winding the watch chain around and around her little fingers. I didn't know which emotion was the strongest—bliss at the reminder of William's love; worry at his dangerous crossing and that his impetuous nature might try such an adventure again; or relief that he was unharmed and that he would be safe in the faraway mountains of Wales.

I felt a cold breeze off the river. Caroline wanted to be off my lap. I folded the letters, put them in my pocket, and picked up the watch chain. It was hopelessly tangled.

TO REGENERATE MANKIND

Dear Annette,

I trust you have had good hunting this summer. Since I am a reformed old aristocrat, I have no time to hunt, myself, but now do several honest days' work before retiring to my château at week's end. A Republican going home to his château is rather a delicious irony, isn't it? Now please do me this honor: see for yourself the patriotic zeal I employ for our new republic. I am enclosing a pass for you to the courts tomorrow morning. Be there at nine, then lunch with me at the Town Hall and discuss the future of Europe; you will find it all unexpectedly enlightening. I trust you have made good use of the old lodge. I have the honor to be, etc.

Château de Beauregard
9 September 1793

An impassive National Guardsman perused my pass, signed by the count—or rather "Henri Thibaut, City Magistrate"—and, like a taciturn valet, opened the old oaken door of the Town Hall, once a sumptuous palace, now a haven for the bureaucracy of surveillance, suppression, and propaganda. Every large room had its desks and occupants, quill in hand and sacred stamps at the ready. Every corridor, instead of hall porters, had its sentries standing silently by doors and busy clerks carrying papers to the next desk for the next stamp. The walls, once adorned by tapestries or paintings, were now as spartan and stark as the morals the Revolution professed, following the example of the "Incorruptible" Robespierre.

As a guardsman, younger than myself, led me toward the courtroom, I glanced into several high-ceilinged rooms, looking in vain for that religious tapestry I had briefly glimpsed the day of my own trial. It was unnerving being here again as a free citizen; so easily, I thought, my freedom could be revoked. What if someone denounced me, having recognized me from Paul's escape or seen me ride out late at night, leaving, past curfew, on one of my excursions? I might never walk out of here, except to go to the Beauvoir again. Why had I accepted this invitation? It could be a trap, the count now working in his new capacity as upholder of the revolutionary laws. I clutched my pass, to show that I was on the side of the powers that be, but no one noticed me.

In small groups, talking conspiratorially outside tall double doors or descending the marble staircase, I saw impeccably dressed men in high-collared cloth coats, silk cravats, and knee breeches, some even with the traditional powdered wigs. These were the lawyers. And they all boasted the tricolor cockade, pinned either to their hats or to their lapels. Apparently one could still look like an aristocrat if one just attached a cockade to one's clothing somewhere.

Women in the market wore cockades now on their dresses or hats. In fact, one was tempting fate if one did not wear a cockade. I had bought tricolor ribbons at the scarf lady's table in the market, and I wore them now on the pocket of my dress. Their colors just showed beneath the edge of my shawl.

My footman in uniform rather than livery now opened the gilded doors that led me into the room of the cherubic ceiling. I felt for a moment my throat dry and my thirst come back. Why had the count asked me here? To see what happened to people who dared to defy the strict authority of the new regime? Was he trying to frighten me into ceasing to use the lodge? Well, I had already stopped, as of last week—told them the Mother of Orléans was going to be just a mother—both because it's always good to stop while you're ahead, and because I needed it less. Whole displaced villages, men, women, and children, were now traveling with their newly formed Royal and Catholic Army.

I sat on a hard bench in the back of the grand room and again looked up. They could strip the walls of centuries-old tapestries or art, but they didn't bother to change the ceiling—those blue fields of heaven where plump, good-natured angels once, perhaps, looked down with some irony on a bishop's feast, and now, with the same irony, mutely regarded revolutionary justice.

The count himself entered from a side door, elegantly dressed as usual, in his curled wig, blue silken coat, white waistcoat and breeches, and shoes whose buckles shone. The cockade hung from his wide lapels like a decoration on a party costume. He walked in with his casual air of old-world authority, sat at the center of a long table, and glanced out at the spacious room. I was one of a handful of spectators—the man in front of me was already writing in a notebook: perhaps a reporter from the Blois *Gazette*. The count's eye briefly caught mine, then looked down at the papers on his desk.

He had a busy morning. I would have been bored had not a rising tide of anger at the absurdity and the injustice of the proceedings kept me continually awake.

The first case was that of four middle-aged aristocratic men, accused of singing funeral psalms as they carried a corpse to the cemetery. The count reminded them of the law regarding freedom of conscience but not of religious expression, sentenced them to sing "La Marseillaise" in the market square from nine to noon the following morning, and told them they were free to go but must wait for the representative-on-mission for possible further questioning.

His second case involved a young woman who had failed to wear a cockade in public. She protested absentmindedness: her husband had been recently called up in the *levée*, she had two children, and she was in a hurry going to market and had simply forgotten to put on the tricolor. The count said he assumed she knew the recent law that women must display a cockade in public and asked her, What if, one morning, the National Guard protested absentmindedness and simply forgot to protect the nation from the Austrians and the Prussians? This elicited some small chuckles from the clerks in the room and my presumed reporter, and the count ordered her to return to the Town Hall tomorrow, prominently displaying her cockade, and to wait now with the others on the benches to the side of the great room, where I had sat.

The next case, of hoarding candles, actually had a witness, a seemingly vindictive neighbor, whom the count asked, Would you still have turned your neighbor in if you would not receive the reward for reporting hoarders? She said she expected none, so the count dismissed her, and she, angrily, demanded the reward that the government said was rightfully hers. The count told the alleged hoarder to give twenty candles to the neighbor, who left outraged, and the hoarder took her place with the others.

A refractory priest was then shown in, who had refused to take the new oath of allegiance and had been caught hiding in the old cloisters of Saint-Saturnin, near where I lived. One side of his face was discolored, as if he had been beaten during his arrest or some time after. The count sentenced the priest to deportation.

Then a group of farmers stood, accused of resisting giving grain to the army. One of them was a giant peasant who said, boldly, that he needed every ounce of grain to support his family. The count said mildly that we all must make sacrifices now and ordered them to bring to the Town Hall their next twelve bushels of grain.

The next case seemed especially absurd. An upper-bourgeoisie mother and daughter (much like Maman and Angelique, I thought) had been overheard expressing opposition to the Revolution. They had called the Committee of Public Safety "boorish" for shutting down their favorite magazine, the *Journal of Style and Taste*. I almost laughed aloud, then realized they were accused of being counterrevolutionaries. The count told them that, under threat of imprisonment for six months, as difficult as it might be, they were to keep their private opinions private. They were free to go after further questioning.

In the count's last case of the morning, perhaps the most pathetic, a farmer and his son had evaded the new *levée en masse*. When the representatives-on-mission came from Paris to oversee the conscription, the father had hidden his son in nearby woods and brought him food until the representatives left their village. The father protested, without his son, how would he run his farm? The count said that thousands were in the same situation and sentenced the son to immediate enlistment and the father to return to the farm and desist from any more obstruction of the law.

It was near noon now, and the accused, surrounded by four armed guardsmen, crowded the benches. I saw the giant gaze up at the cherubs. Finally, the representative, introduced simply as "Citizen Carrier," strode in quickly, and the count vacated his seat and sat further down the table. The representative was dressed in a smart black frock coat with a carefully tied neckcloth, but he also wore the symbol of the extreme revolutionaries, the *sans-culottes*—long trousers rather than knee breeches—except these were of fine cashmere, not the coarse cloth of the Parisian workingman. The count crossed his arms and seemed to regard narrowly the representative, who, without asking for a review of any of the cases, addressed the accused, the few spectators, and the lawyers and clerks in the room.

He was a tall, very thin man and had a gentle voice when he spoke, like a tired father trying to make a recalcitrant son see reason.

"I have already made myself familiar with all these cases," he said, as if it were a matter of little concern. "You all know, or at least have heard, that we are on the threshold of a new world order. No, we have passed through that door and are about to bathe in the glorious sunshine of liberty and equality. And I refer not just to our great nation but to humanity itself." He paused.

"But to do this," and he continued with the same sincere, even friendly tone, "we must work as brothers; we must have a fraternity of common will. You will agree, then, if one has the opportunity— no, the *responsibility*—to regenerate mankind"—and he paused again—"the only crime, and indeed a heinous one at that, would be in some way to *obstruct* that sacred process. This obstruction could be large—threatening the nation with invasion, for instance, as is the case with the allied front of Austria, Prussia, and Great Britain, aided and abetted by the perfidy of the émigrés—our own depraved aristocrats. Or"—and now he looked thoughtful, almost sad—"the obstruction could be seemingly small. Perhaps one merely *forgot* to wear the beautiful tricolor rosette that proclaims one's love of one's country; perhaps one just wanted to sing songs, that in the darkness of superstition, have always been sung; perhaps one forgets one's neighbor's needs and keeps important items, such as candles, all for one's own use; perhaps one thinks that our glorious fighting men can defend our nation without food in their bellies; perhaps one carelessly casts aspersions on a Republic that espouses greater virtues than those of the vanities of fashion, or"—and here his gentle, but insistent voice, grew in intensity—"or perhaps one has forgotten the invaders on all our borders. One has forgotten that France stands alone against the world—and thinks that one's own harvest is more important than the harvest of liberty and of peace, or perhaps"—and now his voice raised itself almost to a fury—"one has stubbornly and brazenly refused to offer allegiance to this great Republic and insists, in ancient priestly arrogance, to think oneself above the law."

He paused once more, and when he resumed, his voice was again soft and his tone reasonable. "These offenses may seem small in themselves, but I tell you, they constitute an even greater threat than all of the allied armies combined"—and suddenly his pitched intensity returned—"for these are the crimes of the haters of liberty. These are the people who work from within the nation to destroy our brotherhood of freedom; these are the real enemies of *la patrie*, our country.

"Whether he acts from stupidity or from intention, he is of the party of the tyrants who make war on us. We have new masters now—not the old barons and counts"—he paused—"but no less cruel or insolent. These are the enemies who stand, unseen, among us. To ensure the security of the nation, one must punish not only the traitors, but even those who are indifferent, or careless, or selfish. Through the Revolution, the French people has manifested its will, and all that is outside of that will is the enemy."

I wondered how long he could go on in this harangue. The count looked utterly bored. He must have heard it all before. I was not bored; I was scared. Now Citizen Carrier's voice grew gentle again. "There are only two types of people in France today—the patriot and the counterrevolutionary. The guilty parties here have shown where their sympathies lie."

And the representative stood up, his fingertips pressing the table. "Therefore I will overrule the magistrate's verdicts." I looked at the count, and he was staring at the table. "In his capacity as a newly appointed local official, he was unable to see the gravity of these crimes in terms of the crisis of the nation as a whole. There is no hope for prosperity or peace as long as the last enemy of liberty breathes. All the guilty parties here—without exception—shall be delivered to the guillotine. That is the sovereign will of the people, of whom I am the representative, chosen by the Committee of Public Safety with absolute authority in these matters." He paused and looked at the aristocrats who had sung the hymns, then at the priest. "I might add that it has become abundantly clear that—as it is said in Paris— France will never be secure until the last aristocrat is strangled in the bowels of the last priest," and Citizen Carrier strode from the grand room, as if he had more important matters to attend to.

THE KEY

"So you see, my dear," the count said, "that I do earn my money after all."

We were in a small dining room reserved for the lawyers in the Town Hall. It only had two pillars and one chandelier. Because of Citizen Carrier's speech, we were late, and only a pair of men talked at a far table by the window; we sat in a corner on embroidered chairs that must have once known bishops' velvet robes.

"The man's quite insane; he should be in an asylum," I said softly. "*He* is the threat to the security of the nation."

"He has the force of the government behind him," the count said. "What I think you don't realize is—" He paused as a waiter brought in the bread. The waiter poured a glass of red wine for the count and me, and left. The count sipped his wine and made a face. "The new order doesn't know about wine," he said.

I thought the bread was good. Bread was, once again, becoming increasingly scarce. "For the true Jacobin," the count continued, "politics is a religion. Perhaps that is why they hate priests so. *They* want to be the only priests. Only the Jacobins can claim the right now to regenerate mankind, as Carrier put it. And you know, my dear, you and I, all those poor people on the benches—we are as nothing before the will to change the world. Any nonbeliever must be purged. Carrier and his friends would have done well during the Inquisition. They just would have been wearing hoods. The point is, religious zealots have always been the ones who are the most willing to kill their fellow man. Just look at history."

The waiter brought in our lunch of eels with mushrooms and prunes. "I hate eating here," the count said. "Eels should be simmered in mature wine."

"Why did you invite me here?" I said.

"To enlighten you on the future of Europe, I believe I said in my letter. The little drama of Citizen Carrier should have done that."

"So now I've seen cases that make me angry. I already know of the injustice of the new regime, believe me—"

"And you're already doing something about it—"

"In a small way, thanks to you."

"I have nothing to do with it and know nothing about it. Do you care about the fate of these people today?"

"Of course. They do not deserve to die for their noncrimes."

"Would you be willing to do something about that, too?"

I paused with a piece of eel flesh on my fork.

"Would you be willing to risk more than taking a ride on your horse at night?" the count said. "If you say no, that is fine; we will just enjoy our eels and prunes and you can say how splendid I was in my useless capacity of magistrate."

"How long has Carrier been here?" I said.

"Almost a week, and he has undermined every case I have heard since then. I might as well stay in my slippers in my château. You see, it is partly revenge against Carrier that I want." He glanced over at the two men, who were leaving their table now. "Sip your bitter wine," the count said, "and don't be hasty in your response."

"Can you tell me more about what you are referring to?"

He leaned over his plate. "I'm talking about releasing them all from prison. Illegally. At night. In a plan of genius. My motives are simply revenge, as I said, against the mockery of justice that is flooding this nation. It will be amusing, if it works. They will see they are not invincible. That people can resist them. Carrier and his crowd will be publicly embarrassed. I, of course, will be comfortably at home. I know you have taken risks before, and they don't seem to bother you. You are really just as mad as your Englishman, who tried to oppose the Jacobins by writing sincere articles for the Girondins—"

"How did you—"

"Seriously, are you interested?"

"Let me judge the level of 'genius.' I don't have an army for a prison break, Count. I have a horse and sometimes a groom with a limp."

"That is quite satisfactory. Only you'll need a boat, and Edouard, my exquisite valet, will conjure one up, with the help of a couple of royalist sailors in need of money and a noble mission. They will have contacts downriver, part of a network with which I believe you're familiar."

"You're a royalist spy," I whispered.

"No, nothing that romantic or dangerous. By being magistrate, I merely gain security from the new order and some soothing of conscience by occasionally helping the old. I can't do much. It was your asking the use of the lodge that put me in this frame of mind. You're the daughter of my old friend who would not be afraid to act, were he here. You shamed me, my dear, so, with the help of Edouard, I have made a few contacts. But as I said, I take no risks."

The waiter entered the room, picked up our plates. "We will need nothing more," the count said. "Just leave us the water," and the waiter left.

"You could have asked me about coffee," I said. "I haven't had any for months."

"Not even here," the count said, "though some restaurants get it through the black market. Do you know what this building used to be?"

"Of course. The Bishop's Palace." The count nodded and filled my water glass.

"Once, deep in the old cellars, among the racks of fine vintages, when the bishop was showing me a Chinon '65, I asked him, Where does that rusty iron door lead? He said it was an escape route, built during the religious wars—though I myself think it was really used to smuggle in a woman. It led to the cathedral crypt, so she must have been a brave or a well-paid woman."

I laughed. "Etienne and I discovered that door when we were kids. While our parents thought we were at confession, sometimes all of us children would play hide and seek in the crypt. One time, it was only Etienne and I, and when I found him near the door to a marble vault, he remarked that it was slightly ajar and dared me to enter it. We always brought candles for our game, so I went ahead. Once inside, I found a passageway and couldn't *not* follow it, and then poor Etienne had to follow me. After that, we went to confession."

Now the count laughed. "You are truly the most bizarre young woman I have ever met." He shook his head, as if he couldn't believe what he had just heard. "This makes it a bit easier for me. I mean, I thought I was going to have to ask you not just to free prisoners but to enter a crypt. You know, then, that the door at the end of the passage is now behind the bars of the the the new holding prison in the cellar of the Town Hall, the wine being long gone—"

"I didn't know that. I thought that door led to the Underworld. I thought the River Styx flowed on the other side of that door."

"Just a pack of helpless prisoners, I assure you." He was speaking softly now, and anyone peeking in the room would have supposed he was trying to inspire me to acquiesce to a rendezvous—which, of course, in a way, he was. "Do you know that the key to that door is in my possession, is even on my person at this moment? That Edouard located it, secured to the back of a painting of the Madonna and child that the *boors* had placed atop a pile of the palace's useless, decadent items they were about to burn? That Edouard saved the painting, discovered the key; that I pondered its use; that my valet satisfied my curiosity by trying it out on a number of doors on a pretext of looking for files for me—the endless bureaucracy of the Revolution—and as he pretended to interrogate prisoners in the old cellar, he found its home? Edouard is the true genius. He will now need to do further questioning for me, tomorrow night. That is, before the prisoners are sent on to the guillotine at Orléans."

"At what hour would he be doing this questioning?" I asked.

"At midnight, when only two guards are left on duty. And their post is at the head of the stairs leading to the cellar, not actually in the cellar itself. He will tell the guards, as he has before, that the prisoners are tired and vulnerable and easier to interrogate at that hour. He will also bring, as a present, two bottles of one of the fine vintages that used to be in that cellar. Instead of interrogating the prisoners, he will tell them of their immanent escape and to be calm and quiet and remove the empty barrels in the corner, in front of the ancient door. By three that door will open, Edouard will tell the prisoners, and the guards should be dutifully sleepy themselves, and I myself will be surprised if they have not sampled the wine. So the wine, the hour, and the smell and filth of the place that once aged some of the best wines in the Loire Valley should keep the guards from checking the cellar too often."

"Won't someone know," I said, "that someone inside engineered the escape? That your valet was there?"

"It's an old, rusty door. They could easily have forced it. No one knows a key exists. And Edouard will have left long before the escape happens; that is, if you decide to do it at all."

"Why me? Why not one of your contacts in the network?"

"I have never met any of those contacts. I only—and very occasionally—send information as to when representatives-on-mission will be visiting certain villages, to give the people time to hide. I don't know anyone. I certainly wouldn't trust someone to whom I had only and very indirectly delivered a note. You have proved yourself a number of times to be prudent and discreet—"

"My mother's favorite words again—"

"And resourceful and courageous, like your father, who went to help others even when a riot was in fury all around him—"

"Put the key on my knee under the table," I said. "If anyone looks in, they'll think you are just getting friendly."

I felt its weight suddenly on my leg, and I reached my hand under the table, felt the old bigness and heaviness of the key, and slipped it into the pocket of my dress under the cockade.

"Those were good eels, Count," I said. "I don't know why you're so fussy."

"You're brave to eat them all," he said.

"What really takes courage," I said, "is to enter that crypt at night."

When I left the Town Hall, the cobblestones were wet from the first September rain and the air smelled fresh and sweet. The old cathedral seemed to stand out boldly against the afternoon sky, lit behind it. Caroline would be safe with Claudette. William was safe in England. I breathed the air in deeply. I felt some strange mixture of dread and excitement.

THE CRYPT

I crossed the bridge well before the evening curfew and sat at the Café de Liberté at Saint-Louis Square, across from the cathedral. I drank a glass of cider and read from a small book that contained part of *The Romance of the Rose*, which always reassured me, and which I kept in one of the large pockets of my riding cloak. When the café closed and curfew was about to begin, I crossed the square and entered the cathedral through a small door in a side chapel, which the ubiquitous Edouard had left unlocked. I sat in the dim silence of the huge cathedral and waited for Jean and the appointed hour to arrive.

Like all cathedrals now, Saint-Louis was officially called a "Temple of Reason." But few people, I think, sitting in a cathedral at night, staring into the vast, empty nave, with its large arches disappearing into a darkness of infinity, could take its new name seriously. I was not disturbed by what William would call a Presence, palpably, in the silence that loomed around me, and I welcomed it and prayed quietly to Lucette. I closed my eyes and rested now in a dark, luminous space that knew nothing of the dangerous expedition on which I was about to embark, nor about Committees of Safety, nor even about English poets.

I finally heard the chapel door open and close, and the slightly unsteady gait of Jean, with his old limp, making its way across the nave. He had walked all the way down from chez Vergez after curfew, keeping to the shadows. He had become quite fond of intrigues. I whispered his name: "Monsieur Verbois," I said, and Jean, groom to my father, a symbol of the security of my old family, grinned a gap-toothed grin before me in the semi-dark. He had taken his hat off when he entered the cathedral, and his bald pate shone. "Madame," he whispered, *"Allons-y,"* the same phrase I whispered to La Rouge to make her go.

I rose, and he followed me to the door that led to the crypt. But when I opened it, and it creaked and broke the silence I had become comfortable in, I suddenly wanted to turn back. I had never felt that before on an intrigue. This was not, I thought, like letting tired people into a secret room that was once the assignation place for your mother and her lover. Nor was this like riding through the moonlit night to an old hunting lodge and providing soup for hungry people. This was entirely different. This was the stuff of dares: enter a crypt, go into the mouth of a tomb, and free prisoners of the state. Well, Etienne and I had done the first two things long ago. I had tapped then on a tomb for good luck because I liked the name on it—Chevalier Destigny—then went down a tunnel that I thought was leading me on a winding path to hell.

I kept going now, down the dark and even darker stairs, partly because Edouard had presumably been in the cellar tonight and had raised the prisoners' hopes, and if those hopes were destroyed and those prisoners led to an undeserving end at the blade of a guillotine, all because of my timidity, that would not do. That would not do at all.

Jean and I now lit the candles we carried in our pockets and proceeded into the crypt. It had the same cold, dead air as any time of day or season. What are hours or months to the dead? The smell of dust was strong, and Jean sneezed, which resounded in the crypt like Jove's thunder. We stood still a moment, and Jean, who had never been here before, followed me around the broad tombs. I remembered to pat the dust of Chevalier Destigny's as I passed it. But I hated it down here.

Jean could not show fear because he was a man in the presence of a woman. I could not show fear because I was the leader—and because I was a woman leading a man. Nevertheless, it was not with great *joie de vivre* that I stood in the oppressive darkness of an ancient crypt, stared at the door, slightly ajar, of a marble vault, and told myself that I was going to open that door again and walk right in. Jean shook his head.

"Courage," I said, as we pulled opened the door of the vault. "Something to tell your grandchildren."

I went first by the corpses of the bishop and his mother. They hadn't changed since I saw them last. What were six or seven years to them? Jean stifled a gasp. We went past her ragged blue velvet gown, the remnants of his red robe and a glimmer of his silver chain. I had to glance at her face. I had to think of her kissing him as a baby, of her holding him close to her breast. Then we were in the narrow passage. Jean walked bent over. Maybe all the people in those days were more my height. Maybe it was just too hard to build a bigger tunnel. Jean's shoulders almost brushed the sides. I saw the fast, sliding movement of tails, heard squeals, and felt a soft body against the toe of my riding boot and others scurrying over its top. I felt some scampering under the hem of my skirts and a tail slap my ankle. I danced a bit and kicked some. I remember I screamed here when I was a girl. Now I just didn't want any rats up my legs.

The passage again seemed endless. I had great respect for the courage and fortitude of Jean. It made a huge difference to me that I had been here before. Finally we saw the big iron door in our flickering candlelight. The quiet was unearthly. What if the guards had discovered the escape attempt and were waiting to arrest us on the other side of that door? Or what if there were more than one vault with a passage, and we were at a different door than the one the count intended?

I drew my pistol from one pocket, gave it to Jean, and from another pocket of my cloak pulled the large key, flat alongside *The Romance of the Rose*, and inserted it in the rusty lock. The count said that Edouard had tested the key from the other side. I turned it slowly, and a scraping sound followed that echoed up the lonely dark corridor. Then the key stuck. I turned it again and nothing happened. I was about to have Jean try when I twisted it to the right once more, and the jarring sound of an ancient bolt being hauled out of its resting place tore through the silent, still air as if another vault behind us had suddenly opened. I pulled the key out, not wanting to leave any evidence, and turned the rusted bronze knob. Jean pushed the door slowly open, with a minimum of creaking sound, and in our paltry candlelight and the dim flicker of a torch in the cellar, I saw silent, wondering faces give way before me.

I heard a woman gasp, a man whisper, "Mon Dieu," and someone else start a Hail Mary, and I stepped into the fetid cellar. I noticed some faces from yesterday, but many more than I had foreseen, perhaps a hundred, crowded together: all silent, all looking at me with expectant faces. Children slept or sat quietly in mothers' laps; old, young, and middle-aged eyes returned my gaze. A black velvet coat edged with dirty lace at the cuff, or a white muslin gown whose hem swept the filthy floor, rubbed shoulders with a coarse brown wool jacket or dress. Everyone shared the same fate.

A small, older man in a high-collared gray coat came up to me. "Madame Williams?" he said softly. I thought I recognized one of the aristocrats arrested for singing hymns. "We are all prepared. Notice how quiet we are, as if we are all sleeping." He smiled. He was proud of their efficiency. "You should know that one of the guards periodically comes to chat with one of our ladies. An inopportune attraction and a reason to move quickly. The gentleman in the corner will require some assistance." I noticed an older peasant, whom I thought was asleep, lying near the wall. "They say they will manage, though," the small man said. "We'll follow you now?"

"You'll follow Monsieur Verbois," and I pointed to Jean. "I will stay here until you are all out." I motioned for Jean to hand me the pistol. "Monsieur Verbois," I said to the cell, in a loud whisper, "will also give ten more candles to individuals on your way out. He will lead you to the quai, where a boat will be waiting. Listen. No one, I repeat, no one, must run or go before Monsieur Verbois." His slight limp would keep them at the right pace, I thought. "The boat will not leave until you are all on it. We will use the bishop's own escape route through the church crypt. Do not be disturbed by it. If it was good enough for a bishop, it is good enough for us. Now, proceed."

I stood back and let them file past, some nodding their heads at me, some looking straight ahead. All the faces seemed tight and strained. Then I heard a relaxed voice beside me. "You are on the hunt again, Mademoiselle Vallon." I turned to see a short, portly, black-bearded man in a green woolen riding cloak like mine, but his was trimmed with gold braid. I recognized the baron de Tardiff, one of the count's old circle whom I had hunted with on autumn mornings in another age. "You have that fine mare with you?" he said.

"We're walking tonight, Baron. What are *you* here for?"

"An artillery and a cavalry officer were arguing over whether they would use my horses to pull cannon or to ride directly into musket fire. As that would be a great injustice to my horses, I set the dogs on the men and led my horses, as fast as I could, to a hidden ravine in the forest. They arrested me as I returned home. Excuse me." Most of the people were past me now, and the baron helped prop up the ailing farmer; this didn't work, so he joined another farmer in carrying the sick man. The baron grinned at me as he walked past. *Fate and danger have made us all like old friends*, I heard the young chevalier saying in my mind.

Cool air blew from behind me into the stuffy, foul air of the cells. Everyone was moving quietly and efficiently.

"If nothing more is required of me, Madame," said the self-appointed leader of the prisoners, the older aristocrat who had first approached me, "I will leave too. But I'd watch that one, though," and he jerked his head. "The others have shunned her because she answered the attentions of the guard."

I thanked him, and he vanished into the crypt, leaving in the cellar only two women with a sleeping boy of about four or five: the younger woman who, I remembered now, had liked the *Journal of Style and Taste,* and her mother, who seemed very agitated, standing beside her. The young woman was looking up the stairs that must lead to where the guards stay, and her mother was pulling her arm. "Leave me alone," she said to her mother.

"Don't be an imbecile," her mother said, but the young woman didn't move, and her mother ran past me, crying.

"It is time to go," I said.

The young mother roused her sleeping boy, who cried out and waved his arms, as in a bad dream. She instinctively put her hand over his mouth, and, as his eyes were still closed, this brought on more of a panic.

Then I heard a door open, the sound of boots on stairs, a voice calling, "What's the matter, then?" and a young National Guardsman appeared, a stunned look on his face, his open mouth immediately silenced by the sight of my pistol pointed through the bars at his chest.

"You will be quiet, Monsieur, or you will die. It is very simple. I am not afraid to sacrifice your life for all of these others. Enter." I motioned him to enter the cell, and he took out his keys with a steady hand and unlocked it and entered.

"Now lock it," I said. He reached through the bars and did so.

"And give me the keys."

The woman who liked the *Journal of Style and Taste* finally spoke.

"Georges," she said. "Georges, listen, you do not have to be left here."

"Yes, he does," I said.

"No, Madame, he can come with us."

"Look at his uniform," I said.

"Georges, come with us," the *Journal* lady continued.

"Madame," I said, "either you come with us, or you stay here. I don't care, but make your choice."

"Georges, do you love me?" she said.

"We don't have time for this," I said.

Georges nodded.

"Georges, will you come with me?"

Georges nodded again. The present situation seemed to render Georges beyond the capacity of speech.

"Georges," I said, "do you care more about Madame here than about your position or your cause?"

George dutifully nodded again. "Well, it might be safer not leaving you here," I said. "Madame, are you willing to let him be responsible for your child's life and carry him to the quai?"

"Of course. Georges has always been caring to *petit* Charles. He brought Charles milk in the prison."

"Georges," I said, "do you realize I will be right behind you, and if you try to escape or to warn anyone I will shoot you, or if that is too noisy, I will stab you with my dagger, just as the famous Charlotte Corday did to Citizen Marat in his bath. A woman can do it. Do you understand?"

Georges nodded once again and picked up the boy, and with the muzzle of the pistol, I motioned for him to go in front of me. "Now quickly, Madame," I said. I was growing worried that the others were too far ahead of us. And I wanted to be there when they all boarded the boats. "Fast, now," I said. "There is nothing that will harm you in there," but Madame was afraid of entering the dark passage first. All the others had someone right in front of them and periodic candles. "Georges, you go first," I said, and pushed him in front of Madame. "Just stay where I can see you, Georges," I said. "You'll both have to use the light from my candle. Hurry."

Georges, to his martial credit, walked quickly through the passage. Madame only gave one gasp at the corpse of the old bishop, and I directed Georges through the crypt. I patted Chevalier Destigny's tomb with the pistol in my hand, and it made a clicking noise, at which both Georges and Madame jumped and turned around. I shrugged, then dropped the prison keys on his tomb. By the time we were in the cathedral, we saw the others trailing out through the door of the side chapel. And from the foot of the cathedral I saw under a crescent autumn moon a strange and wonderful sight: a long, dark, silent line of moving figures wound down a narrow alley, crossed back upon itself at a stairway farther down, and curved into another alley. Jean, gored with that boar's tusk years ago, was leading them well.

I hurried the loving couple, now looking like a little family, until we were right behind the last ones. The young woman's mother turned around and saw her daughter and grandson. She let Georges and the boy pass, then showered her daughter with kisses, without either of them slowing their pace. Then I saw the baron, still helping carry the ailing farmer, stumble on the stairs; the sick man fell and moaned loudly, and a hiss of whispered voices reached me. Immediately the line took shape again and wove, like a black phantom serpent, through the oldest quarter of the town. I saw the dark broad body of the river through the narrow opening of the last alley, and I knew my work was almost done. I wanted to make sure the people didn't crowd the open quai, but kept to the shadows and quietly boarded the boat. "Watch him," I said to Madame, and ran ahead to the front of the long line and saw Jean's scared face.

"Where's the boat?" he said.

THE SAINTE LUCETTE

*I*stood on the quai Abbé, with no boat moored up- or downriver, and a crowd starting to murmur behind me. Some would see this as a plot: they had been betrayed into further proving their guilt by attempting to escape; others would simply start to panic.

"It must be here," I said. Now I started to doubt the count.

"What is that there?" I said. I pointed about twenty yards out, to a large vessel with a sail sixty feet high.

"That can't be ours," Jean said. "All these people can't swim."

"Light your candle again." He did so, and held it up, and immediately a light answered. I dimly saw a rowboat detach itself and heard the dipping of its oars. When it reached the quai, one sailor tied it to a post and stood up. He had a white feather in his cap. He jauntily mounted the stone steps.

"Long live Louis XVII!" he said.

The young prince was guarded heavily in prison, and I thought this a most absurd greeting. "All these people can't fit in that boat," I said. "We don't have time to make many trips. The night patrol will be along soon."

"I am sorry, Madame," the royalist sailor said. "The only vessel we could get had too big a hull to come into shore. But she's fast. I brought a rope."

"A *rope*?"

"Yes, Madame. The old or too young can make one or two trips in my boat. The others can pull themselves along the rope."

"Are you insane?"

"It's quite easy," he said. "I've done it many times."

"These are women and children and farmers," I said, "not sailors."

"Is the rope secure?" It was the voice of the baron, again beside me.

"Yes, Monsieur," said the sailor, "I just tied it myself and my knots never fail."

"Then I suggest women and children step into the boat," the baron said, "and I will be the first on the rope."

"There are too many women," I said

"Annette, some will have to follow on the rope," the baron said. "They will do it if they see one person do it first. And you know that some women can do things well that are thought unnatural for them to do." And he went over to the dark mass of people at the edge of the quai and explained what they had to do. I added to the young women that this would be the adventure of their lives, something to tell their children and grandchildren. What else could I say?

"Who is this?" The baron pointed at the guardsman, carrying a little boy.

"That's Georges," I said, "he's the new father."

"Well, you better stay quiet, Georges," the baron said, "or she will slit your tongue." He pointed at me. "I've seen her do worse."

"I still don't trust you, Georges," I said, "and I'll watch you." Georges nodded. He had grown on me. "Madame and the child will take the boat. You'll have to take the rope." The compliant Georges nodded again.

"I'll go with him," the *Journal* lady said. "Charles, you get to go with Grandmère in the boat," and she handed the boy to his grand-mother.

The first boatload of the very old and young rowed off, and the baron, complete with boots and cloak, lowered himself into the cold, dark water. The men started to follow him. "Women should go in between the men," I said, "not all at the end."

"You go first," a woman's voice said to me in the dark.

It was my job just to bring them here. I had done that. I wasn't escaping with them, as was the baron. But I didn't want to explain all that, then, to the voice in the dark and to the other fearful women. I just wanted them off the quai and onto the boat. It endangered us all, every minute they stayed here. And I could see her point. As their trusted leader to this point, I didn't want to ask them to do anything I myself wouldn't do. I removed my petticoats from under my riding skirt, stepped out of them, undid the skirt's lower buttons, then sat down on the cobbles and pulled off my boots. I gave Jean my hat, pistol, riding cloak, and boots.

Going willingly into dark water in the middle of the night was, like entering a tomb in a crypt, unnatural. I think it was the idea of the cold that made me hesitate, when I couldn't afford to hesitate. Again, showing fear was out of the question. So I went in. At the first shock of the water I gasped involuntarily. The Loire is just trickles between sandbanks in the summer, but after the first autumn rains it immediately swells on its long journey, and now the river piled up heavily against me and pushed me away from the rope. I had to hold it with all my strength, and, since my arms are not strong, kick with my legs under the water toward the boat, and the skirt hampered my movements. Now other women were undressing on the quai and entering the river. I heard a series of gasps at the coldness. "Tell them to kick, not just pull themselves," I said, teeth chattering, to the young man behind me on the rope, and he passed it on.

I was at the side of the boat when I saw a woman, several people down the line from me, lose her grip and slip away with the current. The man next to her; the one I had thought of as a giant, caught her with one hand and slowly pulled her back to the rope. Now two strong sailors were hauling us up to the low deck. A big, bearded sailor said to me, "Welcome aboard the *Sainte Lucette* , Mademoiselle."

I was taken aback. I prayed to Lucette daily. It was quite a coincidence, as no boats had saints' names anymore. But this was a royalist boat.

"Thank you," I said. "Do you have any blankets on board?"

"There's some below," he said distractedly. "These ones are moving too slowly now. Look at them. The shore patrol comes in twenty minutes."

I went belowdecks and gathered blankets, and when I returned I saw the rowboat make a third run back and the rest of the dark blurs on the quai gradually disappear without sound into the water. It seemed as if it took an hour. The sailor who greeted me was now helping the last ones up on deck. The other I met was tying his rowboat up to the side of the boat. "Wait," I said, "I have to get back."

"You want to go *back*?"

I plunged in and grabbed the rope as I hit the water. It was harder alone, with only the swift dark water swirling around me and wanting to take me all the way to Nantes, or to the Atlantic. I was also tired. I didn't realize how tired I was. The quai seemed so far away. My hands felt too numb to hold the rope tightly. If I just put one hand in front of the other on the rope, I thought, and concentrate on holding on, the quai will get closer. Jean's worried face grew clearer slowly, looking at me, glancing east along the quai, then back at me. I kicked and tugged and grunted against the power of the river, coming up and slapping me in the face for my impudence with each lunge I took along the rope, then my feet felt the wooden pile of the quai, and Jean knelt and hauled me up, like a limp fish, out of the black water, and draped my riding cloak around me. As I put on my boots we heard the sound of other boots on cobbles, the night patrol, walking downriver from the quai Saint-Jean. The bridge would obstruct their view for another minute. I tried to untie the rope, but my hands were too cold to do anything. "Let's go," Jean said.

"We can't leave it dangling here," I said. Jean cursed under his breath, loosened the rope, and it slithered quickly back toward the boat, now floating west with the current, its large sail full.

Jean had gathered up all the petticoats and thrown them in a nearby alley. He handed me my effects, and with his limping gait, we ran across the open quai into the alley we had emerged out of and hid in the darkness until the sound of the boots and of the voices passed. They apparently had heard nothing from the Town Hall. It was better, I think, that Georges had gone with young madame.

Because of sentries on the bridge at night and the curfew, I couldn't return to the cottage, so I followed Jean home. It was a long walk, back through the winding alleys, up the stairs, around the edge of the square, and up more steep streets to what I still called, in my mind, chez Vallon, on its hill over the city. By the time I got there, my wet clothes clinging to my body all the way, I was stiff and aching with cold.

Jean woke up Angelique, who brought a blanket and a dry shift and met me in the stable. With my riding cloak and the blanket, I arranged a bed on the straw of La Rouge's old stall. I was shivering now, and Angelique hung my wet clothes up on hooks in the stall and regarded me in the lantern light. "Are you comfortable now, you old mare?" she said.

I nodded, but could not speak because of the shivering.

"You're really quite absurd, you know," she said. "Look at you. How many people did you save tonight? Twenty out of the thousand that the Committee of Public Safety will arrest again tomorrow? I wanted to bring you something warm to drink, but I didn't want to alert any of Vergez's servants, so I just brought this. I'm sorry I didn't have time to grab a glass." She handed me a small decanter. I was shivering too much to hold it.

"You're so ridiculous," she said, and drank some herself. "It's fine without a glass," she said, "apricot brandy from Angers." I felt its warmth flow through my veins. I took a second sip and gave it back to her. Angelique put the bottle down and brushed my wet hair back from my forehead with her hand. "You're the most ridiculous person I have ever known," she said. "You think you can take on the whole Revolutionary Army by yourself. You and Jean with his limp. Someday you'll get yourself killed and leave me alone with stinking Vergez and Maman the Queen of Protocol and your little baby and Claudette, and I'll have to help Claudette and cook and work in the garden like you two do and destroy my hands and never go to dances. Oh, they still hold them. See what you're missing. I know you like dancing, and you were so good at it." She was still stroking my forehead, and she gave me another sip of brandy. My limbs were quieting down.

"There, you're all right now," she said. "It's too bad you had to go and fall in love with an Englishman, Annette. Really. And Marguerite gone. You have no idea how lonely it gets. Oh, Etienne and his friend went to all the dances with me. Etienne has an eye for the ladies now, and they for him. And his friend almost got into a fight with a National Guard officer. I calmed them down. I'm going to bring you some water, now. I'll have to take the brandy. I don't know what you were doing tonight, and I don't want to know, but I think nothing's worth you ending up like this in the middle of the night and sleeping in a horse stall. You're the most ridiculous person I know," and she kissed me on the forehead and left. A few minutes later she came back with a jug of water and blew out the lantern.

Early the next morning, after a few hours of sleep, I rolled up my still-wet clothes, hid them under my riding cloak, and walked down through the quiet town and across the bridge with the first carts. A sentry looked at me as if he knew what I had been up to all night in town. I passed the cloisters of Saint-Saturnin, then saw the smoke rising from the chimney of our own cottage and heard our clucking chickens as I opened our little gate. I was still exhausted, physically and emotionally, from the night before. As Claudette opened the door with Caroline in her arms, and I saw my friend's relieved expression and my daughter's beaming face, I thought, it's time to retire from the Chouans. Caroline reached out to me, and I picked her up and nestled her in my arms.

hen one keeps animals, tends a garden, cooks, cleans, goes to market, and cares for a young child with only one other woman to help, one does not need to risk one's life in the evening to keep ennui from the door. But once I had let the Chouans know that I had other responsibilities besides riding horse-back and swimming in rivers at night, William suddenly occupied the place in my thoughts that had been packed full with the details of the next or the last intrigue. I realized that in helping others, I had been also in some way preserving myself from a fearful loneliness. What I simply wanted now was William in the quotidian of my life: hoeing in the garden, walking to market, in bed each night while the stars quietly changed positions outside the window and we quietly adjusted ours within—or to wake beside me, his eyes as eager and alive for the day as his daughter's. Was it too much to wish for, these common-place joys, to which every married couple had a right?

In what sort of illusion, I asked myself once more, was I living? I knew beyond doubt that William ached to return. I knew also that it was impossible. But since when were one's dreams bound only by the domain of the possible?

Once a week Angelique came to dinner at the cottage. She never asked about my intrigues, though she knew I had been doing them all summer. This time she brought a guest, a young officer with gold braid on his blue coat and a red sash about his waist. I was concerned until I saw it was Philippe, the count's son.

"Oh, didn't you know he'd been levied this spring?" Angelique said. We were sitting at our table, and Philippe was opening a bottle of wine he had brought, a rare treat.

"Father was furious," Philippe said. "I was visiting the château when representatives came with the conscription notice. Father told them to leave his property at once. 'What's the use of being a city magistrate,' he said to me, 'if I can't keep my own son from being conscripted?' He actually threw a glass of marc across the room. And you know how Father prides himself on his sangfroid. I told him, though, 'I've finished at university at Tours. I have nothing to do. Fighting Austrians is at least useful.' But Father didn't talk to me for a day, as if it were my fault. Then he burst into tears when I left for training. I've never seen him like this. I don't think working agrees with him. Soldiering is a very honorable profession. Especially defending one's homeland from the barbarian hordes."

"As long as those hordes are truly invaders," I said. "As long as wars of defense don't become wars of aggression. As long as they don't use you against your own countrymen—"

"Oh, no fear of that." He filled our glasses. Caroline sat on my lap and wanted some. I drank from my water, then gave her some. "I'm off to the Rhineland," Philippe said, "in a week. I've completed all my training. One thing Father said before I left was, 'I'll get you into the artillery, that's what I'll do. No cavalry charges for you.' I don't mind. I was never that good on horseback, not like you, Annette. And I became a second lieutenant in three months. They need more officers."

"Because they all get killed off," I said.

"No fear of that," Philippe said. "I have the luck of the counts of Blois in my blood. Look who's by my side," he added, and put his arm around my younger sister. She was beaming.

"You shouldn't say things like what you just said, Annette," she said. "It's bad luck. Besides, it doesn't apply to artillery officers."

"Quite right," Second Lieutenant of Artillery Thibaut said. Then he nudged my arm with his elbow. "Look at this, Annette," he said, and he lifted Angelique's left hand from her lap, and a ring with a small diamond sparkled on her finger.

"No," I said.

"Yes," Angelique said, "but the marriage is put off until Philippe's two years are up. It's a long time." She sighed. "They don't want their officers to marry, but engagement is all right. Maman is ecstatic."

"I'm glad," I said. Angelique sipped her wine and smiled at me.

"Now he'll be gone, and I'll have another war widow, so to speak, on my hands," Claudette said at my elbow, as she placed two big dishes on the table, then sat beside me.

"Don't talk like that either, Claudette," Angelique said.

"It's just an expression," Claudette said and began serving the dinner. "Monsieur William is sipping tea in England, where they don't have a shortage of sugar. Lieutenant Thibaut—that *does* have a good ring to it—will be sipping Rhineland wine—and there will be more lonely women here."

"Oh, Philippe said I can still go to dances," Angelique said. "In fact, he joked that he really just proposed to me so all the officers in town don't get any ideas." She smiled coquettishly at her fiancé.

"Any serious ideas," I said. "*Bon appetit*," and we started eating.

"Now don't tell me," Angelique said, "that you and Claudette caught this trout in the river."

"No, but I've found that food tastes best when it's from your own garden," I said. "Isn't that what Voltaire suggested is all one can ultimately do—tend one's own garden?"

"The potatoes, tomatoes, onions, and thyme in the casserole," Claudette said, "I had Madame Annette gather this afternoon."

"You're still one of the oddest persons I have ever known," my sister said to me. "Now you're a farmer."

I gave Caroline a bite with her own little spoon. I was pleased she liked it.

"Have you heard about the prison break?" Philippe said. "A counterrevolutionary ring, right here among us, engineered the whole thing."

Angelique's eyes were now wide as two moons and blazed on me. I looked down. "It also seems," continued the lieutenant, "that a Town Hall guard was their spy in our midst."

"No," I said.

"Yes, a Georges Lefevre. Disgraced forever. Must have run off with them to Brittany or wherever they went. Apparently he masterminded the plot—as complicated and bizarre as could be—a secret door, an ancient escape route through the cathedral crypt, a boat waiting on the quai—"

"No," I said. My sister was staring at me.

"They think Lefevre could be one of the top men in the Chouans," Philippe said, "those murderous brigands we hear about."

"A Town Hall guard?" I said. I was laughing. I couldn't help it.

"She's not used to the wine," said my protective little sister.

"It's not funny," Philippe said. "The representative-on-mission from Paris—a Citizen Carrier—humiliated that it happened when he was here, has left Blois. I told Father how embarrassing that was for his town, and he just laughed too—said Carrier was a 'boor, and we're well rid of him.' Sometimes I wonder about Father."

"I think the count has always proved himself rather wise," I said. But what I said no longer held any weight with Philippe.

"He's of the old world," his son said. "He told me to be careful at the front because one day *I'll* be count. He doesn't realize that there are no titles anymore—or the only ones that matter are military ranks."

"Oh, my," I said, "I think I should check on the pear tart."

"From your tree, of course," Angelique said.

"Of course," Claudette said.

While I was in the kitchen, Philippe continued. "Have you heard that some old marquis has organized a band and is terrorizing the Loire Valley?"

"How can 'some old marquis' be so dangerous?" I asked.

"He's wild," Philippe said, "fought side by side with Indian savages in the American war and uses their tactics. We can never find him."

"We?" I said from the kitchen.

"They're talking about pulling troops away from the front to fight him and his band. A tragic displacement of manpower."

"I remember," I said, standing by the table with the tart in my hand, "when you were ready, that night of July 14, '89, to go fight the mobs of the Revolution with your father and the other men. Now you're defending their government."

Angelique shook her head.

"I'm defending France," the lieutenant said.

I served the tart. "The wine was such a treat. Thank you," I said. "And congratulations." I kissed Angelique, then the lieutenant, and wanted to cry for my anger and frustration at a government that makes innocent young men believe in the value of perpetual war, and out of fear for my sister. "Excuse me," I said, "I need to put Caroline to bed."

The next night, I sang Caroline the same lullaby twenty times in a row before she fell asleep, and though she awoke the moment I put her down and I had to sing it at least once again, she finally stayed asleep. I went downstairs to sit with Claudette and work on a wool winter suit for Caroline. Though I was slow and clumsy with a needle, it was only mid-September, and I had plenty of time. Claudette was working on new curtains.

I was a retired intriguer now. I had been lucky and knew it. When Caroline greeted me at the door after the escape through the crypt to the river, I swore to myself as I held her that *she* was all I was living for now—and to keep myself healthy for William's return. Others could carry on the dangerous work. There were plenty of angry people out there who would be happy to do it, I thought. It was a warm autumn evening; the kitchen door stood open onto the garden. The needle was in my hand when I heard the hoot of an owl. I put the needle down and looked up. Claudette stopped too. I had told her of the Chouan signal. "If it's *them*," I said. "I will tell them I've retired."

I walked out to the garden, filled with a subtle scent of lavender and sage. "If any here desire the services of the Mother of Orléans," I said to the vegetables and herbs, "she is retired. She just tends to her daughter and to her garden now," and I went back into the cottage and resumed my sewing.

A minute later, with no sound of footfall, we heard a soft knock on the open door. I looked up to see a tall man with a round, black beaver hat, a black riding cloak, leather breeches, and boots to his knees. Long black hair fell from under his hat, and a scar sliced across his cheek. His coat was open, and one couldn't help but notice the silver hilt of a rapier and two pistols at his belt. He doffed his hat, bowed, and said, "The Marquis de La Roques at your service, Madame."

"Madame Williams, Monsieur, but you already probably know that, and Mademoiselle Valcroix," and Claudette inclined her head. "I won't say I'm 'at your service,' for, as you've just heard, I've retired. But if you're the terrible marquis I've heard about, and I think you are, this is still a friendly house to those who resist the Committees. If you have a thirst you may come in and serve yourself some water from the jug on the table. Please forgive us if we continue our work. One must take advantage of a sleeping baby."

"That is very kind of you," the marquis said, and did as he was bid.

"Please sit at table, Monseigneur, if you like," I said. Claudette couldn't take her eyes off of him. He looked so dangerous, yet had the manners of the count.

"'Monseigneur' is a title rarely used now, Madame," he said. "I knew of a young marquis who, to avoid conscription in the infantry, joined the cavalry of the Revolutionary Army. He brought along his valet as an aide-de-camp, who inadvertently one evening called his master 'Monseigneur.' The marquis was arrested on the spot and shot the next day. I learned this story from his loyal servant—he's now one of us."

"That is a very tragic story, Monseigneur," I said. "The world abounds in tragic stories now."

"Would you like to hear one with a happy ending?"

"Please; knitting, if you have never done it, leaves the mind free and often in need of entertainment."

"I'll give you two."

"If they are not too long," I said. Claudette giggled and looked down at her needles.

"If you are in need of nourishment, Monseigneur, please partake of the loaf on the table," I said.

He cut himself a generous slice. "This is excellent bread," he said. "Did you make it in that oven that looks from the outdoors like a giant beehive attached to your house?"

"Mademoiselle Valcroix did," I said.

"You have no idea," continued the marquis, "what it is like to taste good bread when you have been eating crusts and dried pork. This is heaven."

"What would possess a marquis to eat in such an uncivilized manner?" I said.

He took another bite of his bread. "It's time for my stories," he said. "There was once a young marquis of nineteen years of age who sought glory and honor fighting for his king against the British, far on the American continent; no, not the famous Lafayette, but one of the same age, who traveled with him. While Lafayette dined with and became as an adopted son to the top-ranking American general, this other marquis slept in the woods, learned the ways of survival and the methods of fighting of the Indians. He led backwoodsmen in deerskin clothing, not trained soldiers in blue uniforms, in raid after successful raid on the unsuspecting British in their bright red coats in the dark forests. At the end of the war, he stayed with his men and their families for some time, for he liked them and the wildness of their rivers and mountains. But he was called home by the love of his own region, of his own river that flowed through it. The end."

"That is very charming, but that's not quite an ending, is it?" I said.

"You wanted it short."

"One more sentence to bring us up to the present day," I said.

"So he used these methods," the marquis continued, "that he had practiced in the service of his king, now to protect his own region that he loved, and perhaps even, some day, to restore the monarchy that he also loved; as his men fought from hedgerows and in woods that they knew in the dark, or fired a musket, hidden in their fields, and continued with their plowing as if nothing had happened; so these fighters, both men and women, have never been beaten and have never been found. The End."

"That was rather a long sentence," I said.

"It all connected," the marquis said. "It even has a postscript: they formed themselves into an association—not just the loose bands called Chouans, of which you have doubtless heard, but an organization called the Philanthropic Institute."

I laughed. "This is the age of grand names," I said.

"Yet this name is not a menacing name," he said, "as in 'Committee of Surveillance'—or a hypocritical name, such as 'Committee of Public Safety.' This name simply reflects the beneficent purposes and actions of the institute itself; that is, relief for barns burned, for crops or homes destroyed, for widows and orphans."

"I thought you had two stories."

"Ah, the second one might be familiar to you." He smiled, and his scar crinkled; his black eyes danced. "There was a young woman," the marquis went on, "a young mother, actually, who took it upon herself to bring aid to those who needed it, who even dared rescue from prison victims of an unjust government, who led them through

the paths of the dead and through the freezing current of a river in
the dead of night to safety and freedom. This is the sort of woman,
Madame, of whom songs and legends are made, don't you agree?"

"Sounds like rather a rash and foolish woman," I said, "especially
if she is a mother."

"Ah," the marquis said, "but there are larger loyalties to which this
brave woman might also feel allegiance—to the family of humanity, to children who have been betrayed by their nation. Why do you
think this woman undertakes these dangerous missions?"

"I really have no idea," I said. "I suppose, after all the rational reasons have been examined and exhausted, she would simply say that
she had to do it."

"And that is the kind of courage I respect," the marquis said, "pure
compulsion, but for noble ends. And others who have expressed similar, though perhaps not as great, courage for such ends have become
members of the Philanthropic Institute."

"Did you not hear that that woman, despite what she may or may
not have done for the family of humanity, now just wants to be a
simple mother and not neglect her own child?"

"In that child's world," the marquis said, "not far from her safe
garden, the men from Paris are now enacting what they call the
'Policy of Desolation.' These people actually talk like that—the
great bureaucrats of murder—and other children are falling victim
to this signed and stamped government policy. Rather than ambush-
ing patrols from hedgerows, or shooting from behind trees, I thought
that this mother, who has heard the call of duty and adventure combined, this extraordinary woman who chose to do something—" the
marquis paused. "I thought, I merely had the thought," he said, "that
she might have some fun in procuring money for the Philanthropic
Institute to aid the victims upon whom that policy of desolation has
been practiced."

I laughed. "Monsieur le Marquis—all of your stories and speeches
were just to try to get me to steal money for you?"

"And have fun doing it—"

"No risk, no violence, just fun—"

"There is always risk," he said, "but violence is often an option. A
Vendéan general freed five thousand republican prisoners as a gesture

of mercy. Do you think the other side would have done that? Violence can be a choice."

"But you are a soldier—"

"And you are a mother," he said. "This choice, of making more stories that could be told someday over a jug of water and a loaf of bread—and helping people in the bargain—I leave for you to consider."

"I am honored, Monseigneur, that you came all this way to inform me of this institute, but I remind you that I have retired from intrigues. Yet I have enjoyed your stories and your company. We get few visitors, you know."

And the marquis rose and bowed deeply, "I thank you for the fresh bread," he said. "The clear water, the enjoyable feminine company, and I beg your forgiveness for the length of my stories." He donned his hat at the door. "Something I learned from the red man," he added; "the land is our mother, yet, like a mother, she is also, sometimes, under our protection. If ever, Mother of Orléans, you should change your mind about the institute, just wear a simple white ribbon in that straw bonnet of yours when you're at market, and a friend of mine will talk to you. You might be interested to know that you have a new title. They now call you the Fearless Chouanne of Blois." And he entered the garden and melted into the night.

"The Fearless Chouanne of Blois, Madame?" Claudette said. "That is quite a title."

"I fear our marquis could have made it up." I said. "He is fond of stories."

"But of true stories." Claudette paused, then added, "And he was certainly handsome, Madame, not 'some old marquis,' as Monsieur Philippe said; though he looked as I imagine a pirate would look—with that scar and sword and black eyes."

"A pirate with manners," I said.

THE LETTER

I was out in the garden several days after our visit from our mysterious marquis. My tall tomatoes, intertwining with each other, round squash with yellow flowers, and climbing beans were a world in themselves now. A melon hid itself beneath overarching leaves. Caroline was in her place beneath the pear tree. It was Claudette's turn to go into the tobacconist's, and she returned with a letter from my mother.

This was rare. Maman and I had had no communication since my letter after the *boucherie* incident, as I referred to it, if I referred to it at all. I opened the letter quickly. But it was not from my mother. She had merely written my address on a letter and enclosed within her page another letter. That one was short and signed by the Committee of Public Safety.

Claudette heard my scream and came running from the house. She first looked at Caroline, to make sure she was all right, then at me. I had immediately dropped the letter, as if its pages were fire. I felt turned to stone. I stayed still, in the same position as when I had dropped the letter, my hand open and hanging at my side. Caroline had begun to cry when I screamed, and I just stood there. What I had read in the letter could not be. Claudette picked up my child, "Madame?" she said. I managed to point at the letter. "Is it Monsieur William?"

I shook my head. I still couldn't believe what I had read. I couldn't say his name. Finally, "Etienne," I said. "They've—" and I sat, or sank, down in the middle of my garden, crushing the lavender. I lay there, like a stone in a bed of lavender. Out of the corner of my eye I saw Claudette, while carrying Caroline, kneel down, pick up, and fold the letter. I heard her talking to Caroline in a light tone, and crying as she spoke, as they went back in the house. I could do neither. I could not cry, and I could not pretend to be happy for the sake of my own child. I could only lie there, looking blankly at the autumn blue sky, as if at a wall, smelling faintly the lavender around me. I had no desire to move and felt as if I couldn't, even if I wanted to.

I don't know how much time had passed when Claudette came back out to the garden. I was still in the same place. I noticed shade had moved over the tomatoes. Claudette brought me a cup of water. "Drink," she said.

"No, thank you."

She placed the cup in the thyme by my head and left again.

The shade had crept up my legs when Claudette returned with Caroline. "Sit up on your elbow and drink," she ordered. "You've been lying for hours in the sun. You'll get sick. You'll turn all brown. Your daughter doesn't know why she can't see her *maman*. At least sit up."

With effort I leaned on my elbow. I felt like a dried-up creek bed in autumn. Nothing flowed. No tears. No feeling. No words. I sipped the water and put the cup down in the thyme.

Claudette sat beside me, with Caroline in her arms, quiet, playing with Claudette's pendant. She fingered the chain about Claudette's neck. It was such an innocent gesture, but anything having to do with the neck now made me think of Etienne's fate, and I felt vaguely nauseated. I had to look away. What could my child know of these things, of this world of which she was a part, and into which she would grow and want to love? With that thought, my numbness suddenly began to thaw into anger and into the urge to protect. I hadn't been able to protect Etienne.

"Did you read the letter?" I finally said to Claudette.

Claudette shook her head. "I could guess its meaning," she said. "What happened?"

I took another sip of water.

"He was arrested under the new Law of Suspects. For—" It was so difficult actually to say it, as if that made it more real. "For traveling with false papers," I continued, "for attempting to flee the country, for consorting with known counterrevolutionaries. They executed him in Paris as an enemy of liberty," and with the saying of it, suddenly something changed in me. "Sweet Etienne!" I said softly, and I couldn't stop crying now and lay back in the faded lavender, my body convulsed with sobs against the herbs and the cool earth.

And when there were no sobs left I felt myself alone in the dark garden. I only felt the sharp autumn coldness now and an emptiness that stretched from me to the vastness of the sky I looked into, and toward which the lavender around me faintly seemed to float.

That night, as I lay unsleeping, Etienne as I last saw him came to my mind, clearly, as he stood in the dark by the gate, opened his watch, looked at my portrait, and said I should send him a new one, for he checked the time often.

I crossed the bridge on foot (the count had warned me against La Rouge being seen by army officers), walked up the long hill to my mother's house, and met her in the drawing room. The Queen of Protocol, as Angelique called her, the fearful figure of my youth, seemed to have grown frail overnight. She sobbed as soon as she saw me—perhaps because Etienne and I had done so much together, and I reminded her vividly of him—and we sat down together on the couch. I didn't say anything. My own hatred and bitterness had fallen away in the wake of Etienne's death. Sitting beside Maman, I suddenly wanted to embrace her, for my sake as well as hers. I forced my arms up. Then they found their own way. I held her, as I would hold Caroline to comfort her when she would wake in the night, and thought, Etienne had been Maman's baby.

Monsieur Vergez had discreetly absented himself.

I murmured something to Maman that there was another world, and she suddenly said, "I cry also for you." She pulled away to look at me. "I betrayed you," she said. "Etienne was always happiest when playing with you—running, riding—perhaps he knew something I didn't. And I thought it was a weakness in your father, indeed in any man, that he loved you with such abandon—as if heaven had sent you just for him. But he too, perhaps, knew something I didn't." She dried her eyes now with her embroidered handkerchief and looked straight at me. "You were the recalcitrant one, the independent one. Now I want to say this before it is too late. Listen. I misunderstood my authority, Annette. I considered only what would give you the best advantage in life. I wanted to help you with my experience and stifled my desire to show you sympathy as a weakness in myself. I thought I was fulfilling my duty to you, but I misjudged. I neglected another duty—the natural one of a mother to her child's happiness. I don't want you to die and think I never loved you. In this world one can choose severity over sympathy and think one is doing right."

"I'm not going to die, Maman, and, now that I am a mother, I know how difficult it is. Every time Caroline cries, should I pick her up?"

"Just do not harden your heart, my dear. The Revolution has shown us that the advantages and opinion of society, which I thought everything, are really nothing, and always have been nothing. It is only our vanity that led us to believe otherwise, and one is not rewarded for vanity. I, for instance, am severely punished for mine. Etienne was always a gentle child, of an open heart. I choose now to bury my vanity in his virtue. And you—you go marry your Englishman, if you like."

I almost laughed through my own tears. "There is a war on, Maman. And his country is on the other side."

"We could all go anytime," she said. "Bring Caroline to me. Let her know she has a grandmother."

Angelique entered the drawing room, and she ran to me and sat on my other side on the couch, and buried her blonde head on my shoulder, already wet from her mother's tears.

DELICIOUS REVENGE

wo days later was Saturday, the busiest market day, in which we, with our humble goods, would not be participating. I left Caroline with Claudette and went to market with a basket on my arm. It was half full of sausage, leeks, Normandy cheese, and perch when I heard, at my elbow, "That simple silk ribbon is very becoming in your straw bonnet, Citizeness."

I turned and saw a woman younger than myself, about Angelique's age, with a long brown apron over her dress and a green scarf knotted into a cap on her head, and a striped yellow and green kerchief around her shoulders. Long black curls poured out from under her scarf-cap, and she had big, serious eyes. "Would you like to see the ribbons I have for sale?" she said, and I followed her over to a small table on the side of the market, where silk and cloth ribbons of black, red, blue, white, and yellow lay draped over a tablecloth. Others twirled in a breeze like tiny banners in a type of wooden lattice she had for displaying them. Various striped and plain scarves were folded also on the table. "No green, though," she said, "it's still a bit risky. Though I've always liked the color myself, as you can tell from the one I wear."

"You are different from the other scarf and ribbon lady," I said. "Is this your table now?"

"Things are always changing," she said.

I fingered the fine ribbons. "I could use another white one," I said. "It goes with anything."

"With an aigrette for one's bonnet, perhaps? I am Jeanne Robin, and I am a member of a certain philanthropic institute."

"Madame Williams. I have heard of the good work you do. And I have changed my mind about helping you."

A middle-aged woman and her mother approached the table.

"Look at these pretty ribbons," said the older lady. "Wouldn't you like to wear these at a dance?"

"They can make any hat, no matter how plain, look like it's a holiday," Jeanne Robin said.

"What holidays?" the old lady said. "As I recall, Michaelmas came and went without anyone noticing."

"Come, Maman, I need a new hat before I get a new ribbon for it," and they walked on.

"A certain officer named Lieutenant Leforges—" Jeanne Robin said, in a soft but lilting voice over the scarves.

"Excuse me, you said *Leforges?*"

"Yes, you know a Lieutenant Leforges?"

"I knew someone of that surname, a long time ago."

"People make new identities for themselves these days. He may be the same man, or—"

"It's no matter, please continue."

"This officer, together with a sans-culotte—you can't miss them, one elegant, one straight from the streets of Paris—will be in the square in front of the Louis XII fountain tomorrow around ten. This morning there the lieutenant forced locals to watch him and the sans-culotte almost destroy the beautiful fountain because of its name. Now the people can't use it. You've heard that ancient church properties—here in Blois, Saint-Louis Cathedral and the churches of Saint-Nicolas and Saint-Vincent—now pay rent as 'national buildings.' This lieutenant, working for the new representative-on-mission from Paris, is collecting rents from these national buildings throughout the Loire Valley. (I understand he also gives dance lessons to officers' wives in the evening.) He will move on to Amboise in two days. Just observe him tomorrow morning. We'll decide later, after he has collected his rents, how we can make better use of them than he. I'll be by the fountain in the square by noon."

"That is all?"

"Scouting the enemy is the the first stage of an engagement. If you wish to do more, decide after that. The founder of our institute has great faith in you."

"Until tomorrow, then," I said. "These are pretty," I added, my voice raised to a regular marketing level, "but I don't need them now, thank you," and proceeded to a table piled high with heads of lettuce.

"Annette! Annette!" My friend Isabelle Tristant, whom I had not seen in a long time, rushed up and kissed me. She said she had heard I had been in trouble. Was I all right now? Where was I living? She said she liked my bonnet with the white silk ribbon. She would like one like that. She had heard I had a daughter! She didn't even know that I had married my English friend! Shame on me for not telling her. And how like me to be so secretive. In convent school, I had always kept from her, Isabelle, what I was reading or writing. But how charming to have a little baby! Isabelle was sure my baby was a very pretty little girl. But Isabelle never saw me at dances anymore. She saw Angelique. It must be dull, sometimes, being a mother, Isabelle said.

I remembered what Maman had said about Isabelle and her mother's visit to chez Vergez when I was in prison. I wanted only to disappear. But I was saved from responding to her barrage of questions and comments when a fashionable older lady joined us. Blonde ringlets danced above her shoulders, and silver earrings in some design I couldn't recognize peeked out from the curls. Isabelle smilingly said, "But you remember my *maman*, Annette." True, I remembered her as always a "lady of style and taste," but with dark, not fair, hair. I recognized her eyes and features now.

"Ah, Annette"—Madame Tristant laughed—"don't be confused. It is I. It is just the new mode, from Paris. I secretly always wanted to be blonde, like your pretty sister Angelique. Well, now, it's all the rage to be blonde, and it's inexpensive. Would you like to know my secret?" She leaned in as if to whisper to me, and as she did so, I saw her earrings closer, and I inadvertently stepped back. My shopping basket slipped from my arm, and I just caught it before all its contents tumbled out. As it was, only one head of lettuce fell on the ground. I picked it up, leaving some leaves on the paving stones.

Madame Tristant's earrings were in the shape of little guillotines. I didn't want to know about the hair, now. "The new mode, Annette," Madame Tristant said, not in a whisper, "and I'm *surprised* you don't know it—is a blonde wig made from counterrevolutionaries who lost their heads!" She sounded excited, as if she were a girl finding out about a new fashion that she was going to wear now to a dance. "I know it's wicked," she said, "but when else will one have the opportunity to be blonde, ever? Usually good wigs are so expensive. And these earrings came with the wig, too. Can you believe it? An ensemble for the *femme patriote*. You know fashions change with the times, and Monsieur Tristant always says, 'Show that you're a good republican; let them see that you're a good republican.' It's like wearing a cockade, but much more *à la mode*."

"I want to get one too," Isabelle said, "but Maman says we must wait till the next shipment from Paris." Isabelle giggled.

I felt light-headed and dizzy. I was afraid I would fall onto the table of lettuce heads. I grabbed the table edge. "Angelique is doing well, thank you." It was the only thing I could think of to say. I added, "Excuse me, I have to go. I'm late—my daughter," and I almost ran from the square. I heard the din of the market behind me now, but I was in my own roaring, silent world.

Later that day I asked Claudette to go back to the market to purchase a Normandy cheese and to give a simple note to the lady at the ribbons table. When I had recovered my reason, I realized Madame Tristant had given me an idea.

> *Please provide me with a blonde wig—but not from Paris. I would like, once again, to go to a fancy-dress ball.*

> —*Madame W.*

I sat with Caroline in my lap at the Café de Liberté (formerly Café Louis XII, named after the fountain) and sipped a tisane. The morning sun sparkled in the remains of the Louis XII fountain. Not far behind it were the abbey and the church of Saint-Nicolas. And there, giving orders by a wagon at the edge of the square, stood my old dance instructor: he who first had inspired me to love; he who had betrayed me, and he who had denounced William and the count and would have been responsible for their deaths. His boots sparkled like the water in the sunlit, ruined fountain. His belt buckle and buttons shone. His white trousers were pressed smooth and tight. He had more gold braid on his blue coat than any officer I had ever seen, and he was only a lieutenant. A tall red plume topped the cockade on his black hat. He always had on some costume or other.

His assistant, on the other hand, a large man, wore a short, stained brown jacket with a red collar, no waistcoat, ragged striped trousers, and the red woolen bonnet that was at once the identity and the symbol of every sans-culotte. Stringy, greasy hair hung down his face. A pipe seemed glued to his mouth, and, like some old primitive, he carried about with him a small wooden club.

I had heard a lot about his kind from the people whom I had helped in the secret room at chez Dubourg and at the count's lodge. The sans-culottes, a real political force for the Jacobins in Paris, had also become infamous outside of their city for terrorizing the provinces, for whom the sans-culottes had nothing but contempt. Usually in a gang of about six to eight, they accompanied representatives-on-mission from Paris, beating and hauling off villagers who resisted conscription, searching for and arresting refractory priests, and setting fire to crops of the families who had protected the draft evaders or hidden the priests.

Now the sans-culotte in our square in Blois placed the club down in the wagon and lifted out a statue. Lieutenant Leforges was commanding him to place the statue at the edge of the erstwhile fountain. The fountain, I thought, should be lapping with water and noisy now with sounds of women washing and gossiping. It is unnatural to see a fountain in the middle of a square, in the mid-morning, deserted and still.

Now that the statue was in place, I saw that it was of the head and torso of a naked woman. The sans-culotte went around the square informing locals that, if they were true patriots, they had to come now and witness the ceremony that the lieutenant was about to perform. I knew that Monsieur Leforges loved to hear himself speak. When his sans-culotte had intimidated about forty people and stood on the side of the square, holding his club, watching them, Lieutenant Leforges strode in front of the crowd, rested his left hand on his gleaming sword hilt, raised his right arm, and called out: "Citizens! In Paris recently, an ex-aristocrat, now enlightened citizen, celebrated our liberation from the bonds of religion by dutifully performing a 'republican mass.' Since, in all things, the provinces are ordered to follow Paris, it is my privilege to enable you to witness, and to participate in, our own 'festival of freedom.' Behind me you see the ruins of what was once a grotesque medieval homage to a despot"—with a flourish, Leforges waved his arm to the smashed fountain—"and beside me you see a beautiful resemblance to the female figure. I hereby baptize this statue Goddess of the Republic," and he scooped up a handful of water from the fountain and poured it over the head of the statue.

"Now Citizen Gauchon will act as my assisting priest," and Gauchon left his place watching the crowd and lumbered up to his superior. After Lieutenant Leforges had whispered to him and gesticulated impatiently, Citizen Gauchon cupped his big hands and commenced pouring water over the head of the statue. As he did so, Leforges took a wooden cup from his coat pocket and held it between the breasts of the statue. When the cup overflowed, he lifted it above his head and said, "Behold, the Chalice of Liberty. This water from a king's destroyed fountain, blessed by the Goddess of the Republic, is your wine; I, Lieutenant Raoul Leforges, am your priest. Drink and be reborn!"

And he first lowered the cup to his lips, then held it to Citizen Gauchon's, then Gauchon with his club herded as many of the locals as he could—some hurriedly left the square—into standing in line and sipping from the cup as Lieutenant Leforges lifted it to their lips. He made them wait as he took a pretty girl aside and had her perform Gauchon's part now, pouring the water over the statue so the lieutenant could refill the cup from between the statue's breasts. His back was turned as he did so, and some of the citizens who had just had their communion spat the water out not far from the fountain. Lieutenant Leforges turned and praised the pretty girl to the crowd as a true lover of liberty and of *la patrie*.

I had had enough. If Jeanne Robin wanted me to see Monsieur Leforges's character, I had known it for a long time. I paid for my drink and, with Caroline in my arms, left the café. Then I heard the lieutenant exclaim, in a classically trained voice that rang over the square: "It is now time for the climax of our festival of freedom! Only the unpatriotic would want to part now." The crowd, which had other things to do that morning, now threatened with being called counter-revolutionaries, gathered again.

Lieutenant Leforges took a small blue vial from his pocket and held it up to the crowd. "Behold," he said. "This vial speaks of your oppression by the hated priests and kings. With *this* they held you in awe of their power—it is the vessel that holds the *Holy Tear of Vendôme!*" Even though Gauchon was watching them, one could hear a collective gasp from the people in the square. "I see you recognize it," said Leforges. "And well you might. It kept you in thrall for centuries, coming back to receive its 'magic'—a supposed tear, almost two thousand years old! Think of it! What deplorable ignorance! If your Christ ever did shed a tear, do you honestly think it would still be here?"

At this point I shouted from the back of the crowd, "My own father, a learned doctor, was once aided by the Holy Tear!" People turned and looked at the mother holding her baby. Monsieur Leforges couldn't see who it was and seemed amazed at the oddity of being interrupted. I went on, "Furthermore, *mass, priest, chalice*, and *goddess* sound like religious words to me. I'm sure the the good lieutenant is aware of the law that grants him the freedom of his conscience to believe what he likes, but not the freedom to express his religious beliefs. And I'm sure the lieutenant would want everyone, *equally*, to abide by all the laws of the republic. But is not a 'communion with a goddess' an expression of religious belief?" Some of the crowd actually dared to laugh. And being laughed at, being humiliated, was the one thing that Monsieur Leforges could not abide.

Before he could think what defense he could muster, I addressed the crowd. "Now, how many of you have known someone or have heard of someone, an uncle, a grandfather, an old neighbor in your quarter, who has been healed by the Holy Tear of Vendôme? Go on. Don't be afraid. I am not asking for an expression of religious belief, but for a report of actual cases."

"I," said a man's low voice.

"That's right. Let the others hear," I said. I was walking now to the front of the crowd.

"I," said another man, a little louder.

"And I," said a woman's voice, loud and clear.

Then almost the whole crowd rang with, "I, I," like a chant.

I glanced up at Monsieur Leforges now and saw the shock of recognition on his face when he realized who it was who had been inciting the crowd. This was my delicious revenge. The poised dancing master looked from me to the crowd now, in open defiance of him. "Would you not say, Lieutenant"—the crowd quieted when I spoke, and I assumed an air of aplomb I could never have summoned up when he was my master—"that before you now is evidence that this Tear, real or not, can help ordinary citizens, and is it not the will of the Republic, Monsieur Leforges, to help all citizens with no regard to rank, just as the Holy Tear is oblivious to rich or poor, just heeding sincerity?" I glanced at Caroline, and she seemed fascinated by the crowd and by the figure with the red plume on his hat.

It gave me great satisfaction to render Monsieur Leforges speechless. I added, "An inscription on that vial reads, 'The Holy Tear of Christ, wept on the tomb of Lazarus, brought from Constantinople by Geoffroy Martel, 1171.' It is a healing tear. It is not the superstition, but the compassion, Monsieur, that you cannot understand."

Gauchon approached me, but the crowd pressed around him and wouldn't let him through. Monsieur Leforges stood on the fountain by his goddess. "Don't listen to her. She's a witch," he finally said, resorting to superstition himself to sway the crowd, but his words trailed off when he saw their faces. He had pushed them too far. I always knew Monsieur Leforges was just words, that if he ever were required to show genuine courage, his panache would melt like butter in the sun on a summer's day.

"Go back to Paris," I heard one man cry, and a woman: "She has a baby; leave her alone"; and a third, "The Holy Tear of Vendôme!" and that last cry was picked up by many of the others. It had been the old battle cry of the Vendôme knights. And upon hearing that complete rejection of his own authority, Lieutenant Leforges raised the vessel above his head, held it aloft a moment, and dashed it at his feet. Some liquid poured out.

"Let it bring the stones back to life, if it can," he said.

Monsieur Leforges caught the look of shock and dismay on my face and laughed. I was familiar with that laugh. That was his victory. Now he could leave the square with some dignity and go about collecting his rents. It hadn't been an entirely successful morning for him.

And that was the last time I saw the man I had once wanted to marry.

The crowd rushed and shoved and knelt to touch the wet stones. Some brushed their fingers across the dampness and held their fingers to their foreheads or lips or eyes. (The Tear had been supposed to be especially effective against eye disease.) Others tried to kiss the remains of moisture. Soon it was just dry stone and bits of shattered blue glass beneath a destroyed fountain, and the people left and went about their business, delayed so long by the man from Paris. And the Holy Tear of Vendôme went forever into legend.

THE BLONDE CHOUANNE

When the crowd thinned, I saw Jeanne Robin, washing a blouse on the other side of the fountain from where the Goddess of the Republic, now ignored, still stood. My mission had been simply to observe, I thought. And I have made a spectacle of myself. When the last person had left the square, I walked up to Jeanne Robin rather sheepishly. "Ah, the Fearless Chouanne of Blois," she said quietly. "The Institute, you know, prides itself on its *invisibility*. In this rests its success."

"I am sorry, I—"

"You said you knew this man, Leforges?"

"Yes—"

"We all have personal animosities, Madame, but you must retain a *sang froid* or you are useless to the Institute. You can betray yourself, others, our cause, and revenge is *not* what we are here for."

I felt embarrassed, holding a baby in my arms and being lectured by a woman the age of my younger sister. But she was completely right.

"We are here to help others, not ourselves. That is why it is a *Philanthropic* Institute. The marquis gave you our name?"

"Yes."

"Now you *may* have compromised your mission, but it is possible that the lieutenant and the sans-culotte will only collect the rents, then give that collection to a third party. Then you can truly help, if you still want to and if you can keep your hot blood to yourself—"

"I am normally—"

"Oh, I respect your passion, Madame. Without it we would all be like those people in the square herded into taking a communion they didn't believe in. And you were right about one thing."

She paused and I waited. "You'll have to change your looks. Here's some things the marquis wants you to have—" She reached into her laundry basket and handed me a sack.

Caroline was getting fidgety in my arms. I put my foot up on the base of the fountain, rested her on my knee and opened the sack with one hand. The butt of a pistol showed beneath blonde curls. Now I will have two, I thought.

"Return to the café around four. Without the baby. We'll see who gets the collection, where he goes, and the marquis thinks you can come up with a creative way to divert the church rents—tithes from the people—back to the people."

"I?"

"He seems to value your intelligence as well as your courage—"

"I didn't plan that release from prison—" I whispered, even though no one was about.

"But you carried it out and didn't lose your head when the boat was too far away to board." This Jeanne Robin seemed to know everything. "Do you still want to help us, Madame?" she said.

I nodded.

"Your passion will serve you well," Jeanne Robin said. "Just don't go making fools out of old lovers who now are in the service of the patriot army." She smiled.

I didn't have anything to say.

"Get some rest and change your clothes. We might do some riding—but don't bring your pretty horse to the square. Until this afternoon, Madame," she said, and went back to her laundry.

At home in the cottage, when I inspected the contents of the sack, under the wig I also found a stiletto, for which, during the quiet of the afternoon, I embroidered a pocket on the left shoulder of my coat. I hoped the look of it would be intimidating enough. At the bottom of the sack I came upon a dark green velvet mask, with a note attached:

I hope you enjoy going, once again, to a fancy dress ball,
   M R

On my walk back to the Café de Liberté, though, I felt concerned that this time I was out of my depth—it seemed that Jeanne Robin and the marquis played a game that was far more complex than the ones I had played—and even more dangerous.

Yet I was also glad to be doing something. During the day my many chores occupied me, but at night I'd lie awake and think of Marguerite and of her children in England. How tall was Gérard now? Did he talk of his aunt? Was Marie still doing her drawings? Were they both learning English?

And William would wander into my thoughts, wearing different faces: the anguished face of the lover who doesn't know the fate of his beloved; the eager face of the poet with new lines to share; the soft face of a man whom the world has not touched, singing me songs in the firelight. And with each face a different emotion would be summoned within me. I would try always to end with the soft face and even to hear his voice, but one is not always in control of one's thoughts at night.

I lay open also, in the dark, to the finality of Etienne's death. I would awake in a rage; or with the certain clarity of just having heard his voice in a dream; or lie there engulfed by the black hollowness that was my own room. Sometimes I would get up and light a candle and stand by Caroline's crib watching her sleep and reminding myself in this way of life and of the love that I owed to it.

I could not do anything about my brother's death. But I could do something of which, perhaps, he would be proud.

I entered the square a little before four and felt the strangeness of it again without the sound of the fountain. Jeanne Robin was nowhere to be seen. I was blonde now but also wore my three-cornered hat *à la jockey*, my cloak, and boots. I looked as if I were going riding but I had no horse. La Rouge was now carefully kept in a stall that Jean helped us build, hidden in the back of the barn, past the goatpen and hen roost—*her* secret room—lest any officer felt the need to requisition her.

I sat at the Café de Liberté. Coffee was too expensive now, so I ordered a glass of cider and watched the square. I made the one glass last, and it was near five when I saw Citizen Gauchon lumber across the square from the direction of Saint-Nicolas church with a metal box in his hands, and hand it to another sans-culotte, identical looking though not as large, with a pipe stuck in his mouth and wearing a coat that looked too big for him.

A National Guardsman was at his side. At the same time I heard the rumble of a carriage entering the square and stopping in front of the café. The driver hopped off, talked with the second *sans-culotte*, and entered the café. I heard the driver complaining to the patron that he was going to have to miss his supper and drive this official and a guardsman to Bourges, and what could he have now, before he had to leave. I saw at least one other head in the shadow of the coach.

I wished Jeanne Robin were here. The marquis had asked me to steal this money for his institute. I had now accepted. I saw the first star come out and realized I had to make up my mind without Mademoiselle Robin. I paid for the cider and left, walking quickly back across the bridge to our cottage. I took a slice of bread and cheese for my supper and told Claudette that Jeanne hadn't shown up, and that I was going on a ride into the forest to help the marquis's Philanthropic Institute.

She then reminded me that I didn't have to do this, that I was by myself, and I said I thought that I did have to do it and that it was easier and quieter by myself.

I tied my blonde hair back in a long queue, kissed Claudette, and didn't say good-bye to Caroline, who was just waking up from a late nap, for I didn't want seeing her to weaken my resolve.

It was in the barn that I truly felt that I had made the right decision: as soon as I heard La Rouge's whinny as I approached the false back of the barn; as I carefully opened the door that looked as if it were just part of the old wall; as I saddled and talked to her; as I walked her out past the goat nipping at my sleeve; as I lifted myself onto the familiar saddle, tucking my leg in on Rouge's left side, and as I felt the autumn dusk come whipping into my face and made for the road that would take us south, into the forests. At every step that led me on the mission I knew one thing: if I knew on what coach the *collection* was and where that coach was headed and I didn't act, I would not be able to sit comfortably at home and work on Caroline's winter suit. I would think that I had abdicated a responsibility I had taken on. I would think that my father would not approve of such an act. I would not approve of myself. I would want to be out here, riding into the dark.

And from the refugees I had talked to, I knew something of the plight of the people whom the Institute helped, of the violence to which their villages were subjected. Their stories filled me with horror and with repugnance for their tormentors, the Revolutionary Army from Paris, who saw the Vendéan villagers in the west as poisonous rebels who needed to be purged from the system of the new republic.

The colors of the changing woods glowed dimly, and I was reminded of evenings in another world, coming home from hunts with my father, looking forward to the big meal and the fire and the tangy taste of hard cider. The carriage was well ahead of us by now, and soon there was only the sound of Rouge's hooves and the blur of the scented forest. And all the while I rode I was thinking.

We raced onto the old path, barely discernable now, uphill toward the lodge, and down again, across the stream, the meadow, and into the thicket where I had first heard the wild boar. But before the ravine we turned back along the dry streambed and followed its course to where it ran beside the road the carriage would take to Bourges.

There was still some light through the oaks, beeches, and chestnuts here, and I could see no recent wheel tracks in the dust. I dismounted and looked for any branches fallen in recent September winds or from the dryness of summer. I dragged one after another and laid them across the road. I worked fast, for I didn't want the carriage to arrive when I was off in the forest. I made an adequate but not a big obstacle—with all the branches sticking up it seemed taller than it was—enough, I hoped, to spook a horse suddenly coming upon it in the dusk—and mounted La Rouge again and waited under the growing dark of the trees at the side of the road, where I donned the velvet mask.

I heard the sound of sixteen hooves, the roll of the wheels, and the rattle of a fast moving carriage slow down to make a sharp turn and saw the lead horses balk at the knee-high pile of branches and heard the curse of the driver and the jostling as he stepped down to the road. He continued to curse as he cleared the branches. The guardsman stepped down after him and walked to the side of the road. He grasped his musket and peered into the dark forest looming around him. He was on my side of the carriage, or I could have quickly poked my head into the coach and pointed my pistol at the sans-culotte.

As it was, I urged Rouge forward and knocked the guardsman down before he saw us coming. I pointed one pistol at him, and with my left hand tucked the reins under my leg and reached for the other pistol in my coat.

"The Chouans welcome you to the Forest of Boulogne," I said to the guardsman and the driver. "Leave the musket on the ground." The guardsman stood up. "Both of you, clasp your hands behind your heads, now."

I had a pistol in each hand now and nudged Rouge with my leg to the door of the carriage. "I believe a citizen wearing a red cap is within. Will he please come out here, and anyone else who is in the carriage. And Citizen, please do not forget your metal box. Come now. I would be glad to shoot through the window of the carriage to encourage your haste."

The sans-culotte, clutching his box, and a young, pretty woman in a dark blue cloak stepped down from the carriage. "You're a woman," she said.

"And so are you," I said. "Put the box in this saddlebag, Citizen, slowly." I kept a pistol pointed at his head as he did so. "Very good. Now you both clasp your hands behind your heads also."

"Even Rousseau says women should not be involved in politics," said the blue-cloaked woman, as she put her hands behind her head. "You should be ashamed of yourself."

"Monsieur Rousseau, Madame, is still a man," I said.

"My husband is captain of the Revolutionary Army stationed at Cholet," she said. "He will hunt you down. No rebels have a chance with us."

"Far better, Madame, that he hunt you. After all your travels, you want him off chasing me?" I said. "I do not want to delay your reunion any longer, but do you know what goes on in Cholet and other places in the Vendée? St. James himself says we are to help widows and orphans. So know, Madame, that the *collection* in this box will go to help children whose parents have been murdered; to mothers who have seen their daughters raped on the side of the road and then shot or stabbed; or to old ones who have seen soldiers carry nursing infants on their bayonets or on the pikes that had pierced mother and child with the same thrust."

I watched her face unwittingly turn from scorn to horror. "This is the world that you enter to the west, Madame," I said. "Just ask your husband. I do not exaggerate. Now you two," I pointed with my pistol to the Guardsman and the sans-culotte, "one at a time, first you, sit down right in front of me, take off your boots, and throw them in the carriage." The Guardsman did so. "Now you, Citizen." The sans-culotte stared at me maliciously, sat in the road and pulled off his boots, and threw them in the open door of the carriage.

"Now toss in your red cap," I said.

"Not my cap," he said.

I tucked a pistol in my skirt, drew the stiletto from my sleeve, rode beside the frightened sans-culotte and with the tip of the stiletto picked the cap off his head and tossed it onto the side of the road where it lay like a red leaf in the brush.

"No Parisian sans-culottes out to terrorize the provinces here," I said. "You're in the Forest of Boulogne now." I put the stiletto back and drew the second pistol again.

"You are the worst kind," the sans-culotte said, pipe still in his mouth. "The kind who weep at night for the death of the King. Well, his little son you call Louis XVII is rotting away in prison as fast as he can. Weep for him all you want," and his hand darted into his coat.

I shot into his open coat and heard the bullet hit metal. The sans-culotte jumped back, white-faced, and inspected his hand to see if it had been hit.

"You're all right, Citizen. Just place the gun on the ground, now, slowly. Thank you. I think you better start your march to Blois now. Both of you, go." And I watched them walk in their stockinged feet to the bend in the road. "Beware of horsemen riding fast in the dark who may not see you," I said. "Or horsewomen."

I motioned to the driver with my pistol to remount his seat. "Now, Madame, back inside. I'm sure your journey will be much more comfortable without the odor of the sans-culotte so close beside you." I took a note from my pocket and handed it to her as she climbed into the carriage. "That is a receipt, signed by me, *La Chouanne*, on behalf of the Philanthropic Institute, for the contents of that metal box. Rest assured, as I said, that their new destiny is far preferable to their old one. Tell your husband, the *blonde chouanne* wishes that the tenderness he bears for his pretty wife engenders in him at least one degree of mercy for the poor people of Cholet. *Adieu*, Madame.

"*Allez*," I said to the horses, and the driver cracked his whip, the carriage trundled on, and I tucked the pistols in my skirt. Then La Rouge and I plunged into the darkness on the other side of the road.

I shouted to the first gleaming stars, "Your daughter is a thief! Your sister has robbed a carriage! What do you think of that?" I let out a long, high, triumphal cry as I galloped across the old meadow. Then I thought of my brother and of the people of Cholet and of my puny victory, and I took off my mask and rode quickly home.

Jeanne Robin, late from stealing back a friend's horse from a small patrol of the Revolutionary Army, never missed another rendezvous. She was a fine horsewoman who had served in the cavalry of the Royal and Catholic Army of the Vendée, and with her help that autumn we raided more coaches that carried rents collected from church properties, always on different routes, as far west as Amboise, as far east as Saint-Laurent, or north toward Vendôme or south past Cheverny. Sometimes even the marquis himself and a few of his men came along. I think it amused him to sit on horseback behind the two women as they parleyed with the people in the carriage. No road in the region was safe from us, and the money was passed on through the efficient network of the Institute, which found homes for refugees in Normandy or Brittany, or occasionally used the money to bribe officials or National Guard officers to set prisoners free. No one ever traced the masked blonde Chouanne with a pistol in each hand and a stiletto on her sleeve to the amber-haired mother who, child in arms, sold fresh vegetables, fruit, eggs, goat cheese, and live rabbits at the market.

*I*n early October I had come back at dawn from the raid on the coach near Amboise, and as I didn't want to disturb the sleeping Caroline or Claudette, and as, in any case, I wasn't ready to sleep yet, I busied myself in the dew-filled garden, picking ripe tomatoes, plucking off ones half eaten by birds or other creatures, and pulling some ever-present weeds from the damp earth. It was after some fifteen minutes that I became aware that I was being watched. I could feel it, on the back of my neck. I realized I still had my Chouan costume on—blonde wig and tricorne hat with the white feather—and heard someone say, in a familiar accent, "Excuse me, do you know if an Annette Vallon lives here?"

I answered, without moving from my crouched position near the tomatoes, "A Madame Williams lives here," and I looked up and there was my precious William himself, his face so full of confusion and surprise, relief and wonder, tiredness and worry, that I ran the few steps to him, embraced him, and said, "It is I, just in costume for a while," and I threw off my hat into the rosemary, pulled off the wig, tossed it on top of the hat, and shook out my long amber hair.

"But—" William started.

"How did you get here?" I said. "Come in the house—" Before I could finish my sentence my lips found his, or ours found each other, and our arms wound us into one creature, shadowed in the thin light above the mint and lavender. There was no question now of moving into the house. Without a word we fell to our knees at the edge of the garden; then, falling into the herbs, we kissed and unbuttoned and lifted muddy skirts. There was no lengthy kneading of back or shoulders, no gradual warming of limbs that had once again found each other. The smell of his sweat and mine, of his dirty linen shirt, the fresh smell of the morning and of the dew-wet leaves under us, mixed with the danger that I had known that night, his sudden inexplicable appearance, and the unbelievable reality of his flesh and lips.

We lay quiet, breathing hard next to each other, his hand still on my thigh, and we laughed when we got to our knees, returned to the world, and saw the lavender bed crushed. I took his hand and led him to the kitchen door.

"Now, softly, we leave our boots and coats here," I said. William knelt and gently took my boots off and let his hand stay a moment on my ankle.

I poured us both cups of water from the jug on the table and looked at him and laughed again, and said, "How?"

He smiled, and I shook my head.

"Come see your beautiful daughter while she is still asleep." And I led him silently, even though I was full of a thousand questions: Did he plan to take us back to England, or even to stay in France? Both seemed fraught with insurmountable difficulties. Most of all was the question I had already asked: How in the world had he gotten here? But now was not the time for talking; I just wanted to feel his hand in mine, to watch his face as he watched his daughter's.

We stood above her simple crib, the walls above it adorned with pictures I had drawn of the sun and of a deer in a meadow, and one of a foal standing on its feet for the first time. And before us dangled another crude horse I had carved and painted red, and attached on a long cord so it hung from the ceiling above Caroline's bed. She often just lay and stared at it, sometimes her legs kicking the mattress with happiness as a breeze from an open window stirred the horse and made it dance, or she might bat it with a hand to watch it spin. I stood there, watching the toy horse that I had thought William would never see, never share in this little joy of hers.

"What's wrong?" William said.

"Nothing, nothing; I can't believe you're here. I am so happy you are here."

"She is beautiful. She looks like you."

"You will see she has your eyes. Your deep poet's eyes. And look at her English nose. It's a nice nose. A nose of character."

"Babies don't have noticeable noses."

"What would you know of babies?" We were whispering, and backed away from the crib.

"Annette, I tried to come—"

"No, I did not mean that," and I took his hand and kissed him again. It was a long, slow kiss now, and I reached my arms up around his neck, and he held me against his slender and sturdy body, which had just walked so far to be here, in this room, at this moment. We bent to my small bed, and now discarding the clothes that, in our impatience, we had hardly noticed before, letting them lie beside the bed like old skins dropped off, lazily and leisurely, taking all the time in the world, we explored again the geography of the landscapes that we had known only in dreams. This time we fell deeply asleep.

We had three small bedrooms upstairs, but I wanted to be near Caroline if she needed me in the night. I heard that other babies cried when they awoke in the morning; mine cooed, or hummed a tune that climbed or descended in pitch and seemed to bespeak some inner contentment on opening one's eyes to the world, of which only babies and lovers in one another's arms know the secret. This morning her soft sounds did not wake me, but Claudette, with her own spontaneous cry upon entering the room, did. The cherished moment of William and I waking together became a confused and somewhat embarrassed one.

But Claudette went straight to Caroline's crib, picked her up and said, "I think your *maman* and papa are asleep. We won't disturb them," and left.

Soon we heard and smelled something good floating up from the kitchen. I washed my face, put on my old worn satin slippers, and joined Claudette. I decided, in this rare and celebrative occasion, we should use our hoarded bit of coffee. I was dipping the spoon into those fragrant and precious grounds when Claudette finally said, "How did he—?"

"I don't know. He arrived at dawn, just before I did."

"You didn't ask him?"

"It wasn't the time to talk."

"Well, someone needs to know what to do if the Committee of Public Safety comes around, asking about someone with an accent, traveling without papers. By the way, I picked up a blonde wig and a cap with a royalist feather in it from among the rosemary leaves. You're getting careless. Did you greet each other without words out there, too?"

"Thank you." I shrugged.

"Ah. Well, I'm making him an English breakfast, thought he'd need it."

"Claudette, he's here. He's actually here!"

"Does he know what you've been doing?"

"We didn't—"

"That's right. First things first. Well, here's the sleepy Englishman."

With her hands full, Claudette kissed both his cheeks and flipped an omelette a second later, catching it in her pan. "You've always amazed me," said William. "I'm so glad you are still with Annette."

"Where else would I go?" she said. "And I'm Caroline's guardian, don't forget. She's the lucky girl with two mothers. Now, Monsieur William, how would you like to do the offices of third mother and feed this lovely child? That way your fiancée and I can finish making your big English breakfast." And before he could answer, Claudette placed Caroline on his lap and a spoon and a bowl of mush before him. William seemed somewhat hesitant, but Caroline didn't seem to mind, with the familiar bowl before her, and, after taking a cursory glance at the stranger and seeing that, with her two mothers close by, it was all right, opened her mouth for the first spoonful.

"You're doing very well, William," I said.

"Mush on her mouth only accentuates her natural beauty," he said.

We sat down to a feast of cheese and tomato omelette, sausage, and coffee. I took Caroline from William's lap and let her sit with me, occasionally giving her a bit of omelette from my plate.

"France is not in such a deprived state as I have heard," William said.

"We have our own supplies here," I said. "Did you see our barn?"

"I thought of hiding in there until daylight, but two goats pushed me out and a fat pig grunted at me."

"That would be Emilie, Frederick the Great, and Horace," Claudette said.

"Horace?"

"He is a very wise pig, with literary ambitions," I said. "But I don't know if they will ever be realized. He may go to market soon."

"*Dulce et decorum est pro patria mori*; 'It is sweet and fitting to die for one's country,'" William said. "Horace wrote that."

"Then he'll definitely be going to market soon," I said.

"Who's Horace?" Claudette said. "I just thought it was a good name for a pig. When you two used to talk," said Claudette, "I rarely did understand half of what you were saying. Now, Monsieur William, how did you know to find this house? How did you get across the Channel? How are you going to keep your head on? If Annette doesn't care to know, I need to satisfy my own curiosity."

"I visited the Dubourg residence in Orléans, the last place I knew you to be, and was told of your new address, and I must add that I think it is a fine improvement, in spite of Horace's temperament. By the by, I found out that the landlord of my old residence in Orléans, who was fond of letting rooms to officers ready to emigrate, lost his head just last week: that's the casual way I hear it said here, as if it's just part of daily life, and unfortunately, I suppose it is. To the second question, I crossed on a smuggler's boat from Torquay to Saint-Valéry. They said it was my lucky day. They usually don't sail that far, but can get more money if they put in closer to Paris, so they chanced it this time. I am to meet them for the return trip at Cateret, on the Cherbourg Peninsula, in a week's time—Annette, this was a Cornish smuggler, who comes from a long line of successful smugglers, not one of the new ones on the Isle of Wight trying to take advantage of the recent situation and working within sight of the British fleet—did you get that letter?"

I nodded.

"Amazing," he said. "I didn't get any. So you see, I was more careful whom I chose this time, then I traveled safely with the smugglers to Rouen, with a few all the way to Paris, avoiding, with their practiced skill, any committees or troops checking papers; although, to the third question, regarding my head, I do have a Civic Certificate." And he reached into his waistcoat and pulled out a slip of paper, which he waved with a flourish, then put back in his pocket.

"How did you——?" I said. "Do you know how hard those are to get?"

"As I wrote to you, I have a lawyer friend in London, James Losh——"

"I didn't get that letter," I said.

"Ah," William said, "well, Losh managed it for me. It took two months for him to request it and have it sent to England from France. But it seems France welcomes me here now because I work for the Society for Constitutional Reform, and I'm here doing research into the advances the Revolution has made for the world in constitutional government."

"You mean, that's what your friend wrote on the form," I said. "So you're here under false pretenses."

"I actually did know a John Frost, here in Paris a year ago," William said, "who worked for that organization. He wrote favorably about his findings but is in prison now, in England. You see, we have our own Committees of Surveillance."

"How long is that certificate good for?" I asked.

"As long as I need to conduct my research."

"You know a Civic Certificate can be revoked on the whim of any representative-on-mission," I said, "who can claim absolute authority from the Convention itself. Then your next stop is prison and——let me see that certificate."

"I never let it leave my pocket," William said. I reached over Caroline toward the inside of his waistcoat, and he held my hand and I shot out the other. Caroline watched in amazement at this sudden and unknown game at the breakfast table, and this time I pulled out the sacred paper, unrolled it, and read it.

"It is true," I announced. "This is a Civic Certificate with the seal of the mayor of Paris on it. Only it is good *from August 30 to September 15*, 1793. It is now the *twelfth of October*. Monsieur William, this is an invalid document, and traveling with improper papers can be even more dangerous than traveling with none. If you don't have papers, you may be illegal but not counterrevolutionary; if traveling with false papers, you are immediately seen as an enemy of the Republic, and"——I looked at Claudette——"that is how my brother died."

"Etienne?" William said, shocked. "I—"

"I wrote to you about it," I said. "William, how did you avoid anyone checking your papers?"

"I walked, looking, I suppose, like any lone person minding his own business, hid when I saw any troops. One man walking does not excite a lot of attention, and he can easily step behind a hedgerow or—"

"William, you're foolish. You don't know what kind of a world we live in."

"I had to see you," he said. "After war was declared, I received no mail. I was desperate. What was I to do? All I heard was news of terror coming from France. I had to know if you and Caroline were all right. I had to see you," he repeated.

"William, you wonderful imbecile," I said, and I threw the letter back at him, stood up, and placed Caroline alone on the chair. I picked up my plate. "Have you finished?" I asked him.

"This is the first decent meal I have had for weeks," he said. "I'm going to eat every bite."

"Caroline and I need to go visit the barn," said Claudette. "Emilie needs milking, and everybody else needs feeding. And Horace can take anybody's unfinished portions." And she picked up my plate from the kitchen and carried it and my daughter out.

"You are an intelligent man," I said. "I can't believe you did such a thing."

"I am sorry about Etienne."

"*He* was trying to get to England." And I started to cry, standing in the kitchen, and William stood up and put his arms around me.

"I'll be careful," he said. "I'll be very careful."

"You're such an imbecile," I said. "Thank you for being such an imbecile."

And he took my hand and led me back to the table.

"You received letters?" he said.

"None for months and months, and then suddenly *two*—perhaps because they came from different places, arrived at different ports, than the others. I don't know. One said you were about to leave to France, and the other that you had almost been killed trying to get here and were, wisely, going to Wales."

"I did. And my old friend Jones, whom I talked to you of, listened to me endlessly explain my dilemma as we walked among the misty mountains of his country, and when I said simply, I had to try again, he loaned me money and told me Cornwall was the ancient seat of smugglers."

"William, you're a criminal in the eyes of two countries."

"And you? I must tell you, I saw a strange sight. I arrived around dawn, after walking much of the night. Once I had made it to Orléans, and you weren't there, I had to push on. The cottage was dark. I thought everyone was asleep. I went to rest in the barn—barns have been very helpful to me lately—met Frederick the Great as heretofore mentioned, and, deciding to rest under the eaves, I saw La Rouge ride up—strange, arriving at dawn, but more strange, a blonde lady with your cloak, and a white feather in her hat, dismounted and proceeded to lead Rouge into the barn and open up a hidden stall. This lady had your features and figure, even in the dim light, but I had never seen her before. Do you know where she came from?"

"There are three women, William, whom I will tell you of. You know the first two: the woman who lives for her infant daughter and grows vegetables and fruits for market; another who loves a poet whose country is an enemy to hers, and they must live exiled from each other; and a third, who secretly tries to help others in great need."

"And what if something should happen to the third woman, in this uncertain world, and she dies and leaves her infant daughter behind her?"

"She has made plans with a very reliable person who also loves the child."

"Is it worth it?" he said. "And what about that lover in exile?"

"She does not know fully why she undertakes her minor adventures," I said. "I think she feels she owes it, somehow, that it is a debt of honor."

"To what?" William said. "To whom?"

"To a little girl she saw once," I said, "who no longer had any parents, and who was hungry and scared and alone. And, I believe, to the memory of her father and brother."

William filled his cup from the jug of water and looked at me, as if studying me again.

"For a year I've thought of you as the playful person I first met," he said, "isolated in my memory as you were, untouched by the catastrophic events of the world around you. And all the time you were becoming someone else, someone I could not possibly know because I have not lived as you have lived, in a country at war with itself."

"I am still Annette," I said, "your Annette."

"This other person," he said. "Does she have a name, too?"

I laughed. "It's embarrassing. She's called—the Fearless Chouanne of Blois. I'm not fearless, William—"

"I've heard of the Chouans," he said. "They're brigands—"

"And where did you hear that from?" I said. "They are the only ones successfully and tirelessly resisting the intrusion of the government of Paris into their lives. I heard a man singing a song they had made up. You might like it; it's poetry of a sort:

> You've killed our priests and killed our king,
>   And stolen our church bell;
> You want our men for wars you've made—
>   We say, just go to hell.

"And I thought you hated politics," William said.

"I do" I insisted. "I hate it more than ever."

William looked away, ran his hands through his disheveled hair, and said, "I saw it, Annette, when I was in Paris. I saw the Terror. I thought what we heard in England could have been exaggeration. It was not."

"What did you see?"

"The machine itself."

I shuddered and tried to push out the picture that suddenly came into my mind of my brother, standing there, or kneeling there. It was rainy September in that picture. I had seen it before. It felt cold now, in the room in the fall morning, with the breakfast fires waning. That machine was always waiting, an invisible presence in the homes and hearts of so many people. "Did you see—?" I said.

"A journalist I knew, Gorsas, I saw him led up to the scaffold, his hands tied behind his back—I had lodged with him in Paris, Annette. I knew him. He wrote for the Girondins, and we argued sometimes over his more extremist positions—but it doesn't matter now. I heard all my old Girondin friends are on trial. I wanted to go see some of it, but to witness Brissot in his eloquence rip the prosecution's flimsy case to shreds and have his fine words ignored by a judge who has already made up his mind would be too sad to see. They have actually accused the Girondins of being in league with the prime minister of England! It would be laughable, if it weren't so tragic. Anybody can say that someone else is 'not a true patriot,' and that person is destroyed. That is the real Terror."

"And here are you," I said, "with a false Civic Certificate, and think you're not tempting fate?"

"For a mission such as mine," he said, "to see you and my daughter—the gods protect such a one."

"What if you were to climb trees and help a couple of helpless women pick some pears and apples for market this afternoon?" I said. "Is that noble enough of a mission to merit the protection of those gods?"

"If you are referring to you and Claudette," he said, "I've never known either one of you ever to be helpless, but I'd be happy to harvest some fruit for you. On one condition—that I then get to accompany you to market, and see one of those three women you told me about at her work."

The rest of that morning William stood perched precariously on various boughs and stretched himself as far as his long arms could reach, risking his life for a single isolated pear or for an impertinent apple that swung just out of his fingers' touch, until he lunged for it and grasped it, and I shouted up that it *wasn't worth it*. From below, he was half lost in the leaves and intertwining branches. I could just see his legs and hear his voice from another world. I loved having him working there: my husband and friend and Caroline's father, as she watched his movements far above her.

That afternoon he accompanied us to market, carrying baskets of ripe pears and apples. He stood beside me at our table now and said we had the best fare at the market, with our fruit and vegetables, goat cheese Claudette had made, and a few rabbits in a makeshift wooden cage. We did well that day, and I smiled at Jeanne Robin, at her table behind us at the opening of an alley behind the square, at the edge of the market.

Then I noticed Citizen Gauchon weaving up to us. I thought he had left to collect church rents throughout the Loire Valley long ago, with Lieutenant Leforges. He looked as if he had been drinking. He still had his red cap and pipe. He came straight to our table.

"Do you have a permit to sell here?" He sounded as if he had been drinking.

"Yes," I said, "would you like to see it?"

He grunted, and I took the paper from my pocket and unfolded it in front of him. I kept it in my hand. I saw him looking at the seal of the town of Blois on it. Then he looked back at me.

"You look familiar," he said. "Little baby with you, told everybody in the square that the Holy Tear of Vendôme was real. The real tear of Christ. Are you some kind of idiot or just a counterrevolutionary wench?"

"I think you must have me confused with someone else, Citizen. Excuse us, we must serve our fellow citizens here. You've seen our seal. We have a right to be here."

"What about this one?" and he pointed to William. Now *I* felt like the imbecile. In my bliss at having William with me, I had forgotten that, of course, most of the men his age would have been conscripted. Benoît was gone now from the count's service.

"He helped us pick the apples," I said. "He's not clever, just tall." I didn't want William to speak and betray his accent.

"Where are you from?" Gauchon said. "Why aren't you in the army?"

"His mind is slow," I said. "He can't follow orders or talk right. The army didn't want him."

"The army wants everyone," said Citizen Gauchon. "Why doesn't he talk? Hand me your papers," he said to William.

William unfolded his invalid Civic Certificate in front of Gauchon, as I had done. I could only think of Etienne's fate with his false papers. Again Gauchon looked at the seal.

"This isn't proper," he said.

"Why?" I said.

"This is the seal of Paris. We are in Blois." Citizen Gauchon was not too drunk to forget the Revolution's obsession with official seals.

"But this seal allows him to be anywhere in France," I said. "He just comes from Paris. He travels, picking apples and pears in the fall."

"Then he must get new certificates from the towns he is in."

I realized that Gauchon had only looked at the seal. He couldn't read. He couldn't see that the dates were wrong and the purpose of doing research on constitutional reform was absurd for someone picking fruit. He only saw that the seal was wrong. But that was bad enough.

"I will have to bring this matter up with the representative-on-mission from Paris," Gauchon said. "A man must have the seal from the town he is in. Come with me."

Just then, as he was about to grab William's upper arm, Gauchon's bleary eyes left us, and he looked over our shoulders. I followed his gaze to where Jeanne Robin, behind her table but in full view, was squatting down, lifting her skirts and baring her bottom. She seemed to be about to relieve herself.

"Holy mother of God," said Gauchon, "what a sight," and he immediately half-stumbled on, in a hurry not to miss the view. Jeanne seemed to be taking her time.

"Leave now, Madame," Claudette said, "I can take care of the table," and I lifted up Caroline and hastened William away from the market. If we were lucky, I thought, Gauchon would be too drunk to remember the encounter. If he asked Claudette where we were, she would say the right thing.

"Don't you know," we heard Gauchon saying loudly to Jeanne Robin, as we left, "that women can't do that?"

We were almost back to the cottage when William said, "France is a strange place."

"That woman behind us, she's a Chouanne too," I said.

"I see. A singular distraction, but it worked. That fellow seemed to recognize you, wig or no."

"That was before I had the wig. My one indiscretion, for which I will not be able to go to market now until that citizen goes back to Paris."

When Claudette returned that night, she said that Gauchon had followed Jeanne into the alley behind the square, and Jeanne had returned alone.

After supper I asked William to sing to Caroline, and while she lay in my arms he sang the ballads of his country in the north of England. "Sing the Annachie Gordon song," I said. "She knows that one, only in French, with happier words."

I was glad he had come. He had seen his daughter. He knew I still loved him, even if the *I* was different from the one he had known and loved. And I knew he had risked his life just to see me.

Late that night, in the quiet of the house and of his soft breathing next to me, as he lay near sleep, he said, "But Chouannes are wild people. Are you really a Chouanne?"

"May I be a Chouanne with a romantic heart?" And he was asleep before I had my answer.

William stayed for two more days. The second evening after dinner he said, "Annette, I want to show you something." He pulled a slim book out of his rucksack and handed it to me. I noticed his name on the cover.

"Is this——?"

"It's for you," he said, "I carried it all the way from London. I didn't want the Committee of Public Safety to get their hands on it. There're not many copies." His voice was nonchalant, but he couldn't stop smiling.

"And you've waited all this time. Why didn't you show it to me the first day? This is exciting."

"I was saving it."

"Read the title to me, in English," I said. "I want to hear how it sounds."

"*An Evening Walk* and *Descriptive Sketches*, by W. Wordsworth, B.A. of St. John's, Cambridge," he said. "That is I. Open it; I wrote something inside for you, in French."

Caroline was just getting used to William when he had to leave. He had stayed as long as he could, and I was anxious for him. On the third morning I wrapped my worn velvet dressing gown around me and went with him in the dark and held his hand by our little gate.

His face was in shadow, and the faintest line of light lay behind the dark trees beyond him. It was still cold from the autumn night. Dew coated our garden with silver. You could smell the river. He pressed my hand, shouldered his old rucksack, and went down the deserted road. He was already lost in the dark. It was a long way to the Normandy coast.

When I came back inside, I noticed the whiteness of a sheet of paper slipped under the porcelain water jug on the table. I took the paper over to the window and stood in the pale light and read the lines William had left for me. Translating his poetry was always a slow process for him, and I wondered when he had composed these.

> *Tonight, my Friend, within this humble cot*
> *Be scorn and fear and hope alike forgot*
> *In timely sleep; and when, at break of day,*
> *On the tall peaks the glistening sunbeams play*
> *With a light heart our course we many renew,*
> *The first whose footsteps print the mountain dew.*

He wrote that these next lines were a fragment from a work in progress,

> *. . . He who feels contempt*
> *For any living thing, hath faculties*
> *Which he has never used.*

> *True knowledge leads to love.*

At the end of the month all of William's Girondin friends were executed. Journalists at the trial wrote of the Girondins' passionate extemporaneous speeches in their own defense, but the verdict, of course, had already been decided. I could only think that William so easily could have been among them. They sang "La Marseillaise" as they rode through the streets of Paris in the tumbril, and each shouted "Vive la République!" before he stepped valiantly up to the guillotine. But Paris had turned against them. The Jacobins had convinced the people that the Girondins were, after all, traitors: propaganda, for the most part, works. One of the Girondins, upon hearing the verdict, had stabbed himself rather than give the Jacobins the victory of his death. But the Jacobins insisted upon the letter of the law: his corpse stayed in the cell all night with the condemned Girondins, accompanied them to the scaffold, and was beheaded along with them. The twenty-two leaders were killed in forty minutes.

And on October 16, 1793, one day after William left, when, even with his sturdy legs, he was probably still in France, the Queen was brought to what was now called "Sainte-Guillotine," all witnesses commented on her composure, her hands tied behind her back (unlike the King), and in an open cart. She even apologized to the executioner for stepping on his toe.

It is true that if one says a thing enough times, it comes to be believed. The gossip that had sold pornographic pamphlets since long before the Revolution, which depicted the Queen as a depraved, licentious monster, now became the spurious lies that made up the bulk of the prosecution. Antoinette was not tried before the National Convention, as was her husband, but by the extremist prosecutor Hébert and the Revolutionary Tribunal, hastily and righteously disposing of their political enemies.

But most of the people I talked to in Blois were still surprised. They thought the queen would be ransomed and sent to Austria. But the regicide had to be complete. I will not repeat here Hébert's vicious and obscene accusations, which the queen would not lower herself to answer. She appealed to the mothers of France, and some of the market women in the courtroom even called for the trial to stop. But Hébert wanted her head as his own political trophy. When he himself mounted the scaffold six months later, his screams were far different than the quiet dignity with which Antoinette lightly stepped up onto it. Perhaps they both knew where they were soon bound.

THE NOYADES

That October we heard distressing news from the Vendée. The Royal and Catholic Army, about 40,000 strong, and with at least as many women and children in tow, had crossed the Loire, north, into Brittany. They were on their way to meet British troops and an émigré army from England that would land on the coast. Their new leader, the twenty-year-old Count Henri de La Rochejacquelin, inspired them. They had marched all the way to Granville by mid-November, in harsh weather, and found no trace of the British—some said the fleet was detained by contrary winds, others that the British had never intended to meet them. Then the huge, hungry army headed back south. Once out of the hedgerows and woods of their home territory, they lost the advantage and suffered loss after terrible loss, as Count Henri tried to attack cities. By Christmas, the remains of the 40,000 were starving in the marshy lands at the mouth of the Loire. The freezing river was now a barrier against their return home. By New Year's we had heard of their final defeat near Nantes. The Republic was publicizing it as a great victory.

It was on the night of Epiphany, the sixth of January, that the marquis paid another visit to the cottage. He made his owl call, more as a greeting than anything else, and the next minute, as soon as I opened the door, he stepped out of the darkness with a bundle in his arms. When he had seated himself at table and accepted some hot tea, he unfolded his package and showed us his gift of venison, ready for the cooking. "My Twelfth Night present," he said.

"This is extremely kind of you, Monsieur le Marquis," I said, "but we have nothing to give in return but our tea and what's left of the *Gâteau des Rois*, the Three Kings Cake, that Claudette baked today. Who knows, perhaps you will be the one to get the elusive bean in his piece; we have not found it yet."

"Thank you; I would be more than grateful. And the company of two civilized ladies is more than enough reward for bringing you this lean deer. I was hoping to bring you a *wapiti*—that's a very big deer, in an Indian tongue." I served him a piece of the cake, and he did find the bean.

"I think, with all your exploits, you could use the luck of the bean this year," I said.

"It is on another matter that will require luck—but not mine—that I have come to talk to you."

"Ah, no mere social visit from the busy marquis."

"I'm afraid the news from the Vendée is taking up all my time. You've heard of the defeat at Savenay?"

"If one goes into town, one hears little else—'Brigands defeated! Royal and Catholic Army destroyed!'"

"Well, they are not all destroyed, though their victors were ruthless, using their bayonets and the hoofs of their horses, but they could not stab or crush all of them—including, of course, many women and children—though they shot prisoners by the thousands in the next several days. Still, there are many left who now crowd the prisons in Nantes. That is what I have come to talk to you about."

"Not to manage an escape from Nantes! That's a hundred miles away, and one would need an army, more than an army—"

"Peace, Madame Williams; you do not have all the facts. The facts are not agreeable, and I will lay them before you plainly: Nantes was not made to keep thousands of prisoners, nor can the Republic afford to feed them, even though prisoners in Versailles were dining on rats. Word got out about the mass executions, and as that didn't square with the professed morals of the government, they had to stop them. The representative-on-mission there, one Carrier—"

"Carrier! He's the one who ordered the deaths of the people whom I helped escape from the Town Hall!"

"An enthusiast, this Carrier. He apparently has devised a new plan, a creative one, I'm sure he thinks, that would, in one stroke, empty the prisons, rid the Republic of deadly enemies—remember, many of these are still women and children—and do so in a manner that would not tarnish the principles of the Republic, for it would be done in secret."

"How do you know about it?"

"We intercepted a messenger from Carrier to the Committee of Public Safety; his note referred to solving the problems of the prisons through cargoes. This was curious enough to lead us to make sure the next messenger, a week later, didn't get through. Now Carrier was more specific. He had grown bold from his success. His plan uses nature itself as a means of solving his 'problem.' His letter read: 'The miracle of the Loire has just swallowed up 360 counterrevolutionaries from Nantes. Others are going to follow them. Oh, what a revolutionary torrent is the Loire.'"

The marquis paused, but Claudette and I were silent. This was my beautiful river, which I had loved since I was a child. The Revolution had now invaded even its waters.

"There are a few witnesses," the marquis continued, "even though it is done in the dead of night. It seems they bind the prisoners and take them out in old barges, which they then scuttle and let their 'cargo' sink."

"What do you want me to do, Marquis? As I said, Nantes is a long way away."

"I would not mention this to you, but if we are to do anything about this new terror—and nightly, I fear, more people are lost—we are in a desperate situation. Most of the Chouans of the West joined Count Henri's expedition and are themselves dead or in the Nantes prisons; the ones who didn't cross the Loire are hunted by the Revolutionary Army, and my men and I—have you heard of the Hell Columns, Madame?"

I shook my head. I hardly wanted to hear of more horrors tonight.

"In short, they are what they say they are. They march across the Vendée, killing all locals they come across as counterrevolutionaries—and this means largely widows, orphans, and the elderly, and even some republicans, but the Hell Columns have gone mad with killing and then burning villages and lands. Whatever one column doesn't destroy, the next one will. I read one report. It ended, 'Pity is not revolutionary.'

"So my Philanthropic Institute will try to save and hide villagers before a column comes, or, if we are late, between one column and the next. I cannot spare the time to go all the way to Nantes to rescue prisoners."

"How can I? I cannot ride that far. I am only one person—"

"You are two, or more than two, with the formidable Jeanne Robin. And you would have a barge, fitted with hay and even some livestock, to make your journey downriver credible. That is, should you decide to do it at all. Your work for the Chouans of Blois has been fearless and constant. You do not need to do work outside your region for those who perhaps cannot be helped. But please think on it. I wish you good Day of the Kings and will await your answer tomorrow night, when I will pass by your gate." The marquis rose, and I thought even he looked a little tired and worn. I walked him the few steps to the door, and he bowed deeply to us both.

"Thank you for the venison, Marquis. That was very thoughtful."

"I wish I could do more. And I apologize for bringing you this news. It is an unnecessary burden. In retrospect, it was wrong of me to ask."

"You were wrong, Marquis, when you said that Nantes, as far as it is, is outside of my region. I think wherever our river flows may be part of my region. An American, whom you fought for without knowing it, once told me, when I was a girl, to remember to be true to my own land. I've thought of that often lately. It is winter. I will need scores of blankets—all you can steal—and I suppose you have a crew—"

"I'll find a bargeman or two."

"And, may I ask, how would one return upriver?"

"There is a group of *gabares*, sailing vessels, leaving Nantes in about a week. I can arrange passage for you and Jeanne Robin in the cabin of a barge."

"And the prisoners? Once they are free?"

"If they can be ferried safely to the south bank, by the time you get there I can have Chouans who can emerge at night take them to safety. They are mainly local farmers who are willing to hide refugees, but not to ride a barge through Nantes and rescue the prisoners themselves. What happens to the prisoners is not your concern. Your task is to get the prisoners, bound and guarded, off a sinking barge in a freezing river, and onto your own healthy boat."

"I see."

"There are fortifications at the harbor at Nantes. You will have to float by them silently."

"In any case, it is far better than riding between Hell Columns with your band."

"If those are your only choices. You are a very odd and wonderful woman, Madame."

"But you knew, once I heard about children being drowned, I really had no choice."

"You are still rare, you and Jeanne Robin. Extreme times can also bring out honorable qualities."

"And you?"

"If I weren't fighting for a Philanthropic Institute, I'd probably be raiding vessels on the high seas." And he kissed my hand and vanished into the cold night. I never learned, on the marquis's unexpected visits, where he came from or where he went.

At dawn I was awakened by loud sounds like fireworks suddenly going off, and I realized they were volleys of muskets. I thought at first the civil war had come to Blois, then realized it was far away, and crushed, at least for now. No, I thought, as I sat bolt upright and stared at the closed shutters, these were executions of prisoners, now being held at the Château. The sound of the volleys echoed over the blue slate roofs of Blois all the way to my cottage, with its ripe pears on the boughs. These were prisoners I couldn't save. There were probably women among them, taken upriver from Angers, which had full prisons now. No trials, no lawyers for the defense, no witnesses, just tribunals exercised by the representative-on-mission from Paris. "Pity is not revolutionary." Jeanne Robin had mentioned to me something of the reports from Savenay, the highways piled high with corpses, in some places piled in pyramids. I counted twelve volleys before silence once again surged back over the town, wakening into another day of the Terror.

I was now riding with the current down the longest river in France, with the fragrance of hay and the earthy smell of cattle, and the cold winds blowing upriver from the Atlantic, the banks spotted with snow, and now, on my left, the stern château de Chaumont, where

Queen Catherine de Médicis had exiled Diane de Poitiers, her husband's favorite, after his early death. At least Diane still had the river
as a view.

"Our river" was now taking on a new connotation for me. I did
not know if it would ever be the same—La Rouge's and my river, by
which I had ridden in the summer by the *luisettes*, the trickles between
the sandbanks, or in the rainy autumn, or snowmelt of spring, when
its waters swirled high under the arches of the bridge; Gérard's and
my river, that we had watched, gray or blue, from Marguerite's terrace and had made up songs about; and William's and my river, by
which we had walked and performed our make-believe and so serious
wedding: the river that, like Monsieur Jefferson's Shenandoah, ran
through the heart of all that was dear to me. Now it was polluted near
Nantes with the deaths of perhaps thousands. These drownings now
had a name—*noyades*—and the Chouans had also reports of them at
Saumur and Angers, and other towns. Citizen Carrier's plan had been
so successful, it was being copied.

But they were still performed at night, with no witnesses, as if the
republicans were fearful that word of them would show the Revolutionary Tribunals and the Revolutionary Army for what they were.
The marquis's feeling was that if just one *noyade* could be stopped,
the Committee of Public Safety would fear that they were no longer
secret and that public opinion, told constantly that the atrocities of
the Terror were only conducted on a high moral plane, would be hard
to manipulate in this case. The guillotine was one thing, ridding the
Republic of dangerous counterrevolutionaries, one by one, in public
view. Mass drownings of women and children in the dead of night
was another. The Revolution would be finally hard-pressed to justify
its actions. Perhaps the patriot Carrier had gone too far. But first the
ubiquitous committees would have to know that people had found out
about the *noyades* and were willing to do something about them: at
least, two women on a barge full of cattle were going to try.

Jeanne and I slept in a cabin at the back of the barge and on a coal
burner there cooked soup and porridge, which we also served to the
two bargemen, who reminded us that they were just hired to man the
boat: if there was any fighting, they would not participate; if we were
captured, they would say we had forced them to ferry us downriver.

After all, we had weapons, and they didn't. Jeanne had her cavalry sword and a pistol. I had my pistols and a stiletto.

It took five days to float downstream to Nantes, and in that time Jeanne Robin and I came to know each other better. She had joined the cavalry of the Royal and Catholic Army last June with her brother, father, and fiancé. Both her brother and fiancé were about to be drafted into the Revolutionary Army. The army had imprisoned their priest, whom they had known all their lives, and had taken their draft horses to pull their cannon, and before they could take their three best hunting horses and themselves, her father and older brother decided to ride against the army that would ride against them. They did not try to dissuade Jeanne from joining them. Her mother and younger brothers and sisters stayed behind at Loches—first protected by the successes of their local army, then having to flee. Jeanne had saved them all but her fifteen-year-old sister. Her father had been also killed, and when her brother and fiancé decided to move west with the army, Jeanne stayed behind.

She had no desire to traipse a hundred miles north to meet the British, and she couldn't comprehend fighting outside of her region. She didn't really care about *la patrie*, about the abstraction of a nation. She cared about her family, about the way of life that had been destroyed by outsiders, about the people of her village, and finally, about her horse. I liked her. She was pretty, selfless, and unbelievably brave. She had seen horrors of battle that I did not want to imagine, and she spoke matter-of-factly about other horrors I would rather not have known about.

"You have not heard about what they call the 'republican marriages'?" she asked me as we passed the mouth of the Cher, and I was thinking about a summer long ago, when my parents had brought us to a large fête at the château de Chenonceaux, along the Cher: a ball was going on in the large hall built on arches over the river, as Marguerite and I walked outside in the warm night, with two boys at our sides and a chaperone behind us, and on the other side of the hedge we heard the cries and laughter of the older girls and boys in the maze, and the music from the hall floated over the river, and the torches on the arches cast orange lines that quivered on the dark

water. I thought, vaguely, that republican marriages were some type
of wedding performed without a priest.

"I'm surprised you don't know of them—they've been going on for
a couple of months now, starting in this part of the river we're on now,
west of Tours. They think it's quite amusing. They strip a priest and a
young royalist woman naked, tie them facing each other, and take them
out in boats and lower the bodies into the Loire. You see, drowning
prisoners in the Loire is not a new idea. I think Citizen Carrier came up
with his plan after the popularity of the republican marriages."

I had nothing to say. My river had changed utterly.

The next day it was hard to keep warm, and Jeanne and I stayed
wrapped in our blankets, huddled over the small coal fire in the
cabin.

"Have you heard of the ebony trade, Jeanne?"

She shook her head. I could only see her black eyes. She held the
gray blanket up over her nose. She had on a green woolen cap, and
below that her black hair fell over her shoulders. She was a lot taller
than I, and even sitting I had to look up when I spoke to her

"Well, most people haven't," I said. "The ebony traders like it like
that. It's still going on. It's very successful. People in Nantes, like
my grandfather, became rich through the ebony trade. I visited him
once in Nantes. He was about to die, and my father thought his father
should meet his granddaughters. He and Papa had quarreled long ago
over the ebony trade."

Jeanne nodded. She pulled the cap down over her ears. "I can still
hear you," she said.

"He had a sugar cane plantation in Martinique. He was in the West
Indies often and went there by way of Africa, where he picked up a
black, or ebony, cargo. You understand? It's all in the wording, like
Citizen Carrier's report about the *noyades*. If you call it 'cargo,' it's all
right. And in both cases the 'cargo' was human."

Jeanne reached her hands out of the blanket to hold them over
the coals. She was a farm girl who had become a soldier and who
knew many horrible things. But that this business was conducted by
people so close to her home was new to her. "Your grandfather traded
slaves?" she said.

"And probably his father. Oh, they traded sugar too. But my father refused to go into the business. He was a disgrace to the family, the only son. He went to Paris to study medicine, and worked all his life. He could have been a gentleman of relative leisure. His name was respectable from his family's wealth. And on my grandfather's death, Papa still inherited most of the fortune. His friend once told me he thought Papa worked hard as a doctor as a type of penance for his family. I never knew about the ebony trade until this friend told me. I never knew why Papa worked when we had enough money. I think Maman always thought his working a little distasteful."

"I would have liked to know your father," Jeanne Robin said.

Soon I would be passing by the city of his childhood. His family had a mansion among other mansions, I remembered, along the quai. But I didn't see it, or recognize it when we got there. I had other things to worry about.

On the afternoon of the fifth day, we let the cattle off at La Che-buette. We dropped anchor just outside the harbor of Nantes so that we would arrive at the scene of the *noyades* late that night. I had been asleep for a few hours when Jeanne awakened me. "We're passing in front of the fortifications, now; we should be coming to their barge soon."

I got up to watch as we passed the harbor. Jeanne was at the bow, talking with the bargemen. I stood outside the cabin door and reached down and rested my hands over the pockets of my cloak. I felt my pistols there, in their familiar places.

Nantes was the last stop for river traffic. It would be odd for a barge to be going beyond the harbor. We would have to pass unno-ticed, by two islands on the south side of the river, only a dark blur in a quarter moon, in and out of storm clouds.

But I could still make out the snouts of cannon on the west tower of the old castle, under the torches that gleamed on them and made paths that we crossed, noiselessly, on the black current. The harbor was filled with barges with square sails, with *sapines*, the big rafts already discarded on the shore, for they were only used to go downriver, and with dozens of *gabares*, which towed smaller boats, including a barge with a cabin, upstream.

Now the masts of the *gabares* stood silent and ghostly, packed
against each other, with a thin moon seemingly caught in their rigging. I was glad when the harbor was suddenly behind us, and then
before us, a black bulk on the black river, was the destination of our
long voyage.

With the moon and the clouds, sometimes we saw the barge clearly
and sometimes lost it entirely. I could tell it was either moving very
slowly or not at all, which was both a good sign, as we could easily
catch up to it, and a bad sign, for if it were still, that would mean it had
already been scuttled and was in the process of sinking. I noticed a
rowboat tied to the side of the barge, presumably so the guards could
escape before the barge sank, so they had to be still aboard, finishing
their grisly work.

Now a few cries reached me, indistinct through the darkness. The
barge appeared to be stopped, and a cold rain started pattering on our
deck. I couldn't see a thing, then suddenly the moon ducked out from
the thick clouds, and a slice of light fell directly on their deck: a man
had got free of his bonds and was trying to free his neighbor's hands.
A large guard ran out from the cabin, his sword raised, and cut off the
arm of the man who had escaped. The arm just fell right there on
the deck, silently from where I stood. The man's scream cut clearly
through the rain. The guard was raising the sword again now, either
to finish off the man or against the other prisoner, who was now strug-
gling free of his ropes, and I aimed my pistol and shot quickly. The
guard staggered, still raised his sword, and I fired my second pistol.
The guard fell, like a heavy sack of flour, into the river.

The rain was turning to hail now, pounding loudly on the decks as
we came smoothly up beside the barge, and Jeanne and I jumped down
onto it. Jeanne had a cloth in her hand, and she knelt and wrapped a
tourniquet around the bleeding arm of the first man who had got free.
I was cutting wrist bonds with my stiletto, working as fast as I could
against time. The barge was covered with hundreds of prisoners, half
naked, crowded close against each other in the lashing hail. Once
free, they untied their ankles and started to run, with difficulty, for
they had been tied for hours, toward our barge, and I yelled at them
to free their neighbors first. Most of them stopped, their memory of

humanity flooding back. Men and women bent over children, untying their ropes. A young man asked me, "Who are you?"

"A Chouanne," I answered.

"Who's the other woman?"

"A Chouanne. Now help me free the others."

And it was not easy to loosen their bonds. Often, in the hail and in the fear of the sinking boat, the prisoners' fingers would not work right, and the ropes were tight, and I had to go from huddled figure to figure, slicing my stiletto in the dark, with some screaming, frightened now that I was going to stab them. It was worse for them when Jeanne approached, for she wielded her cavalry sword with swift assurance, cutting between their wrists and just an inch away from their neighbor, lying in a rising flood of river water, the boat now growing noticeably lower. Finally Jeanne said to me, "We'll never get to them all. Just cut the bonds at their feet and have them jump to the other boat."

Then someone shouted, "What about those below?" My God, I thought, there's more. Jeanne ran first to the hatch that led below, and as she did so, a guard emerged out of it, his pistol pointed at her. Before he could pull the trigger, her long, sharp sword had sliced him from his mid-chest up to his neck. Mademoiselle Robin was a strong woman. To avoid people tripping over him, she rolled him into the river.

I finished cutting the ankle bonds of the ones on deck, and now we were both below, and I couldn't speak any reassuring words to them because their screams filled the hold. Many were sitting with their knees up in three feet of water. Mothers, or surrogate mothers, had scooped children onto their laps or their knees, but the water was rising every minute. The guard had left a torch burning on the wall, and by its dim glow Jeanne and I sloshed along through the hold, cutting bonds again, first the mothers, who could then help the children. These people were also desperately cold, for, like those on deck, all their jackets, waistcoats, dresses, and skirts had been taken by their captors (whom, I learned later, got good money for them): women in thin shifts, men in cotton shirts, often without any trousers, children in underclothing; all of them without shoes and most without stockings.

Suddenly the barge lurched, and all the people sitting in the stern had the Loire up to their chins. They lifted their legs above water for me to cut their bonds, then waded out with their hands still tied. I finally got to an old man and woman in the corner, who, somehow, had survived the long march, the battle, and the massacres, and leaned peacefully against each other, now entirely underwater. I lifted them up and saw that they had left, together. Then I heard a soft humming sound, and, the river up to her lips, a woman sang to her little girl, poised on top of her knees. The girl was still asleep. "I thought," the woman said, as I approached her, "that if I sang the song she's used to, she wouldn't notice anything."

Then the water suddenly poured into the hold. I cut the bonds from the woman's ankles. She held onto the waking, crying girl, and I swam, pulling the mother with one arm, the stiletto between my teeth. I shoved the mother with her girl up the hatch. The torch went out, and the water flowed over my head. I was under the numbingly cold, black water now, and I couldn't reach the hatch. Through it the river was pouring in on me and pushing me down and back into the hold. I swam with all my might and bumped into the side of the barge. I had gone in the wrong direction in the dark. My lungs were burning. I pushed myself once more hard against the current and reached up toward where I thought the hatch was. I only felt air. I sank down, then kicked and reached again. I felt a strong grip suddenly grab my flailing hand, and Jeanne Robin pulled me up, and I felt the hail again, like pebbles on my face. "Look at you," Jeanne said, "a knife in your teeth."

"Holy Mary," I said. "Holy Mary."

The deck was well underwater now, and tipping violently. Jeanne strode across, helping the mother and child onto our barge, and I jumped behind them onto our deck, crowded with hundreds of wet, confused, relieved, and frightened people. Jeanne and I made our way through them, and I disappeared down our hatch and started to hand up piles of wool blankets that the marquis had stolen from a barracks when the regiment was out looking for him. Jeanne passed the blankets out, women and men soon coming to her aid, until all of the prisoners either had a blanket around them or one to share.

I realized I was shivering myself now, and went into our cabin to grab the blankets I had stayed under all day. There I bumped into two people standing under one blanket, taking up most of the room in the cabin. I asked them could they please stand outside, that at least the hail had stopped, and I heard, "Annette, this is Michel, my brother," and the two people turned around, and I saw Jeanne, her eyes wet and shining, and the young man who had asked me who Jeanne and I were. They couldn't believe their luck, and neither could I. Out of the thousands of people killed at Savenay, the thousands executed afterward, the thousands probably already drowned in the *noyades*, here was her brother on the one barge we saved. It was a miracle. But if the Virgin were to smile on anyone in this war, if any one deserved a family member to be brought back from the dead, it was Jeanne Robin. Her fiancé, I learned later, had been lost in the attack on Angers.

I left the cabin and directed the bargemen to take us about three miles downriver and pull in to the south bank. I hoped the marquis's men had made it through to the local Chouans, or we would have a lot of helpless people on the banks of the Loire. The rain had stopped now, and when we landed, with the white feather again in my hat, I jumped ashore and gave the owl call into the trees along the bank. Within a minute, a dozen armed men surrounded me, and in less than half an hour, they had a dozen wagons, covered with canvas, driving in two different directions into the night. One middle-aged man wrapped in a blanket and passing by me toward a wagon asked me, "Are you the one they call Madame Williams, the Mother of Orléans?" I said yes, and he clasped my hands and said he was Count Dufort, and that he would make sure that someday, he would thank me properly.

They did not tell me where they were going, but I found out later that the Chouans ferried the refugees before dawn to two locations, one in the woods by a lake south of Nantes, and the other at a farm just west near Bonaye, where the Philanthropic Institute, living up to its name, would hide, feed, and clothe them, and gradually ship them off to safe homes.

Jeanne and her brother planned to stay together and eventually rejoin their mother and surviving siblings at Azay-le-Ferron, where Jeanne had taken them, about twenty miles south of their hometown of Loches, but out of the fighting. Jeanne said her days as a Chouan were over now; she had fought for her family, and now they needed her more than the Chouans did. Once her brother had been brought back to her, they would never be separated again.

I was loaned a Chouan horse, and two stern and silent older men conducted me, shivering embarrassedly under a blanket, the fifteen miles back to La Chebuette, east of Nantes. They waited with me, had hot tea and cold biscuits at daybreak. I drank the tea gratefully. Snow started to fall in the vague dawn, and I felt that I might never be warm again, while my guardians sat mute and still until the *gabare*, with its convoy of small boats, sailed up from Nantes. They made sure that a dinghy detached itself from the convoy and picked me up before going on to perform some other secret, philanthropic task. The efficiency and the thoroughness of the marquis' institute again impressed me. Everyone knew what their task was, and everything had been planned and communicated, although it took days to get information from Blois to Nantes. I didn't doubt the communication system of the Chouans, which had a voice in every village and hands in every harbor along the river.

My new host was a round-faced, rough, and cheerful bargeman in a round black hat who wanted to wait on me as if I were royalty, but soon found out I was not an appreciative guest. By nightfall I was in a high fever. All I remember about the voyage upstream was shivering or sweating under blankets, the round-faced bargeman scolding me for throwing them off, him forcing me to drink hot broth and, at night, singing me river songs. His voice somehow reminded me of William; I asked him several times where in England he had learned such old French songs, and he told me that he had never been in England, that he grew up on the river, and that it was his only home. He cared nothing for republic or monarchy, just for the river itself, which was much, much older than either of those governments and would be here when kings and revolutionaries had all rotted and become soil washed into the river. At least, that is what I remember him saying.

I asked him if he knew Jeanne Robin, for I missed her, and he said he didn't know that song. On a fifteen-day journey upriver, he was my father, mother, and best friend, some benevolent spirit that chose to hover by my bed and put cool rags on my forehead or another blanket over my feet. When I was able to stand and walk on deck the last day, suddenly I saw the Beauvoir Tower and the spires of Saint-Louis Cathedral, and there was so much hustle and bustle as he unloaded the barge that, in my dazed state, I disembarked and never thanked him properly. I never learned his name.

PEACE

hen I had recovered, like Jeanne Robin, I found that after Nantes my taste for intrigues had waned. With no exaggeration, perhaps the most blissful moments of my own life occurred when, just a few days after my return from the barge in the pelting hail, Caroline took her first steps—or, I should say, raced her first steps. She never really did cautiously walk but went straight from crawling to a type of blundering running. Claudette and I sat facing each other, about six feet apart on our thin hearthrug, and Caroline stood in front of Claudette, with her help. Then my daughter looked at me and suddenly took off, running with the biggest grin possible on her little face, accompanied by her bubbling laughter, and didn't stop until she had run right into my arms. I wanted to take no more risks that she lose her mother, and I slowly curtailed my intrigues with the Philanthropic Institute.

I did not go with the marquis on any of the daring rides that he made throughout January to save towns between the Hell Columns. I did help stop a few more carriages in the winter woods, but the rent collectors were getting more and more wary, so I needed a patrol with me, and I mainly went because the men said I was good luck. On one memorable raid, without a shot fired, a patrol was disarmed by about two hundred Chouans around me, surrounding the patrol and singing the song that I had quoted to William.

Another memorable night occurred when Angelique came to dinner in a green cloak and a white-feathered bonnet. She said it was all the mode now to dress as the Blonde Chouanne at fêtes. Philippe had taken her to a ball in which perhaps thirty women, she said, showed up in blonde wigs and green masks. Some even had stilettos embroidered on their sleeves. One woman, though, not in Chouanne costume, took Angelique by the arm and told her that she had really seen the Blonde Chouanne, who had ambushed her carriage, that the Chouanne was as cold as ice and had a pistol in each hand, and that it was uncanny how much she, Angelique, looked like her. "I told her not to worry, that I had enough jewels," Angelique said. "Now isn't that a story?" she said. "Isn't it?" I agreed, and we left it at that.

After dinner Angelique looked at her teacup and said softly, "Philippe said that the Blonde Chouanne's last fête will be on the guillotine. Don't you think she should be more careful?"

"Perhaps she should wear a red wig, or take a holiday," I said.

She didn't take a complete holiday. The Royal and Catholic Army had been destroyed at Nantes, but no one could stop the Chouans. No patrols of the Revolutionary Army or visiting sans-culottes from Paris were secure on the roads in the Loire Valley. For many months now, despite all their efforts, the officials had not arrested a single draft escapee or deserter between Blois and Nantes—they had just gone to swell the ranks of the Chouans.

Things were changing in Paris. The ones who loved to call themselves patriots, who had exulted over executions and been intoxicated, insatiably, by them, slowly grew tired of head after head falling into the wicker baskets on the scaffolds of France. One can even get tired of Terror.

And they turned against its architect, the Incorruptible, Robespierre. He sent his friend Danton to his death in a last effort to save his own head, but by July Robespierre himself went the way he had sent so many. The only difference was that, when so many had gone quietly, or, like the Girondins, singing, Robespierre, already wounded in the jaw from an attempted suicide, screamed in pain when they ripped off his bandage so his head could fit in the guillotine. His leaders followed, the crippled and now injured Couthon dragged to the platform, Saint-Just as haughty as ever.

And with Robespierre gone, attitudes shifted in the National Convention. In August, the Convention promised amnesty to all Chouans and twenty livres in silver to all who handed over their muskets, though even that was not enough of an incentive for most.

By the end of October 1794, Citizen Carrier himself was brought to trial. I had been in correspondence with Gilbert Romme, whom,

I heard from the marquis, was the head of the internal commission indicting Carrier. Here there was no hasty tribunal, like the one that had condemmed my brother, but a lengthy process where justice was emphasized. If they wanted justice, I would give them first-hand accounts as a witness of the *noyades*. Carrier defended himself as a patriot dedicated to his duty to protect France, but no one was convinced anymore that the drowning of women and children was protecting the nation. The selling of their clothes added to Carrier's turpitude, and in the end the Convention ruled that the *noyades* were not a "pure reflection" of the Republic's ideals, and Carrier and two others found their way to the guillotine, though twenty-eight others who were complicit in the *noyades* were acquitted. I wondered if they were more "pure" than Carrier.

That winter the Convention also had to deal with complaints from the public: people were dying from starvation, even near the statue of the Goddess of the Republic in Paris. The winter was harsh, and since farmers had only grown about half of their usual crops because they didn't want the government to take any surplus away, food was scarce, especially in the cities.

We had our chickens and winter vegetables, though bread was hard to come by, and one night, again we heard the owl call, followed by a knock, and Monsieur le Marquis was there with his venison, and this time also with a large sack of flour.

He sat in his usual place at the table and poured himself water from the porcelain jug. "The Philanthropic Institute wishes to practice some philanthropy," he said, "close to home, to the Fearless Chouanne of Blois. I also have news, ladies, that the National Convention itself is frustrated in dealing with the Chouans and wants to deploy their forces elsewhere, and we might finally have peace at hand in our region."

Two weeks later, in mid-February of 1795, the National Convention made an official peace treaty with the Chouans. By April most of the Chouan leaders had been found, parleyed with, and received a reward for keeping the peace—Charette, from whom the marquis himself took orders, was given a gratuity of 200,000 livres.

On a mild spring night, the marquis did not make his owl call; he simply knocked, and he had no venison, only a wild white lily in his hand.

"I give this to you, Madame Williams, for all you've done in bringing about this peace. For me, it's a bit like a lily that honors the dead—both the thousands of lives lost, and, selfishly, the loss of my own raison d'être," he said. I got up to put the lily in some water.

"Though, you see," the marquis continued, opening his coat to reveal his sword, and one of his pistols at his belt, "I did not surrender. Part of me thinks we're being tricked into joining their Republic. I've sat at endless civilized conferences beneath tents in forests and watched every Chouan leader I have known and respected for years being bought off, as if we were fighting for money."

"But the Vendéans get back all the property taken from them during the war," I said. "They have freedom of worship; they are exempt from military service."

"Though that is not a little ironic," he said, "as they have lost a third of their population. No, you are right, of course, but it's still a pacification, not a victory. I did not come to speak of that, though; I bring you a warning. Despite the peace, the Chouans will rally sometime next year to meet a British-backed invasion of the émigré army, which has been waiting in England for years. Have no part of it. I know the man who is behind it. I'm afraid it will end up in disaster."

"Thank you, Marquis, but I have no intention of helping an invasion."

"One never knows about the generous heart of Madame Williams, where it might lead her."

"And what will you do now, friend of the American revolutionaries and of the French royalists?"

"What does a man do, raised in luxury, accustomed to privation and fighting? You do not know my hidden aspiration, Madame. Ever since I saw the grand landscapes of the new world: I shall paint forests and rivers. And where does a man go, who wishes to paint these things?"

"He returns to America?"

"Precisely. He paints rocks and trees and mountains where no beings who call themselves 'civilized' exist to spoil the beauty. No Chouans, no Patriot Army, no king, no National Assembly, just a few wild Indians left, plenty of game, and people who like to do things themselves, like me."

His attitude toward civilization sounded like that of someone else I knew, who lived as far from it as he could, in the wilds of the Lake Country of England.

The spring night entered through the open door, and with it the spirit of adventure. Claudette said, "Good. It sounds like a good place."

"I think it is," the marquis said, "especially after the kind of world we've lived in. So, Madame Williams, with our war effectively over, but with who knows what still in store for France, what about going to America with me? You too, Claudette, of course, and Caroline."

Claudette gasped. I took a petal of the wild lily and held it between my fingers.

"I still have some money from my inheritance, and whenever I get my land back, I will sell that," he said. "There is nothing left for me here. And you and I have always worked so well together."

"You flatter me, Marquis, but there are things that still keep me here."

"Ah. You refer to the mysterious Monsieur William."

"And a feeling that this is still my region. We have run a lot of risks just to abandon it when we no longer have to fight for it."

"Enjoy the peace, Madame. This Monsieur William, I believe, is a lucky man. May I ask when he might return?"

"That is up to the war with England, and to fate."

"Ah, well, I shall not argue with either of those. Madame, you have been the one light in these dark years; may I say my short, and, I'm afraid, unannounced visits here always made up for the months of living like an animal, speaking only to rough men. The small time in your company always reminded me of what I was fighting for, which I regularly forgot, and now I completely forget. To me, you will always be the Fearless Chouanne of Blois," and he kissed my hand and was at the door in an instant, where he bowed deeply and departed swiftly into the spring night. His lily sat in a wooden cup of water, in the center of the table.

I knew the difference between a good friend and a true love. Besides, what if the war should suddenly end, and William fly to France, only to find me retired to America with a marquis? There was never any question in my mind.

And the marquis was right, as usual. The invasion came in June, and it was a disaster. Almost a thousand Chouans made it to the beaches to greet the great French émigré army, but it was only about three thousand strong, and the British unloaded supplies, but none of King George's Redcoats. Four thousand men is not enough for an invasion force. General Hoche of the Republican Army efficiently cut them off on the peninsula, and all the Chouans were either killed in battle or executed afterward. I was glad the marquis was painting American mountains.

PERPETUAL WAR

With the permission of the count, I had reopened the hunting lodge and, off and on, continued for the next ten years to hide deserters from the glorious army, or draft evaders, or refractory priests, or anyone who was hunted for voicing dissent.

I also used a cave a few miles to the west of town, where the first inhabitants of the Loire Valley had lived, thousands and thousands of years ago. At a time when I judged it safe to take La Rouge out, as dusk turned into evening, the sinking sun had shone on a shadowy opening in the white tufa chalk cliffs along the river. I dismounted and peeked into what seemed a small room. I came back the next evening with Jean and candles, and we explored two more rooms that opened from that first one. In the farthest one our light shone high on the cave wall, on the heads of five deer or "wapiti," as the marquis would call them, with grand antlers, alert black eyes, ears forward, and noses almost twitching at us. Who knows how long ago people, not that different from us, drew those figures up there, and what they were thinking? I imagined them—or him—in the flickering torchlight, carefully working.

Whatever they were thinking, it wouldn't have been that thousands of years later a woman finds the perfect place to grow mushrooms and to hide more refugees. No one at market knew how I produced so many and such fine mushrooms. The refugees slept or read or wrote by candlelight right there among burgeoning mushrooms and ancient watching wapiti. I had been looking for some other place to use besides the lodge. The cave dwellers had provided me with a prudent alternative.

After what came to be called the Reign of Terror, the time of the Directory ensued, when a group of men "directed" France in a most disorganized way. The *assignat*, the already worthless paper currency of the Revolution, had become even more worthless. To help bolster their nation, bankrupt through expansionist policies abroad and poor management at home, the Directory reinstated old taxes that the kings had used only in the worst of times: on doors, windows, all goods coming into towns. They also decided to confiscate émigrés' lands more vigorously, again persecuting priests, any émigrés who tried to return, and even their families. Thus the need for the cave.

We all know what arose out of this chaos—that artillery corporal whose first famous act as a general was to turn cannons on royalist demonstrators in Paris. Now he began winning victory after victory abroad. I thought that we would truly have perpetual war, as long as Bonaparte kept winning and the old empires kept creating useless coalitions to oppose him. It all seemed a wicked joke made up by the masters of empires to keep themselves in business.

It also seemed hopeless ever to see William again, or even receive any letters from him. I imagined him climbing the mountains of his youth, composing poems on their windy crags. I continued my own translation of the huge *Romance of the Rose* into a prose story. That was my perpetual project, which I set against the unceasing wars. That and the raising of the beautiful and gentle Caroline, who helped make goat cheese and sell it with us at market in little *crémets,* and whom I taught to ride on the grounds of the château de Beauregard.

The count was now able to keep his château by being a caretaker for it, while Napoleon granted it periodically to different top marshals, so they, in turn, could grant it to their wives or mistresses. So sometimes when I visited the count I would see plumed hussars riding up to the château, or the carriage of a marshal of the Grande Armée stopping outside, but usually it was just a grand lady in a chiffon gown, with several other chiffon- or taffeta-gowned ladies following her, all floating, laughing and talking, through the salons, and I entering the side door in my riding habit and a hat ten years out of mode. Marshal Ney, in his shining top boots, once complimented me on La Rouge. Although I was nervous at first that he would want to confiscate her, I soon saw that this man, who led thousands of cavalry in battle, appreciated a good horse when he saw one. He was very polite. What need had he of another horse?

The count kept to his own corner of his château—to his salon and to his library, with his coat of arms. He dined in his library. The exquisite Edouard acted as if that were always the most fitting and proper place to serve a dinner.

One cold February afternoon I saw Angelique coming toward our cottage. She must have walked all the way from chez Vergez across the river. And Angelique never *walked* anywhere. She rode in the family carriage, or occasionally on horseback. I met her in the barnyard with her hood down and the wind whipping her long blonde hair and her eyes glistening with tears. She looked a vision of the saddest beauty I still have ever seen. She stood before me and simply said, with utter finality, "Philippe's dead. They killed him somewhere in Italy. A place called Rivoli. Where's that? Who cares about Rivoli? Do you care about Rivoli, Annette? Did Philippe die to protect you, or me? It's all a lie. Well, you know it's a lie. I don't have to tell *you*."

I wanted to embrace her, but she, I could tell, would rather stand there, with chickens running stupidly about her feet, and a goat looking interested in her glove, and her hair being blown about by the cold wind. She wasn't seeing anything but a cold, raging anger. I knew that anger. One had to do something with that anger. I waited.

"Annette," she said, "I want you to let me help at the lodge again. I know you're still doing it. Don't say you're not. I know you were the Blonde Chouanne. I'm not stupid. And I'm not a coward. I just never cared before. I'm sorry. Even after Etienne. I thought all this would go away. Now it's just getting worse. There's no end. So I want you to let me help. I want to help hide people, or pass them on to others, or whatever you do. I can keep quiet. I can be discreet. I just want to do something against the wars. Something small. Something a girl with a short memory who can't ride very well can do. I must do something, Annette." And then she cried, and I held her.

I later enlisted her in the Chouans, and she was very efficient at the lodge and at the cave. She was good for morale.

That evening I rode out to the château to console the count. I met him in the library. He was standing on a high ladder, taking down his coat of arms from its place by the coffered ceiling. He didn't greet me. He just said, "Annette, I'm glad you're here. I've got to hand this thing down to someone. Can you please help me?"

I climbed up the ladder behind him, and he passed me the gilt frame that held in it the faded azure background and the three round gold bells. As he did so, the bells rang dully, like the sound of cows grazing in a distant meadow. "Careful," he said. "It's heavy." I held it carefully and handed the coat of arms back to him at the bottom of the ladder.

"Edouard wouldn't help me," the count said. "Something about the pride of the family, for which he has been in service all his adult life. But what's the point, I ask you? What's the point of keeping it up there? It's the first time Edouard's ever refused a request of mine," he added.

"It's the first time he's ever received such a request," I said. I touched one of the bright brass bells. "I'll wager Edouard has polished these many times," I said. "I've always wondered what these bells mean." The count took his coat of arms now and gently placed it on the rosewood table. Then he pulled back a wood panel in the wall, carved with a bell, and unlocked a closet hidden behind the panel. "They're carved in the woodwork," I said. "They're everywhere. They must mean something." The count unfolded a strip of white linen from the edge of the table and placed it over the face of the coat of arms. He carried the coat of arms to the closet and laid it on a broad empty shelf.

"They may have meant something once, my dear," he said. "They may have even rung clearly once, to call the counts to the hunt. Perhaps old Thibaut the Cheat knew what they meant. He was the first count of Beauregard, in the year of our Lord 940. But I've never known. Philippe never cared. He even called them 'Thibaut's balls.' So I'm putting them away, in his honor." He checked one time to see if the linen was on right and closed and locked the closet and pulled the wood panel shut. No future generation would want that coat of arms.

I had dinner with the count in the library. We talked about Angelique and about his crops. "I'm very glad you've come," he said at the end. "You know in the notice to me they called Philippe's death a 'sacrifice' for *la patrie*. Those taffeta-covered bitches out there," he said, "in my château; their lovers made a *sacrifice* out of my son. What kind of sacrifice is that? He was the only one I had." And I embraced him finally, and he held on to me long.

The next time I saw him, while the ladies floated by in the hall, he was planting geraniums in the window box of the library.

Napoleon always had disgruntled citizens in the countryside. What did they care for Italy, or Austria, or Prussia, or, God help us, Egypt? They wanted their sons and husbands to help them eat. Paris liked the victories. And they kept calling for more men. Claudette's Benoît had disappeared on the Egyptian campaign. She kept hoping he would return, somehow, across all those miles of water and land. Napoleon had abandoned his army when he was cut off by the British fleet and sneaked through, to return in glory, wearing Egyptian regalia, claiming the right now to rule France. He just needed a new army, which he quickly gathered. And I just had to be on the alert for those who decided they didn't want to help him. Napoleon's secret police, a much more efficient network than the old Committees of Surveillance or Public Safety, had got some word of me, and sometimes I caught them watching the cottage, but they never saw me do anything more suspicious than harvest my cabbage.

By now the new century had dawned in glory and blood. While most people tried just to live their own lives, the new empire kept expanding. In the autumn of 1801, though, communication eased up with Britain, and suddenly I heard from William. He wrote to me of long walks among rainy hills with his sister, Dorothy, and with another poet, called Coleridge. He said they were forced out of a wonderful big house in the south of England because *he* was being watched as a possible spy for the French. They said that he sent letters to France (which never reached me), and that he and his friend wrote seditious material and didn't work (they didn't consider writing *work*).

But he came back to his beloved mountains in the north of England and was happy there, he said. Now Dorothy started to write to me. She called me "sister" and said that William had taught her French.

I was pleased at first—I felt part of the family—then I realized she was virtually taking over the correspondence. I would ask William something—about the routine of his day, new poems, anything to help me picture him, for he was growing daily into more of an abstraction—and Dorothy would answer in detail, more than I had asked for. The facts were gratifying, but I began to wonder, Were my letters even reaching him?

She said whenever William received a letter from France (she didn't say, "from you"; why was that?), he was so distracted that he couldn't write for several days, or had such powerful headaches that he simply went straight to bed, even in the middle of the day, and was good for nothing. She said she saw it as her duty to do what she could to ensure that William had an undisturbed life so he could write, and that also made *him* most happy.

When I answered that I thought he might want to hear from me and hear about his daughter, even if he did get a headache, Dorothy responded that she herself would pass on all my information in casual conversation as they walked. I imagined her saying, "I received a letter from *France* today. Caroline is doing quite fine, and her mother's tomatoes sold well at market."

Was I becoming merely a conversation topic heard about second-hand? What was he like when he became so "distracted?" Was it so unpleasant that he had no desire to receive my letters anymore?

Then he wrote and said that he read all my letters until he had memorized them, would walk at night for hours in any weather or not say a word all day and climb peaks to think of Caroline and me. Now *that* is what I wanted to hear. He had found a way, he said, to work me into his poems, although he didn't say what it was. He said even lying on his bed after a letter from me (not "from France"), with a headache splitting his brain apart, he was composing poems about me, but in a way that others couldn't tell.

Then I didn't hear from him for months. But I heard from Dorothy. Her news, after she politely inquired about Caroline, was all about Mary. Mary was her old friend who had lived with them all one summer—though William had kept excusing himself to go on walks. *Mary* now roamed the Lake Country with her, William, and Coleridge. *Mary* delighted in discussing poetry with them, and William always asked the opinion of Dorothy and Mary on a new work. Coleridge had fallen in love with Mary's sister, even though he was married. His wife didn't understand him, though, Dorothy said.

I wanted to know what William thought of this Mary. Instead, I wrote that they sounded like a happy group, and perhaps we could all live by each other some day. Dorothy replied that it would be nice to have Caroline and me visit their cottage, though it was rather small.

I told her William could stay in *our* cottage when the war ceased. We had a room he could write in, miles of river by which to walk, and, very best of all, his own daughter to delight him. To this Dorothy didn't say anything at all, except for a reference to France as "a very excitable place" and to her, William, Coleridge, Mary, and Mary's sister all being "like a family."

William sent me a copy, in English, of the book, *Lyrical Ballads*, that he and Coleridge had written together. I could make out his name and therefore which poems were his and not Coleridge's. I could catch a few words, like *nature*, *mountain*, and *hermit*; *love* he himself had taught me. I tried to sound out William's poems, but wasn't very good at it. I would have to wait either for him or someone else to translate them, and the next month he did send me translations of "Lines Written in Early Spring," "The Tables Turned," and one he hadn't published yet, on seeing a rainbow. I liked them all very much.

William said his critics made fun of him, saying they weren't really poems, but he didn't care. His critics called them "simple," and he took that as a compliment. He also said it seemed that the war would go on forever, and that his thirty-second birthday was approaching. I didn't see the connection.

Only Dorothy wrote to me of Mary.

Unexpectedly, in the late spring of 1802, since Napoleon had beaten everybody several times over (except the British, who had wisely only opposed him on the sea, where they always won), he declared a peace. After nine years of war, suddenly there was peace, and no one knew quite what to do about it and whether to trust it or not. But William knew what to do. He wrote, could I travel to Calais and meet him there?

So on August 1, 1802, after almost nine years' absence, we met again. But it was not just us. I brought Caroline, and William brought Dorothy.

BOOK V

1802–1820

MUTABILITY

*W*ith the peace, the émigrés could return for a visit. Marguerite wrote and said they would all cross the Channel in the autumn. She wanted to see my cottage. She longed to see Caroline. Gérard was going to a boarding school now, like most English boys, and she was afraid he was forgetting that he was French. But he still talked of his aunt Annette. Marie had suitors who were naval officers. Paul had just left for Spain and Portugal, purchasing sherry, madeira, and port for the British import company. Then Marguerite talked of the roses in bloom in her garden. She was fond of her English garden. It was like a dream to be going to see them all again, yet like a dream it was also strange. As William once pointed out to me, when you are away from people, you think of them as being stuck in time, as they were when you last saw them. We were all different.

Now, in the *diligence* on our way to Calais, I described each of the Vincents in detail to Caroline, in the way I remembered them, and in the way I had heard from Marguerite. Then she wanted me to describe her father to her. "I've already told you all about him," I said. "But I want to hear it again," she said. We had a long journey. I explained that her father had an even longer one, from the north of England, then across the Channel.

This man of myth and legend, of the pink cap she still had in her room, whom she claimed she remembered singing her good night when she was less than a year old, she would meet soon, and I think she was a little nervous about it, and of course, so was I. She was so used to him being in the realm of myth, it was very odd all of a sudden to be seeing him, like meeting a character out of a favorite story that one has read or heard many times. I told her I had tutored Marie and Gérard as I tutored her, and they, too, had become beloved characters in her nightly fictions. She was nine years old now, and a lovely girl, pleasant to be with.

Caroline and I walked along the seashore together as we waited for William's boat to arrive in the evening. Caroline liked the waves, and we kicked our feet in the shallows, getting the hems of our skirts wet. I gave her the parasol. She was fair, like her father, and I liked to feel the sun on my shoulders.

The boardwalk along the beach was crowded. All the people who had not come out to enjoy the sun and walk by the sea for ten years of war were now out promenading in their shabby best. It seemed like an ordinary hot end of July, yet there was something frantic about it; we all wanted to be here before something started again. But France was on top of the world. That would last, they all thought, as long as Bonaparte lasted, and he was young.

It was hot and muggy, and I shaded my eyes when I looked at the sea. Many gold fires were spinning on it, as on a summer day on the Loire, when Marguerite and I would look down from her terrace. But there we were so far above the river, the sun was not so bright on the water. Here, I could hardly see for the glare.

Caroline liked walking with the parasol. "Do you think that's Papa's ship?" she asked.

There was a bulk on the horizon. "Perhaps," I said.

She held my hand and swung our hands to and fro as we looked at the sea. "How tall is he, Mama?"

"He is much taller than we. He has long legs and loves to walk." I had told her all this before.

"I love to walk."

"Perhaps we can go walking together." Then, *with Dorothy*, I added to myself. But I was anxious to see her too. I wanted to meet this woman who had answered so many of my letters with such friendship and concern, who even called me "sister." She had taken care of William when he had come back from France, depressed, worried, and having no clear path in life. She gave him back his confidence, I thought. Can she give him back his life? Do we still have a life together?

"I'm thirsty, Maman. The ship is too slow."

We waited at a café, and Caroline poured water from a carafe into the pale yellow-green citron juice in each of our glasses. She then put spoonfuls of sugar into each glass and stirred them. I was looking out across the boardwalk at the sea, and when I looked down at our table, I saw she had done all this.

"Thank you. Did you put two spoonfuls in?"

"Of course."

"We like it sweet, *chérie*. You are so grown up. Your father will be proud of you."

"Will we have dinner together?"

"Probably, unless they are too tired from traveling. We have had a day to rest. But we will do everything together. We have a whole fortnight." Two weeks against nine years is not a lot, but to a child, a fortnight is forever.

We ordered some bread and a little jam for Caroline. Butter was too expensive, but the bread did not need it. It was lighter than our bread from the big oven at home, fresh and flaky, and I could not believe how delicious it was. Caroline carefully spread the jam on her bread. She was so beautiful, especially here, with her profile, looking down, being serious over her bread. She did remind me of William, her sudden quick movements and her feeling that every little thing was significant in some way.

We walked to read the charts of the vessels coming in, and we found we had made a mistake, and the Wordsworths' ship would not come in until four the next morning. Or perhaps we had not made a mistake, and the tides had changed and delayed them. I could not tell. It was hot, and I was having a difficult time reading the charts.

"The *Ceylon* will not come in until four in the morning?" I asked.

"That's what it says," said the man behind the window and beneath the charts. Beads of perspiration stood out on his forehead. It must be stifling in there, I thought.

"But I thought it was coming in today."

"Not this ship."

"Is something wrong?"

"Nothing's *wrong*, Madame. That's just the way it is. The *Ceylon*'s coming in on the morning tide."

He looked down at the papers on his desk.

Caroline was very disappointed. She walked by my side and swung my hand listlessly in the heat. The boardwalk was empty now, and the flag on the quai lay limp and still in the heat. Shutters were closed on the windows of the shops, and the street seemed devoid of movement.

"But I will be asleep when Papa's ship arrives. I wanted to see it come in. I wanted to greet him on the quai."

"I know, *chérie*, but we'll see him tomorrow morning."

After nine years, what was another day, more or less?

For some reason I felt that I had got something wrong. I was sure William's letter said he was arriving today. But things change. How could he have known, when he wrote the letter, about the tide? No one can control the tide.

When I saw William again, it was through the fine cambric curtain of our rooms on the rue de la Tête d'Or. We had just finished our rolls and coffee and hot chocolate. A rather tall man helped a woman, dressed in black, out of the cabriolet. She was even smaller than I. They did not look like brother and sister. I could not see his face well. I could see more the top of his head, but I knew it was he.

I had faced dangers in the last ten years with some degree of equanimity. Why was it now that I had the desire that we should not have come? Why couldn't we leave it comfortably in the realm of fine memories and the legend of the English father, the great poet who lived across the seas? My stomach knotted as if the old Committee of Safety were at my door. After all, what would we say to each other? I was glad his sister was here now, for she could help us talk. But what could she say, either? He had traveled hundreds of miles, and I was afraid I would disappoint him. I wasn't the young woman he remembered. I was almost middle-aged. I didn't know any English. I had a sudden impulse to pretend we were not home and to go back to Blois in the afternoon. Caroline, sticking a roll in her mouth, noticed me staring out the window.

"Is it them? Is it Papa?"

She squeezed in between the window and me, then wriggled out and ran out the door. I stayed and watched him go under the eaves of the house and heard him knock at the door. I heard the concierge, Madame Avril, scurry to the door downstairs and open it.

Below the window that same English voice said, "Is Mada—" Before he could finish, I heard Caroline squeal "Papa!" Madame Avril's shuffling tread came up the stairs to get me.

"Madame, they are here, your *English* husband"—she emphasized the word disapprovingly—"and his sister. They are here. Shall I have them come up?"

But before I could answer, I heard Caroline's footsteps running up the stairs, "Come, Papa! Come! Maman is upstairs!" and I heard his boots on the stairs and slower steps behind him. Then Caroline burst in the room from underneath Madame Avril's arms.

"Maman! They're here! Here is Papa!"

Madame Avril retired.

William stood at the open door, and Caroline held his hand. Behind him in the hall was a small black figure.

I wondered what I was supposed to do. I had thought so much about this moment. We had embraced, of course, in those thoughts. Now, for some reason, that seemed out of the question. I didn't want to shake hands, like English gentlemen. I took a step forward. I felt a bit paralyzed. Caroline was swinging his arm. William had been looking at me, standing still in my silence. Suddenly he lifted Caroline in his arms, kissed her cheeks, and said, "Now *here's* a beauty. Annette, you did not convey accurately the extent of her beauty. Shame on you." His French was good. And Caroline hugged him with both arms around his neck.

"This is Papa," she said to me, as if I, myself, did not know that fact. William came up to me, our child in his arms. "She's going to be taller than you soon," he said. And with our child between us suddenly it was easier, and he bent down and kissed me on both cheeks. "You should be proud of her," he said. "You should be very proud."

I felt my confusion melt and was about to embrace him, standing before me carrying Caroline. We would embrace awkwardly, with her between us, and that would be fine. Then he ushered the small black figure in front of him.

"Annette, I want you to meet someone," he said.

She smiled at me.

"Dear sister," I said, and extended both my hands to her and leaned forward to kiss her cheeks. She stood her ground and took my hands in hers, and I had to lean far forward to kiss her. I felt as though I had done something wrong.

"It is a pleasure to meet you," she said.

"Thank you for your many letters," I said. "You've taken good care of William for me." She smiled again.

"You have raised a very pretty daughter. You have done well, yourself," she said, in slow, deliberate French. Apparently it was easier for her to write, than to speak it.

"Oh, Caroline, this is Dorothy, the sister of Papa," I said.

"I know, Maman," and she stuck out her cheeks, still half full with unfinished roll, to Dorothy, to be kissed, as she still held William's hand. Dorothy took Caroline's other hand and pressed it.

"You are a lovely child," she said, "and an excitable one."

"She gets that from her father," I said, and laughed.

"She gets that from her mother," William said, and smiled. I had not seen him smile in nine years, and I felt a sudden desire to wrap him in my arms and kiss him. But that seemed as impossible as if he were still on the opposite side of the Channel. Instead, I reached out my hand, and William held it.

"It is good to see you," he said. "You are looking well; the years have been kind."

"Not exactly kind," I said.

We would meet that evening at their lodging for dinner, William said. But when that evening came, he sent us a note that Dorothy was tired and ill from the voyage, and they would just have a small meal in their room. Would we please meet them the next morning at ten, at the Republic Café near their lodging? We would walk by the seashore then, together. William was glad that Caroline and I both looked so healthy.

"We didn't see them very much today," Caroline said.

"They will be here a whole fortnight."

"Good, and we can go bathing?"

"Yes, if it continues to be warm."

Caroline went to bed early. The night was hot, and we slept with the windows and shutters open, and a slight breeze from the sea blew the white lace curtains in front of the windows. I felt the cooling breeze on my face and listened to Caroline's quiet breathing.

I had Caroline; he had Dorothy. I had wondered, before I came, if we would make love, and what it would be like. I had assumed, actually, that we would. But that seemed another world, now, another lifetime, those thoughts and those actions. They belonged in another century. Still, if we could just walk alone. If we could hold each other for a moment, wouldn't we feel all the old feelings? Was he perhaps afraid of them? Why? Had he urged his sister in between us on purpose, when we were about to embrace, or was that coincidence, or a nervous movement, or something he thought he *should* do? She had stood behind him, ignored, when we met. Perhaps he was just being polite. But there was something wrong. I knew it. And it wasn't just my own fears. I wanted Dorothy to be gone, back in England. How could we talk with her here? She wasn't a traveling companion; she was a chaperone.

"Papa is very nice, but I want to talk to him more," Caroline said over breakfast at the Republic Café.

"He was tired yesterday."

"I want to ask him things."

"Like what?"

"Like what is it like in England? Are you going to take us there? Are you going to marry my mother in an English church? Now that the war is over, are you going to live with us in our cottage? I'd tell him I'd prefer that. Am I ever going to have any brothers and sisters?"

"I think it would not be appropriate to ask all those questions yet."

"Why not?"

"Perhaps he doesn't know all the answers yet."

"But you've said that we would go to England some day when the war was over."

"Didn't I say, 'might go'?"

"No, you said, when I was a baby, that my father was coming and we were going to live where my cousins lived. I did not know where that was then. I thought it was across the river."

"It is." I laughed.

"Yes, very far across." She laughed back and forgot, for now, what I had said when she was a baby.

"And I have a hard time understanding Papa."

"His accent's good, for an Englishman."

"It's even harder to understand Aunt Dorothy."

"I'm not sure if you should call her 'Aunt Dorothy.'"

"Why not?"

"I'm not sure if she thinks of herself as an aunt."

The delicious bread was finished, and the coffee and hot chocolate.

"You ate all the jam again," I said. Caroline grinned up at me. The morning sunlight caught her blonde curls, like Angelique's.

"Remember those shells we saw yesterday, Maman? I kept one for Papa. It has the white ridges on it. I will show it to him today. It is my present, welcoming him home, after the war. People do that, yes, for men coming home?"

"Visiting home. Most of those men are still in the Grande Armée and must return. They are on leave."

"I like your new gown, and mine." She twirled her blue sash a little, at the table. "Does Papa know they are new gowns?"

"I don't think so."

"Why does Aunt Dorothy—why does his sister dress in black? Was someone killed in the war in their family?"

"That may just be the style in England."

"If it is, I think I will wear French clothes when we go to England."

It was ten o'clock, and the Wordsworths had not arrived. I asked for a piece of paper and some ink from the waiter, and gave it to Caroline, and she drew a picture of the ship we had been waiting for the day before. At the bottom of the picture she wrote, "Papa's ship."

When we saw them approach the café, Caroline ran up to her father. "Look what I've drawn," she said. He stood there, her hand in his, and studied the picture.

"It's remarkable," he said. "It looks just like our ship. How did you know?"

Caroline beamed. "May I keep it?" he said.

"Of course," she said, and he folded it carefully and put it in the inside pocket of his coat.

"I was a bit ill yesterday," Dorothy said. "I need to take William's arm. Why don't you two walk in front."

It *was* clumsy for us to walk four abreast along the street, so Caroline and I walked together. "We'll show you the way," Caroline said. "Maman and I were there yesterday."

From behind me I heard William's voice, "Another hot day. Do you not have a bonnet, Annette?"

I turned, "I prefer the sun. And I thought it was always *you* who did not wear a hat." I smiled teasingly, and then felt awkward. It was almost as if any allusions to our past life were in bad taste. Well, the biggest allusion was walking by my side.

"I think you must be mistaken, Annette. William always wears a hat out of doors," Dorothy said. "I've never seen you without a hat out of doors, William."

On the boardwalk, we suddenly had to walk together. The sea was on my right, Caroline was between William and me, and Dorothy was between William and the rest of France. Suddenly William stopped. He squatted by Caroline. "I have a present for you," he said.

"And I have a present for you."

"Mine first," and he pulled from his pocket a small box of chocolates. They were very expensive in France at this time, and almost impossible to find.

"Chocolates!" screamed Caroline, and jumped a couple times. She opened the box and unwrapped one and popped it in her mouth and asked me, with her mouth full, if I would like one.

"Thank you."

Then she offered one to Dorothy and William, but Dorothy said, "They are for you. William brought them from England for *you*, dear."

"England must be a good place, with chocolates. Can I go there, Maman?"

All eyes were on me. "We will see."

"Do you want my present, Papa? It's in my pocket. We both brought our presents in our pockets," and she pulled out a delicate small white shell and held it up to him. "See, it has ridges in it. It is the only one we found that was not broken."

"It is beautiful," William said. "It shines in the light. Where did you find it?"

"This way," and Caroline pulled my hand, then suddenly realized she could pull his hand too, and she pulled us both farther down the boardwalk.

"Wait," I said. "You run ahead. We will follow you. Just stay in sight."

"She is a spirited girl," Dorothy said.

"Like her mother," William said.

"Like her father," I said.

It was a very sultry day, and when we caught up with Caroline at the edge of the boardwalk, where she and I had gone walking by the ocean the day before, Dorothy said, "It *is* rather hot. I'm still a bit tired from yesterday. Do you think we could continue this walk later?"

"It will be cooler in the evening," William said.

"I found your shell right down there, Papa," Caroline said. "There are others. Come and see."

"We will walk after dinner, *chérie*," I said.

Caroline walked slowly by me, and unwrapped another chocolate.

"It's all melted," she said.

"We must get back and let it cool in our room."

We let ourselves cool in our room, with our fans, and Caroline dozed, and I looked out the window at the sultry sea. I wrote in my journal:

> *I was uneasy about meeting this woman with whom I have exchanged many letters, mutually addressed as Dear Sister. She has given me so many facts of William's life and hinted that that life is no longer with me. It is with her. I was right in thinking that she is, in her own way, jealous of me. How I wish William had come alone!*

I put my pen down and dressed for dinner. With a fortnight ahead of us, William was not going to see a great variety in my dresses.

At dinner, I asked the Wordsworths about their home in the north of England, and William got very excited and talked about their walks around the lake of Grasmere and up to Loughrigg Tarn. I remembered his wonderful northern names of places, but not this one. I had him write it down. But the strange name made it seem even more like it was another world, up there.

"Tell me about that place in the south of England, the big house, where you got in trouble because you wrote to me in France."

It was the first time I had said anything to imply that we had a relationship besides, somehow, being the parents of Caroline.

There was a pause, then William said, "Well, that was part of it. It was also because of Coleridge's writings and lectures. A place called Racedown. Now, there we walked every morning for two hours, up to Pilsdon, or to Lewisdon or to Blackdown Hill or Lowdett's Castle. Later we lived in Somersetshire, on the edge of the Quantock Hills, near Nether Stowey, where Coleridge lived." He was speaking French, but with all the proper nouns it sounded like a foreign language.

"England has very strange names," Caroline said.

"Like Wordsworth," William said, and laughed. It was the first time I had heard him laugh in almost nine years. I had been waiting to hear that laugh. It hadn't changed. Things like that don't change. They just come less often, I suppose. "Your mother can still not say the name," he said.

"I can too, it just doesn't sound right when I say it."

"What is the difference?"

"*Le bois, le bois,*" I said. "You told me that is what it means when *I* say it, 'Woods woods.'" Caroline laughed. "Or should I say, '*La Valeur des Mots*,' the worth of words?"

"I can say *Vallon*," William said.

"I think we had this conversation ten years ago," I said.

"At least we are consistent," William said.

I liked hearing that.

"William would often want to take longer walks, though," said Dorothy, continuing the previous conversation. "Just a two-mile jaunt up to the coomb would not do."

"Up to the what?" I was laughing. I was enjoying my second glass of burgundy. "The what?"

"A coomb," she said patiently, "is a small deep valley, like a basin in the hills."

I twirled my glass with my fingers. "And what did *cher* William want to do instead?"

"He wanted to go walking for forty miles."

"How can anyone walk that far in one day?" Caroline asked.

"I put on what I call my 'woodland dress' and joined him," Dorothy said.

"Your legs are about the length of mine," I said. "Did William walk slowly? I always had to take two steps for his one, and skip beside him."

"Do you like to skip?" Caroline asked her.

"I kept up," Dorothy said. "Now when we walk, there are more people, some with longer legs, but I still keep up with them."

"Whom do you walk with now?" I asked. I thought I knew, but something in me wanted to see if they'd mention Mary.

"Coleridge, of course," she said. "The miles we put under our feet," she said, "as those two talked or composed poetry. I don't know how they memorized it all. They always asked my opinion on lines they had questions about. Then they would change them. They wrote it all down later. That's the last thing they did. But we haven't seen as much of Coleridge lately. We walk a lot with Mary."

"Did I ever send you a translation of that poem about the rainbow?" William said.

It was very curious, a conversation with Dorothy and William.

The *patronne*, a plump woman, came by and filled my glass again from the bottle on the table. Dorothy put her hand over her glass, and William shook his head. I sipped the wine and tasted its subtleties. A good glass of wine was so rare.

"William likes to write about things like rainbows," Dorothy said. "They move him, but they are transitory."

"But that's not exactly how that poem goes, is it?" I said. "You did send it to me, William. It's only eight short lines, yes? And at the end you make a little prayer that your feelings will stay the same throughout your life, that you will not lose your joy—"

"That 'my heart leaps up when I see a rainbow,'" he said, and smiled.

"You're missing the deeper meaning," Dorothy said to me. "It's about *mutability*."

"I like rainbows," Caroline said. "I will try not to lose that when I get older."

"Bravo," William said to her. "'The child is father to the man.'"

"What?" she said.

"William, you're always talking over people's heads," Dorothy said. "It's about how things change, dear," she said to Caroline.

It was a warm night at the restaurant. We sat outside, and I felt a soft breeze come from the Channel. William stretched out his arms on the table. He put his palms together.

"How is La Rouge?" he said. "Is she still alive?"

"Just this spring I decided to let her retire at the château de Beauregard. It was finally time." My voice broke unexpectedly. "She changed my life."

I brushed my eyes and felt embarrassed.

"I thought she was marvelous," William said. "She saved my life."

"If it weren't for La Rouge, I wouldn't know how to ride," Caroline said.

"I'm a *walking* person myself," Dorothy said.

The woman came with the tray of different cheeses, and I chose three, to enjoy the contrasts, Dorothy took none, and William chose one. Caroline took her chocolates from her pocket.

"These French cheeses are too strong for me," Dorothy said.

"Dear sister, what cheeses do you like in England?" I asked.

"The Stilton, yes, and the cheddar is good. In Germany they have some cheeses that resemble the English ones."

I remembered a letter that mentioned the trip to Germany. They could not visit France because of the war, but they had been so close.

After dinner we walked again along the pier. It was cool now, and a pale glow shone on the sea.

Caroline ran ahead of us. "How is the little Gérard?" William asked. "I liked him."

"He wants to be an English admiral," I said.

William laughed. "The irony is too much." Then, "That was a good meal. I forgot how agreeable a French meal can be. And the wine."

"You should sing," I said. "I'd love to hear you sing again."

"Here?"

Caroline came suddenly running back down the pier.

"Come, look, look!" she shouted.

"What is it?" I asked. I was afraid it might be the dead body of some sailor, washed ashore. In the bad days of the Vendée, there had been bodies sometimes, along the banks of the Loire.

"Come, you must see."

She pulled at our hands again, and led us, straining, as if she were a horse pulling a heavy load, her two small arms outstretched behind her like two reins. We arrived at the end of the pier. "There," she announced. Her mouth, in the half-dark, had a dark ring of chocolate around it and her hand, in mine, was sticky with it. "There, do you see?"

"What? What is it?" William and I asked.

We were parents, for an instant, asking our daughter a question. "Do you see anything?" I asked him.

"No."

"You mean the shining on the water?" Dorothy asked.

"Yes, the shining colors on the water. What is it? Is it not beautiful?"

"William, you were this excited when you told me about a glow-worm," said Dorothy. "She is truly your child."

I didn't know whether that was a compliment or not.

"It's simply phosphorescence," Dorothy said to Caroline. "Egg-shells are phosphorescent."

"You mean if I take an eggshell into a dark wardrobe, the shell will glow?" asked Caroline.

"For a brief time, yes. And if the temperature of the phospho-rescent object is the same as the temperature about it, the light may last a long time. I suppose the warm evening and the warming of the water from the hot day make these lights last." She paused, and then her tone changed. "They are like streams of glowworm light! Aren't they beautiful, William!"

Her scientific voice had suddenly become like a little girl's.

We were all excited then, with the colored lights in the sea, and I took William's hand and reached up and kissed his cheek. It was dark, with the light only on the water, but I think Dorothy and Caroline saw. I did not mind. They should see. I stood on my tiptoes and kissed his cheek again. He bent his head down and put his arm around me. For a moment I could feel his breath next to my ear, as if he were going to say something, but he did not.

Then he kissed me briefly on the cheek. My hair was coming undone, and he partly kissed it instead of my cheek.

"Oh, I'm being too excited," said Dorothy, "I *am* sorry."

"No, it's beautiful," I said.

"Ah, but you are French," said Dorothy. "You are an excited people."

William withdrew his arm from around my waist, but he squeezed it briefly first, as if saying he was sorry he had to withdraw it.

The waves broke under us in a greenish fire.

"Maman, I want to sleep here," Caroline said. "I want to sleep right here."

"I want to go bathing tomorrow," said William. "Will any one join me?"

"The water's too cold for me, but I'll wade," I said.

"William loves cold water," said Dorothy. "But this is not cold. You should touch the water of our northern lakes." Then she paused. "I have a cold and cannot join you, William," she said.

"I'll go!" shouted Caroline.

Back in our lodgings at the rue de la Tête d'Or, I wondered, Why does it have to be so furtive, our touching? He was never ashamed before. Why did Dorothy apologize after she got excited? My God, I was right to be afraid yesterday. There were moments today more terrifying than entering that old crypt. It *was* like a crypt, with Dorothy there, in black.

Caroline was asleep, and I got up and went to the window. The fort, at the entrance of the harbor, was a shadow lit with lights of the sea occasionally flashing beneath it and with a few of its own lights. The army still occupied it, now, even though the war had ceased.

I lay down on my bed and wept.

THE HISSING FOAM

*T*he next day William sent a note chez Madame Avril that asked us to meet them at the pier at one in the afternoon. Dorothy was coming, after all. Caroline was excited that she would get to go bathing.

The tide was low, and we walked along the sands. William went up to a changing cabin, argued a while with a woman at its door about a tip, and then gave her one. Then Dorothy and I watched William, holding Caroline by the hand, walk far out in the low tide. There were more than a hundred people bathing, far out from us.

"It's a delight to see so many people enjoying themselves again," I said. Dorothy looked at William and his daughter and didn't say anything. "You have kept him happy," I ventured.

"It was not always easy," she said. "We started walking together. That helped me keep track of him. We became good friends again. You know, we had not seen each other for a long time when he came back from France. We had gone out of each other's lives. I looked after him when we were children; though I am a year younger, when our parents died, I was the mother. Then I had not seen him for so long, and when I saw him again he was strange, distracted. I even feared for his sanity, as well as for his health. France was very hard on him. He believed all those ideals, and they were dashed; then, when he came back, our uncle would not even let him set foot in his house."

"I am sorry," I said.

"I had to fight hard to have William even half accepted back into the family. He was supposed to go into the ministry, you understand. And for him to have an illegitimate child, and by a *Catholic* and a *French* girl—" She broke off. It was as if she were talking about someone else, not me. I thought I saw her eyes glisten with water. Then she took command of herself. "When I started to take care of him again," she said, "we realized what good friends we were. We were all we had in the world. Now we have made a happy home. And I see that he is now, and will become even more, a great poet. It is worthwhile to make sacrifices for that."

She paused, and in the heat I put my hand on the back of my neck and wiped away some sweat. Caroline, out in the waves, held William's hand. He was lifting her over a small wave. I wanted to be out there, with them, laughing with the striking of the cold water against one's skin. Anything but talking to this woman who had taken my beloved and who spoke with such composure about her conquest. I wanted to shake her complacency, but didn't know if that was possible.

"William was almost dead inside," Dorothy went on, "from disappointment, from heartache, from guilt. I gave him his life back. He is an amazing man," she said carefully, "but he must, he *must*, have the proper conditions to show his genius to the world."

"'True knowledge leads to love.' That's a beautiful line he translated for me."

"It is hard to appreciate his poems fully in translation, though," said Dorothy, "and I am afraid our French is not good enough for you."

"On the contrary, your French is very good. I can understand everything you say, without straining in the least."

I understood that Dorothy was asking me—no, *telling* me—that I must give William up once and for all. But what did she know, what *could* she know, of William's and my life together?

"William always prized his independent mind," I said, "his freedom of spirit."

"I think what he most values now is his tranquillity," she said. "He needs peace to write. Peace and his long walks." She had a tight black bonnet that shielded her face from the glare, and she pulled on one of its long strings with her hand. It tightened the bonnet even further.

"He was happy with me," I said. "You didn't hear him laugh or sing or—" I summoned up my courage as if I were on an intrigue. I must face this little woman. "Love like his doesn't go away," I said. "If you knew anything about him, you'd know that. It can be covered up by new friends and the tranquillity of your cold hills, but it doesn't pass. He has had just as fine walks along our river as along your lakes. He has said so. You didn't hear him, but he said so. He needs peace to write, sure, but he needs something else that you or your friend Mary can never give him as I can—he needs passion, Mademoiselle. Do you know what I am saying? Can you understand me? Is your French good enough?"

"You will never take him away from me again," she said. "He was carried away by the emotions excited by the Revolution. Everyone knows that. That is why it is forgivable. He wasn't in England. He was in a world gone insane. That never would have happened in England. William is a man of self-control." Her chin was trembling, and she pulled at her bonnet string again.

Suddenly I laughed. "You've got a poet whose spirit ranges beyond the mountains in control, you think, but you don't. You control him through fear. If he leaves you, he will fall into the abyss again. If he leaves you, you yourself will fall apart, so he will stay. But his spirit is beyond you, beyond both of us. You don't know what it is like to face uncontrollable forces, Mademoiselle. And you'll never, never know what William and I shared. What we still share, if we could walk alone. Have him walk alone with me, this evening. Or are you afraid?"

"I understand William, and you do not. That is clear. You may walk unchaperoned if you like. He has things to say to you."

"Very well."

"But Mademoiselle Vallon—we know in England about French girls. We know that—what *happened*—was not William's fault. We know that, most likely, William was not your first, and will not be your last. William is beyond French temptation now."

"It sounds to me," I said, "as if the war between our nations is still ensuing. I think it is time to enjoy the peace, Mademoiselle, that you so highly extol."

I looked toward the sea and saw William lifting Caroline, effortlessly, high over a wave, and dipping her feet down into its foam. I heard her scream with delight, over the happy screams of the other bathers. "Everyone is enjoying the peace out there. I'm going to wade now, dear sister. It is getting far too hot here."

I took off my shoes and stockings, scooped up the length of my skirts over my left arm, and started down the hot sand.

"There's one other thing, Mademoiselle," Dorothy said to my back. I turned and stood in front of her black-clad self, my ankles bare. I could feel her disapproval. "You don't know poetry, as we do," she said. "William *asks* Mary and me our opinions on his work. He may argue at first, but he always takes our advice. He couldn't write without us. He knows that. Coleridge's wife, for instance. She doesn't understand, doesn't appreciate literature, and she doesn't fit in our circle. But Mary's sister, she does, so Coleridge prefers to be with her. So we have a complete circle, Mademoiselle. You wouldn't want to feel left out, like Coleridge's wife. You wouldn't want to deprive the world of the great poetry William can create by thriving within our circle."

"I think," I said slowly, "that he created great poetry before that circle existed. He asked my opinion of his poems long before he ever asked yours. I am working on a prose version of *The Romance of the Rose*, Mademoiselle. Maybe you've heard of it. It's 22,000 lines long. I know literature. I have faced the Committee of Public Safety and the Revolutionary Army. Don't think you can intimidate me so easily. Whatever happens here will be because William and I *will* it so, looking at fate full in the face and taking stock of our respective situations. Not because it's part of your plan."

I waded out. The cool water was a delight, and I thought, I should have joined them from the start. I called, "Caroline, William!" It felt good to say their names together. I wanted to kidnap him. He would make a good father. There he was, with Caroline, giggling.

"Watch, Maman!" she shouted. They turned and faced a wave that was over her head. She screamed, and William did not pick her up. I gasped. At the last fraction of a second, William snatched her up and held her over the top of the wave. She squealed.

I said in a voice which the sound of the waves covered, "William, your sister is in love with you! Your sister wants to marry you! Do you know that? I, though, am the cause of your family almost disowning you! I am no good! I am a whore!" A wave, when I was not looking, flung itself over my knees and got up to waist. "What do *you* want, *mon cher*?" William turned and walked through the water, with Caroline holding his hand.

"You should join us," he said.

"Papa rescues me just in time."

"Your dress is wet," he said.

"I might as well not have worn it." It was a bizarre thing to say, but I was beyond caring.

William laughed. "Caroline is a delight. Can you hold her hand a minute? I want to swim out beyond the waves. I will be right back."

I watched him dive into two waves that collided together and swim out. Caroline and I played in the waves ourselves, for a while. We jumped when they came and fell back in the hissing foam. We laughed. William was still out beyond them. We were thoroughly soaked when we walked back to the beach, where Dorothy stood, waiting for us all.

Other people strolled by us, some arm in arm, and three old fishermen leaned on the rail, smoking in the twilight and looking down at the water.

"It's pleasant to walk in the evening after a hot day," William said.

"Yes, it is."

I suddenly felt as though I had nothing to say to the man I had waited so long to be with. Here he was walking beside me in the twilight on the beach, and I had nothing to say. Or I had so much to say I did not know where to start, so I said nothing. I felt *he* wanted to speak, and I waited. I didn't know, though, if I wanted to hear now what he had to say.

"The air is so still," William said.

I decided to help him.

"When I was a girl, going to school at the convent, we called this the 'holy time,' because it was the time of evening prayer."

The evening was so calm, the waves coming in sounded like an intrusion. I looked back, and the pier was a speck, with the bulk of the fort seemingly just on the other side of it.

William finally spoke again. "Except for the sea, the evening, then, is as quiet as a nun."

"Nuns are not always quiet. Sometimes they can be quite noisy, singing, laughing, yelling at one to do this or that. They are only quiet in prayer."

"As quiet as a nun in prayer, then."

We were silent again.

"Caroline loves the seashore," I said.

"Caroline, like Dorothy, has a deep love for the things of nature."

We kept walking. William was not looking at me but at the sand at his feet or out to sea when he spoke. He continued where he had left off. "Caroline's excited joy is like what I used to have—a joy arrived at not through contemplation, but through innocence."

"You had that when I knew you."

"You have that; Caroline is like you in that respect; my sister has that."

He stopped and looked out to sea, toward England. "Dorothy and I were separated, you know, after my parents died. So in seeing her again, I was seeing another soul that had been lost to me. She became my best friend. She has a brilliant mind. Coleridge calls her my 'exquisite sister.'"

I thought of mentioning to him something about Dorothy's and my conversation that afternoon, but decided it wasn't the time. "You have been happy together."

"In our humble way, yes. Growing peas and carrots, so poor we are living on air, walking in the country in all weathers with Coleridge, and the three of us rowing on the lake at night and reciting poetry, or fishing for pike."

"It sounds idyllic." Then I couldn't help myself. "Your sister's very attached to you."

"Yes, she is. She's very protective of me. She ought to be. She's taken care of me long enough. I don't even have to say something, at times, and she knows what I mean, or what I'm wanting. But she's not as strong as she seems. She has headaches that put mine to shame, that debilitate her for a week. She can walk in the cold rain up steep hills; then for no reason one day she is in bed, can't get up to heat water for tea. We help each other."

I thought I knew the reason for the headaches, but it wasn't mine to say.

We started walking again and were on sand that was still hard from being wet at high tide, but was now dry. Near us, as the waves washed up, stars were briefly reflected in the thin film of water over the sand, then it would go dry, then another wave would come up. "Do you think this peace will last?" William asked, and looked at me, then away.

"I don't trust Bonaparte," I said. "What has a man like him have to do with peace?"

"I don't trust Pitt. Even though he is out of office, he will try to get back at Bonaparte."

"You don't trust your country; I don't trust mine. What will we do, *cher* William, if the peace does not last?"

"What will we do? Let us walk up to the dunes."

We walked up to the dunes, and he spread his coat on the sand for me to sit on. The dune in front of us was high, and you could not see the beach, but over the top of it, far across the water, you could see two little lights glimmering on the English shore.

"Sometimes I feel that so much has passed from my life that I cannot retrieve," William said. "I feel old, as if I've lived more than one life."

"You're only thirty-two."

"Part of my life died when I left France." He sat close beside me on the edge of his coat, but without touching. He hugged his knees and stared straight ahead. "I overcame that death in our brief reunion when I walked across Normandy to your cottage. Then it engulfed me again." He glanced at me and held my gaze. "I was happy coming here," he continued. "I rode atop the coach, and as we passed through London in the early morning, I composed a sonnet sitting up there watching the river, the great city about to awaken. I was *happy*, Annette. I was coming to see you. But I had completely forgotten *why* I was coming to see you."

"I don't understand."

"I was thirty-two—what was I waiting for? my family asked me. No one knew what I was waiting for, except Dorothy, and she did her best to have me forget it for my own sake, for my own happiness." He kept glancing across at England, to me, intensely, then away again. He had something to tell me, and he would do it in his own time. I could wait. I could wait all night. I had been waiting nine years. "Suddenly, there was your voice again, in the letters. It was a shock. We had been isolated up there in the Lake Country, on our own happy island, so to speak. Have *you* been happy, Annette?" He rephrased the question. "In spite of the war, have you been content in your own life?"

"I suppose I have, with Caroline, with Claudette, with our cottage and my garden, with my . . . work with the Chouans."

"Are you still helping those dangerous people?"

"It makes me feel I can do something. So often I feel that I can do nothing. I also write."

"Those pages you sent me from your prose version of *The Romance of the Rose*, even with my inadequate French, were most wonderful." He touched my hand and seemed to forget whatever it was he had been trying to say. "I'm so proud of you," he said. He was holding my hand now. "That's what France needs, what the world needs. A renewal of the hero's quest, to put things in perspective in these modern times. I told you I'm doing one about my youth—it's really just for Coleridge; I don't think anyone else would be interested—the *quest* is the growth of a poet's mind. I put in it the love poems I wrote to you in France, only fictionalized the situation."

"So no one will know."

He laughed. He was himself again, discussing writing. "Even a work about oneself is still a fiction, once one puts pen to paper, is it not?" he said. "What one *chooses* to say, what one chooses *not* to say, *how* one says it? It is all a fiction."

"I will remember that if I ever write about my life."

"I created my own fiction about you," he said, "living so far away. I would see you, sometimes, up on Helm Crag, or Hammer Scar, or Loughrigg." He recited the names of the mountains as a type of litany.

"I'd be hiking with my sister or by myself, then suddenly I'd see your shape, your face even, with the wind blowing your hair, up on a peak. You'd be looking at me. I'd get dizzy. I'd have to steady myself with my hand on a rock. Then I'd go on, ignore it, but I'd look back and see you. It got so I became afraid, if I took off toward a peak—Dove Crag, it happened once there—that I would see you. Then I'd be silent the whole rest of the way, thinking about you and what I had lost. My sister thought I was just being meditative."

I looked into his intense blue eyes. I was a myth, a woman on a mountain.

"And I had dreams. In all of them I was looking for you. Sometimes revolutionary tribunals would catch me and put me on trial, and I couldn't speak a word of French. In others I'd find you briefly and talk to you, hear your voice clearly. I could smell the river and hear it moving behind you. And then I would have to leave in a hurry; it was

always a life-and-death matter. I'd wake up well before dawn. Sometimes I'd be in a sweat from the tribunal. Sometimes I'd just lie there
and listen to your voice, still in my mind. It was my secret, waiting
for it to get light, letting my heart calm down, listening to your voice.
Once the day got started, I'd forget the dream. A few months later I
would have it again."

William was weaving a narrative together for me, like a long poem.
It had side paths, but I knew it was all leading to a place he had in
mind. I thought I knew what that place was, now. He was sometimes
slow with his French, but he was certain. I was silent and followed
him. It felt like my heart was beating very slowly.

Then he put his hand on my walking shoe, which, with my knees
bent on the sand, was next to him. He let his hand rest on my foot. I
looked up, and there was this new moon, just a thin crescent, luminous, with nothing around it but the violet sky.

"When your letters came," he said, "they reminded me of what
I had forgotten, of what I *had* to forget, except in my dreams or in
a vision on a mountain. I had created my life again, with Dorothy's
help, in the land that I loved. I prayed that you be well, nightly, you
and Caroline. I prayed that God keep you. And I made adjustments
to go on with my life. I didn't realize what I was doing, but I wrote a
series of poems, about a fictional character. She has the name of your
patron saint, only in English. Of course, in one of the poems she's
English and represents all that I missed about England when Dorothy
and I lived in Germany—but symbols can shift."

He scooped up a handful of sand. His other hand still rested on my
foot. It felt good there.

> *The stars of midnight shall be dear*
> *To her; and she shall lean her ear*
> *In many a secret place*
> *Where rivulets dance their wayward round,*
> *And beauty pass into her face.*

He spoke the verses as if they were just part of his natural conversation, when in truth he must have worked long at their translation.
Had he prepared, then, for this speech? I looked out at the Channel

and thought I saw a British ship, still patrolling. "How are those lines an 'adjustment'?" I said. "They sound like part of a love poem, to me."

"They are. But she unexpectedly dies. No one knew what she meant to the narrator of the poems."

She lived unknown, and few could know
When Lucy ceased to be;
But she is in her grave, and oh,
The difference to me!

"Your beloved *dies*?"

He did not answer me, but with one hand let the fine sand pour, like a fast hourglass, from his palm to the beach. Then he scooped up another handful and did it again. He seemed totally occupied with that. But he continued. "She lives on, of course, in a song in the wind, or as part of 'rocks, and stones, and trees.' In that way, she is always around the narrator. But sometimes she's only 'the memory of what has been, / And never more will be.'"

"I never 'adjusted' like that."

"Didn't you? What did you do, again and again?"

"I faced death—" I said. I felt a cool wind from off the Channel and shivered. William noticed it. I hadn't expected it to be like this. I had expected him now to talk about Mary, but not about death, about us both adjusting to "the memory of what has been." I saw that ship out there, blocking the Channel. It had no business to do that. We were in the middle of a peace. Then I saw the thin moon above it.

William took my hand and held it on his knee. He put his arm around me. We looked together out to the Channel. "Is that a British ship out there?" I said.

"Yes, they're not taking any chances."

I felt we were approaching something that we had to reach the end of now. I waited.

He lifted my hand to his cheek and rested it there. "Many poems," he said, "about deserted women and orphaned children. And a ballad in which an old man looks back thirty years to when his daughter died.

> *To the churchyard come, stopped short*
> *Beside my daughter's grave*
> *Nine summers had she scarcely seen.*

"You understand her age? You understand?" He was almost crying now. "The old man turns from her grave. People thought I was merely writing of the common people, resuscitating the ballad form. Coleridge thought the Lucy poems were about what I would feel if my sister died, but I was *writing of my life*. What else can a poet do? I had to do it, or else I couldn't 'turn from the grave.'"

"But we weren't dead. I was riding La Rouge at night, hiding people in our old lodge. Caroline was milking the goat." But I knew what he was saying. "I never so much as kissed the cheek of another man," I said.

"How does one go on?" He laid my hand back on his knee. We talked of the death of love and held hands like young lovers.

"One finds other things to feel passionate about," I said.

"Exactly. I had my poetry." He took his arm off my shoulder. He gazed at me with his old piercing eyes. "And then I turned thirty-two," he said, returning to his earlier point. "I, and everyone else, thought the war would continue forever. Bonaparte's power was absolute over Europe. I did not believe the preparations for the treaty would lead anywhere; none others had. Dorothy thought, no, I thought too, her best friend, my companion also; we all get along well together; I could not stay a bachelor forever." He looked back out to the Channel. "My family asked me again, what was I waiting for, and I proposed to Mary." He ended abruptly.

"So this is what this is all leading up to? You're engaged to Mary? Why didn't you just come out and say it?"

"I had to explain—"

I felt a smooth devastation, as in a clearing I had stood in once when I was a girl, in the forest where there had been tall chestnut trees, where you could see the light coming through their leaves in the summer. Now they were gone. I had realized that, standing in the clearing, remembering the light-filled leaves. They are not coming back.

Grass will have to grow here now, I had thought.

And it became ankle-high grass, sweet to walk through.

A breeze picked up on the sea and blew my hair in front of my face. Maybe the breeze had been there before, as William was talking, but I hadn't noticed it. The British ship had moved on. I had feared *this* was coming. And now, when it came, somehow, it wasn't as bad as I had feared. The one thing that I wanted most not to happen had happened, and now, for some reason, I felt strangely lighter. I myself would never marry. I knew that. But that didn't matter either, right now. The worst was over. He had told me. I pushed the hair back from my face.

The breeze blew some clouds over, and the two twinkling lights in England vanished. There was just the sound of the sea, and the stars far above us. I leaned my head back and looked at them. Some constellation spread brilliantly down the southern dome of the sky, across the European continent. What was the war and two lovers and their problems against *it*? I laughed. I suddenly laughed, and it shocked me as much as it did William. He was sitting there like a ghost beside me.

"William," I said. "We're already married. Have you forgotten your vows by the river?"

"Of course not—"

"They can be real, and they can also be our secret. I think you're right—we have both 'turned from the grave' in the past nine years, but something's also still alive, yes? In the depths of your heart?"

"Yes."

"Then kiss me. Let's not talk about anything anymore. Kiss me as if you were going to England and never coming back."

And he turned to me, held my chin lightly, tentatively, in his hand, then brought his face to mine. It was a feeling of coming home. Suddenly, there were no nine years, there was no Mary, or Dorothy, no war—in that familiar touch they were all erased. He kissed me again, and our arms went around each other. We were home, and I leaned back against the sand.

"No."

"I'm your French wife."

"I can't kiss you, I can't be with you," he said. He put his arms at his side and sat up. "Duty forbids it."

I sat up beside him. "I don't believe you. What about the depths of one's heart? What about duty to that? God knows that *it* knows. If one doesn't follow that, one feels ill. Why do you think you were getting all those headaches? It's not as complicated as you make it."

He dug the toe of his boot several times into the sand until the toe was covered up. Then he sprinkled sand over the top of the boot. He shook his head. "I'll tell you something I've thought about a lot and never told you," he said. "This simplicity is one of the things I love in you, that I marvel at. You come naturally to what I arrive at after long thought and suffering."

"The suffering is only because you are not listening to your heart. It's making you suffer because you are ignoring it. And then you call that suffering 'philosophy.' It's quite amusing, really."

"You're making fun of me." He put his hand on my cheek and stroked it, pushing my hair back now. I felt twenty-two again. Above us the summer stars were spreading out.

"Tell me that constellation, William. I never learned all their names."

"Where?"

"That long line of stars, there." I pointed to the south.

He leaned closer to me, to see where I was pointing. "The one that dips down there, and curls up, that goes all the way down the sky? That's Scorpius. Do you see the triangle there at its top? That is its head. Then its long, brilliant body. The fishhook shape is its sting." His pointing hand moved slowly in front of me and up the night sky. "To me, Scorpius means that it is summer. And summer, I've thought, ever since I was a boy, seems that it will never end. That the warm days will just go on and on."

His hand rested now on my cheek. It just stayed there. He was staring at me. "It's really the first time I've looked at you in nine years," he said. "You have the most perfect skin."

"I'm a thirty-three-year-old mother, but I am your French wife."

He kissed me on the mouth then, and my mouth opened, and his hand held the back of my head. I felt it all gratefully vanish again, the need to talk, the need to figure it all out, to explain it. How could one possibly explain it all anyway?

"Oh, Annette," he said. Above him I could see the glimmering tail of the Scorpius curling above the sand dune and all of France. I could hear the sea pounding and hissing and lying silent, and I could feel my beloved once again come home. It was our hour, which we had waited almost a decade for. It was the hour William had denied could be.

From a long way away, William said, "Now, I can sleep."

"What do you mean?"

"I did not write you this, but every time I received a letter from you, I would lie awake, thinking about you and Caroline. Sometimes it would last for night after night, and would almost drive me mad. One night my sister knelt with me in prayer that I might sleep."

"Poor William. I did not mean them to have such an adverse effect. They were just simple letters. What Caroline was doing. How my apricots were golden, my tomatoes red. Nothing to give you head-aches about. I think it was seeing Mary, not my letters, that caused the sleeplessness, yes?"

"You are right."

"I like to be right."

But it did not matter now, of course, who was right or not. My head lay on his chest, his arm about me. I felt wonderfully lazy, lazy in a good way, as I had never felt in my life.

I think neither of us wanted to move. It got later; the waves came and went. William now lay with his head on my shoulder, my arm about him.

But I knew someone had to say something. Someone had to say that we had to walk back, that people were waiting for us, that if Caroline awoke in the middle of the night she would want me to be there.

I sat up and took his hand. "Come, my love," I said.

I felt happy, leading him down the dune. We ran. I fell down once on my knees and laughed, and William lifted me up and we kept run-ning.

It was a warm night, and we walked over the carpet of reflected stars in the wet sand. "Let us dance," I said, and I took his hand. "I have not danced in years." And there, with nobody looking, we traced some of the old steps from long ago by a river, on another summer's night.

"You are very good; you don't forget."

"It all comes back to me," he said.

We moved forward and backward with the tide, and twirled, and laughed at ourselves. William whistled a tune that he said was from a country dance. I hummed an aria from Rameau's *Orpheus and Eurydice*. We kept dancing. We could never get tired. We danced with the cliffs of England in the distance as if wars and lost marriages and future marriages never existed. Green flames shot through the waves. The tide washed softly up to our shoes, and when it receded, stars of Scorpius glimmered beneath us.

William bowed and gave me his hand.

Williiam and I had decided to extend our stay for two more weeks. When would we three ever get to be together again? With William's marriage and another war looming, we didn't know. Dorothy read in her room, William said, great poets of the past—Milton's *Paradise Lost* and Sir Philip Sydney's *Arcadia*. She had brought the books with her. She said the French seashore was too hot, and she preferred her room. William thought it strange that she had stopped writing in her journal since she had come to France. "She always keeps up her journal," he said, "even if it's just to mention a walk to town to get flour to make gingerbread." But she hadn't written a word since coming to France.

She seemed civil to me, now. Perhaps she was not pleased with the extension of their stay, but she knew the wedding would occur in October as planned. There was no doubt about that. William would marry her best friend, and his childhood friend. If she had had doubts when she first met me, William had laid those to rest. I had renounced all previous claims. Perhaps he said something like that to her; I don't know. One evening when Caroline, William, and I returned to the door of their lodging after dinner, she took my arm and led me aside, while Caroline said good night. "I'm sorry for what I said about French girls," she said. "That's just a silly English way of thinking about them. I wish you'd forget what I said about French girls."

"I never took it seriously," I said, and I hadn't, really. I had forgotten her as soon as William and I were alone that night. Now she wanted to be friends. It was important, for Caroline, that we all be friends. I was no longer a threat; how could I be an enemy? Dorothy taught Caroline how to play chess, how to construct some basic sentences in English, and Caroline taught Dorothy how to organize a shell collection.

They corresponded for many years.

On the last evening of our stay together, Caroline swung her parents' hands, one on either side of her, and we watched the sun slowly, slowly, approach the horizon, then suddenly, almost imperceptibly, slip over it. We thought it was all over and started to walk on, when Caroline shouted, "Two sunsets!" One was on the sand, washed by waves. The colors shone beneath her feet. Caroline took off her shoes and waved them over her head.

Golden rays shot up and flecked the clouds over France. The water turned lavender and pink. William and I finally sat down on his worn frock coat. Other people stopped their promenade on the boardwalk. It seemed everyone on the seashore paused at once and quietly looked out. What was there to say? It would all be over in a minute, and we didn't want to lose any of it. We wanted it never to be finished and knew in a few minutes the sea would subside to silver, the sky darken, and the first star appear.

Caroline chased seagulls now, then bent down, looking in the sand for shells.

"I have two new translations for you," William said.

I thought it would be a long time before I heard him read a translation to me again. "Read them," I said.

"The first is a line from an old poem, written directly about you and never published. It is a young man's work—

Those auburn locks which now exceed
The breathing woodbine's hues.

"I thought you should have it, for it is the only poem without any fiction. There is more to it, of course," he said, "but those lines are so sad, I'd like to forget them now. Though 'vermeil lips' you might like," and he smiled. "My main translation is about one of our evening walks here, at Calais. It takes place in what you called the 'holy time.' But it's also *our* short time, between wars, between lives. When it says, 'Dear child,' that is Caroline, and when it says 'dear Girl,' that is both Caroline and you."

"No one will ever guess."

"Others may not know; but you will know."

As he read, he kept one hand over my hand, on my knee. I did not look at him, but at the dimming gold in the sky. It is my favorite of his poems.

It is a beauteous evening, calm and free;
The holy time is quiet as a Nun
Breathless with adoration; the broad sun
Is sinking down in its tranquillity;
The gentleness of heaven broods o'er the Sea:
Listen! the mighty Being is awake,
And doth with his eternal motion make
A sound like thunder—everlastingly.
Dear Child! dear Girl! that walketh with me here,
If thou appear untouched by solemn thought,
Thy nature is not therefore less divine:
Thou liest in Abraham's bosom all the year;
And worship'st at the Temple's inner shrine,
God being with thee when we know it not.

"And so it will be when I am not with you, when I have gone back to England," William said. "The Supreme Being is with you when I am not, as is this poem, as are my thoughts."

arguerite and I corresponded throughout the peace, but when autumn came and they were due to cross the Channel, Paul had been sent on another trip. He worked hard, knew a lot about wine, and had made himself invaluable to the British company. Marguerite was afraid that by the time he came back, though, the war would start again.

She also said that since I had mentioned that William was friends with a writer named Coleridge, she had taken notice recently of a short poem by Coleridge in the *Morning Post* the other day. Had it anything to do with me? She only asked because it had my name in it. But since when was I a "courtesan"? She had perceived a certain attitude that the English had toward French women, she said. It was an epigram, called "Spots in the Sun,"

But always we find the pious man
At Annette's door, the lovely courtesan!

I wrote her back that yes, the pious man did seem to be William, and no, I was not a courtesan. Do they have courtesans anymore? And that probably no one in all of England knew the truth of that poem except she, William, Dorothy, and perhaps Mary. I'm sure Coleridge was having a fine private joke, I said.

Dorothy wrote to us that William had married. She said she had become very ill and couldn't attend the wedding, but by the time the wedding breakfast was finished, for weddings in England *always* were in the morning, she had recovered and accompanied the bride and bridegroom on the journey back north, to "our" home, she said. She wrote that, loving the fresh air as he does, William preferred to walk behind the carriage, and that while she and Mary rested at an inn, he walked up to a waterfall in the rain. My brother can sniff out a waterfall, she said. But I don't think you have waterfalls along the Loire, do you? It's rather a flat river. She said where they lived they could see mountains every day, and that made William happy. That and how she and Mary cared for him. She wished us well and that we might avoid the belligerence of France, which must be all about us.

Apparently, they had a happy life together. Dorothy was a great help in the house and in raising the children. Many years later, her illnesses overcame her, and William and Mary ended up taking care of her for the rest of their lives.

William Wordsworth was a product of a short era. He did not belong to his generation, nor did he belong to his uncle's. His was a short time of great hopes when anything was possible. Somehow, I had got entwined in the fall of those great hopes. I do not think he could separate anymore the fall of his ideals for the world with the fall of our ideals together.

So he was an exile in the lovely land of his youth. His youth, with its unbounded hopes, was forever around him untouchable. His personal sorrow he translated into world sorrow, and he came to believe that things not working out as he had wanted was symbolic of something larger.

> *. . . those first affections,*
> *Those shadowy recollections,*
> *Which, be they what they may,*
> *Are yet a fountain light of all our day. . . .*
> *Though nothing can bring back the hour*
> *Of splendour in the grass, of glory in the flower;*
> *We will grieve not, rather find*
> *Strength in what remains behind.*

*I*t would not be wholly objective of me to say that William's poetry started to wane about a year after his marriage, but I have read all the French translations that we have now, and it seems that one could make that statement. He also kept going back to his youth in his poetry, as if he were trying to find something there that he had lost long ago, or that he had forgotten that he even once possessed.

While we were at Calais, Napoleon declared himself First Consul of France, and the war soon commenced again. The Vincents never had time to visit.

In November of 1804, more than two years after my stay at Calais, and a month before Napoleon crowned himself emperor, a long, tube-shaped package arrived at our cottage. When I opened it, I saw it was an oil painting of a river winding through steep bluffs, with green forests extending on both sides of the river. The river disappeared in the background amid endless forests. There was nothing striking about the painting except for the color of the water and the sheer vastness of the landscape. One could notice a little figure on the shore of the river, perhaps fishing. The painting was not signed.

The next day Angelique appeared with her new *ami*, Marc, as he simply called himself, whom she had met in the Chouans. He had been marooned when Napoleon abandoned his army in Egypt and had made it back across North Africa. His father ran a sugar import business in Blois whose barges traveled upriver from Nantes. But the ships that unloaded onto those barges had to run the British blockade. Besides his own bitterness at having to make a rather long walk home, Marc also wanted to end the war for business reasons. He worked at a warehouse during the day and often with the Chouans at night. If he and Angelique married, I thought, Maman could have her sugar merchant son-in-law after all.

Angelique came in with a new green cloth ribbon in her hair, kissed Claudette, twirled Caroline around in a simple dance step, and said, "A *gabare* from Nantes docked near Marc's warehouse yesterday. It brought something from far away."

And behind her, through the open door, strode the marquis. He didn't have his old cloak and sword dangling and pistols at his belt, but wore a fashionable double-breasted coat with long tails. He doffed his tall hat, bowed, and kissed my hand.

"I apologize," he said, "that I have no venison to bring you, or even a wild lily. But I did send you a painting."

We all gathered around the landscape that I had left on a chair, not knowing what to do with it. "That's how vast America is," the marquis said. "But do you see that little figure beside the river?" We all assented that we saw it, but could not make it out clearly. "That is I, pondering what to do in all this vastness, wondering why I am so far away from another river, which I love. This one in the painting is called 'the Hudson.' What kind of name is that? Is that the name of a noble river?"

"So what brings you back?" I asked, "when you had all that land to paint?"

"I have so many paintings," he said, " I filled my rooms with them. I couldn't go out my door without bumping into paintings. I finally got tired of them. Gave almost all of them away, except this one and one that is now hanging in the château de Beauregard, if I may say so. But it wasn't having too many canvases of rivers and woods that made me leave."

"He was back to his old tricks," Angelique said to me. "I didn't know who the Marquis de La Roques was during the Terror, but I had heard of him. Apparently he had something to do with the creation of the Blonde Chouanne."

"But who's there to fight in America?" I said. "Indians?"

"No, they were my friends, and they're all dying off. A tragedy right there. One of them, though, brought a black man to my back door one night. Without a lantern, they just stood there in the dark with my candlelight on them. The Indian in a waistcoat with his sleeves rolled up, who helped at the farrier's now, and a tall black man in tattered clothes, with bare, bloody feet and frightened eyes. He had come hundreds of miles on those bare feet, helped by others like my friend. Now I became an outlaw again, by aiding him. Then my rooms became a regular stop for others. I even went south to a place called Kentucky and helped people cross a river. It was called the O-hi-o; that's a little better than Hudson, I suppose. But that's where I got in trouble. Angry men who had lost valuable investments followed me up the Hudson. I gave my paintings away, went downriver and across the sea and so to the door of—who is this lovely lady?"

He bowed and kissed Caroline's hand.

They all stayed for dinner of cabbage, onions, roast chicken, and fresh bread that Caroline had baked.

"I always thought you were a pirate," Claudette said to the marquis.

"I'm now a civilized gentleman," he said.

"No," I said.

"The distinguished Edouard finally retired from the count's service. I'm the new valet of the château de Beauregard. I've had experience. Everyone in America works, so I became the butler in the household of a man who owned a shoe factory. Can you imagine? They liked my accent. He made very nice shoes, and I got a free pair for working there. So you'll have to call me 'valet,' and not 'marquis,'" he said and laughed.

We all laughed. It seemed so absurd.

"His château and lands were confiscated long ago," Marc said to me.

"I was never a very good marquis."

"What *was* your château?" I said.

"Poncé sur la Loire," he said nonchalantly.

"It's beautiful," I said.

"You've seen it?" the marquis said. He poured himself some tea made of mint from our garden. "When?"

"Years ago. My father and I were returning from his pilgrimage to Vendôme. He had had me read all the Greek myths that year and now wanted me to see paintings of them done on ceilings of a giant stone staircase. So we asked permission at the château and soon were looking up at Perseus holding his shield in front of Medusa's ugly hair; at Jason slipping the fleece from under the sleeping dragon. I loved them. But then we paused on the next landing, and do you know what we saw? Pegasus," I said, "drinking from a well by a young man holding a golden bridle, then flying, his white wings spread wide over the blue sea. It was the most beautiful thing I had ever seen."

"They were on their way to kill a monster," the marquis said.

I suddenly remembered something else. "There was a young man, a boy, really, sitting on the floor, painting the Pegasus."

The marquis had lifted his cup and he put it back down. He stared at me. "That was *you*?" he said, "the little girl who peered over my shoulder and asked, 'What are you drawing?'"

"You were rather rude. You didn't answer."

"I was *working*. I saw you later, wandering back and forth in the maze. I heard you finally calling for your papa."

Angelique and Marc laughed.

"You were the one who showed me the way out, who shouted down from the window and pointed," I said. "Don't you remember?"

"I haven't thought about the château for a long time," he said. "In '89 they burned it. Left my father's body there before his own door. The gardener and I put out the fire, finally. I think we may have saved about half the château. But I didn't care anymore. I haven't been back."

He drank from his clay cup of tea. Caroline and I had made that cup. If the marquis noticed it was an odd shape, he didn't say. I had never heard him talk about his personal life. I didn't even know he *had* a personal life. He was always just "the marquis," the head of the Philanthropic Institute.

The table was silent. He looked at his cup a moment, then smiled at me.

He wanted to let me know that it was all right, I think.

"The château de Beauregard is the place for me now," he said. "It's more grand. More things for a valet to do."

"Well, what shall we call you besides 'valet'?" I said. "We don't even know your Christian name."

"Call me Jean-Luc," he said. "My name is Jean-Luc. I hear we're getting an emperor soon. We'll be like a lot of ancient Romans."

"But haven't we been stupid?" Marc said.

"What?" said Angelique.

"Look who's staying at the château de Beauregard regularly. Top marshals of Napoleon. What better way to find out information, to pass it on? All one has to do is keep one's ears open while one glides down the hall like the perfect valet. I think our marquis hasn't retired at all."

We all looked at him.

"I'm just a humble valet," he said. "Why would I want to be anything else?"

No one said any more about it. I thought perhaps Marc was right, but I liked the marquis now simply as Jean-Luc.

After dinner the gentlemen built the fire up, and Jean-Luc told more stories of America, then Angelique and Marc left, and Claudette and Caroline went to bed, and Jean-Luc and I told stories of long ago. He wanted me to start, so I told him of dances, and of hunts, and of meeting a forbidden lover in the steep dark streets, and of fleeing enemies through snowy forests, and of a priest who never stopped telling his beads for the five days I hid him, and of a marquis turned outlaw, who was a friend in a friendless world. Then he told of bribing prison guards with money I had stolen, of Chouans singing, of a green mask that, on a whim, he had placed at the bottom of a sack, and of a fast horse.

"I saw her," he said, "grazing peacefully at the château de Beauregard. She's eternal."

"I'd like to see her again," I said. "I never get out to Beauregard without a horse."

"I'll arrange it," he said.

And he did. I went often to Beauregard, where he was a splendid valet to the aging but lively count. Jean-Luc also came often to our cottage. He became my very good friend.

He supplied me with a mare sired by Le Bleu, and together we used the old caves in the tufa cliffs as well as, occasionally, the lodge in the service of the Chouans. But we went on no more raids. "A valet is a more dignified person than a marquis," he said. "He cannot also be a pirate. Besides, you and I, Madame," he said to me, "when I came back, I found out they had made legends out of us. It's quite amusing. There are all sorts of things I didn't know I ever did, or you—now *you* may have done them. But don't you think it's better to keep some things in legend?"

*S*everal times I wrote to William regarding prisoners of war who were kept in the north of England, not far from where he lived. These prisoners were sons or husbands of people who, looking for their loved ones, had contacted the Chouan network, and William used his influence as, now, a respected postmaster, to free these men and send them back to France. Each time he asked them first to come and pay their respects to Caroline and me.

One was already known to me, or, rather, especially to a dear friend of mine. Benoît appeared at our door, looking a little older after years of imprisonment, first in the southeast, then in the north of England. Like Marc, he had been stranded in Egypt, but his general had eventually surrendered to the British. Claudette almost fainted, then couldn't talk, and Benoît couldn't believe that she had waited all this time for him, believing in her heart that he was still alive. Now we had another reason to visit the château de Beauregard, for the count immediately gave Benoît back his old position as groom. It wasn't long before Claudette married him and moved there.

That was a blow for me. I had never lived on my own without Claudette. Caroline had learned everything that Claudette could teach her and was more adept at caring for the animals, and certainly at cooking, than I. But I had got used to Claudette's greeting me in the morning, sunny or cheerless. Or, after checking on the animals at night, one of us first saying good night to the other. How does one live without someone who has become such a part of one's life?

In the summer of 1812 a young cavalry officer, recently released from prison in England, came to our door with greetings for a Madame Williams from a Monsieur Wordsworth. His name was Eustace Baudouin, and he had a locket with a miniature portrait of William, looking older and very serious, his hand against his head, for Caroline.

He also had a handsome younger brother, Jean-Baptiste. They both kissed Caroline's hand. Jean-Baptiste couldn't stop staring at Caroline. When they left, I asked Caroline if she thought he was rude, staring at her like that. She said she hoped he would never stop staring at her. And so, indirectly through her father, Caroline met her future husband. I'm not the first one to say that it's a strange world.

It was at that time that Napoleon, full of his own hubris, invaded Russia with his Grande Armée of 400,000 men, and the Russian general wisely drew them further and further into his heartland, finally battled him before Moscow, then withdrew again, burning his own city and his people's land, so the Grande Armée had nowhere to stay the winter and nothing to eat and had to turn around and walk thousands of miles back: and so Napoleon was finally defeated not by an enemy but by nature herself, who had decided to pay him back through a Russian winter.

As Napoleon fought his way back across Germany with a small and hungry army, Jean-Baptiste and Caroline courted, and after Cossacks did not stop their horses until they reached the banks of the Seine, and Paris fell and Napoleon was exiled to Elba, the young lovers decided to marry. That was the spring of 1814, after twenty-two years of war. Caroline would be twenty-two in December.

I wrote to William and Dorothy to come to the wedding in the fall, and Dorothy answered that William was still in mourning over the loss of two of his children, just over a year before. Could we possibly wait until the next spring?

Caroline decided to wait. Jean-Baptiste worked as a clerk in a local law office, and he would dine with us, then I would hear the lovers talking or laughing downstairs until late at night. It made me feel old, and one evening I saddled La Noire, the mare Jean-Luc had given me, and rode to the château de Beauregard to stay with people more my age, and the count, who always made me feel young.

But when the spring of 1815 came, any wedding was out of the question, especially with foreign guests. Napoleon had escaped from Elba. What we thought was over forever had suddenly returned and overturned our lives.

The emperor had to raise an army, quickly, and Jean-Luc and I created many posters that told the young men, eager for some glory, that France had given enough of its blood. They didn't need to add themselves to the sacrifice. We put these posters up before dawn, in outlying villages and in the market squares of Blois. One early morning, as market began in the old Saint-Louis Square, I waited for Jean-Luc and lingered in the square, watching some people idly reading the posters.

Then I suddenly stood up on the Louis XII fountain, which still hadn't been rebuilt. Just in case I needed to hide my identity again, before setting out that night with Jean-Luc I had put on the old blonde wig. I stood on the ruins of the fountain now and called out to the people that when the conscription officers came this afternoon, they should not cooperate with them. They should leave the town, hide, defy the officers openly if they dared. "You, parents," I said, "do not let your sons be carried away by dreams of glory. That glory is a chimera. We must call it so to its face and refuse its lure, when it calls us."

A small crowd had gathered. One older man even shouted, "It's the Blonde Chouanne!" and the man next to him laughed, but others didn't laugh. And the faces of women looked up at me and nodded.

Then Jean-Luc, who had been putting posters up on the hill, in the small square in front of the church of Saint-Vincent, suddenly took my arm and led me from the fountain. "Remember what she says," he shouted as we left, "for this woman is a prophetess!" We mounted our horses and rode toward the château before any new representatives of the emperor could arrive. "You're incorrigible," he said to me as we rode. "Something about that square makes you reckless. Jeanne Robin told me about a speech you made there long ago."

I listened to the rhythm of the hooves crossing the stone bridge, the spring river swirling high beneath us. "When will they learn that it's all a waste?" I said, "just a terrible waste?"

In mid-June, a few days after my forty-sixth birthday, I heard children playing in the morning in the road that ran by the cottage. I thought how strange it is that children play when there is a war going on, that marvelous obliviousness that lovers also share. Lovers often have the pressure of the world right behind them, though, just out of earshot though ignored, but children genuinely do not know another world exists. I was thinking this while savoring the sound of the children, which I have always loved, when I realized there were adults screaming.

I ran outside and grabbed an older man by the arm, "What *is* it?" I asked.

"The emperor is defeated!" he wailed. He and the fellow with him seemed to be self-appointed town criers, although perhaps it was really that they couldn't bring themselves to believe it, and they were releasing their grief and shock to the world.

"*C'est la fin de l'Empereur,*" the other man cried, in a lamenting voice that I will never forget.

Then market women came by in a panic, saying that Prussians were burning and pillaging Paris and raping the women. Their cavalry would be in Blois by tomorrow. Then a man said that the English had captured Paris and that the emperor had surrendered to them. The man had only one arm. I thought I'd believe him.

It was all over, in any case, all over again. I wondered how many of the men who died had come from Blois.

British soldiers were bivouacked now in the Bois de Boulogne, and the English were not popular. It was not a time for English tourists. We postponed the wedding again, until the new year.

February of 1816, with the muddy or icy roads of winter, was not a good time for travelers from the north of England to make it to Blois, but some from the south could. All the Vincents were coming to the wedding. William sent enough money to provide for ample food and drink, and the count supplied any reserves of nourishment that anyone could need. The wedding itself was held in Saint-Vincent, the church on the high hill, with its broad steps down which Caroline's train flowed. Guests who desired to make the short journey to the château de Beauregard would be fêted there far into the night.

It was a cold, sunny day. My daughter, whom I had spent almost every day with since her birth, took her vows under her white veil, under the high ceiling, vaulted to heaven, and Jean-Baptiste lifted her veil, and I beheld her radiant face.

I can tell you that Marguerite did not look at all twenty-four years older, and Paul, with his gray hair, still had his discerning eyes and ready smile, and that I didn't recognize Marie, who had a daughter by the hand and an English doctor on her arm, nor Gérard, in the uniform of a British lieutenant in His Majesty's navy. When I exclaimed at that, he said, "I always liked knots, Aunt Annette, I liked tying you up." His ship had been part of the British blockade, and he spoke French with an English accent. We embraced, and I cried like a baby. He kissed my cheek once like an Englishman, until his mother reminded him.

At the château de Beauregard, I danced first with Paul. "In his letters home from the navy," he said to me, "Gérard said he was loath to fire on any boat coming from France for fear it was his aunt, escaping. He did not forget you."

I danced with Gérard, and asked him about it. "It is true," he said, "every French woman is my aunt. I want to protect them all. I'm afraid I've told the story many times of my aunt who risked her life to save me and my family. I've impressed young ladies with it. Though I've frightened some away, I believe. I've embellished a bit, for drama. Told them my aunt was guillotined. I think they're afraid I would expect such a sacrifice from them, if the time came. I make it sound like you're the most fearless woman in the world. How could they possibly compete?" What would he say to them if he knew what I had actually been doing all these years? I thought. "I loved the version of *Romance of the Rose* you sent," he said, "though my French is a bit rusty and it was tough going. When will you finish it? I read Chaucer's version in school, you know. It wasn't as good."

I smiled. "I'll finish it someday," I said.

I glanced past Gérard's tall shoulder at my mother, dancing with the old count. They looked very well together. Monsieur Vergez had died the year before.

Angelique had married Marc, and their son, Charles, scampered under tables laden with breasts of duck in apricot sauce on little white-and-gold china plates, with cheeses, with fountains of fruit, bowls of nuts, and wines and champagne and cakes. William couldn't have paid for all that, I thought. And little Charles sat there under the table eating cakes while his mother and father danced.

Gérard showed me a two-handed card game as we sipped champagne, and I watched Caroline and Jean-Baptiste glance in secret happiness at each other as they each talked with separate guests. Caroline wore the locket her father sent her from England, but it was Paul, whom she had never met, who had walked her down the aisle.

Caroline greeted Claudette, her second mother, and held both Claudette's hands in hers. Claudette was talking fast and crying at the same time.

Now Marguerite clapped her hands together, saying something to Caroline. My older sister had escaped living in a country of war for more than twenty years; she had always lived a charmed life, I thought. I had never told her of my work, for fear of discovery, and the whole Vincent family, as well as myself, was surprised at what soon followed.

* * *

The count stopped the small orchestra. He waved to get everybody's attention. I thought he was going to give another toast, but we had already done that. Perhaps the old count was a little drunk. But he didn't look drunk. He said a few words about the auspicious occasion. And then he said, So, it is high time Caroline's mother be honored. What did he mean? Everyone looked at me, and I felt embarrassed. "And a few others would like to say some words on this matter," he said.

Jean-Luc stood now beside the count. "Some of you know," he said, "that I was engaged in resisting the Paris government's interference with our own lives. But many of you don't know that I had a secret partner, who continued in the work long after I retired to America to paint landscapes, which only a few of you have had the misfortune to see. If I wanted any task to be done, the one person I could count on, no matter how dangerous the mission, was the one who became known throughout this region as the Blonde Chouanne." He looked over at me. There were some stirs at this.

"Needless to say, she wore a wig and a green mask, and I heard this way of dress even became the mode at parties!"—some scattered laughter followed—"among those who had no idea into what dangers the Blonde Chouanne rode. I will not recount for you her adventures, better left in the long years of strife, but you don't have to take my word for all this." And he withdrew now a paper from his pocket and unfolded it. "This police missive somehow found its way into my hands a long time ago—" More laughter here. "I have kept it for posterity's sake. I quote from Corbigny, Prefect of Police, Blois, March 16, 1804, responding to a summons from Napoleon's secret police, March 8, 1804, 'to have the conduct carefully observed of the demoiselle Vallon . . . married to an Englishman named William.'" He read that last phrase quickly. "'The woman Williams', Napoleon's police say, 'is particularly known as an active intriguer.' Now, they are a bit slow, and that's a good thing, for at this time Madame Williams had been an 'active intriguer' for over ten years!

"The new prefect of police of Blois, Guillemin de Savigny, gathered some information for us in preparation for this our moment of honoring her. He writes, 'Madame Williams, born M. A. Vallon, she it was who saved the head of Monsieur Delaporte, reported by informers to the Revolutionary Tribunal, by hiding him as well as Chevalier de Montlivault; she also who got Count Dufort out of prison, and others. . . . Blois was known to be the haven of the unfortunate outlaws. To her they were directed from everywhere.'" There were some mumblings of awe among the guests, and I felt acutely embarrassed. Why had Jean-Luc decided to do this now? This wasn't my night. And I didn't want any recognition. People knew of the Blonde Chouanne. They didn't know of me.

At this point Paul stood up and said it was I who had engineered his escape from prison and enabled his whole family to flee the country. I wished all this would stop. Then I saw Marguerite crying. Marie's face was pale. Gérard was looking at me with a worshipful gaze.

Then the baron de Tardiff, the old hunting friend of my father, whom I had met again in the escape through the crypt, emerged from behind Jean-Luc. With him were others, some who looked vaguely familiar. I didn't know where they came from. They weren't at the wedding. "On one side of me is Count Dufort," the baron said, "whom Madame Williams saved from drowning in the infamous *noyades*. On my other side is the chevalier de Montlivault, whom she helped to safety by hiding him." A sound escaped my lips and I put my hand over my mouth. It was the nineteen-year-old chevalier whom I had talked to the first time I had used the lodge. "Others whom she saved stand behind us now. Some have come long distances to thank her. They are but representatives of many, many more who owe her their lives. Her daughter and new son-in-law have helped arrange this happy reunion." Caroline beamed mischievously at me. So it was *she* who had engineered this. Jean-Luc must have had a hand in it. "And we want to present her with this."

The count came forth again. "In response to a petition that we here have written and signed, King Louis XVIII has granted a life-long pension to Madame Williams for her service to the people of France—*this*, ladies and gentlemen"—and he pointed to the parchment in his hand—"is the seal of the King of France—and I quote, 'Madame Williams has hidden and helped a large number of emigrants and persecuted people. She has aided in escapes from prisons and by her devotion, selflessness, and courage has saved many subjects from death.'" The count ceremoniously walked over to me and placed the parchment in my lap. He made a little bow. Everyone applauded.

I stood up and waved them to stop. "Thank you very much," I said. "But what I did I could not have done alone. You must thank Jean Verbois," and I pointed to the old groom, his foot up on a cushion, for his limp was worse in his old age. He grinned his marvelous gap-toothed grin. He had a cup of wine and a large slice of cheese in his lap. "My sister, Angelique"—she hid her face behind Marc's shoulder—"the bravest woman I've ever known, Jeanne Robin, who, unfortunately is not here today; and of course, the great Marquis de La Roques, now simply known as the valet of the château de Beauregard—my gratitude to you all." And the room filled with applause again.

Before I could sit back down, I was surrounded by many faces, some with tears in their eyes, which I remembered as in a dream. They all thanked me, and I felt that they were not thanking me, exactly, but someone else who had done those things. Suddenly my mother kissed me and said, "You never did as you were told." She added, "I wish your father and Etienne were here," and then I cried.

That was when Jeanne Robin came up, with a mischievous glint in her eye. Where had she been? Where had they all been? "An ambush, as always," I said. I hadn't seen her since the *noyades*, twenty-two years ago. I recognized her immediately. Perhaps it was her black eyes. Her brother was with her, and she, like Angelique, had a husband and a charming son. I spent the rest of the afternoon with Jeanne. She and her family had come all the way from the village of Azay-le-Ferron, to the southwest, and had to return the next day.

The Vincents stayed for two weeks, and we rode through the old forests and talked until there was no end of talking. Marguerite gently scolded me for risking my life, and Gérard said he only hoped he could be as brave as I. Paul talked politics with the count, and Marie and Jean-Luc discussed painting and went out together to draw the light and shadow of the winter woods about the château de Beauregard. In the evening we played cards with Maman and with Dr. Thompson, Marie's husband.

Then all of a sudden the flurry of reunited family faded, and I found myself watching the Vincents' carriage disappear. It went down the long entryway, around the bend toward Blois, and the road was empty between bare chestnut trees. Caroline, back from her honeymoon to the seashore in Normandy, took my arm.

Though the Vincents did visit us once a year now, I never went to England, and they never moved back to France. And whenever they came to Blois, Marguerite made it a point not to go by what had been chez Vincent.

By the end of the year I was a grandmother. Naming her child partly after her aunt was also, I believe, the closest Caroline could get to including her father in the name: Louise Marie Caroline Dorothée.

We all lived together in the cottage now, but in 1819, the law firm for which Jean-Baptiste was a clerk offered him a promotion to their Paris office. He and Caroline invited me to move with them, so I left my beloved river to live near another one. Jean-Luc promised to visit regularly, and he did. I missed my garden.

Holding her little hand tight in mine or carrying her, I took Louise through the narrow, crowded streets of Paris out to the Seine, and we watched the light on the water and the slow barges and waved to the rough-voiced bargemen. It was important to me that a river ran near to my door, and I wanted to pass that on to Louise.

Then it turned out that the voyage of William and Dorothy to the Continent had only been postponed after all. With hostilities between the nations well in the past, the Wordsworths were traveling through Switzerland and wanted to stop in Paris. Jean-Baptiste arranged for them to stay in our quarter.

It was October of 1820, and I was fifty-one. We were to see them at the Louvre, at one o'clock. William would meet his granddaughter, and I would meet his wife.

THE HEALING WELL

I was not afraid, as at Calais. What was left that could happen between us? Dorothy held no surprises for me either. But I was excited to see William, a luxury I could not have felt eighteen years ago. And my heart lurched when I actually did see him, and I surprised myself.

We were strolling now through a grand room with huge paintings. Louise had my hand, and Caroline my arm. Her other arm was linked in her father's. Dorothy walked on his other side, then Mary. William had been going on and on in slow French, with Caroline straining to understand him, about how he had felt so young because he had found the most important place in his life, again, in the Alps. I kept smiling. William was trying to explain an experience in wild nature. The two women with him were talking among themselves. The person he was conversing with could hardly understand him.

"What?" Caroline said. "You felt what?"

"He's saying he felt the same," I said. "Thirty years were nothing. They all vanished."

"That's exactly what I was saying," the great poet said.

We stopped to rest on a bench, and Louise was tugging at her mother's dress to go on. She then looked up and pointed to a painting of the revolutionary extremist Marat's murder in his bath. The artist, David, had done a fine job of making the madman into a martyr.

"Oh, look what we've been sitting under," said William. "That was the death of the Girondins, that murder by the well-meaning Charlotte Corday. They were all hunted then."

Dorothy looked at him, and he looked directly at me. The painting seemed to shake memories in him, not just of the Alps thirty years ago, but perhaps of fleeing with me in the dark twenty-eight years ago.

"Let's leave this room," he said.

"I think Louise would agree with you," Caroline said. Louise was running ahead.

"She's like you, William," Dorothy said. "You kept running up those hills in Switzerland like a mountain goat." She said something to Mary, and they laughed. Mary had not spoken at all, except quietly to Dorothy. But that was all right; I had hardly said a word myself.

Then Caroline walked fast to catch up with Louise, and William followed. I was suddenly next to Dorothy. We passed ancient Egyptian kings and queens, wrapped up in gauze.

"You got a bit wet waiting for us outside the Louvre," Dorothy said.

"We were just coming in because of the rain."

"Parisian women are very adroit at avoiding splashes on their dresses," said Dorothy. "I have seen many colored garters."

"Did you see ours?"

"I think yours were a gold color, and Caroline's red?"

"Our stockings are splashed, and our dresses are perfectly correct."

"It is an art in Paris, I believe," Dorothy said.

William turned back to us. "Let's leave these relics and see another room," he said.

We finally found some Fragonard paintings, which pleased me, with ladies swinging high on swings, all their petticoats frothing, and gentlemen below them, playing guitars and flutes. Dorothy pointed to the lady on the swing.

"You see, it is an art in Paris," she said and smiled.

I tried to see Mary's face and couldn't. When we briefly met, I thought she had a very kind face. Now she looked down or off at a painting near her.

We met Jean-Baptiste at a café just outside the Louvre; the rain had stopped, and the streets were bright with the sun on the wet cobbles. Jean-Baptiste tried talking in English, but he was very slow, and William was obliged to help him translate, so we talked in French after a while.

The Wordsworths wanted tea, and there was none, and William started to tell the waiter they should have tea, and his wife put her hand on his arm. She looked tired now, from the traveling, or the walking. She caught me looking at her once, and she looked down. She truly looked like a sweet soul, as William had said. She was fair-haired with lots of gray, and I felt sorry for her, for her lot as a mother had not been easy; she had lost two children in the same year; perhaps it was because they lived in the cold north of England. But now the other children were grown or off at school; it was her first time on the Continent. She sipped coffee and looked as if she would rather be resting at their lodging. Our eyes met again, and for a moment I looked at the woman who had been the wife I had never been, and she looked at me. I think there was more curiosity in her eyes. I smiled, and she looked down at her small cup of coffee and lifted it. There was nothing in it. I looked away, so she would not be embarrassed. I liked her immensely in that moment, and I could feel how she and William had been such good friends over the years.

The men were talking about the forest of Fontainebleau, about a wild and lonely spot William had found, called the Healing Well.

"You *drank* from it?" Jean-Baptiste said. "People used to go on pilgrimages to it. I hear it's not a well, actually, but just a broad, bowl-shaped rock that's always full of water to the brim, no matter what the season, or during drought. It's not a spring. It's supposed to bring you good fortune if you drink from it, even a small cup."

"I think we should all make a pilgrimage to that well," Caroline said.

"We got lost, looking for it," William said, "and as soon as I drank from it, an old woman, a beekeeper, came up and showed us the way out of the forest."

"That was not a beekeeper," Jean-Baptiste said, "that was an enchantress. But the office and duty call; I must get back."

Jean-Baptiste was gone. Louise put her head in her mother's lap. Everyone seemed tired.

"Would anyone like to go to the Jardin des Plantes?" William said suddenly. "The sun is out, and I'm tired of walking indoors. I've always wanted to see the Jardin des Plantes."

"I will show you," I said.

* * *

It was autumn in the *jardin*. "Whichever way you turn now," I said, "there are golden leaves."

We sat on the bench under the oldest tree in Paris and were silent.

William picked up a twig fallen from the tree and made designs in the path. "Do you know what sort of crop they grow in the forest of Fontainebleau?" he said.

"I didn't know they grew any crop."

"We thought they were sheaves of corn. They're placed side by side, in an open space in the forest."

"It doesn't sound like corn."

"Imagine two thousand of these, side by side."

"What were they?"

"Beehives."

"Ah."

"The woman there, a poor woman who lived alone with her children, told us that only fifty of all those beehives were hers. She was a steward of bees. She grew flowers for them. She had been doing it most of her life."

"Thirty years," I said. "In the Louvre you kept repeating 'thirty years ago in the Alps' to Caroline."

"I kept being reminded. And I was feeling the same feelings. And the places were the same."

"Why could not the woman in the forest own all the beehives?" I said. "She had nurtured them."

"At the end of summer all the bees are removed to another part of the forest, where the owners get the honey."

"Why couldn't they stay with her?"

"The heath plant, which they need for the honey, is more abundant in the other place. She helps bring them there."

"I think, though, that the bees think they belong to her."

"They wouldn't hurt her. It was extraordinary. They'd swarm all over her and land on her and she would talk to them, and none of them ever stung her, unless by accident."

"A poor woman, with children. I believe she wished she owned all those two thousand hives, instead of just fifty."

William traced almost indecipherable lines in the gravel with the twig.

"Annette, I have finally published that poem I wrote long ago, about two lovers, in France."

"Thirty years ago?" I smiled and looked at him. We had mostly been looking at the trees, or at the path, as we talked.

"It's the only love poem I think I've actually published. You remember, I translated parts of it for you, long ago? The young man stands beneath her window in the spring evening and feels he is in paradise. She opens a door."

"It doesn't end happily."

"But they had shared these powerful feelings."

"Remind me: what happened to them?"

"They had difficulties with parents, families, the law; the times were against them."

"Did their love survive?"

"They belonged to each other, but they couldn't be together."

"Other people owned their life; that wasn't fair. I don't see why the old woman with the bees couldn't own all of her bees. They belonged to her. She knew that. She cared for them and nurtured them and led them away to other ground." I suddenly started to cry and looked down at the gravel path and a puddle there, reflecting some of the red and orange leaves of the ancient tree above us. The puddle grew blurry. I thought I was beyond all this.

"I can't help it," I said.

"Let's walk to the river," said William. "But not past the animals in cages."

We walked, without touching, but close beside each other, silently down a wide, smooth avenue now, lined with thinning and flaming trees.

"There's the herb garden," I said. "They say there are cures for all ailments in those plants."

"Perhaps just walking by it will help us," William said. "I've a heaviness in here that I need a magic plant to cure."

"It's not magic; it's simply the knowledge of the plants."

Then we were by the river. We followed it back, until we found a bench looking toward the Ile Saint-Louis. We looked at the river.

"It was very hard on Mary and me when Catherine, then Thomas, died in the same year," William said. "I think part of our love died then. We had seen ourselves as lucky, as blessed even, then *that*—and ever since, but perhaps even before that, I have been sort of dying, Annette, slowly dying, for the lack of the powerful feelings that I felt up there in the Alps. There are only three new poems in my new collection—which, by the way, will be translated into French—I would especially like Caroline to see it, to be proud of me, I suppose. I have written that poetry is the spontaneous overflow of powerful feelings that are recollected in tranquillity. I have the recollection, the tranquillity, but no longer the powerful feeling. I have been dying—from that—not literally, my health is fine, but no longer anything to overflow. I translated this for you, to try to explain—

> *Now, for that consecrated fount*
> *Of murmuring, sparkling, living love,*
> *What have I? shall I dare to tell?*
> *A comfortless and hidden well."*

"But it came back in the Alps," I said.

"Yes, that's why I was so excited, jumping around like a child."

"And you found the overflow in the forest of Fontainebleau—the Healing Well that's always full. I liked Caroline's idea of going on a pilgrimage to the Healing Well."

"I already have," William said, and he looked at me, and it was the face that helped me into the carriage at Vendôme and tried to smile, when his chin quivered slightly, and when I looked back, he had been standing alone in the square. When I saw him again, he had traveled with invalid papers during the Reign of Terror to see me.

"So have I."

I put my hand on his, on his knee. There were yellow leaves scattered at our feet, and I watched one slowly spin down and land on William's shoe. The river looked full from the rain and was very blue and fresh-looking after the storm. Even a dirty barge, full of refuse from the city, looked clean.

"The air tastes like spring," I said.

He put his other hand on top of mine on his.

"Annette—"

"Don't talk. You don't have to talk."

He finally said, "Let's walk back; the others are waiting."

He managed a smile at me, as our feet crunched on the gravel and the large grayness of Notre Dame approached.

"I must not talk now," he said.

William decided to extend their stay to a month again, and we saw them almost every day. He spent much time with his daughter and granddaughter, and they walked together to the river. Once a friend of his, a writer, Crabb Robinson, came to dinner. He took me aside in the hall between courses and said, "Madame Baudouin—"

"I am Madame Williams; my daughter is Madame Baudouin."

"Madame, excuse me, but isn't it indelicate for the young Madame Baudouin to continue to call Monsieur Wordsworth 'Father'?"

"I think it would be indelicate for her not to, Monsieur Robinson." That ended our conversation, and Monsieur Robinson did not return to chez Baudouin.

At the end of the month, William said simply, "I will return to Paris; I will see you all again."

It was evening, and one could feel that it was the end of October. A soft autumn rain fell. William stood by himself outside our front door, and the light from the hall shone on his face. In that light he looked older than I had ever seen him.

"Until then," Caroline and I said, and he turned and went down the steps of chez Baudouin, opened and carefully closed the gate, then walked slowly down the dark rue de Charlot toward his lodging. We saw his dim figure turn and wave once, and we waved back, but we couldn't see his face any longer. I closed the door and went back into the warm, lighted parlor with Caroline.

I felt a hush settle over me that heightened other sounds: the rain in the eaves, Louise on the stairs singing in her high soft voice to her doll. Caroline sat on a footstool in front of me and took my hand. We said nothing. I sat in my chair by the lace curtains of the dark window and played with the patterns of the lace as they lay along the arm of the chair. The intricate lace pattern felt good between my fingers, and I understood how Louise must enjoy still holding her blanket, tattered now, that she had held and enjoyed since birth.

A month ago, in the *jardin*, along the Seine, even in the Louvre,

William told me something that was not easy for him to say, something that I know to be love, about things not changing in the green high Swiss valley he had seen as a young man, and I saw a man now, young again, running to the banks of the Loire to fetch me a reed for a ring. Things were the same in a place where they could not be touched by anything else, a place we knew to be true. And I understood that place to be where I was, now and always.

I did not know if I would ever see William again, but I could hear his voice saying nothing had changed, and see his shining fifty-year-old eyes, and thought I truly knew what he meant now, and I suddenly laughed for the obvious joy and absurdity and sorrow of it all. Only the joy mattered now.

I let my hand drop from the lace pattern to the top of Caroline's head. It rested there. She leaned her head against me. We sat there like that. Louise continued to sing on the stairs.

L'ENVOI

One could tell by the morning air that it was early summer, and at the end of a double row of overgrown lime trees, we saw the dark façade of the charred château.

My hands were clasped in the crook of Jean-Luc's arm.

"Poncé sur la Loire," he said. "Most of it may be burned, but it's all mine again."

We walked toward the staircase tower now. It alone had remained untouched by the fire.

"I want to see if I can still draw it," Jean Luc said, and he took paper and a pencil from inside his coat and sat down on the floor where I had first seen him. "What do you think about rebuilding this pestilential monster of a home?" he asked as he drew.

Outside the narrow window, the winding paths of the maze in which I had got lost were now lost themselves in the hedge run wild. "It's good to be here," I said. "More than you thought remains intact." I heard the coo of a dove. "That vast dovecote is still here. Not one of the trees was burned."

I glanced over at Jean-Luc's sketch. His quick pencil strokes already conveyed the moment when Pegasus lifted off the ground.

I looked up. On the ceiling, as when I first beheld it as a girl, the great horse still flew, unimpeded, powered by the beat of his own bright wings.

AUTHOR'S NOTE

This story is fiction, yet based on the lives and times of known people, especially concentrated on a year that William Wordsworth spent in revolutionary France. I have taken liberties, as is the wont of a novelist, but tried to be faithful to what we know of the young Wordsworth, to the little we know of Annette Vallon, and to the complex array of facts and of interpretation of facts known as the French Revolution.

There are many sources on the French Revolution, on the life of William Wordsworth, and on the Loire Valley. These are the ones I found most useful:

David Andress, *The Terror, Civil War in the French Revolution* (2005); Antonia Fraser, *Marie Antoinette* (2001); Stephen Gill, *Wordsworth: A Life* (1989); Jacques Godecot, *The Counter-Revolution: Doctrine and Action*, 1789–1804 (1971); Kenneth R. Johnston, *The Hidden Wordsworth* (2000); Georges Lefebvre, *The Great Fear of 1789* (1989); Émile Legouis, *William Wordsworth and Annette Vallon* (1922); Colin Lucas, *The Structure of the Terror* (1973); R.R. Palmer, *The Twelve Who Ruled* (2005); *La Nuit de Varennes*, French film (1983); Aileen Ribeiro, *Fashion in the French Revolution* (1988); Simon Schama, *Citizens* (1989); Elisabeth Scotto, *France, The Beautiful Cookbook* (1989); Jason T. Strand, *Chateaux of the Loire*, Michelin Guide (2006); Donald Sutherland, *France, 1789–1815: Revolution and Counterrevolution* (1985); Jack Tressidor, *Eyewitness Travel: Loire Valley* (1996); Dorothy Wordsworth, *The Journals*, edited by William Knight (1930); William Wordsworth, *Poetical Works*, edited by Ernest Selincourt (1936) and *The Prelude* 1799, 1805, 1850, edited by Jonathan Wordsworth, M.H. Abrams, and Stephen Gill (1979).

ACKNOWLEDGMENTS

I would like to thank my brilliant editors, without whom this novel would not be in its present form: Courtney Hodell, for her faith in the story and for leading it into a new incarnation, and Alison Callahan, for her support and vision of the whole. I would also like to thank my insightful editors at home: my wife, Lorraine, especially for her knowledge of horses and of a woman's perspective, and son, James Devin, for his poetic ear and ideas for revisions.

In addition, I would like to thank the following people for their help: Candance Cafferty, for her unexpected enthusiasm for the first draft of the beginning chapters; Juanita Hoffman, for telling me Wordsworth needed me to write this book; Dr. Terry Fairchild of Maharishi University of Management, for finding me a copy of Legouis's book on William and Annette in the University of Iowa library; Susan Keller, Janet Mackintosh, Kathleen Merner, Allan Mosher, David Rollison, and John Watanabe for reading the first draft and encouraging me; Professor Ted Margadant at University of California, Davis, for his suggestions for research material; Jeanette Perez at HarperCollins, for her friendliness, efficiency, and ideas for the afterword; Karen Perrin for her assistance with things French; the intrepid research librarian Linda Perkins; Deborah Schneider; Carolyn Tipton; Thomas Tipton; and especially my parents, Elizabeth and James L. Tipton, for their support. I would also like to thank Loreena McKennitt for her singing of "Annachie Gordon" on her album *Parallel Dreams* and Tracy Chevalier for mentioning lavender in a kitchen garden in *The Lady and the Unicorn*.

THE HISTORY

BEHIND

THE STORY

FACT AND FICTION IN
Annette Vallon

*I*n writing fiction about people who actually existed, the novelist balances the biographical parameters within which one must operate with the creative license to make the most dramatic turn of events take place. Few times in history can have more dramatic turns of events, however, than the French Revolution. My job, then, was not to change what is known but to use my imagination to fill in the gaps of what isn't known. I tried to do that in such a way that it all *could* have taken place.

So I wove the plot around biographical and historical events: the death of Annette's father when she was young; Annette's "estrange[ment] from her mother by the latter's remarriage;"* the dates when Wordsworth was in France; the poems he would have been working on; what we know of his behavior when he returned to England; the Battle of the Tuileries; the September massacres; the execution of the king, the queen, and the Girondins; Annette's resistance work from 1792–1815; the infamous Noyades, engineered by Citizen Carrier; and William's trips back to France: to Calais in 1802 and to Paris in 1820.

The evidence we have for William's actions is, of course, documented in many biographies, although biographers don't always agree, especially on the episode of his life that involves Annette Vallon. We have only the broadest parameters for his actions during his year in France in the Revolution: He met Annette in Orleans; she was his language tutor, then lover. He then followed her to Blois, where he also became good friends with the patriot Captain Beaupay. William sympathized with the Girondin cause, met some of their leading characters, and spent time in Paris before returning to England, shortly before the birth of his daughter, in mid-December 1792. Such a general outline of facts leaves ample room for biographers to

---

* Émile Legouis, *William Wordsworth and Annette Vallon*, 1922, 9

interpret and to disagree, and for a novelist to imagine scenes and the emotions that filled them.

And what is the evidence we have regarding Annette? In researching who Annette Vallon actually was, I found that many of Wordsworth's biographers—especially the British ones—treat her frigidly, as if to give her her due would be somehow to diminish the stature of the great poet. Even Émile Legouis, who is usually sympathetic to Annette, and whose 1922 work is still the foundation for all later Wordsworth biographers who deal with her, calls her "devoid of intellectual curiosity;"* "prone to effusions and tears;"† and "ill-fitted for prolonged ecstasies in nature."‡ Mary Moorman, in *William Wordsworth, A Biography: The Early Years* (1957), asserts that Annette is "easily moved to tears," and then goes on to describe her as "finding her interests entirely in those whom she loved. . . . There was in her nothing that could have reciprocated [Wordsworth] . . . in all the deepest springs of his being."§ Juliet Barker's recent *Wordsworth: A Life* clearly tries to discredit Annette.

And from what evidence do they draw their conclusions? On two surviving letters, one addressed to William and one to his sister Dorothy, both written when Annette was distraught over her new plight as a single mother, wondering when and how her lover could return when her nation was at war with his. But would that not be a situation in which one could be "easily moved to tears," one that does not call for either great "intellectual curiosity" or "ecstasies in nature?" These biographers' treatment of Annette has to spring from their desire to justify William—a poet of great moral rectitude—in a situation that seems to belie that rectitude.

It is far better when drawing conclusions, instead of looking at two letters written during a time of distress, to look at evidence of the two lovers' characters. Only a brief perusal of Wordsworth's poetry shows us an incredibly serious and sincere nature. Wordsworth was no Lord Byron, with illegitimate children spread over the continent. It follows that his "natural child," as they were called then, would

---

* Ibid., 33

† Ibid., 13

‡ Ibid., 69

§ Moorman 1957, 180–81

be the result of a relationship in which he had deep feelings—and his guilt and sorrow and extreme state of distress upon returning to England seem to indicate this. William himself writes that he only returned "dragged by a chain of harsh necessity."[*] We should not see his despair at this time as arising only from the collapse of his ideals regarding the Revolution. I think we can read a far deeper emotional source for his wandering the southwest of England, for his spending, in the summer of 1793, a month on the Isle of Wight—as close as you can get in England to the French shore—and for his poems based on orphaned children and abandoned women.

Legouis tells us that, after war was officially declared between their countries, "the lovers, who had, when they parted, hoped for a near reunion, found themselves divided by an almost insuperable obstacle. William could only run the risk of another journey to France at the cost of the utmost difficulties and perils. Did he run that risk?"[†] Legouis thinks he probably did. Kenneth Johnston, in his meticulous biography *The Hidden Wordsworth* (2000), devotes two chapters to the probability that William made a secret trip to France at the height of the Reign of Terror. (I was happy to read those chapters, for I had just written my own chapter in which William makes such a return.) Johnston even thinks Wordsworth went to rescue Annette, failed, and hid out in caves and forests,[‡] just as the lover Vaudracour in the *Prelude* "lay hidden for the space of several days."[§] In additon to Wordsworth's poetry, information that Legouis reveals provides a basis for this scenario: William told the English historian Carlisle that he had seen Corsas, the Girondin journalist, executed in Paris. Now, Corsas was executed in October of 1793, and Wordsworth left France in December of 1792. Yet in December of 1792, the Reign of Terror had not begun, and Wordsworth could not have seen any of the executions. It is unlikely that Carlisle, a highly respected historian, is in error. It is far more likely that Wordsworth let slip—consciously or not—something he was usually at pains to hide.

---

* *Prelude*, X. 222

† Legouis 1922, 34

‡ Johnston 2000, 287–88

§ *Prelude*, IX. 734

Wordsworth disguised his relationship with Annette. Yet in referring to his famous lines that characterize the heady enthusiasm of the early days of the French Revolution—"Bliss was it in that dawn to be alive, / But to be young was very heaven!"*—Johnston points out that "we must appreciate Annette's part in creating Wordsworth's bliss," and that "there are also not many expressions that better capture the transfiguring effect of young love at first sight than Wordsworth's description of Vaudracour's vision of Julia:"† "he beheld / A vision, and he loved the thing he saw . . . Earth lived in one great presence of the spring."‡ But Wordsworth himself said first that this was simply a story he had heard from Captain Beaupay, and later that he got it entirely from a French lady and did not make up anything at all.

Wordsworth does not refer directly to Annette in any of his poems, though we can find indirect allusions to his feelings for her and also to his guilt and distress at his having to abandon her and Caroline. Legouis concludes that "as a poet he helped to blind the world. . . . He allowed an image of himself, more edifying than exact, to take shape in his verse. . . . He practiced . . . the deceit which consists of omission of embarrassing facts."§ William's family is also complicit in this effort. Legouis laments, "It is a great pity that all traces of Annette and Caroline should have been carefully destroyed by the poet's nephew and biographer,"¶ although he believes that "it is certain that the correspondence was not closed with the visit in 1820" and that William and Annette kept up a lifelong friendship."**

One poem alludes to Caroline—the famous sonnet "It Is a Beauteous Evening, Calm and Free." When I was a freshman in college being introduced to the Romantic poets, a professor explained to the class that the footnote to this poem referred to the poet's affair with Annette Vallon. She wasn't even mentioned in the footnote, only Caroline, and my teacher's brief reference to this young poet in love

---

* *Prelude* X. 108–9

† Johnston 2000, 217–18

‡ *Prelude*, IX. 582–3, 586

§ Legouis 1922, 116

¶ Ibid., 102

** Ibid., 112

in the midst of a revolution became the seed that grew into my novel twenty years later, when, teaching the class myself, I came upon the same footnote and wondered about the story behind it.

At the time Wordsworth published that sonnet, however, no one knew to whom it referred—some mistakenly thought he was writing about his sister. They didn't know the real reason why he was in France during the brief Peace of Amiens in 1802, just before he got married. Those who downplay the importance of Annette Vallon in Wordsworth's life may think that he was at Calais only to secure some financial arrangement for his daughter (of which there is no record). But if one were to meet an ex-lover and the parent of one's child for these purposes alone, how long would one stay? Several hours, a day, two days? Wordsworth stayed a month, during which time his sister and chaperone, normally a meticulous recorder of daily events as simple as fetching gingerbread from town, also joins in the disguise and abandons her journal. (Or were there more emotional reasons for her abandoning it?) The couple of entries she does have seem to have been inserted later. In Dorothy's letters and in the journal itself, she usually refers to Annette only as *A*, or, "We had a long letter from *France*," or as "C's [Caroline's] mother."

Indeed, the only reason we do know at all of Annette is that Guy Trouillard discovered Annette's two letters, which had been impounded by the Committee of Surveillance, among the records in a sub-police station in the Loire Valley in the early 1920s. The name of the famous English poet *Monsieur William Wordsworth* fortunately alerted Trouillard. Unfortunately, the address *London, Angleterre*, had alerted the Committee in 1793. How many other letters were lost? The two letters make references to other letters of which we have no knowledge. But the story came out, and when it did, in the early 1920s, it rocked the British literary establishment, which I think never forgave the French for discovering these letters. Wordsworth had by then become a Victorian icon, and now he was known to have had an illegitimate child by a French woman. But baptismal records show that Wordsworth owned the child as his and gave it his name.

I quote from Annette's surviving letter to William in the front of my book and in a few sentences in one of her fictional letters in the novel itself, but for the most part I have used the tone of her letters and not her words themselves. I will translate more of the letter here, dated March 20, 1793:

> *Come, my friend, my husband, receive the tender kisses of your wife, of your daughter. She is so pretty, this poor little one, so pretty that the tenderness I feel for her would drive me crazy if I didn't always hold her in my arms. She resembles you more and more each day. I believe that I hold you in my arms. Her little heart beats against mine. . . . [I say to her,] "Caroline, in a month, in fifteen days, in eight days, you will see the most cherished of men, the most tender of men." . . . Always love your little daughter and your Annette, who kisses you a thousand times on the mouth, on the eyes. . . . I will write to you on Sunday. Goodbye, I love you for life.*

This letter gains poignancy when we realize that Wordsworth never received it. And the parting sentiment is no lover's hyperbole, for she kept his name, "Williams," for the rest of her life.

Legouis, and before him, George Mclean Harper in his *Wordsworth's French Daughter* (1921), explained something of who this Annette Vallon was. From his work, we have a much clearer basis on which to establish conclusions as to her character than that provided by two emotional letters. We find her a major figure in the resistance movement against the Reign of Terror and, later, against Napoleon, risking her life to help save the lives of others. Johnston writes that "she took initiatives in hundreds of matters in dozens of different ways, braving the secret police of, successively, the Terror, the Directoire, and Napoleon. . . . She was a dynamo of action."* It is easy to see her as a kind of Scarlet Pimpernel, and it is hard to reconcile the figure "easily moved to tears" with the unrelenting underground fighter, as it is hard to think that "there was in her nothing that could reciprocate" Wordsworth when one simply thinks of her passion for her cause and the passion behind Wordsworth's poetry.

The primary document that shows her involvement in this service is the 1816 petition to the newly restored king on behalf of Annette

---

* Johnston 2000, 216

Vallon to secure for her a pension for her services of almost twenty-five years. The list of names signed to this petition reads like a who's who of the restoration—two peers of France, a number of marquises, counts and viscounts, duchesses and chevaliers. (One, the Marquis d'Avaray, we learn from Legouis, is most likely a personal delegate to the king, for his brother was the king's closest friend in his exile.) Such an impressive list represents the respect that Annette Vallon had earned over the years.

On the petition, a chevalier "declares that Madame Williams saved his life," and a viscount and major general "attests that Madame Williams rendered services at the time of the insurrection of the Vendée." Annette asked for any reward to be given not to herself but to her daughter, Caroline. I will roughly translate below a section of this petition. The full petition can be found, in French, in the appendix of Émile Legouis's book.

> *Madame Williams, born Vallon . . . has, for the past twenty-five years, hidden and aided a great number of émigrés and other persecuted persons. She has engineered escapes from prisons and has, by her zeal and her courage, saved many loyal subjects from death. She has performed all this service with an absolute selflessness. In recent events [the return of Napoleon from Elba] she again showed her courage without any thought of personal gain: she posted proclamations at night, distributed them during the day, helped brave men escape to serve the King. . . . I attest that in this unfortunate epoch there did not exist in all of France another of such zeal, such devotion, and such courage as she.*
>
> —Le Baron de Tardif, Field Marshal and
> Superior Officer of the Gardes du Corps,
> Paris, March 6, 1816

We also have reference to her in police records, as in the following:

> *Have the conduct carefully observed . . . of the demoiselles Vallon, one of whom is married to an Englishman named Willaume.*
> —Napoleon's secret police, March 8, 1804[*]

---

[*] Legouis 1922, 89–90

The woman Williams is particularly known as an active intriguer.
—Corbigny, Loir-et-Cher prefect of police, March 16, 1804[*]

Some facts I did change for reasons related to my plot. Annette was actually the youngest of six children. Two of her sisters, not just one, aided her in her underground work. She did not have a brother who died on the guillotine, but Angelique did die when she was young, in 1809. Since she was part of the underground network, it is certainly possible she met her end that way. Jeanne Robin was killed leading a cavalry charge against the Revolutionary Army. Annette did not have an older sister who emigrated to England, and Paul, who came so close to the guillotine and spurred Annette to enter the world of intrigue by causing her to come to his aid, was her brother, not her brother-in-law.

Other details in the novel come from biography and history: After Caroline's marriage, Annette lived with the Baudouins, on rue Charlot, on the left bank in Paris. The marquis in my book is based on the swashbuckling Marquis de Rouairie, who fought alongside the Indians against the British in the American Revolution and returned to use the tactics of guerilla warfare against the armies of Paris. To dramatize the beginning of the Reign of Terror, history handed me an apt metaphor: A full eclipse of the sun actually occurred on the same afternoon that the National Assembly placed "Terror on the order of the day."

The pink cap that Annette is knitting in my story, which she carries in her basket to Vendôme and bids William to kiss just before he boards the carriage for Paris, is one which the real-life Annette mentioned in her letter: "The first time she had it on . . . I said to her, 'My Caroline . . . your father is less happy than I; he cannot see it, but it should be dear to you, for he put his lips to it.'" I also refer to the odd fact that William became friends with Caroline's future brother-in-law, a French prisoner of war in the north of England; in actuality, Eustace Baudouin visited William so often that Samuel Taylor Coleridge thought that Wordsworth had a French son, not a French daughter.

---

[*]   Archives nationals, F6410, 5 division: Police secrète, Dossier n 8171

One curious event I could not use, though, happened after Annette's death. The year after she died, at age seventy-five, Wordsworth published a rare French translation of a poem about young men who died fighting for the Chouans. Why would he choose to translate a poem on such an obscure topic unless he was, in doing so, writing an elegy for Annette, who had fought so tirelessly and so long for the Chouans?

Annette Vallon AND THE HERO'S ADVENTURE

With the death of her father, which coincides with the death of the old order, we see Annette at the edge of a world whose day is done. She will have to make the transition on her own from the decadent but pleasant world of her class and of her sheltered youth into the young, chaotic world that has lost all boundaries in its search for new ones.

She says, "Some tried to change the world. I only tried to live in it, which became increasingly difficult." But Annette is a little modest here, for as she "only tries to live in it," she also tries to help others do the same. And in her battle against the impersonal forces of the modern world that overtake her own, she uses the weapon of compassion as well as that of courage.

Fighting chaotic, cruel, and chthonic forces is traditionally the lot of the hero—Odysseus against Polyphemus, the cyclops; Beowulf against the monster Grendel; or Rama, in the ancient Indian epic, against a ten-headed demon that has ravaged the world. All these heroes battle irrational, valueless forces to establish a society based on reason and order. And all these heroes are men. Annette Vallon also fights embodiments of irrational, valueless forces, not to establish a new order but to deliver compassion, however briefly, in a compassionless world and to treat others as *others*, not as abstractions, no matter what their class. Annette "tries to live" in the world with the courage of compassion.

For her, that means risking her life to save others—to hide them, to help them escape from prison, to cut their bonds on a sinking barge in a freezing river. It is a striking aspect of her heroism that she doesn't act out of duty or from a clear intellectual understanding of what she is doing but from compulsion, out of her allegiance to the family of humanity. The world is her larger family, and she pits this loyalty even to unknown individuals against the loyalty to impersonal abstractions—the only loyalty that the new order seems to know.

She is also unwavering in her loyalty to the first real love of her life while maintaining a self-sufficiency that renders that love ultimately unnecessary for her well-being. The hero must stand alone.

Annette, in keeping with the "hero's adventure" so brilliantly explained by Joseph Campbell in the *Power of Myth* video series and in his book *The Hero with a Thousand Faces*, enacts all the traditional aspects of the male hero in legends. This universal adventure is made up of trials and revelations. Annette experiences these early on: in being used by her dance tutor, an embodiment of his decadent world; in realizing her own self-reliance as she saves her father's life; in coming of age into a world that is no more; in keeping steadfast in her allegiance to love and passion in a society that believes in marriage as a commodity; in finding that love in a foreigner who is an outsider, even in his own society, a poet who, like her, has a unique vision of the world; and in willingly putting her life at risk, not for glory, like a male warrior, but because her heart dictates that she can act in no other way.

Campbell points out that another aspect of the hero's adventure, along with trials and revelations, is going into the "belly of the whale:" the hero's descent into the dark. Odysseus journeys into the underworld to consult Tiresias; Beowulf dives into monster-infested waters to fight Grendel's mother; Rama endures his dark night of the soul when his wife is stolen by the demon. In her first descent, Annette is alone, lost in the forest that she knew in her youth, which has taken on a new menace as the world has changed; chased by brigands, she makes her way through a dark ravine and almost freezes to death. She experiences the "belly of the whale" in her imprisonment, during which she is befriended by another woman, a mother with her child, who, along with a sliver of light from a high, small window, gives her hope and a will to live. She descends into the dark of the crypt itself, which for her as a child before the Revolution was an innocent field for playing hide-and-seek; now in this same location, the mouth of a tomb, she embarks on a dangerous mission down a narrow passage to free enemies of the state. On another adventure, after freeing prisoners from the hold of a sinking barge, she is trapped in underwater darkness and saved from drowning only by the helping hand of her comrade.

In all her descents into the dark, Annette receives some form of divine aid, another universal aspect of the hero's adventure, as, for instance, Odysseus, in his most pressing times of need, frequently is blessed by Athena's assistance. Annette's supernatural aid is simply the personal saint she was given as a child, Lucette, or *light*, which makes an appearance as the star above the dark ravine; the slant of light when she is alone and bereft, imprisoned in the Beauvoir Tower; the name she invokes as she closes her eyes in the cathedral and feels she is in a "dark, luminous space" before she enters the crypt; and the name of the boat that rescues the prisoners she has freed. Her belief in aid from a higher power manifests in the only words she utters when she emerges from the freezing water of the sunken hold, "Holy Mary."

A participant in HarperCollins's First Looks program, a layperson, not a critic, read an advance copy of the book and wrote that Annette "shows us what being a hero is all about." For me, Annette incarnates William Wordsworth's lines "that best portion of a good man's life, / His little, nameless, unremembered, acts / Of kindness and of love." But of course, she is a good *woman*, who, over and over again, risks her life in those "acts of kindness and of love." The marquis, as well as the first refugees she helps in Orléans, compares her to Joan of Arc. The Baron de Tardif, in his real-life assessment of her exploits, praised her selflessness and asserted that there was no other woman in all of France like her. The heroism of Annette Vallon is an unassuming victory of the human spirit in an everyday reality of hypocrisy and violence.

I am glad that she was finally recognized by her nation at her daughter's wedding and that, at the end of my story, she takes the arm of Jean-Luc and walks toward the remains of his burned chateau, where together they envision, for the future, over their vanished world, the glint of Pegasus's wings.

ANNETTE VALLON AND THE POETRY
OF WILLIAM WORDSWORTH

*I*n 1800, William Wordsworth defined poetry as "powerful feelings . . . recollected in tranquility."* But in expressing that emotion he is as adept at using masks and metaphors as any poet. It is in his manner of disguises that we can understand and identify references to Annette Vallon.

The clearest expression of Wordsworth's passion for Annette Vallon is in his story of Vaudracour and Julia, originally placed at the end of the ninth book of the *Prelude*, where the poet recalls his experience in France. That's where it belongs. But the poet "may have been afraid lest marks of his personality should be discovered in the poem if it found a place so near his own adventures,"† and Wordsworth published the story separately in 1804. Legouis asserts that "It is the only place in his works where he [describes] the intoxication of passion." (I quote from the poem in my chapters "Different," "Nature's Child," and "Overbless'd.")

> *—he beheld*
> *A vision, and he loved the thing he saw.*
> *Arabian fiction never filled the world*
> *With half the wonders that were wrought for him:*
> *Earth lived in one great presence of the spring,*
> *Life turned the meanest of her implements*
> *Before his eyes to price above gold,*
> *The house she dwelt in was a sainted shrine,*
> *Her chamber-window did surpass in glory*

---

* *Lyrical Ballads*, Preface
† Legouis 1922, 15

All the portals of the east, all paradise
Could by the simple opening of a door
Let itself in upon him . . .

(IX. 582–93)

As with William and Annette, events force Vaudracour and Julia to separate; they meet again briefly and are again forced apart. Vaudracour hides out and in despair eventually retreats to a hermitage, where he stays for the rest of his life. Through a convoluted story about ill-fated lovers, Wordsworth shares with us the elated passion and terrible desolation of a man alone with his sorrow, which he is unable to express but through disguise.

We can certainly see the powerful feelings Wordsworth encounters in France recollected in the *Prelude*. His descriptions of the Reign of Terror sound like they are coming from someone who is not just recording history but expressing personal grief and anger:

Domestic carnage now filled all the year
With feast-days . . . the maiden from the bosom of her love . . .
                    —all perished, all—
Friends, enemies, of all parties, ranks,
Head after head, and never heads enough
For those who bade them fall.

(IX. 329–36)

These lines can remind us of Wordsworth's friends the Girondins, who were executed, as well as of Annette, torn from "the bosom of her love." But even more striking than his images of this time are his dreams:

Most melancholy at that time, O friend,
Were my day-thoughts, my dreams were miserable;
Through months, through years, long after the last beat
Of those atrocities (I speak bare truth,
As if to thee alone in private talk)
I scarcely had one night of quiet sleep,
Such ghastly visions had I of despair,

And tyranny, and implements of death,
And long orations which in dreams I pleaded
Before unjust tribunals, with a voice
Labouring, a brain confounded, and a sense
Of treachery and desertion in the place
The holiest I knew of—my own soul.

(IX. 368—80)

Wordsworth says he is speaking "bare truth" (without his customary disguises?), and to his friend, Coleridge, "alone in private talk." But what is so personal here? His nightmares themselves? Or that they betray his secret trip to France, in the middle of the Terror (as in my chapter "Tonight, My Friend")? Or is there further need for privacy? Kenneth Johnston, in referring to the last two lines of this excerpt, comments, "if there has been treachery and desertion in his own soul, does this not mean he feels that he has betrayed someone else, who could only be Annette?"* More private even than his trip to France is his sense of guilt.

When we have the story of Annette and Caroline in mind, we don't have to look far for evidence of them in Wordsworth's early poems. The connection is not subtle, but it has been missed, between Annette and Caroline and many poems with subject matters of abandoned women, orphaned children, and guilt. Just a quick look at some of the titles should tell us something: "Guilt and Sorrow," "The Forsaken," "The Complaint," "The Emigrant Mother," "The Sailor's Mother," "Maternal Grief," "The Affliction of Margaret," "The Childless Father."

The Emigrant Mother, for instance, who is from France, laments "Across the waters I am come, / And I have left a babe at home . . ." Why would William Wordsworth, whose formula for poetry is based on the recollection of powerful feelings, choose these topics unless he were giving us his own experience through the poet's mask of *personae*, or voices? Wordsworth's own daughter left behind in France, not the emigrant mother's, is the source of pain behind the poem.

Many of these poems also have as their subject the loss or death of a child. In "The Affliction of Margaret," the mother cries, "Seven

---

* Johnston 2000, 286

years, alas! To have received / No tidings of an only child." The Oxford edition of *Wordsworth's Poetical Works* puts the probable date of composition for this poem at 1801. Because of the war between their countries, Wordsworth would have "received / No tidings of [his] only child" for at least "seven years."

"The Complaint" deals with a mother who has her child taken away from her, as Annette had Caroline taken from her for fear of scandal and "put out to nurse." It's possible Wordsworth had heard of this event from Annette, writing, "My Child! They gave thee to another, / A woman who was not thy mother." Besides speaking figuratively of his feelings, these poems themselves are empathetic acts: through female *personae* the poet imagines and identifies with the plight of his beloved.

Wordsworth's best-known poem that refers to Annette still does so indirectly, for it is addressed to Caroline. This is the lovely sonnet "It Is a Beauteous Evening, Calm and Free," also published as "On the Beach at Calais" and quoted in full in my chapter "A Beauteous Evening." "Thee" at the end of the poem, however—"God being with thee when we know it not"—could certainly refer to both Caroline and Annette. It's also interesting to note that, on the way to that monthlong visit, Wordsworth writes a poem of reverie without any sense of loss, "Composed upon Westminster Bridge." In this poem, his mood seems to be one of unusual happiness as he passes through London on the top of a carriage in the early morning, and as Annette and Caroline wait for him in Calais. But would this betray too much to admit he was happy to see the woman he was *not* going to marry? Intriguingly, he publishes this poem with the date September 3, 1802, in the title, although he actually composed it July 31, 1802: on his way *to*, not *from*, France. Is this more disguise?

Through the intense emotions that characterize his involvement with Annette Vallon, Wordsworth finds the poetic voice that shall express in everyday speech his powerful feelings recollected in tranquility. If it weren't for Annette, would he have found the powerful feelings needed in order to come up with his formula in the first place? If he had married Mary without having met Annette, I would say no. He needed intensity, not sweet docility, to become a poet, or at least the unique poet that he was. He needed passion, and passion tinged with loss, such as we find in the language he uses toward nature in "Tintern Abbey."

In Wordsworth's poetry we often find behind the glad refrain of nature "the still sad music of humanity." Civil war in France and a seemingly unending war between his country and that of his beloved had "betrayed his heart" before. In "Tintern Abbey," he directs the language of passion toward the healing and reassurance that nature gives, "knowing that Nature never did betray / The heart that loved her." This is a poem of gratitude to nature and to Dorothy, his partner in nature, for bringing him back from the brink of despair. Before he met Annette, he was "more like a man / Flying from something that he dreads than one / Who sought the thing he loved." In "Tintern Abbey," Wordsworth returns to himself, but it is a self he never would have known without the profound passion and loss he knew through Annette.

The most transcendent expression of Wordsworth's theme of loss is "Intimations of Immortality." The essence of *Paradise Lost* is here in eleven short sections, not even three pages in the Oxford *Wordsworth's Poetical Works*. But every line is full of the utter poignancy "that there hath past away a glory from the earth." He speaks of "the years that bring the philosophic mind," but he is himself still a young man of thirty-two and in fine health. He tells us that "the things which I have seen I now can see no more . . . nothing can bring back the hour / Of splendour in the grass, of glory in the flower." This is not a poem about mere childhood innocence lost; the sense of loss is here so profound it asks us to look for a deeper cause. What brings a man in his early thirties to write a poem about adjusting to the loss of childhood? He's made that adjustment long ago. It is far more likely that this is a man in love saying goodbye to that love. Yet it is a transcendent poem because the poet finds the ability to move on:

> *Thanks to the human heart by which we live,*
> *Thanks to its tenderness, its joys, and fears.*
> *To me the meanest flower that blows can give*
> *Thoughts that do often lie too deep for tears.*

Reconciliation of loss is perhaps an odd theme for a poet in the first year of his marriage, as is probably the case here with Wordsworth. And that is another way to look at "Intimations." He finds "strength in what remains behind:" The poem may be his acceptance that he will never marry Annette.

Here Wordsworth's gratitude is to the heart. His experience with Annette has taught him the fundamental impermanence of all things: the beauty of the world and the poignancy in the passing of that beauty. He shares it intimately with the reader in the simple, direct, clear language of powerful feeling honestly expressed. It is the style of verse he has now perfected: the recollection of youth's passions and losses distilled into a language that would transform modern poetry.

ADDENDUM

With reference to my chapter "The Window," any discussion of William Wordsworth's poetry and Annette Vallon ought to include the great ice-skating passage from the *Prelude*. In my story, he gets Annette, Captain Beaupay, and Annette's servant and friend, Claudette, to ride out to a frozen pond, where he gives them ice-skating lessons. They soon all give up, and he is left alone to enjoy himself. Apparently he really was an accomplished ice skater. The Nobel Prize–winning poet Seamus Heaney has even written a poem titled "Wordsworth's Skates."* It seems a perfect sport for William, especially at night when he retires "into a silent bay," alone on a lake with the mountains and the stars for company. Here is part of his recollection:

> —*All shod with steel,*
> *We hissed along the polish'd ice . . .*
> *So through the darkness and the cold we flew,*
> *And not a voice was idle; with the din,*
> *Meanwhile, the precipices rang aloud,*
> *The leafless trees, and every icy crag*
> *Tinkled like iron . . .*
>
> > *Not seldom from the uproar I retired*
> *Into a silent bay, or sportively*
> *Glanced sideway, leaving the tumultuous throng,*
> *To cut across the image of a star*
> *That gleam'd upon the ice: and oftentimes*
> *When we had given our bodies to the wind,*
> *And all the shadowy banks, on either side,*
> *Came sweeping through the darkness, spinning still*
> *The rapid line of motion; then at once*

---

* *District and Circle*, 2006

Have I, reclining back upon my heels,
Stopp'd short, yet still the solitary Cliffs
Wheeled by me, even as if the earth had roll'd
With visible motion her diurnal round;
Behind me did they stretch in solemn train
Feeble and feebler, and I stood and watch'd
Till all was tranquil as a dreamless sleep.

(I. 460—489)

The lighter side of HISTORY

❋ Look for this seal on select historical fiction titles from Harper. Books bearing it contain special bonus materials, including timelines, interviews with the author, and insights into the real-life events that inspired the book, as well as recommendations for further reading.

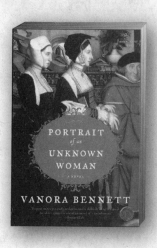

PORTRAIT OF AN UNKNOWN WOMAN
A Novel
by Vanora Bennett
978-0-06-125256-3 (paperback)

Meg, adopted daughter of Sir Thomas More, narrates the tale of a famous Holbein painting and the secrets it holds.

THE SIXTH WIFE
She Survived Henry VIII to be Betrayed by Love...
by Suzannah Dunn
978-0-06-143156-2 (paperback)

Kate Parr survived four years of marriage to King Henry VIII, but a new love may undo a lifetime of caution.

A POISONED SEASON
A Novel of Suspense
by Tasha Alexander   978-0-06-117421-6 (paperback)

As a cat-burglar torments Victorian London, a mysterious gentleman fascinates high society.

THE KING'S GOLD
A Novel
by Yxta Maya Murray   978-0-06-089108-4 (paperback)

A journey through Renaissance Italy, ripe with ancient maps, riddles, and treasure hunters. Book Two of the Red Lion Series.

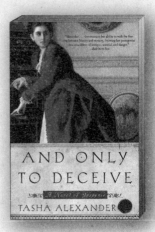

AND ONLY TO DECEIVE
A Novel of Suspense
by Tasha Alexander
978-0-06-114844-6 (paperback)
Discover the dangerous secrets kept by the strait-laced English of the Victorian era.

TO THE TOWER BORN
A Novel of the Lost Princes
by Robin Maxwell
978-0-06-058052-0 (paperback)

Join Nell Caxton in the search for the lost heirs to the throne of Tudor England.

CROSSED
A Tale of the Fourth Crusade
by Nicole Galland   978-0-06-084180-5 (paperback)
Under the banner of the Crusades, a pious knight and a British vagabond attempt a daring rescue.

THE SCROLL OF SEDUCTION
A Novel of Power, Madness, and Royalty
by Gioconda Belli   978-0-06-083313-8 (paperback)
A dual narrative of love, obsession, madness, and betrayal surrounding one of history's most controversial monarchs, Juana the Mad.

PILATE'S WIFE
A Novel of the Roman Empire
by Antoinette May   978-0-06-112866-0 (paperback)
Claudia foresaw the Romans' persecution of Christians, but even she could not stop the crucifixion.

ELIZABETH: THE GOLDEN AGE
by Tasha Alexander   978-0-06-143123-4 (paperback)
This novelization of the film starring Cate Blanchett is an eloquent exploration of the relationship between Queen Elizabeth I and Sir Walter Raleigh at the height of her power.

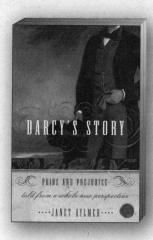

DARCY'S STORY
by Janet Aylmer
978-0-06-114870-5 (paperback)
Read Mr. Darcy's side of the story—*Pride and Prejudice* from a new perspective.

THE CANTERBURY PAPERS
A Novel
by Judith Healey
978-0-06-077332-8 (paperback)
Follow Princess Alais on a secret mission as she unlocks a long-held and dangerous secret.

THE FOOL'S TALE
A Novel
by Nicole Galland   978-0-06-072151-0 (paperback)
Travel back to Wales, 1198, a time of treachery, political unrest...and passion.

THE QUEEN OF SUBTLETIES
A Novel of Anne Boleyn
by Suzannah Dunn   978-0-06-059158-8 (paperback)
Untangle the web of fate surrounding Anne Boleyn in a tale narrated by the King's Confectioner.

REBECCA
The Classic Tale of Romantic Suspense
by Daphne Du Maurier   978-0-380-73040-7 (paperback)
Follow the second Mrs. Maxim de Winter down the lonely drive to Manderley, where Rebecca once ruled.

REBECCA'S TALE
A Novel
by Sally Beauman   978-0-06-117467-4 (paperback)
Unlock the dark secrets and old worlds of Rebecca de Winter's life with investigator Colonel Julyan.

REVENGE OF THE ROSE
A Novel
by Nicole Galland
978-0-06-084179-9 (paperback)
In the court of the Holy Roman Emperor, not
even a knight is safe from gossip, schemes, and
secrets.

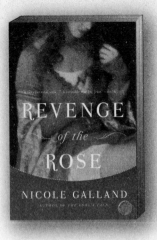

A SUNDIAL IN A GRAVE: 1610
**A Novel of Intrigue, Secret Societies, and
the Race to Save History**
by Mary Gentle
978-0-380-82041-2 (paperback)
Renaissance Europe comes alive in this dazzling
tale of love, murder, and blackmail.

THORNFIELD HALL
Jane Eyre's Hidden Story
by Emma Tennant   978-0-06-000455-2 (paperback)
Watch the romance of Jane Eyre and Mr. Rochester unfold in this breathtaking
sequel.

THE WIDOW'S WAR
A Novel
by Sally Gunning   978-0-06-079158-2 (paperback)
Tread the shores of colonial Cape Cod with a lonely whaler's widow as she tries
to build a new life.

THE WILD IRISH
A Novel of Elizabeth I & the Pirate O'Malley
by Robin Maxwell   978-0-06-009143-9 (paperback)
Hoist a sail with the Irish pirate and clan chief Grace O'Malley.